THE
DRIVER

THE
DRIVER

A NOVEL

HART HANSON

DUTTON

DUTTON

An imprint of Penguin Random House LLC
375 Hudson Street
New York, New York 10014

Front jacket road map provided by Steven Varner, americanroads.us.

DUTTON is a registered trademark and the D colophon
is a trademark of Penguin Random House LLC.

LIBRARY OF CONGRESS CATALOGING-IN-PUBLICATION DATA

Names: Hanson, Hart, author.
Title: The driver : a novel / Hart Hanson.
Description: New York, New York : Dutton, 2017.
Identifiers: LCCN 2016038929 (print) | LCCN 2016055702 (ebook) |
ISBN 9781101986363 (hardback) | ISBN 9781101986370 (trade paperback) |
ISBN 9781101986387 (ebook)
Subjects: LCSH: Chauffeurs—Fiction. | Limousine services—Fiction. |
Disabled veterans—Fiction. | Extrasensory perception—Fiction. |
Celebrities—Fiction. | Attempted murder—Fiction. | Los Angeles
(Calif.)—Fiction. | BISAC: FICTION / Suspense. | FICTION / Thrillers. |
GSAFD: Suspense fiction. | Mystery fiction.
Classification: LCC PS3608.A72275 D75 2017 (print) | LCC PS3608.A72275
(ebook) | DDC 813/.6—dc23
LC record available at https://lccn.loc.gov/2016038929

Printed in the United States of America
1 3 5 7 9 10 8 6 4 2

Set in Bulmer MT
Designed by Spring Hoteling

For Brigitte, who doesn't approve of soggy public declarations of love
so the best I can do here is declare the simple truth that she
is the best part of my life.

THE DRIVER

SOMETHING GETS
IN MY EYE

Five minutes before a pair of overconfident, underaged, undercooked, tweaked-out, teenage-skater-boy assassins swagger through the front door of an upscale bar in a tourist hotel just south of the Santa Monica Pier, I'm innocently killing time in the manner of all limo drivers since the invention of the wheel: wiping down my vehicle with a chamois while listening to a less car-proud driver complain about the weather. He isn't wrong to complain, considering how the two of us are being sandblasted by Santa Ana winds in the limos-wait-here alley behind the hotel.

"Fuckin' Santa Anas," he said, squinting into the grit. "White people freak the fuck out, level a black man the evil eye."

Black man referred to him; *white people* referred to me. Which was fair because I am, in fact, an astoundingly vanilla man: brown hair, brown eyes, five foot eleven, medium build—your average kind of white man, milquetoast invisible average—but while I admit to regarding him with interest, "leveling the evil eye" parlayed too much spin on it.

(Yet . . .)

There was something about the guy that didn't ring true.

He wore a dark-blue limo-driver's suit made for somebody maybe two inches shorter than himself unless he'd recently undergone a growth spurt, which seemed unlikely given that he was pushing thirty. His shoes were not the standard black wingtips or cap-toed oxfords; they were patent leather laceless boots, sporting flashy silver toe and heel caps (though whether gaudy-cheap or conspicuous-expensive was beyond me).

His hair was rusty colored in a way that said beach bum more than limo driver. As did his cigarillo packed with primo weed. Plus, he checked his phone with manic regularity. Normally, I'd have written him off as a moonlighting soul surfer obsessively checking an app that tracked storm waves from across the ocean. Except the Santa Anas blow out any kind of decent surfing; even junk surfers don't need an app for that.

Most likely Mr. Chelsea Boots was new to the limo business, nervous, checking for texts from a particularly demanding client—but if that was the case, then why was he getting high? To calm his jitters?

So yeah, come to think of it, maybe Chelsea Boots was right and I was leveling him the evil eye. Or maybe he was paranoid from the weed. Maybe a little of both.

My mobile buzzed. I removed my sunglasses, shaded the screen from the setting sun and gusts of grit with my body. It was my mechanic, Tinkertoy, calling. I answered in my most soothing voice.

"It's me."

Dead silence (not unexpected). Sonic blackouts are a quirk of Tinkertoy's post-traumatic stress paranoia, an awkward unwanted intermission as she evaluates whether or not the person on the other end of the call is for reals the person she herself just dialed.

"It's you who?" Tinkertoy asked.

"This is Michael Skellig," I answered.

Crickets.

"Your boss."

Silence.

In college, in addition to required math and engineering classes, I took an elective survey course in Great Thinkers in which we studied the birth of medicine, featuring protodoctors, half scientist / half magician, starting with a Greek named Hippocrates. (You've heard of his oath.)

Hippocrates set out to label and categorize human beings by separating us into four basic groups based upon (I shit you not) a personal predominance of the following: snot, black bile, yellow bile, and blood. He labeled these *Humors*. We all have one, a humor, like a sign of the zodiac. Hippocrates would have diagnosed Tinkertoy as a *Melancholic*, meaning she suffered from a surfeit of black bile.

Eventually, Tinkertoy decided that I was, in fact, who I claimed to be and, in the jerky, tumbledown telegram way she speaks once she decides it's safe, she said, "Two is ready. Fuel injector was fucked. Not like from sabotage. Nuh-uh. Just old. So I replaced it. Hundred seventy-five bucks. Secondhand. Could not. Be rebuilt."

Two referred to the second of the three limos I own. I was currently leaning on our flagship: Number One.

"Good job," I said, and waited for Tinkertoy to analyze that controversial response for hidden meaning.

You're wondering where I get the patience to deal with Tinkertoy, and the answer is that I appreciate the way she fends off her PTSD demons by immersing herself in the minutiae of all things mechanical (typewriters, binoculars, clocks and compasses, fuel injectors, air-conditioning units, cameras, whirligigs, toys, guns, stereos, computers, lawn mowers, and anything else you can think of with spinning, clicking, percolating, conducting, gyrating, or ambulatory properties).

The Veterans Health Administration psych wizards categorize Tinkertoy not as *Melancholic* but as *Ego-syntonic suffering from Obsessive Compulsive Disorder derived from Post-Traumatic Stress with Serotonergic Imbalance Resulting in Adjustment Disorder with Anxious Features*—indicating, to me at least, that shrinks could learn a thing or two from Hippocrates and his humors.

Chelsea Boots huffed noisily on his doctored Black & Mild blunt, quick, shallow, urgent puffs like trying to keep something alight that wants to go out.

The major limo companies do not sanction that kind of behavior. They maybe look the other way if a driver is obliged to take a friendly hit off a doobie (I know, but that's what I call it) to assuage the nerves of a pot-paranoid client who worries about off-duty cops moonlighting as limo drivers. But Chelsea Boots sucked back on his shit with Snoop Dogg levels of enthusiasm, the end of his cigar glowing red even through all this crashing sunlight.

Tinkertoy finally ticked the last box on her exasperating mental list and said, "Ripple says should he call in Lucky since Two is ready?"

Ripple's another employee Army vet with issues. I hired him to handle scheduling and dispatch for my company, Oasis Limo Services. The other full-time driver is named Lucky. Lucky owns a ten percent stake in the company but he has to trust me on that because he's an illegal alien coasting along on forged documents (yes, another veteran—we all have our tribes).

I named our company *Oasis Limo Services* on the advice of my mother, who, as a politician, knows a lot about branding. Mom said that if I called it *Stars and Stripes Limo Services* it would scare the limousine liberals on the west side of Los Angeles, who happen to be my target clientele. Plus, according to Mom, the word *oasis* works on the subliminal level to seduce prospective clients into feeling "like Bedouins eating dates in a tent near a cool water hole after crossing the Sahara."

(Like everyone else who doesn't know better, Mom views Los Angeles as both a literal and a figurative desert.)

"Ripple needs to do his job," I told Tinkertoy, which resulted in the muffle of Tinkertoy covering the phone with her grease-stained palm, ostensibly repeating to Ripple what I'd just said.

Ripple is barely nineteen years old and looks younger, a luminously pale freckled boy with crazy hair like copper wires. He draws cartoons all day, all of them horrifically violent in the way that sets off alarms for the VA wizards. Just over a year ago, Private Second Class (E-2) Ripple had a bad day in a shithole called Wal-akan, southwest of Kandahar, Afghanistan, when he lost his right leg from just above the knee to a sniper and his left leg at the hip when an HMMWV (which was rushing to block a second kill shot) accidentally ran him over.

Hippocrates would label Ripple *Sanguine,* which means his predominant humor is blood, which tells you just about everything you need to know about the kid.

I heard Ripple's voice in the background, a jumble of words followed by a clearly discernible, "Tell Skellig to go fuck himself!" followed by Tinkertoy's muffled, "Why don't you? Go fuck? *Your-self?*" followed by escalating classic Sanguine-versus-Melancholic insults. I hung up to let the two of them work it out.

"Famous poem about the Santa Anas," Chelsea Boots continued, as though our conversation had never been interrupted, "concerning a wife and a knife. You got a wife?"

I shook my head.

"Why not?"

How do you answer a question like that? I'm single for all the usual reasons plus a couple of ancillary snags and detriments, for example: an eye-catching scar on my forearm left by an obstinate pit bull whose windpipe I was forced to (honest to God!) wrench out in panicked self-defense—please, no grief about the humane treatment of animals. Killing a dog is not a meet-cute anecdote on a first date (especially if the woman in question is an animal lover), and yet due to the prominence of the dimpled scars on my arm it has never not come up, unless I wear long sleeves, in which case, this being Los Angeles, the woman in question assumes I'm a junkie. I could go for Gila monster attack as an explanation, but then I'm lying on a first date, which, as any relationship expert will tell you, does not bode well for the future of the relationship.

Putting aside the dog-killer excuse, the main reason I do not have a wife is that I'm hopelessly in love with a woman who not only refuses to marry me but decided that the fact that I'd asked (and she'd refused) meant that we should take our whole relationship to a much more casual level.

Instead of admitting all that to baked Mr. Chelsea Boots, I changed the subject.

"It's not a poem."

"What's not a poem? Wife with a knife? What is it, then? Doesn't sound like no kind of joke."

"It's a story."

Which is when a speck of grit blew into my eye and burned like an ember. Santa Anas are the katabatic devil winds that blow no good from the high deserts—everybody knows that, not only wives and knives, poets and surfers and limo drivers, especially getting late in the afternoon, after twenty-eight hours of no sleep, driving around a client who obviously does not ever want to go home, the sun banging on your eyeballs from both the sky and the reflection off the ocean.

I heard a burst of calliope music from the Santa Monica Pier amusement park, blown up the alley behind the hotel on a back eddy of the Santa Anas, and my eye watered and stung and the wind spoke to me in the guttural accent of a Chechen jihadist torturer I shot through the eye in Yemen a decade ago.

What the Chechen said was *Troubletroubletrouble.*

Yes, yes, I know, on top of the dog story now you're going to be all freaked-out about my mental health, but those ghostly wind warnings have saved my life a dozen times, always keening in the spectral voice of somebody I'd killed. Of course I've never admitted that to the wizards. I tell them that I experience an overwhelming sense of déjà vu and disconnection from the world. They tell me I suffer from a form of PTSD-induced protomigraine known as an *aura.* Why don't I tell the wizards about my whispering ghost voices? Because they will take it much too seriously and plunge a needle full of Thorazine in my ass.

. . . *troubletroubletroublebadtrouble* . . .

"What up?" Chelsea Boots asks, because I'm tossing the chamois onto the limo's hood, tucking my sunglasses into the breast pocket of my shirt, and turning to trot along the broken asphalt of the alley, instinctively reaching for a phantom sidearm that isn't there and hasn't been there for three years.

I slam into the dented metal door at the rear of the hotel like I'm trying to escape a burning building, then thump on it with my elbow until it opens a crack. I shove my way past the shocked Malaysian dishwasher kid wearing eyeliner and rubber gloves, moving fast and low, like I'm leading a strike team, through the coolness of the corridor, smelling cleaning fluids and raw refrigerated beef, olive oil, spilled liquor, antiseptic. I zigzag through the kitchen, scanning, scanning, ignoring the whoops and hollers of the Mexicans and Guatemalans who work there—*"Hey! Choo can be dere!"*— bursting from behind the bar into a cool place of wood warmth and air-conditioning and mirrors and an infinity of bottles and indirect light and people and music throbbing at 180 beats per minute (like the heart of panic).

"Jesus Christ!" grunts a barback; then there's a bouncer who plants himself in front of me, chanting, "*Stop. Stop. Stop!*" in the singsong, patronizing, faux-weary voice bouncers affect to hide their own anxieties in a physical confrontation.

When I outzig his zag, he tucks in behind and chases me.

"Buddy? Buddy?"

This bouncer moves well but his nose has never been broken, which indicates that he's a martial arts type, which means that, unlike a boxer or a cop, he cannot take a hit and keep coming, so when he grabs my shoulder I spin, elbow him once, solar plexus, and keep going. I consider shouting my client's name, which is Bismarck Avila (that's right, the wunderkind skateboarding hip-hop mogul from the reality show), but then I see Avila rising as the culminating sound of the disturbance I'm causing roils over my head and breaks over him like a wave, so I jostle my way through the evening drinks crowd, managers and agents and call girls and tourists, muttering "'Scuse me, 'scuse me, 'scuse me . . ." in a way that really means, *Get the fuck out of my way or I will hurt you.*

Two three-hundred-pound bodyguards rise in front of me like darkness looming, twins, buttoning their Hugo Boss suits in the way large African American men do in order to intimidate average-size Caucasian men like me, the same monumental bookends who followed my limo in a tricked-out black Navigator as I drove their boss from club to club to sex club to hotel suite to restaurant to private party to bar—a different woman or women in the back servicing the client on each leg.

"Get him out," I advise the twins, pointing at Avila but scanning, scanning, for the threat that the Chechen had warned me about but had not yet presented itself in reality.

"I don't think so," Tweedledee says.

"Who you talkin'?" Tweedledum asks.

"That's the limo driver," says Tweedledee just before the bullet slaps his gut, right through his Hugo Boss buttonhole, the crack of a nine millimeter following a microsecond later and the awful wet-clap sound of bullet meets flesh, and for the two seconds before hysteria and panic hit, the whole place goes as silent as Antarctica.

Tweedledum looks down at the spreading red on Tweedledee's shirt while Tweedledee looks at me accusingly, like I was the one who shot him.

I pivot to see two kids approaching. The one leading the way is short, Slavic-looking, free-weights blocky with steroid zits and a shaved head. His wingman is tall, skinny, and pasty white, with dyed black hair. Both sixteen, seventeen years old, both wearing board shorts, and—judging by the generous display of butt crack when he pirouettes to scan the crowd—the Slavic zit kid is going commando where the Goth boy favors dingy plaid boxers. Both wear unlaced combat boots, white tank tops under brand-new black hoodies, and sun-faded multicolored Ogio backpacks with trailing skateboard loops flapping around like black ribbons at a Portuguese funeral.

Both brandish crap Hi-Point nines, bought on a corner for a hundred bucks and whatever drugs they carried in their backpacks.

The crescendo of shouts and screams breaks and recedes like a messy wave as people get the hell out.

The Slavic-looking kid fires again and I feel the hot streak of a bullet crease my armpit, because I'm already turning to grab Tweedledee's Glock as he slumps to his knees, gripping his spreading-red gut (maybe praying, probably praying), definitely crying because he is shot and dying. I flick off the safety as I bring the gun around and the Goth boy makes a sound—*OH!*—like someone threw a bucket of cold water on him and then executes some kind of movie-action-hero somersault move, intending, I guess, to pop up and shoot me.

Except he loses the gun and pops up facing me with nothing but an irritated look that his killer move hasn't worked out.

I cannot bring myself to shoot his stupid young life into a ghost voice in the wind, so I blast Tweedledee's cannon into the ceiling three times above him. The Slavic zit kid grabs his buddy by the collar and yanks.

"He said *don't get caught*," Slavic Kid yells into Goth Boy's ear. They turn to run, Slavic Kid firing his gun into the air, agents and managers and tourists and a familiar-looking local TV traffic girl flailing out of the way.

I turn to see if Tweedledee is still breathing.

A flash of light blinds me and I think it's a camera, but the flash isn't light, it's pain, and flashing light turns to flashing dark and I almost have time to laugh before everything goes away: the electric copper smell of Tweedledee's blood, the mewling sound he makes like a tortured cat, cologne and perfume and sweat and expensive liquor spilled everywhere, and the musty softness of carpet on my cheek, and I think about how Los Angeles is really a chain of restful nooks where happiness and comfort dwell but between them is a wasteland of purgatorial hell or hellish purgatory and I think, *Shelter from the devil wind*, and close my eyes, resting and happy.

TWEEDLEDEAD

I open my eyes in the ambulance. I can't hear anything. No voices, no siren, nothing. On the gurney next to me, Tweedledee spasms and expectorates a blast of bright-red arterial blood into his clear plastic oxygen mask and transitions from Tweedledee to Tweedledead. The EMTs rush and pump and smash and inject and push and shock, but it's all over for the big man. His ghost drifts up to the ceiling of the ambulance like an accidentally released helium balloon, looking down at his own dead self, finally realizing his sad situation. I catch eyes with his ghost (nothing I can do to help; Tweedledead's never going to speak to me because I didn't kill him and those are the only ghosts who haunt me).

We both fade away, each of us dissolving. Me, figuring I've been shot in the head, it hurts that much, wondering if I am on my way to everlasting peace or if this time purgatory will stretch from here all the way through eternity.

I'M NOT DEAD

"Mr. Skellig? Mr. Skellig? Could you please open your eyes, sir?"

The voice is female, reassuring and warm, insistent, a slight note of reproach implying that laziness is the only thing keeping me from waking. The same tone my mother took Sunday mornings when I was fourteen and pushing back at her on the whole go-to-church issue, even though I knew it was important to Mom's constituency that her family be God-fearing and churchgoing and gun-toting and free.

It was out of respect for Mom that I opened my eyes. It took a moment to focus. Leaning close into my face was a teenage Asian girl, solid and solemn in a reassuring way, like she had her priorities in life straight.

"Can you tell me your name, sir?"

"Michael Skellig."

My throat didn't hurt. Good sign. It meant I hadn't been intubated. Or embalmed.

"Do you know what day it is, Mr. Skellig?"

"That depends."

"Depends on what?"

"How long I've been black."

The girl pulled back, fresh worry etched on her face. "I'm sorry, Mr. Skellig, you believe you are black?"

"No. Sorry, no, Army lingo. How long have I been unconscious?"

"Approximately three hours."

"Saturday, seventeen January," I said. "Approximately eight P.M." (Showing off now.)

"Do you know what happened to you?"

"Excuse me, who are you?"

A tiny flashlight appeared between her face and my left eye, strobed, then moved over to my right eye. Painful. During this, she explained that she was Dr. Quan, an emergency room resident here at the UCLA Medical Center. I made a joke about medical licenses being handed out in high school; she countered with "I'm older than I look," in a way that told me she'd done it a hundred times before.

"What exactly happened to me?"

"You were bludgeoned on the top of your head."

Tweedledum. Bastard. After I scared away the two shooters, he didn't know whether to shit or go blind, so he conked me on the head to prove to his boss he had everything under control.

"Your skull is not fractured but you required sixteen stitches to your scalp," Dr. Quan said, rocking back so that I could focus on her. Considerate. My eyes were definitely bollixed; it took all my concentration to keep them from independently rolling around in my head like marbles. "I'd like to admit you overnight for observation."

"No, thanks," I said, sitting up—which turned out to be an awful, painful, unpleasant adventure. Struggling to keep a straight face, Dr. Quan gave me a moment to fight my way back from nausea, tunnel vision, and the spins before advising me not to sit up too quickly.

"Funny," I said.

"Sorry. But I knew you'd be one of those guys who says, 'I got this!' then passes out."

"I did not pass out."

"I've cataloged your scars pretty thoroughly," Dr. Quan said, handing me a sippy cup for grown-ups. "You've been blown up, savaged by a dog, stabbed, and shot three times. And those are only the injuries visible to the naked eye. Your X-rays are a horror show. I assume you are some kind of tough hombre? Military?"

"Former military," I said, "so only a former tough hombre."

"Thank you for your service," Dr. Quan said, the way sincere people do when they don't know how else to thank a veteran, not realizing that the stock phrase sets up a kind of discouraging buffer between us and them, between a returned soldier and the world.

"Unfortunately, Mr. Skellig, I'm not the one you have to convince to let you go."

Dr. Quan pointed to where Detective Delilah Groopman of the Los Angeles Police Department, Major Crimes, Pacific Division, leaned on the doorjamb, smiling at me and waggling her fingers, like a beauty queen. Foulmouthed, sexy, armed, scary smart, tough, and streetwise—that kind of beauty queen.

"Oh no," I said.

"Now, fuckwit, be nice," she said.

"Do I need a lawyer, Delilah?" I asked.

"Considering the situation," she said, "let's go with Detective Groopman."

"Ah, crap."

"I've got other patients, so . . . ," Dr. Quan said, pointing to the corridor, and who could blame her for wanting to get the hell out?

"Dr. Quan? The guy who was in the ambulance with me?"

Dr. Quan looked at Delilah for permission to speak, which answered my question.

Delilah said, "Dead as God's grampa."

I was in the middle of a homicide investigation.

Dr. Quan patted me on the foot in an encouraging manner and left. Delilah poked around the end of my bed and then pushed the button that raised me so that we could speak eyeball to eyeball. I felt like my head was about to pop off my shoulders and roll down my chest to rest in my lap, which (knowing Delilah, and you will see that I do) is exactly the effect she was going for.

As I drew level with her, I could see that Delilah looked a little ragged. Puffy eyes, carrying maybe fifteen pounds more than the last time I saw her, but even so, carrying it well, a statuesque woman with blond hair and warm light-brown eyes, lines on her forehead from the effort of projecting herself into the mind-set of dumb-ass criminals all day every day. I hoped she wasn't drinking again or getting jerked around by yet another shitbird from SWAT or, worse, Drug Enforcement.

"You drinking again, Delilah?"

"Oh, Skellig, aren't you just the sweetest vanilla cupcake with shit frosting?"

Hippocrates would categorize Delilah Groopman as *Phlegmatic*: ruled by snot (which, despite how it sounds, is not disgusting).

I asked if I could borrow Delilah's chewed-up pen and cop notebook. She watched as I found the first clean page and scribbled on it.

"If that's a confession, you gotta sign it."

"It's a license plate."

I told Delilah about Chelsea Boots. I told her that he was African American, approximately thirty years old, sun-rusted surfer hair, a weed-packed cigarillo, and why I called him Chelsea Boots.

"What the flickety-fuck are Chelsea boots and why the fuck shouldn't a black man wear them if he wants?"

"The Beatles wore them."

"Who cares about the Beatles? The Beatles are irrelevant. They all died fifty years ago."

"Chelsea boots are slip-on. They got elastic on the sides to hold them tight. This guy's had bling on them."

"How's about if you aren't going to say anything worthwhile to me, have the decency to shut the fuck up?"

Sometimes you just have to give people what they want. Especially cops. So I stopped talking. Delilah crumbled after thirty seconds of silence.

"You're implying that Mr. Beatle Boots is a possible person of interest?"

"It's worth checking out."

"Why did you enter the bar?"

"To warn my client of impending danger."

"I don't mean, 'To what end did you enter the bar?' I mean, 'What caused you to enter the bar?'"

"My client hadn't paid me yet."

"You drove Avila around for thirty hours, so at your going rate that's what? Thirty-six hundred bucks? If Avila's a good tipper, count on another thousand in gratuities . . . say, five grand in total. Is that about right?"

I nodded. It was like getting conked on the head with a log.

"So your motive for entering the bar to save Bismarck Avila's life was that you wanted to get paid?"

"It makes me nervous, a cop using the word *motive*."

"If I ask you about where you took your client—were there any disagreements along the way? did he enjoy sexual relations with another man's woman? that sort of thing—you gonna plead limo-driver privilege?"

"Oasis Limo Services guarantees absolute discretion," I said. "You get a warrant and I'll provide you details of Bismarck Avila's itinerary. But trust me, that's a tree with no bark on it."

In fact, I'd driven Avila to half a dozen aboveground nightclubs (where he got TMZed and Instagrammed and Snapchatted and self-ied and Twittered) but also to an underground sex club in Korea-town off Western.

"Drugs?"

"Nope. He drank about equal amounts of vodka, Red Bull, and coffee," I told her. "At least in my limo. I have no idea what he did inside any of the destinations."

"Why is that?"

"Because I didn't go into the destinations with him because I was his driver, not a member of his entourage."

"How did you even know Avila was in danger? You said your-self, he was inside, you were outside, in the alley. The hitters en-tered through the front doors. You couldn't see them."

"People started screaming—"

"I have statements that you entered the bar before the hit men, so nobody was screaming yet."

"Not men. Boys. Teenagers."

"Don't deflect, Skellig! What made you go in, knocking over kitchen staff and barbacks and leveling a bouncer?"

Here's the thing about Delilah. If she's cursing you out, you're fine. It's when she starts asking questions that you remember what an excellent investigator she is, able to smell bullshit from three rooms over and two across.

I wracked my brain for a possible answer that did not include crazy-man ghost voices in the wind.

"The guy, Chelsea Boots. He made me suspicious."

"Because of his classic-rock footwear?"

I told Delilah that his suit was too small—like it was stolen or borrowed—that he left his car running for the air-conditioning but the back doors were wide open and the car was pointed the wrong way in the one-way alley, set up for a fast getaway.

"Chelsea Boots was the wheelman for the two hit . . . boys?"

"They sure as hell weren't going to escape on skateboards."

"They were skaters?"

"They wore skateboard backpacks. The loops in the back were flapping."

"Decks are personalized and distinctive," she said. "Like tattoos. Those boys were smart not to bring them along."

I told you Delilah was a good cop. Look what she got out of me that I didn't even know I knew.

"Decks?"

"That's what skateboarders call the board part they stand on," she said. "The wheels they call *trucks*. You should concentrate more on current culture, what's happening in the world *today* and less on what kind of shoes old bands your father likes wear on their fucking feet."

Insults and cursing. Much better than questions. I let myself relax slightly.

"My dad is a Stones guy," I said. "Not a Beatles guy."

"I have eyewitness statements that you prevented one of Bismarck Avila's bodyguards from doing his job by taking his gun from him, which, in turn, led to him being killed."

"Delilah!"

"Let's stick with 'Detective Groopman.'"

"The bodyguard was already shot and on the ground when I borrowed his gun."

Delilah sighed. I sniffed her breath. Delilah is in and out of Alcoholics Anonymous and tried once to be a Scientologist but was declared a Suppressive when her auditor got too aggressive and ended up lying on the floor with one of the magic tin auditing cans jammed up his ass.

Her breath smelled only of coffee.

"I stumbled a week or so ago," she said, catching me at it. "But I'm back working the program. But right now I have to ask you, Mr. Skellig, if you were in any way working with the shooters."

"I need my doctor."

Delilah crossed her eyes at me, then went to the door and waved. A moment later, Dr. Quan reappeared, chewing on an energy bar, hurriedly tucking the uneaten portion neatly into her lab coat pocket.

"Dr. Quan, I am confused about what happened to me, the date, who is president, even my own identity, what I had for breakfast, plus I am in a great deal of pain."

Delilah grimaced at Dr. Quan and said, "He's just tired of me asking him questions."

"Still, I have to ask you to postpone this interview, Detective," Dr. Quan said.

Delilah laughed, accepting my play with good grace. "I was done anyways. Have Connie get in touch and set a time when you feel well enough to answer a few more questions."

Connie is my lawyer and Delilah's best friend, so now you're caught up on why Delilah and I are on such familiar terms. You were probably thinking that it's because I'm Known to Police, an Underworld Informant, a shitheel. Shame on you. Me killing that vicious dog in self-defense convinced you that I'm a shady guy despite my revealing my innermost thoughts in a full and frank manner.

"Later, 'tater," Delilah said. I waved.

Big mistake. I missed Delilah's exit due to the jolts of blinding agony running through my head and down my spine.

"Can I offer you something for the pain?" Dr. Quan asked.

CLEAR SHALLOW WATER

While I'm drugged and asleep, let me tell you about my old man. Hippocrates figured that why and how we do what we do is irrevocably attached to what particular bodily fluids dominate our character. My dad, Abel Skellig, may not be an ancient Greek alchemist, but he is something equally anachronistic (a cowboy), plus he's a deep thinker who has his own take on people.

When I was eleven and my brother, Brendan, was ten, my father worked as manager on a four-thousand-acre mixed-use ranch up in Big Sur called Rancho Pico Blanco, named for the most distinctive peak in the Santa Lucia mountains of Big Sur. The family who owns Pico Blanco deeded Mom and Dad a hundred of the best acres plus the house I grew up in along a dirt road off Old Highway One above the headwaters of Bixby Creek. Since the owners live in New York and San Francisco and Chicago, by any real measure Pico Blanco is Dad's ranch.

These days Mom is a state senator in Sacramento, which means my parents live apart much of the time, though it's obvious (and baffling) that they are as in love now as they were when we all lived together like a normal family on the ranch and Mom commuted into the city of Monterey to teach school.

When I was a boy I loved nothing more than when Dad asked me to help him ranch, because he was (and is) the most competent man I've ever met.

So here we are (me eleven, Dad thirty-five), early spring, climbing from the floor of Bixby Canyon through the redwood groves, up, up, up to Serra Ridge on top of the world. Being a runty kid, I have to take twice as many steps as the old man, but when we start climbing the ridge, my father's long legs lose their advantage.

"Look at you," Dad says, "half mountain goat! Go ahead! Don't let me hold you back."

It's like letting a dog off a leash, I scamper ahead so fast, showing off for Dad and myself and the universe, freer than Huckleberry Finn on a raft.

Which is why I'm the one who finds the calf and runs back to get Dad, like I'm being chased by wolves, about this close to tears, barely able to describe what I've found up ahead on the pasture beyond the ridge.

"Still alive?" Dad asks.

I nod, unable to speak.

Dad shrugs off his canvas backpack and digs through it for his whacking-big cowboy Colt revolver, a chunk of metal and wood he inherited from his father, a Vietnam vet turned game warden in the Sierras who was killed in a back-road hit-and-run when Dad was eighteen. That Colt is old and dependable, fair but firm, worn and reassuring.

"What happens," Dad says, "is the coyotes find the calf and attack it, but then the mother cow comes running, scares them off, and the calf is left to die slow."

"Its guts are hanging out."

"Coyotes melt away until the calf dies, which is smart because, y'know, one kick to the jaw, even from a newborn calf, they're gonna starve to death."

"I wish those damn coyotes would die of starvation."

"Don't hate on 'em, Mikey. They are acting according to their nature, looking to feed their own young. It's not good or bad. But we are cattlemen, so the coyotes are our antagonists. Big difference between enemies and antagonists. Enemies you can hate if you got the energy to spare. Antagonists you deal with respectfully."

"You gonna shoot the coyotes?"

"Right now, it's the calf requires shooting."

"The calf didn't do anything wrong."

"You don't have to do anything wrong to suffer."

"I'll do it."

I have no idea where that came from. Dad lifts his eyebrows in surprise, but he takes me seriously, considers the offer.

"Ranching's a hard life," he says, "and I can use a hand doing the hard work. Shooting a calf counts as real hard work."

Now we're standing over the calf, the grass worn to dirt from where it's kicking its legs and moving its head up and down, like making a snow angel in the dirt only awful and bloody. Its eyes are rolling all over the place, trying to watch us, trying to watch everything, panting and grunting. Dad hands me his father's gun. Heavy.

"What do I do?"

"Stick the barrel in her ear and pull the trigger."

Which is fully what I intend to do, but the calf keeps moving her head and making a desperate noise and suddenly I'm sniffling, then crying. Dad looks off along the ridge for a bit, giving me time to push back on and maybe overcome my emotions, before he takes the gun back.

"That's okay; I'm proud of you."

Dad places a foot gently on the calf's neck, thrusts the gun into her ear, and pulls the trigger, and the calf stops making angel marks in the dirt and we stand there in the silence, Dad letting me pull myself together while he looks at Pico Blanco to the southeast and the fog rolling in from the ocean to the west, clouds scudding only a few feet above our heads. (If you want, you can reach up and touch them, make your fingers wet.)

He's good that way, my old man, giving you a little time when you need it.

I tell Dad I'm sorry.

"No shame here," Dad says. "It's important for a man to be decisive, but that has two parts to it. Are you listening to me?"

I'm listening.

"Part one is making the decision. That should be the hard part. Take all the time you can to do that properly. Part two, taking action, that's the easy part. You got ahead of yourself this time, is all. You put part two ahead of part one. Take your time making the decision so that the action you take is *clear shallow water.* Just like the German poet said."

Dad pulls me into his leg and pats my back.

"Now," he says, "we're going down to the truck, get the rifle. Then we're gonna climb back up here and head over in those ponderosa pines, and we're gonna wait quietly until the coyotes come back to see if the calf is dead yet, ready to eat, and I'm gonna shoot them with the rifle. That's my decision, which I will act upon without hesitation."

"Like clear shallow water?"

"That's right."

I love my father and I've always known that my father loves me, and even when I was eleven, I knew then, as I know now, that I am one of the lucky sons who has a good father.

And I did not hesitate to shoot the lead coyote when he showed up to eat the calf he'd killed. And even though I didn't understand it when Dad said it, I understood when I pulled the trigger and every single trigger I've pulled since that day.

Clear shallow water.

B!$M@R©K!

I open my eyes to the sight of celebrity skateboard mogul, rap figure, and TV reality star Bismarck Avila mean-muggin' me from the doorway of my hospital room. You know Avila (you've seen him thirty feet tall on billboards, selling sneakers and aftershave and wet suits, hats and watches, etc.). Avila eyeballs me in full-on showbiz street mode (serious business, no flashes of humor because life's a struggle skating these hard streets while copyright protected). The second he catches my eye, Avila glides into the room, compact, well muscled, smooth, weird pale-green eyes in a burnished mahogany face under well-coiffed and highlighted short dreads. Only twenty-six years old, famous for more than half his life for his abilities on a skateboard and with a microphone, for his rampaging sex life, for feuds with other skateboarders and rappers and athletes, for fronting a surf-rap-punk band, and today, I assume, for being the target of a high-profile, bungled hit that killed his bodyguard.

None of those pressures showed on Avila's calm, famous face.

He wore black linen pants with panic-blue unlaced basketball shoes, a skintight sleeveless white T-shirt with Buddha smoking a doobie on it (which I doubt is historically accurate), and some kind of multi-colored Laplander tasseled wool cap because, you know, LA is freezing this time of year unless you go outside. I could see a police guard out in the hallway. Obviously, Delilah wasn't going to just let me go. I was officially detained for questioning.

You know Bismarck Avila's story: half-German half-Mexican gambler falls in lust with an African American escort/stripper, she gets pregnant, Dad gets murdered during an altercation after an illegal dogfight, leaving little Bismarck and his crackhead mother to bounce around a series of motel rooms and boardinghouses in and around Lennox. But the kid is gifted and determined and practices his street kicks and airs and grabs, kickflips and lasers and shuvits, all night until he gets discovered in an underground skateboard video sold on the Venice Boardwalk.

Two years later, in a big upset, fourteen-year-old Bismarck Avila wins the X Games for the first time; a year after that, he's an emancipated minor living high on sponsorship. Mom dies ugly during a rape and young Bismarck Avila (now more a brand than a human being) stars in a salacious reality show, which was mostly about a barely legal kid hooking up with models and porn stars; he turns twenty-one and uses his TV money to form his own skateboard company (B!$m@R©k! with two exclamation marks and a dollar sign and other symbols instead of letters!), specializing in clothes, skate and surf accessories, videos, and condoms with street cred.

And now here he was, standing in the doorway to my hospital room, bottleneck in his fist.

"What I got here is a twenty-five-hundred-dollar bottle of Scotch."

Tsunamis of light flooded through my window. I'd slept the night through; it was morning.

Sunday.

"What time is it?"

"I don't tend to know shit of that nature."

"You don't tend to know shit like the time of day?"

"Trivial, brah."

I had to pee, so I got to my feet and wobbled toward the can. I thought I did all right, considering I hadn't been upright for well over twenty-four hours.

"Jesus, ass hanging out," Avila said.

I shut the bathroom door on him. I heard him ripping shrink-wrap off the plastic cups on my bedside table. By the time I emerged, he'd poured two stiff drinks. He toasted me and tossed his back, tossed *mine* back, then poured us each another.

Maybe the strain was catching up after all.

"Drink up," he said. "What's the matter with you?"

"Relax. I'm not going to sue you."

"Sue me?"

"Your bodyguard assaulted me."

"C'mon, brah! It was a confusing sequence of events."

"I'd appreciate it if you told the police I wasn't working with the kids who tried to shoot you."

"I want to hire you full-time." Avila said it like he was bestowing the Nobel Prize for wonderfulness along with a plastic cup holding three fingers of twenty-five-hundred-dollar Scotch. Do the math. Fifty bucks a swallow.

"Drink up," he said, pounding back his third.

"I don't drink," I lied like a lying-dog liar.

"You seriously gonna allow a man to drink by himself after he offers you the best job you ever gonna get offered in your whole life?"

"You seriously gonna talk about yourself in the third person?"

"You think I don't know what that means. Bismarck Avila knows exactly what *third person* means."

Okay, so he had a sense of humor. Still, I knew who this guy was at the core because I've met a version of him in every village I ever fought for hearts and minds in, every street corner and marketplace anywhere I've been deployed. Bismarck Avila was a thin-skinned showboater who does whatever it takes to be the center of attention and get his way.

Which meant this conversation was not destined to end happily.

"Thanks, but I already got a job."

I put down the Scotch, leaned against the edge of my bed, and watched Bismarck Avila come to grips with someone not doing what he wanted the second he wanted it.

"You never even gonna ask how much I pay?"

"Thanks for the Scotch," I said. "Somebody tried to kill you, so my advice is stay home until the cops get a handle on that."

"Cops escorted me here," he said. "I got cops up my ass. What job you already got? You mean that played-out limo company?"

I nodded. I reeled but did not pass out. Let the healing begin.

"I'll buy your shit," he said. "Three limos, three full-time employees, handful of freelance drivers, half dozen vans and trucks you lease out for airport shuttles and moving day and shit."

Avila seemed very well informed—aside from the fact that he had less than a clue about what he was in for when it came to Tinkertoy and Ripple.

"That shit's barely a company," he continued. "You know what's a company?"

"Bismarck? With exclamation points and dollar signs and symbols all over?"

I envisioned *O@$!$ L!mO $eRv!©e$* on the sign above our bays and felt aggrieved.

"My company's not for sale."

Avila drained his Scotch and crumpled the cup, then said, "My bodyguard who died, his name was Brian. His brother Chris is grieving the loss heavy, y'know? Twins. Tight."

Brian and Chris were not the names I'd have guessed. More like Goliath and Gargantua.

"Depending what Chris tells the police," Avila continued, "you come off as either a hero or a suspect."

"You mean depending on what you tell Chris to tell the police."

Avila shrugged and downed another two ounces of Scotch.

"If you want a limo company so bad, go ahead and put one together yourself. It doesn't take much. A few cars. You can afford that, right?"

"Hells yes, I can afford that."

"Then why do you want my company?"

"None of your business why I want what I want."

"My business isn't for sale."

Avila stood, pointed at the bottle. "Keep that for yourself."

"No, thank you."

One thing most soldiers get good at, dealing with officers, is making *thank you* sound like *fuck you*.

Avila blinked. I don't guess lifestyle megamoguls hear even a polite *fuck you* every day, much less twice in a row, much less from a mere driver.

"Bismarck Avila your real name?" I asked. "Sounds made-up."

"Look me up," Avila said, peeved at me for the first time. I must have touched some sort of pride nerve there, not knowing enough about him. Avila tossed the Scotch into the waste can and left.

As soon as Avila was gone, a nurse stuck his head in the door and asked, "Are you ready for your next visitor?"

"Only if my next visitor is a beautiful lawyer."

"Depends on how your tastes run, I guess," he said, "but he looks okay to me."

The nurse disappeared from my doorway and a few seconds later, Lucky entered the room, gazing around himself sadly and itching his ear with a carefully placed little finger.

"No, no, no," I said.

"Apologies," Lucky said.

Lucky's real name is Luqmaan Qadir Yosufzai. He was born and raised in the Herat Province of western Afghanistan about a yard from Turkmenistan. Qizilbash Tajik on his mother's side and Hazara on his father's, raised Shia, it's no wonder Lucky learned to survive at a very young age. Handsome but diminutive in that way where people think he's a yard or two farther away than he actually is, Lucky is a living optical illusion, a fact that he maintains has saved his life on multiple occasions. Lucky was my interpreter when I worked with the anti-Taliban forces in Afghanistan. I smuggled him into the States after his last deployment before Taliban sympathizers or Aimaqs or Balochs or other Sunnis could string him up on a power pole and chuck rocks at him until he died. Lucky speaks Dari, Farsi, Urdu, Pashto, English, Hebrew, Russian, and French. He lives only for women, doesn't care about men unless the man is a guest in his home. Lucky's an observant Muslim mostly because he's deeply invested in the prophet Muhammad's promise of a heaven devoid of men. He watches all-female sports on TV (golf, diving, figure skating, volleyball, tennis, basketball) and he's excited by the fact that female jockeys are finally making inroads in the sport of kings. Lucky despises sexism in every form except leering. I know I can trust Lucky with my life because I've done it plenty of times and come out on the other side with soul parts and meat parts properly conjoined.

"How's your noggin?" Lucky asked, working, as always, on his dated colloquialisms.

"I left five voice mails for Connie. Because I need Connie. Because Connie's a lawyer."

"Yes, and Connie in turn called upon me to Convey Unto You a message."

"What message?"

Lucky extended an Oasis Limo Services ball cap. "May I offer this so that civilians don't Gaze Upon You and vomit?"

Although Lucky speaks English without any discernible accent, he rattles along in a kind of Victorian cadence that suggests he is capitalizing certain words in his head as part of his translation. (Like Winnie-the-Pooh or Henry James.)

"You and I are both civilians now, Lucky. Everybody around us is a civilian. We live in the civilian world and I need a lawyer."

"Why?"

"Because I'm a person of interest in a murder. Which is why I need a lawyer, not an interpreter."

"Yes, I see, but Connie has sent me in her place with a message."

"Let's have it."

"Connie contends that you Labor under the Mistaken Impression that *confer* means the same as *fuck*."

"Connie never curses."

"I Divined the Hidden Subtext from the Vigor with which she declined to attend your summons."

"That's a lot of vigor."

"As you are aware, Skellig, I myself have enjoyed Sexual Relations with Many Women," Lucky said. "Dozens, approaching hundreds, yes, hundreds of women, including lawyers . . ."

I rubbed my eyes, wondering if Lucky was working himself up to quote the Koran, the Upanishads, or Oprah Winfrey. Lucky is a man who gathers his wisdom wherever it finds him.

". . . but never my own Personal Solicitor," Lucky said, "because I possess a Keen Intelligence. Because it's important to keep a Professional Distance when Serious Legal Matters are at stake."

"Connie and I are just friends now, Lucky."

"Friends with Occasional Benefits."

"Very occasional. Christmas. And I ruined even that by telling her I loved her with all my heart."

"Perhaps Connie is under the impression that you are using this Current Imbroglio only in an attempt to have sex with her."

"Yeah, I got that."

"You pay me to advise you."

"I pay you to drive a limo."

"Indeed," Lucky said, "I have fetched Number One from where you abandoned it in the alley—"

"I didn't abandon One; I got sucker punched."

"Nevertheless, One is outside and Readily Accessible. Would you like to Make a Break for it?"

"Yes. Great idea. Let's do that," I said. "Because what I really need right now is to overpower the cop out in the hall and then be in a televised car chase with an illegal Muslim alien from Afghanistan named Luqmaan Qadir Yosufzai."

"Ah, sarcasm."

"Go back to Connie. Tell her this isn't a parking ticket or any kind of excuse. Tell her I'm a yard from being wrongfully indicted on statutory homicide charges and I really need her as a lawyer."

"I will not return without her," Lucky pledged, backing out of the room. "As ever, I will be the Instrument of your Salvation."

CONSTANT TRUTH

Six hours later a nurse wheels me to a pleasant, well-appointed waiting room with comforting furniture and wood paneling and indirect light and a view south to the ocean. This is where the hospital shunts grieving celebrities or their families when they are forced to confront the cruel reality of mortality in their heretofore charmed lives.

Such is the nature of the real Los Angeles.

Secret oases.

Hideaways.

Sanctuaries and harbors.

You are standing on a sun-blasted desert street with smog in your lungs, squinting through your sunscreen and sunglasses and sun-blasted desert grit, wishing you were back home in wherever it was you came here from in the first place, and then you turn down this corridor, descend three steps, follow this wall past a mural and through a gate, and find yourself in a courtyard where goldfinches and orioles warble and fountains tinkle and amber-colored iced drinks are brought to you by beautiful, exotic people and you think you've died and gone to heaven.

That's the real reason they call Los Angeles the City of Angels. You constantly find yourself standing at the right hand of God, amazed by the beauty in the world. Los Angeles is supposed to be all facade, but it's exactly the opposite. It's not until you've burrowed into the city's deep nooks and crannies and bolt-holes that you find the real there that is there. A lot of people never get that: if you think there's no here here, it's because you never found your way through the looking glass.

Despite my current surroundings and my pleasant Vicodin buzz, I was trying (and failing) to run through the relaxation exercises my VA shrink gave me when, finally, the door opened and my lawyer entered. As always, my heart rolled over in my chest at the sight of her.

What am I, fifteen years old?

Let me tell you about Connie: her full name is Constanta Candide, which translates, according to Lucky, as Constant Truth, which would typically be ludicrous when applied to a lawyer, but in Connie's case, the translation is accurate. Hippocrates would have labeled Connie's humors as *Choleric with Sanguine overtones,* meaning—well, let's just say that combo results in a particularly turbulent potpourri of conflicting impulses that can make a person alluring but distant.

In flat shoes—which are the only kind she'll wear because high heels are, I quote, "a way to hobble women"—Connie is approximately five feet two inches tall, which barely brings her up to Delilah's shoulder. Connie downplays her looks, unsuccessfully in my opinion, by wearing her dark hair in what she calls a *lob*—which means a bob that stops at the chin—and rimless glasses in an effort to look severe.

I first met Connie in San Diego when she called me up as a witness for the defense in a court-martial involving a shipboard altercation in which an E-3 (male) was struck in the face, with intent, by Connie's client, an E-9 master chief petty officer (female), both parties serving in the US Navy. The petty officer's guilt was not in question because she admitted striking the E-3, but extenuating circumstances could mean the difference between a stint in military prison, followed by the end of her naval career, and a temporary slap-on-the-wrist demotion and an amusing but respectful new nickname. The extenuating circumstances involved whether or not the petty officer was fending off a sexual assault. This is exactly the kind of case Connie loves.

At the time of the proceedings Connie was a full-on naval lieutenant 0-3, while I was ostensibly an army chief warrant officer W-3, which meant that as a commissioned officer, Connie outranked me.

"Mr. Skellig, could you please inform the court what you were doing on board the USS *Elrod* at the time these events occurred?" Connie asked me at the court-martial sentencing hearing.

"I am not at liberty to say," I said. (Yes, it's cliché, but that's the language a guy like me is advised to employ at times like these.)

"You are not at liberty to say why you were on board the ship?"

"I'm not at liberty to confirm that I was aboard *Elrod*."

"Really? Why?"

"Well, now we're whirling around in some tightly coiled circular logic."

"Can you give us a general idea?"

"I cannot."

Connie looked at the court-martial board. Three of them shrugged. Four willed themselves to be invisible to one another and the brave three who had shrugged.

"Mr. Skellig . . . have you been sheep-dipped?"

"I am not familiar with that term," I lied like a lying-dog liar.

"It refers to military personnel whose security clearances have been upgraded so that they can be seconded to the CIA or other government agencies for detached duties."

The odor of sheep-dip upon me must have filled the entire hearing room if a fairly inexperienced Navy lawyer like Connie had picked it up.

"Are you even really a chief warrant officer?" she asked. "And I will remind you that you are under oath."

I said nothing, which told Connie what I was (sort of and inaccurately).

"Lieutenant," a rear admiral advised Connie, "let's assume this is an area the witness is not authorized to discuss and move on as though he is exactly what he says he is."

She looked at me. I shrugged.

"Tell me, without confirming whether you were there or not, in your own words, what happened," Connie suggested.

"If the petty officer broke the turd's nose, then she did absolutely the right thing and the turd deserves a big chicken dinner."

"Big chicken dinner?"

Showing off, the rear admiral informed Connie that *big chicken dinner* was military slang for *bad conduct discharge* and that *turd* was self-explanatory.

"I'm sure the board appreciates your willingness to do its job and mete out justice, Mr. Skellig, if that's your name—"

"It's my name," I said.

"—but if we could get back to the reality that you were an eyewitness to what the petty officer did . . . ?"

"I'm gonna take the Fifth, Lieutenant," I answered sorrowfully.

"Taking the Fifth doesn't mean what you think it means," Connie informed me and, by extension, the seven-member court-martial board. "When you're a witness, you implicate yourself by refusing to testify and risk being held in contempt."

I asked which amendment was the one that allowed me not to answer, which Connie did not find amusing, and my implied security clearance did not stop her from whipsawing and smacking that board around until I ended up in the brig on contempt charges. But three days later it was Connie who came and got me out of that brig, drove me from San Diego all the way back to her cottage at the butt end of the Venice Canals (talk about a hidden-away slice of heaven), and provided me a few pro bono lessons in self-implication.

Why did Connie take pity on me? Because I'm okay-looking, physically fit, because I did the right thing when I stood up for the petty officer, but most of all, I like to think, because she was determined to plumb the depths of my irresistible aura of mystery.

That first weekend together, I told Connie what I could, which was that my service career had been quite wide-ranging, working for or with every branch. Connie wanted to know what I intended to do when I left the military and I told her what I thought was the truth at the time: I intended to use my politician mother's contacts to get into politics with the express intention of making things better for veterans returning to the world. She said she liked the fact that both of us were interested in making the bigger world a better place.

Connie had joined the Navy to get her American citizenship, her mother being an illegal alien from Culiacán, in the state of Sinaloa, which is in Mexico. The Navy put Connie through law school, in return for which she gave them five solid years of service, mostly as a prosecutor, during which time she met me. Now she works for a white-shoe law firm in Century City.

"I want to help Latinos. Run for governor. Supreme Court. Senate. President. Something *gigantesco* like that."

Now you have increased insight into my relationship with LAPD detective Delilah Groopman. Yes, there are sexual sparks between me and Delilah; you weren't imagining that. In the regular course of events, Delilah and I would have given it a shot. (Delilah has confided in Connie that the only things that keep me from being a solid eight out of ten are that I'm under six feet tall and the fact that I'm besotted with Connie.) But Delilah and Connie have been BFFs ever since Delilah was assigned to protect Connie during a contentious trial that garnered Connie a raft of death threats from anonymous persons of the racist persuasion. As a result, Delilah knows exactly how I feel about Connie and how Connie feels about me, so the vibes between us remain dampened and repressed.

Are you wondering what happened to my political ambitions?

After mustering out, I went to work as an adviser on veterans' affairs for a congressman whose heart was most definitely in the right place. Working for him, I got a solid, firsthand look at how good ideas and the best of intentions drown in the swamp of political necessity and realized that it would be years before anything I did in the political arena brought any benefits to actual veterans.

By that time, I'd smuggled Lucky into the country through Canada. He was bouncing around from cash job to cash job and obviously needed something more stable. I realized that the best thing I could do was start a small business where I could hire him on a cash-only basis, so almost exactly one year ago, Oasis Limousine Services was born. Which is about the same time I made the gigantic mistake of asking Connie to marry me.

"Listen, Gringo," Connie said. "I already explained to you my political ambitions. I can't have a gringo husband and half-gringo babies. *Nada* personal. It's the same reason I don't take drugs or dirty dance in public or send you pictures of my *tetas* even though I'd like to. Big picture, right?"

It was never the same between us after I proposed. It had put too much pressure on the relationship, and no matter how much I tried, I couldn't unring that bell.

Until the perfect excuse to spend time with Connie presented itself: I was being questioned with regard to a homicide and needed a good lawyer. And Connie was the best.

It started out very promising with a hug and three (count 'em!) kisses ranging from my forehead to my nose to the very corner of my lips. But by the time she peered at the sewn-up gash on the top of my head, she'd remembered that we were no longer a couple and pressed down on my shoulder to keep me from rising.

"*¿Estas vivo?*" she asked, utilizing her full-on professional-lawyer tone, letting me know she was showing concern not for me, her wannabe fiancé, but for a mere client.

I took the hint and kept it professional. Instead of saying, *I love you, let's get married immediately*, I said, "How soon can you get them to let me go?"

"Not before they transfer you to the county jail."

"When's that?"

"Two hours."

"But I don't want to go to jail."

"Not an uncommon reaction."

"I didn't kill anybody. In fact, I *prevented* somebody from getting killed."

"Several shots were fired from an as yet undetermined number of weapons," Connie stated in her loveless lawyer voice. Whereas questions from Connie draw you in, statements of fact are her way of keeping you at arm's length.

The exact opposite of Delilah.

"Nine shots from two separate weapons," I said. "The Slavic-looking zit kid fired at Avila twice, the first of those bullets striking and killing the bodyguard. The Goth boy dropped his gun in the middle of a somersault before he could get a shot off. Did they find that gun?"

Connie nodded, signaling me to keep talking and leave the questions to her.

"I discharged the late bodyguard's weapon three times into the ceiling, and the Slavic kid shot four times into the ceiling as they fled the premises. Nine bullets in total. Three guns. Not complicated."

"I'm sure you'll be proven correct," Connie said. "But currently the forensics narrative is muddied. Furthermore, there's an *espectador inocente* with a bullet through his liver and corresponding buckets of confusion about how that occurred, and several witnesses point to you as one of the people who discharged said weapons."

"I admitted firing three times into the ceiling."

"There is an alternate account."

"From the skateboarder whose life I saved? Or the bodyguard who didn't do a damn thing but hit me on the head when it was over?"

"You mean the celebrity owner of a major company? Or the trusted member of his security detail?"

"Connie. It's blackmail."

"You are contending that Bismarck Avila is blackmailing you."

"First with a carrot made of expensive Scotch, then with a stick made of confusion about what happened."

"Blackmailing you for what?"

"Avila's exact words were that he wants what he wants."

"Obviously, he wants you to kill someone for him."

"That's alarmingly specific. Why go straight there?"

"It's not like you've never killed anybody, Michael."

"Only for the United States Army! When it was my job!"

"It's possible you developed a taste for it. What was once your job is now your hobby."

"Are you doing that thing where you pretend to be the prosecutor to emphasize the dire nature of my situation?"

"Tell me what Avila wants from you."

"To drive him places. In a limo."

I have to admit that when I said it out loud it sounded maniacal.

"Avila says he'll pay three times my current hourly rate and buy Oasis for three times market value."

"Three times market value! So he's offering you a box of Skittles and a car-wash coupon."

"Hey!"

Connie must have felt bad because she stopped making cruel distancing statements and started asking questions.

"Is Avila making you some kind of mollifying preemptive offer before you can blackmail him?"

"For what?"

"Did you see him do anything probative or incriminatory?"

"I already went through this with Delilah."

"And?"

"I saw him pick his nose with his thumb."

Connie covered her eyes dramatically, as though she was thinking deep thoughts, then said, "Accept Avila's offer."

"I don't want to."

"Take the job, then quit in a week, after Avila gives the police a statement that gets you off their radar."

Connie removed my cell phone from her purse and waggled it impatiently. Her suggestion was smart and simple and pragmatic. I didn't like it.

"After you make the call and your client's memory of the situation legally adjusts, I'll take you home and pro bono this consultation."

The way Connie said *pro bono* cheered me up. I took the phone and called Bismarck Avila to accept the job. Meanwhile, Connie called Avila's lawyer and told him what steps to take immediately so that Delilah Groopman wouldn't send me to county jail, which is an awful place filled with bad people.

Two hours later, I was a free man.

PRO BONO IS
THE BEST BONO

Connie's cottage is tucked away at the northeastern edge of the Historic Venice Canals, one of the increasingly rare funky remnants of California beach-town Bohemia. Surrounded by a collection of architectural boxes, stubborn throwback cabins, and upscale whimsy, Connie's cottage enjoys a view of two toy bridges under which people paddle and pedal and row in toy boats along the canals, drinking chilled wine or artisanal beer under well-trimmed palm trees that clatter slightly in the breeze off the beach just two blocks away. Tonight we sit out on Connie's canal-side deck, under Fellini lights, breathing in the salty tang from the ocean while Connie serves delicious curly pasta in marinara sauce washed down with the perfect balance of a robust red and legally prescribed painkillers.

Because life, at that moment, threatened to approach perfection, and Connie, like a Navajo blanket weaver, would have none of that, she spiked the mood by grilling me about Tinkertoy and Ripple. Connie entertains grave concerns about both of them, especially Tinkertoy, because Connie knows in torturous detail exactly what befell Tinkertoy in Iraq.

Tinkertoy was a buck sergeant convoy mechanic and driver in the Army infantry. She served three tours in Iraq. Halfway between Abu Ghraib and Fallujah on Route Michigan, a band of Naqshbandi insurgents attacked Tinkertoy's convoy, during which fracas Tinkertoy was exploded, bludgeoned, kidnapped, and scheduled for video execution. To while away the days before her beheading, Tinkertoy's captors broke all four of her limbs with a hammer, tortured her sexually, and raped her tortuously.

I was part of the sheep-dipped extraction team who extricated and reclaimed Tinkertoy a long three days after her capture, by which time something deeper than flesh and bones was broken (of course), and her subsequent erratic and self-destructive behaviors (of course) placed her before a board (of course) and got her dishonorably discharged (you cannot be serious!).

At that point I was still a congressional aide and, aggravated by Tinkertoy's situation, informed Connie. Connie sailed in, had Tinkertoy's dishonorable discharge transmuted to an honorable discharge, and then tried to help Tinkertoy find a job and an apartment. Another reason for me to get out of politics and into a chauffeur's cap. When I established Oasis Limo, I hired Tinkertoy to be my mechanic.

"I don't like Tinkertoy living in your crawl space," Connie said.

"It's not a crawl space."

Tinkertoy lives in a windowless utility area accessed beneath her workbench through a three-by-three plywood hatchway with rope handles. Anyone who notices the panel at all assumes there's a water heater or electrical panel back there. I think of Tinkertoy's room as a monk's cell. She sits back there, eating food out of cans and watching game shows on TV, muttering the answers in pig Latin so the TV won't think she's helping the contestants cheat.

"Return to the womb. She feels safe," I said.

"You should be encouraging Tinkertoy at every opportunity to better her day-to-day existence," Connie said.

I reminded Connie that, due to my callous and unyielding decree that Oasis Limo be a nonsmoking workplace, Tinkertoy had ceased chain-smoking Camels in favor of chain-chewing bubble gum. Same with Ripple. Same with Lucky.

"The fact is," I told her, "I've saved everybody from cancer. Isn't that why you sleep with me?"

"I don't sleep with you," she said, "at least not regularly."

"Yeah," I said. "What's with that?"

"I don't want to give you false hope," she said. "*Toma las cosas como vienen.* How is Darren?"

Darren Cameron Monning is Ripple's real name. Connie's concerns for Ripple are maternal. It's Connie's contention that I should call Ripple by his real name because *Ripple* is obviously a rhyming version of *Cripple* and Connie wants Ripple to overcome that self-loathing, self-defeating self-image. I've tried calling Ripple by his real name a thousand times and he has not responded even once, even stoned out of his gourd or roused from a sound sleep. When I asked Connie why it was all right for Tinkertoy to have a nickname and not Ripple (Tinkertoy's real name is Rose Margaret Vandevere), Connie said it's because Tinkertoy has the right to reimagine herself as a different woman from the one who was degraded and tortured in Iraq, while Ripple must remember that he is still the same man he was before he lost his legs.

"Same man," I agreed, "except only half as tall."

"How are his new prosthetics?" Connie asked.

"The kid's hard to fit because he's lopsided," I said, "so he's back in the wheelchair. Sometimes he uses one fake leg and crutches, but it hurts."

I wasn't positive that Ripple's constant ingestion of THC hadn't blunted his ambition to stand tall but thought it best not to get Connie going on that subject.

"Has Darren found anybody?"

Meaning a girlfriend.

I shook my head.

"It's been over eight months," Connie said. "Darren's nineteen. He should be bonding with a human being, not *masturbándose* to Internet porn."

Ripple does more than masturbate to porn. He reads graphic novels, loves sci-fi and fantasy, and is adamant that God (whom he believes in wholeheartedly) is an extremely advanced cruel alien conducting Mengele-like experiments on humanity who will get His divine ass kicked when the good-guy aliens finally show up to liberate this concentration camp we call Earth.

"Lucky tried to talk to Ripple about women," I said. "But he did that Afghan thing of holding hands."

"How did Darren respond?"

"By drawing an extremely detailed cartoon of a beheaded Lucky eating his own genitalia."

"*Esto es muy desconcertante . . .*"

"Yes," I said, because why not?

"The kind of physical trauma Darren has faced, the destruction of his physical self, he needs time to find himself as a sexual being again."

I nodded, because why argue?

"I imagine he had his fair share of sex before his injuries."

"Absolutely," I said, "if by fair share you mean once."

"Once? You mean one time? *¿Una vez?*"

"Ripple grew up small-town religious in Three Rivers. He and his high school girlfriend saved it for marriage and they only got married two days before he shipped out."

"Darren is *married*?"

"Waiting on his divorce."

"What happened?"

"What happened? The kid lost two legs in two different ways in two minutes. Eighteen-year-old wife takes one look, no, thanks, that's that, end of conjugals."

"The girl was religious enough to want to be married before they had sex but not *lo suficientemente devota* to stay married to Darren after he came home wounded."

"Correct," I said, but what I was thinking was *of course* because religion is bullshit crap. I didn't say that part out loud because I currently put my chances of staying the night at fifty-fifty and didn't want to jinx it by insulting Connie's friend Jesus. As a devout lapsed Catholic (it's a real thing), Connie could be surprisingly defensive on behalf of God.

"Maybe the problem is Ripple still loves her," I said. "Maybe he can't even imagine being with someone else."

"Don't do that," Connie said. "We're having a good time. We're talking about Ripple. If you want to *tener relaciones sexuales* to-night, don't make everything about you."

I shut up because I did want to *tener relaciones sexuales* tonight. When I felt the blip of tension bleed away, I told Connie that I was confident that someday soon Ripple's redheaded horniness would outweigh his broken heart and missing legs and his fury at what happened to him in Afghanistan, and the right (meaning *odd*) girl would come along and he'd make up for lost time.

You'll notice that Connie didn't interrogate me about Lucky.

It's not because she doesn't like Lucky, she does, but Lucky is a client. Connie's working to get him on a path to citizenship so that he can live and work in the States legally. Because Connie takes her responsibilities as an officer of the court seriously, she won't gossip about clients. Believe me, I've tried to find excuses for her to take on Tinkertoy and Ripple as clients too so I'd never have to discuss any of them.

After we finished our meal and I was done bringing Connie up to date on my employees, Connie stipulated that the only way that we were going to make love that night was if I lay perfectly still—my aching, stitched-up head cradled by pillows—while she did all the heavy lifting. I did not argue. (Would you?)

"*Relajarse*," said Connie, completely unnecessarily since I was already relaxed from food and love and desire and pills and wine.

A duck paddled by on the canal just outside her open French doors, on the other side of a stand of black bamboo, which at least provides the illusion of privacy. The duck quacked at us, which, due to red wine and painkillers and joie de vivre, made me laugh so hard that Connie placed her hand over my mouth.

"Just so I'm clear, Counselor," I whispered when she let go, "would this be *conferring* or *fucking*?"

Connie did not answer due to focus and concentration and did something with her timing and muscle control that made life worth living but froze me into a statue, my toes curled so tightly they cracked like starting a fire.

The duck quacked and then Connie quacked, only after which I took my turn to quack—after which I slept like a drunken fat Lutheran in church, my first solid, rejuvenating sleep in days.

Morning came too soon.

One more quick and very satisfying intimate conference with my lawyer (during which I took a more active role than I had the night before), then raisin toast and coffee and Vicodin, after which

I declined Connie's offer of a lift and set out to walk the couple of miles from the Venice Canals to Oasis Limousine Services in Santa Monica, because if there's one thing a soldier turned limo driver likes to do when he's not working, it's walk.

I emerged from Connie's canal onto South Venice Boulevard, up to hipster-heaven Abbot Kinney, grabbed a *café con leche* to go at Abbot's Habit, and continued east on California Avenue toward Lincoln, smelling jasmine, roses, sage, and a hundred other Southern California plants, mixed in with the scent of Venice bohemians and tech geniuses firing up the occasional morning bowl.

I like Lincoln Boulevard; it keeps you on your toes engaging with the three stages of junkiedom: Junkie. Methadone patient. Reformed junkie. I strode past Olympic High School, through knots of keener kids heading in early, grateful that Lucky had provided me with an Oasis Limo Services cap to hide my gashed and bloody stitched-up head. Past Pico, and over the 10 freeway, morning traffic bad in both directions, as usual, but especially coming from the east into Santa Monica. I zigzagged north and west toward Ninth, over to Santa Monica Boulevard, and up to my domicile and place of business.

Oasis Limousine Services squats a little more than a mile inland from the beach, just off the main drag in an alley. A tallish, badly proportioned, charmless, single-story twenty-foot-ceilinged brick building billed as earthquake-proof (I call bullshit), with three mechanic's bays, a tinted-windowed office at the front, and a toolroom behind the bays. There's a frost-fenced enclosure, where we can secure vehicles at night, that we call the Yard. Before I bought the property at police auction it was a chop shop with a reinforced roof atop which a mobile home had been hoisted by a crane.

The penthouse. My home.

I sauntered into the office to find Ripple in his wheelchair, facedown on his desk, sleeping, his copper thatch of hair half covering a comic book featuring zombies eating sexy nuns. Dressed in his unvarying uniform of black khaki cargo shorts, a yellow Minions T-shirt, and his I LOVE JESUS BUT I STILL CUSS fanny pack, Ripple looked more like an innocent choirboy than the furious, morbid, obsessed-with-violence lunatic I knew him to be.

"Wake up," I said, kicking Ripple's wheelchair, and continued through the office into the mechanic's bay, where Tinkertoy was changing out the solenoid on Number Three, a 2011 Cadillac DTS limo and the bane of Tinkertoy's existence. Three challenges Tinkertoy's every assumption about the rational world of mechanics and machinery by displaying a willful and haunted personality (as does Tinkertoy).

I'd become accustomed to approaching Tinkertoy slowly and carefully because when she is startled in any way, to any degree, she screams like she's being attacked by a knife-wielding maniac.

I cleared my throat.

"I heard you. Already," she said. "Telling Ripple to. Wake up."

Tinkertoy is an imposing African American woman, six feet tall, solid, as dark as black coffee. To me, she looks like some kind of royalty.

"Wait. They keep you in jail overnight?" Ripple asked, wheeling up behind us, a big sleep crease in his face that made him look about fourteen. The jaded smirk he affected to indicate that he knew exactly where I'd been all night didn't make him look any more mature.

"Company announcement: we now work exclusively for Bismarck Avila."

Tinkertoy nodded and returned to her work. Ripple was not so accepting.

"Wait, Bismarck Avila? The rapper-skater dude?"

"Yes."

"Why?"

"He's blackmailing me to work for him."

"Wait, so now Bismarck Avila's our only client?"

"That's what *exclusive* means, Ripple."

"So, wait—I cancel all our other clients?"

You may have noticed that Ripple says *wait* a lot. One of the VA wizards told me it's because Ripple is subconsciously trying to slow life down, which is only to be expected from somebody whose whole life got changed for the worse in a couple of minutes. The world spins too fast.

It probably also explains why Ripple is wearing out his medical marijuana card, another effort to slow down time.

"I'll drive Avila. Switch my regulars over to Lucky."

"Wait. Why would Avila hire you?"

"Why *wouldn't* he?"

"You shot his bodyguard!"

"Not even close. Where'd you get that?"

"TMZ. What really happened?"

"I saved his life."

"So, you're a hero?"

"Exactly."

"Wait. Your reward is to be blackmailed into doing something you don't want to do?"

"No good deed . . ."

"Is Avila *paying* us?"

"He's paying us double."

Ripple pulled his lips back from his teeth, shook his orange head, and flared his nostrils in the universal manner of teenagers who think their elders are idiots.

"Any questions?"

"Yes, how do we get blackmailed by everybody all the time?"

Tinkertoy tumbled into the conversation in her typical way, most commonly described as clumsy or offensive. "Why you?"

"Because I'm delightful, Tinkertoy. I'm due at his place in Calabasas in an hour and a half."

"You taking Number One?" Ripple asked.

One is our prestige vehicle: a 2015 Mercedes-Benz S550 sedan stretch limo. Nice. Understated. The vehicle that brought Bismarck Avila to us in the first place.

"Two," I said.

"What about? Three?" Tinkertoy asked, pointing at her nemesis, the Caddie.

"Three will never make it," Ripple said.

"I fixed it," Tinkertoy said.

"You say Three's fixed, but it never is."

"Three. Is fixed."

"Not unless you conducted an exorcism, because Three is haunted and the ghost who haunts Three hates you."

Ripple zipped open his I LOVE JESUS BUT I STILL CUSS fanny pack and dug out a medical marijuana toffee bonbon.

"Half the limos in town had people die in them," I said. "It doesn't make them haunted."

"Wait! Die?" Ripple shouted. "Ha! Try murdered! With a *machete*!"

(Accurate, but it happened before we owned the vehicle so not our problem.)

"I'm taking Two," I said.

Two is my favorite—an elegant 1954 Chrysler New Yorker limo, a vintage slab of yesteryear's Detroit metal, deep midnight blue, fins extended behind like a contrail. Two has no air-conditioning, which would serve Bismarck Avila right because he lived in the hot, hot Valley and there should always be negative consequences to blackmail.

While Ripple and Tinkertoy argued about whether or not the Caddie was haunted, I took the opportunity to slip away to my penthouse on the roof, which involves climbing a ladder to a precarious galvanized rigger's catwalk bolted to the ceiling, which leads to a pull-down mahogany stairway taken from the set of a pirate movie, which leads up to the roof. The rigger's catwalk alone stopped Connie from even trying to reach my beautifully appointed penthouse on the roof of an ex–chop shop off an alley off car dealership row on Santa Monica Boulevard.

When I say *beautifully appointed* I am not being facetious. My penthouse is without a doubt the dopest nonpermitted home on the west side. The chop shop criminal mastermind who owned the building before me was under house arrest for two years awaiting trial, so he put a ton of dough and sweat equity into what started out as nothing more than a mobile home craned up onto the roof. He added walnut crown molding, skylights made from prism-like light collectors salvaged from a decommissioned nineteenth-century lighthouse, floors of reclaimed California oak from Will Rogers's ranch, rugs from a Merv Griffin estate sale in Palm Springs, and a wrought-iron gazebo that has some connection to William Randolph Hearst's San Simeon.

My secret hideout.

Wearing a plastic Ralphs bag on my head to protect my stitches, I exited the shower (fixtures courtesy of a Jeremy Renner renovation in Bel Air) to find my mobile chirping.

Dad calling from the ranch in the mountains above Big Sur.

"Dad!"

"Hello, Mikey, can you hear me?"

I told him I could hear him just fine what with it being the twenty-first century and at least one of us living in a major metropolitan center.

"I was heading back from Salinas in the F-150, listening to news radio," he said in his concerned-father voice, "and heard the damned-est story and thought I'd better call."

Which meant the murder attempt on Bismarck Avila had made the news all the way up in Steinbeck country.

"What'd they say?"

"That a limo driver was being held as a person of interest in a shooting in a hotel bar," Dad said. "I knew it had to be you because who else would it be?"

"Dad, there are thousands of limo drivers in LA."

"The radio said Oasis Limo Services."

I admitted that narrowed it down.

I told my father the whole story from my point of view, very much as you've heard it so far (leaving out the sexy quacking sequence), after which Dad told me he was proud of me and thought I'd acquitted myself well, considering the circumstances.

After which the old man pivoted like a shortstop and blamed those exact same circumstances on me. "I can't say I've ever understood why you have chosen a life that exposes you to so much violence."

"I'm a limo driver, Dad. Not a hit man."

"You joined the military."

"It was either that or join a seminary and I thought the Jesuits might be unsympathetic to the fact that I do not believe in God."

Dad asked about Connie and Lucky and Ripple and Tinkertoy and then Connie again because, like me, he'd like nothing more than to have her join the family as my wife.

"You're all right, Mikey?"

"I got some stitches in my head but otherwise fine, Dad."

"Can you come up north for a few days? Winter steelhead looking good."

I told him I had work but promised to get up to see him as soon as I could.

"Remember what the poet asked, Mikey, 'So . . . so you think you can tell, Heaven from Hell, blue skies from pain?'"

"What's that? William Blake?"

"Pink Floyd."

And he hung up in exactly the same way rappers drop the microphone to claim the win.

I START MY NEW JOB

There are worse things to do under duress on a Monday morning than pilot a perfectly restored midnight-blue 1954 Chrysler New Yorker limousine down the California Incline to Pacific Coast Highway, windows open, wearing your most comfortable lightweight dark suit, slightly (but not unsafely) buzzed on Vicodin, sipping thermos coffee and listening to Lucky's exotic, calming Arabian chill-out music. In Los Angeles, when the Santa Anas do finally stop blowing, it's like Death Valley takes a deep breath and draws cooler ocean air in over the Southland basin and you remember for the hundredth time why this is paradise.

I drove past a jumbled old slide at the Palisades, continuing past Sunset Boulevard, then turned inland at Topanga Canyon—where surfers bobbed in the ocean across from a nursery / art / outdoor furniture store emblazoned SUPPORT OUR TROOPS!—and wound my way up, up, up to the old funky Topanga village center that hippies and musicians have loved since the sixties (and outlaw surfers before them), left on Old Topanga Canyon Road, past the flaky Inn of the Seventh Ray, smelling yucca and white sage, buckwheat on the hillsides, gnarly coast oaks, tang of pigweed (all the stuff I'd miss if I were driving the air-conditioned Mercedes), taking the scenic route to Bismarck Avila's Calabasas mansion to report for my first day of overcompensated indentured servitude. It was so pleasant I figured my petulant plan to make Avila uncomfortable in the New Yorker was foiled, but as the old Chrysler and I climbed inland, the effects of Saturday's ungodly Santa Anas lingered in the red-rock canyon. I felt beads of sweat form on my backbone and ribs.

Calabasas is where lots of actors and athletes and rapper types live: big houses in gated communities on expansive acreages surrounded by the picturesque Santa Monica Mountains. It's not exactly lush back there, tucked among the scrubby hills between the ocean and the huge San Fernando Valley suburbs, but there's room to spread out if you've got enough money to import fountains and pools and palm trees. A couple of miles past the Calabasas Highlands, I made an abrupt right onto an unmarked, unpaved private road, drove another quarter mile, and stopped at Bismarck Avila's gates. They looked like what you'd get if you carved Mount Olympus out of wood instead of marble. When I got out of the New Yorker to buzz in, I thunked the pillars with my knuckles.

They were made of poured concrete but painted to look like wooden versions of marble columns.

(Fake upon false upon bogus.)

A female voice thrummed over the intercom. She told me to drive up to the house. Her voice sounded sexy but exasperated.

I wanted to say to her, *Hey, I'm not nuts about this myself*, but for all I knew, Bismarck Avila had blackmailed her into answering his doorbell. The gates swung open to reveal what appeared to be an estate on Kauai—monstrous leafy plants and peacocks, coconut palms, orchids, and ferns.

The mansion itself (I estimated twelve to fifteen thousand square feet) looked like it had been designed by a dotty British admiral for the governor of Kentucky. White, stately, eccentric, and rambling, with a castle-looking turret on one side and a steampunk-looking copper-topped observatory on the other, with everything jammed between doing its best to reconcile the whack. I couldn't decide if it was awesome or awful, but what it wasn't was subtle. Poking out from the turret side of the house was what had to be the largest private skateboard ramp in Southern California (meaning the world), four stories high, vertical at the top. Made me queasy to look at. On the other side of the driveway, a man-made pond. Was it possible Avila hadn't heard that California was holding a drought? More likely, droughts simply didn't exist in his income bracket.

In the middle of the lakelet, there was a desert island, size of a tennis court, two palm trees, a yellow hammock slung between them, a tiki hut containing a daybed for desert island shenanigans, a treasure chest half buried within arm's reach of the hammock (had to be a cooler). On the driveway side of the pond, there was a small dock and, moored to the dock, a diminutive pirate-ship galleon, hardly bigger than a Boston Whaler, complete with poop deck and sails, a fiberglass pelican wearing a bandanna and eye patch, and a Jolly Roger flag and a topless mermaid figurehead.

I eased the New Yorker behind a colorless Ford Crown Victoria; unmarked law enforcement with a bar of lights hidden in the windshield and a gigantic whip antenna, which I figured for county since Calabasas is one of the dozens of smaller municipalities that contract the Los Angeles County Sheriff's Department to handle local law enforcement. Bismarck Avila himself stood in front of an eight-car garage, dressed in leprechaun-green basketball shorts and SpongeBob SquarePants T-shirt, speaking to a tall, lean, balding man in his early forties wearing a well-cared-for but dated suit like he'd bought it at the same outlet mall where he got his tortoiseshell aviator glasses, a lanyard around his neck, brandishing a document in an officious manner.

I know what executing a warrant looks like and I was pretty sure Bismarck Avila didn't need his driver for that, so I sat happily in my car, reading Patton Oswalt's Twitter feed on my phone, until Avila whistled and waved me over. I sighed, exited the New Yorker, and approached, adjusting my Oasis Limo Services ball cap to hide the unsightly bald patch and stitches on the top of my head.

"Who's this, now?" the cop asked.

"My driver," Avila said.

"Your what?"

The lanyard he wore around his neck identified him as Los Angeles County Sheriff's Detective Willeniec, A.

"His *driver!*" I bellowed, as though Willeniec, A., was deaf.

(Way to go, Skellig! First thing, let's create an adversary out of law enforcement!)

"*You* drive *him?*"

By which he meant, *Shouldn't* he *be driving* you?

"That's what *driver* means. The one who drives. I am the driver. I think of it more as an avocation than a vocation, if you get my drift."

"What's your name?"

"My driver listed in your warrant?" Avila asked.

"Shush, now. I'm talking to your status symbol here," Willeniec, A., said, turning his back on Avila.

Maybe being a mansion-owning skateboard rocker had allowed Avila to forget what kind of world still exists for darker-hued people beyond the walls of the faux-Hawaiian protectorate over which he currently reigned. Willeniec, A., must have been a harsh reminder, because Avila blinked in surprise before adopting his best poker face.

Willeniec snapped his fingers at me. Asshole move.

"Identification."

Willeniec, A., struck me as one of those bitter guys who runs marathons to compensate for the fact that he's going bald, maybe suffers pecker problems, and is not destined to rise any higher in his chosen career. Angry. Tough. A bully. Manhood issues. Woman problems.

I handed over my driver's license.

Willeniec flipped to page two in his brand-new notebook. He licked his pen and took his time copying my name and details, his entire attitude and body language indicating, *I can hold you here all day as long as I keep scribbling in my little book.*

Avila decided to confide in me.

"Man's looking for barrels."

"Makes sense."

"Makes sense how?"

"I read on Breitbart that barrels are behind a new crime wave. Prostitution, drugs, murder for hire, terrorism. Barrels are taking over the underworld."

"You got a very irritating demeanor for a driver," Willeniec said without looking up. "When I enter your name into the system, am I going to find any warrants, unpaid parking tickets, summonses, anything like that?"

I'd like to take a moment to share with you one of my experience-honed theories of life. To wit: AFEO. Which is an acronym for Assholes Find Each Other. By which I mean, well, exactly that. Assholes are drawn to each other like models and musicians or feet and stink. When two assholes meet, it usually gets strangulatory.

AFEO manifests as road rage, bar fights, parking lot conflicts, disturbing the peace, aggravated assault. Murder. When two deplorable human beings come together, like phosphorus and water, they are certain to combust upon each other.

The lanyard noted that Sheriff's Detective Willeniec, A., worked way the hell on the other side of Los Angeles County, down in

Whittier. Malibu / Lost Hills is the local sheriff's station that serves Calabasas.

Willieniec, A., was a long way from home.

"Are you drunk, on drugs, or otherwise impaired, Mr. Skellig?"

"Not currently. You here all by yourself, Detective Willeniec?"

Willeniec shot me a filthy look: he didn't like me saying his name out loud, even with due respect to his rank and profession.

"Why? You think I need backup?"

Strike two for Michael Skellig. We stood in awkward silence long enough for me to notice that Avila's hand was wrapped in gauze.

Like he'd barked his knuckles punching somebody.

"Barrels!" Avila said to me again, like the warrant read *unicorns*, probably thinking how all white people are crazy. "The fuck?"

A woman stepped out on one of the balconies: African American, early twenties, dressed in flowy white, about as beautiful as beauty comes.

"Warrant says he can search my house and all the outbuildings."

"That include Gilligan's Island?" I asked.

"What's that?" Avila asked, which served me right, making a TV reference to a guy his age. I pointed at the desert island paradise in the pond.

"That's Nina's island," Avila said, waving his hand toward the beautiful woman on the balcony. "Don't know about no Gilligan."

"He find any barrels?" I asked Avila, giving Willeniec, A., a taste of his own medicine: talking like he wasn't there.

"Fuck no," Avila said. "Why'd I have barrels?"

"Back in the day, mobsters used to stuff guys in barrels," I said. "Top it off with concrete, weld the lid on, drop 'em in the river."

"Mobsters!" Avila said, disgusted. "Yeah. That's me."

The beautiful young woman on the balcony, Nina, laughed like a cool breeze. No wonder Avila built her a whole private island paradise.

Willeniec stopped writing in his notebook and handed back my license.

"You should take that warrant," I told Avila, indicating the envelope sticking out of Willeniec's suit pocket.

"Why I want that shit?"

"Because that shit is your shit," I said.

Avila jumped at the chance to go alpha and extended his hand. Willeniec ignored him.

"You got a lawyer?" I asked Avila.

"Chrissakes," Willeniec said, disgusted, like I was betraying the Aryan Brotherhood of White Assholes.

"I got twenty lawyers." Avila indicated his estate and holdings dramatically with his bandaged hand. "They just didn't get here yet."

"I'm not required to wait for your lawyer. Anyways, all twenty of your lawyers will tell you I have the right to search the house and the outbuildings," Willeniec said.

"Which you did and which you found nothing!"

"This warrant also lists a number of other addresses I have the right to search, including your storage unit. That's where I'm heading now."

"Ain't no barrels there neither."

I snatched the warrant from Willeniec's pocket, startling him.

"Legally, Mr. Avila is entitled to a copy of the warrant."

Willeniec nodded and smiled before he turned and headed toward his car. He did everything but pretend his finger was a gun and shoot me in the heart.

I handed Avila the warrant, and the two of us watched Willeniec drive off in his ghost car.

Avila spat, visibly calmed himself down, and asked, "What do I call you?"

"What do you want me to call you?"

"Mr. Avila."

"Call me Skellig. I'll add the 'Mister' in my head."

"You should go on over to the storage unit, Biz," Nina said from the balcony. "Make sure Deputy Dog don't plant nothing. Take your driver there for a white witness."

Nina had noticed me! Not only that but she caught my eye, which was thrilling.

"He says call him Mickey," Avila said, looking at me sideways, seeing if it pissed me off.

"Why'm I gonna call your driver any damn thing?" she asked, disappearing back into the house.

Avila jerked his chin at my beautiful vintage 1954 New Yorker limousine. "The fuck is that?"

"She's a classic," I said. "A nineteen fif—"

"We'll take my Navigator," he said. "It's got comfort. Classic is just another way to say old and broke down. Next time, you bring that Mercedes."

Avila had me dead to rights. Proof positive that being kind of a dick doesn't make you a total fool.

I set the address of Avila's storage unit into the Navigator's GPS. Avila sat himself in the backseat, passenger side, staring out the window and muttering complaints into his smartphone to what I guessed were lawyers, telling the same story two or three times, saying he was a victim of racist cop harassment.

I heard Avila suggest that some jealous rivals might be sending in anonymous tips that he was keeping guns or drugs or dead bodies in barrels, flicking his eyes up at me on that last.

"If they suspected dead bodies, they'd have sent SWAT," I said when Avila got off the phone, "not one lousy sheriff's detective."

"You a lawyer?"

"No."

"Then you stay outta lawyering and I'll tell my lawyers to stay outta driving."

"You blackmail your lawyers into working for you?"

"What?"

"Hippocrates would call you a mix of yellow bile and blood, which gives you a choleric-sanguine temperament."

"What's that? French?"

"You like to dominate others; you enjoy playing and winning games; you want people to admire you."

"You an astrologist?"

"No."

"Then stay out of astrologizing and I'll tell my astrologist to stay out of driving."

I ignored the GPS lady's voice, skipped the 101 highway on-ramp, and dropped south to the old Mulholland Highway and headed west again. If you squint your eyes there, you can pretend you're in the hills above the San Fernando Valley of the 1960s, smelling of orange trees, winding along between eucalyptus groves, steep pastures dotted by horses, a few private roads and driveways lined by palm trees, weekend sanctuaries for the rich and famous wannabe ranchers, or at least those who hadn't yet graduated to vineyards farther north in the Santa Ynez Valley.

I jigged right on Las Virgenes Canyon, through some more open grassland to the Stone Creek subdivision, mostly condos, left on Agoura Road at the McDonald's (*man, those fries smell good*), through the entrance to Virgenes Self Storage, set up like a bunch of small adobe suburban garages with tile roofing and (God help us) fake chimneys.

"You take the scenic route hoping I'd fire you?" Avila asked, laughing. "Teach me my lesson?"

I had to hand it to Avila; when he laughed you felt an authentic urge to join in. That's charisma.

Avila let himself out of the Navigator and slouched over toward where Willeniec stood in front of a unit, looking for a handle, the blank door defying him. I sat back in the Navigator's air-conditioned comfort until ten steps later Avila turned around and gave me a look like I was eight years old: *Come on!*

I sighed and exited into Valley heat blasting up at me in tarry waves from the black asphalt. I felt it through the soles of my shoes. My stitches throbbed.

"You can open it or I'll get the manager to open it. Your choice."

Avila eye-fucked Willeniec, then entered seven digits into his phone. The garage door rolled up on tracks. There weren't any corpse-stuffed barrels in the storage unit, but there were eight life-size statues. Angels. I should say the statues were human life–size given my vague understanding that angels are supposed to be taller than human beings. I laughed at the sight of those angels staring out at us from the shadowed storage unit like we'd caught them grabbing a smoke outside the pearly gates.

"The fuck?" said Willeniec.

"They were around the pool," Avila said. "Nina hates 'em but said don't throw out angels for bad luck."

I wondered if Nina knew about all of Avila's other women. Groupies, escorts, models, semiprofessionals. What was their deal? Maybe, being Avila's girlfriend and not his wife, Nina felt she had no leverage, had to look the other way, clear off the angels and build herself an island until the day he decided to marry her.

Willeniec circulated among the angels, frustration written on his vindictive marathoner's face. The floor upon which the angels stood was dusty, but the area where they weren't had been swept clean recently, marked only by a series of crescent-shaped scuffs. On the tracks for the garage door, I noticed a ding, and then, slightly lower, a smear of blood and skin.

I looked at the gauze on Avila's knuckles.

Uh-huh.

Willeniec didn't notice any of that; he was rapping on the

angels with his knuckles (their bellies, their faces, the bases, their smooth, white wings), getting nothing but a solid *tock-tock*.

"That everything?" Avila asked.

"I'll find them," Willeniec said, pushing his finger, not into Bismarck Avila's chest, but into mine. Whatever Willeniec thought I was to Avila, it wasn't a mere driver.

In order to truly ensure that I fucked myself all the way to Baja and back, I handed Willeniec, A., my business card.

"Oasis is a full-service limo company," I said, "providing personalized group shuttle service to and from LAX, Bob Hope, and Long Beach Airports, wine country, Santa Barbara, Palm Springs, Palm Desert, San Diego, Los Olivos, Montecito, Ojai, and Vegas. Discretion guaranteed."

I hit *discretion* hard in a way that suggested he had no idea how full-service and discreet. I still don't know why I doubled down like that and have no choice but to acknowledge my own aforementioned AFEO rule and the fact that it takes two to tango.

Willeniec took the card.

I hoped that when he checked me on his MDCS computer he wouldn't find that I had not yet been cleared as a suspect in an attempted homicide. My luck, he'd ask for a meet with Delilah Groopman and become her new boyfriend and turn her against me. Willeniec was just the kind of bitter squeezings Delilah found attractive.

The thought gave me a pang.

"What does it tell you about a man when he can't find joy in unexpected angels?" I asked.

"You know what's stupid?" Willeniec asked. "Being a small business owner, like a limo driver, who requires permits and licenses and permissions from the county but decides it's smart to put himself on the shit side of county law enforcement."

Then he got into his ghost car and drove away.

Avila spat onto the hot asphalt, typed seven digits into his phone, and watched as the storage compartment door descended, the angels disappearing into the gloaming. I extended Avila the warrant I'd taken from Detective Willeniec, but he waved me off, so I folded it and stuck it into the breast pocket of my jacket.

"Where to now?"

"Home," Avila said.

I could see Avila's jaw bunching in the rearview mirror, but I couldn't shake the feeling that he was more relieved than angry.

ANOTHER JOB OFFER

The Pacific Division of the LAPD handles Venice and LAX, so it's not the sleepy beach precinct you might expect. Nine o'clock in the cool of the evening, away from the Valley heat, if you loiter in the foyer of the substation on Culver near Centinela, between Marina Del Rey and the 405 interstate, you'll see what I was seeing: a constant swarm of cops and righteous citizens and harmless, babbling schizophrenics. The front of the building is a limpid pool of calm compared to the crashing cataracts in the back, where, mostly against their will, the criminal element gathers and sweats and seethes and plots revenge.

I sat on a bench in the foyer, staring at the Pacific Division most-wanted poster, which looked like it had been printed up from a webpage designed by a high school student: two African Americans, an Asian guy, a few Hispanics, and a sketch of what looked like Woody Harrelson in a ball cap labeled UNIDENTIFIED PERSON. One of the black guys had failed to return a rented car, which didn't sound so bad, but still he was considered armed and dangerous. The Hispanics were gang members: one was a heroin addict who'd killed another gang member; another was five foot three, which didn't sound so bad, except he weighed two hundred pounds and none of it looked like fat. He was a carjacker. I assumed that he simply picked up your car, shook you out, and ran off with it. The Asian guy was some kind of serial berserker. He kept attacking people and biting them. Woody Harrelson was a stone-cold murderer. His weapon of choice was a car battery. Which didn't paint a pretty picture.

"You bring me something, Skellig?"

I looked up (which made my stitches twinge) to see Delilah standing at the door beside the desk under the big silver letters—DEPARTMENT OF PUBLIC SAFETY—just the other side of the prescription drug drop-off box. (Did anyone ever use that?) I held up a chai latte and smiled to show I was, indeed, bearing gifts. Delilah sighed and took a seat next to me on the bench, checking her Ironman Timex. She was off at midnight and wanted me to know that her time was precious.

"Shouldn't you be driving your new boss around? Club hopping?"

"Mr. Avila gave me the night off."

"You two finding anything to bond over? You got any mad skills on a skateboard?"

"We both agree his girlfriend is beautiful."

"According to TMZ, the fuckwad cheats on her. You would never do that, right?"

Was it my imagination, or did Delilah sound slightly hopeful?

"Maybe they have an understanding."

After Avila and I got back to the mansion from the storage unit, Avila was visited by lawyers and managers and advisers while I cooked in the hotbox of Two—hoist on my own petard for bringing a vintage gorgeousity with no air-conditioning to the Valley—observing to-and-froing, come-and-going, poking at my itchy stitches with an index finger. The high point of my afternoon was watching Nina, in an all-white bikini and diaphanous wrap, toting a sky-blue tote bag, smartphone in hand, crossing the driveway to clamber onto her miniature pirate ship and sail across the lake to her private island on invisible underwater rails. She stepped off the other side, waded into the water, and splashed herself, at which point her bikini became delightfully transparent, then settled back into her hammock and poked at her phone while I tried not to stare.

Not one of the women I'd seen Avila with over our twenty-eight hours together could hold a candle to Nina.

"Wow, take your fucking time answering the question," Delilah said. "How's your coconut?"

I removed my ball cap and inclined my head so Delilah could see where I was stitched.

"Blech," she said, poking a little harder than necessary at the sutures.

"Are you being semisympathetic because I was right?"

"I'm not being sympathetic."

"You said 'blech.'"

"We may have witnesses saying that two youths matching the description of the hitters skedaddled from the scene in a limo driven by a black male, approximately twenty-eight to thirty years of age."

"Sweet vindication!"

"I'm certain the pertinent details you provided about those boots will lead to the driver's inevitable capture and incarceration."

Sarcasm was as close to an apology as I'd ever squeeze from Detective Delilah Groopman.

She turned on the bench to fix me with her cop eye. "The girlfriend strike you as the jealous type?"

"You mean the type of African American woman who'd hire two white teenage skate punks to kill her cheating boyfriend?"

"Teenage boys'll do pretty much anything a beautiful woman wants them to do if she provides the right incentive."

"Plus persuade Chelsea Boots to steal a limo and act as getaway driver?"

"Ignoring your tone, I'm going to say yeah again. Chelsea Boots could be her brother or lover, something along those lines. Maybe he hired those boys on her urging."

"Avila and Nina aren't married. There's no upside for her, him dying."

"Fuck," Delilah said, her way of admitting I had a point.

"Didn't Avila used to be in a gang?" I asked.

"Bismarck Avila's legend is he came up from the street," she said. "*Gang* is the wrong word. More like a bunch of dim-shit skaters who hung out, dealt drugs, and stole stuff."

"You mean a typical street kid from Lennox?"

"Avila came up tough. Living in motels, mostly. Shelters. Old friends, left behind in the neighborhood, can get envious, figure their homey owes them, get mad when they're denied."

"Did you seriously just use the word *homey*?"

"I work the streets," Delilah said. "I've earned the right. And my theory makes sense."

When a cop says *makes sense* in a confident manner, it means she's not at all confident and is checking to see if she's lying by saying it out loud to hear how it sounds.

Delilah saw my opinion writ large on my stupid unguarded face. "No? Not buying it?"

"It's not a compelling theory," I said.

"And you come to that expert conclusion after—remind me again how many years of training and experience you've had as a criminal investigator?"

"Delilah, I work for the guy. Excuse me for being freaked-out that I could end up with a bullet in my gut from some emo teenage skater hit boy. If you know something real, please tell me."

Delilah sighed and considered what she could say that wouldn't get her fired.

"About six months ago, Avila's cousin got murdered while he was working as Avila's driver."

"What happened?"

"Carjacking. Shot multiple times through the driver's window."

"Was Avila in the vehicle at the time?"

"Nope. Driver was alone. Killer emptied a clip into the kid and vamoosed."

"The shooter forgot to take the vehicle?"

"That's right."

"So, less a carjacking and more an execution?"

"Gangs Unit heard rumors Avila was looking to hire someone to take out the kid."

"Unsubstantiated rumors?"

"If it's not unsubstantiated, then it's not a rumor," Delilah said, toasting me with her frosty beverage.

"What would be the motive?"

"That is a troubling question which I cannot answer."

"Cannot or will not?"

"Cannot."

"You called the victim a kid? Twice?"

"Eighteen years old. I got a proposition for you."

"Forget it."

"It's been authorized from lofty heights."

"Nope."

"Will you at least *hear* it before you say *no*?"

"I'm not working for you as a confidential informant."

"Nothing like that. All we ask is you report Bismarck Avila's whereabouts and doings."

"That's *exactly* the definition of a confidential informant."

Delilah pinched her nose to indicate that I was a grievous and cowardly disappointment to her.

"Delilah—"

"Let's stick with Detective Groopman."

"Everything you're talking about sounds like gang activity. I am not about to wander into that propeller as a CI."

Delilah looked around before telling me something she didn't want to tell me. "Asher Keet."

I didn't react because the name didn't mean anything to me.

"Asher fucking Keet," she said, pumping more foreboding into the name.

"I gather from his descriptive middle name that he's a scary dude?"

"You never heard of Asher Keet?"

I shook my head. I felt my stitches tug. My headache got worse.

"Asher Keet is . . . Keet's part white gangster, full-on bag o' shit, part biker, part meth distributor, loan shark, illegal gambling, member of the Aryan brotherhood, but only when he's in prison."

"What's he got to do with Bismarck Avila?"

"We suspect Keet and Avila are in cahoots."

"*Vamoose. Skedaddle. Cahoots.* What is this? The Wild West?"

"We need a confidential informant to find the nature of the link between Keet and Avila."

"Who is *we*? Homicide? Gangs? Organized Crime?"

This time Delilah was the one taking the Fifth, sipping her latte slowly, yawning, gazing out the front doors, informing me that she was done talking to me.

"Fine," I said. "You can tell them—whoever they are—that I'm a limo driver. Not a CI."

I stood up to leave. Then, because I was crushing on Delilah and wanted her to like me, I told her about Willeniec, A., serving his weird warrant on Bismarck Avila, solo.

"A *sheriff's* detective?" she asked.

"According to his lanyard. I never saw his badge."

"Out of Lost Hills?"

"Whittier."

"What was he looking for?"

"You wanna tell me why you're all excited? No? You're shaking your head no? So I tell you things but—"

"Skellig!"

"Barrels."

"Barrels?"

"Fifty-five-gallon drums."

"Did he find any?"

"Nope."

Without another word, Delilah stood up, tossed her chai latte into the garbage, and trotted through the door leading back to the serious-business part of the building, like she had to tell someone something in a big hurry.

Which led me to conclude that I'd told Delilah more than she'd told me.

NO TAKEBACKS

I'm a block away from the Pacific Division station and about to put
Two into gear when my phone buzzes.

A text from Ripple's mobile: **WE NEED YOU HERE, RIGHT NOW.**

All caps, complete words, no abbreviations, punctuation in the
form of a comma, no hyperviolent emojis.

Most definitely not sent by Ripple.

Someone else was using Ripple's phone. Probably Lucky (who
is not given to dramatics), so I drove home, window open to the
breeze, hoping for spectral clarification, but my ghost voices are not
a phenomenon you can summon at will.

I parked near Enterprise Rent-A-Car a couple of blocks down
the street and trotted up toward Oasis Limo, stitches throbbing every time I came down on a heel. I approached from the Santa Monica Boulevard side and peeked through the office window.

Totally dark except for meager yellow light leaking through
from the engine bays. The main fluorescents had been shut off. My

choices were to go in through the dispatch office, go through the door that opened onto Santa Monica Boulevard, or go around the side to punch a code into one of the three large overhead doors in the bays along the alley. Or I could sneak around back, climb the fence into the Yard, and come in through the parts-storage door.

Which would be great except that the door squeaked like a nail being pulled out of green wood every time it was opened.

My phone buzzed again.

Ripple's number again.

A call this time, not a text.

I opened the connection and held the phone to my left ear but didn't say anything.

"Where are you?" Lucky asked.

I said nothing, knowing that if Lucky could not speak freely he would pretend I'd answered him and respond in a way that provided insights into his situation. We'd worked this way before with excellent results (meaning we'd survived).

"A gentleman wants Something from you. If he doesn't get it, he will kill all three of us. Tinkertoy is Down and Out. Ripple is hung up. I'm handcuffed to the vise on the workbench and covered."

From that I got:

One bad guy.

Male.

No extra players, just the bad guy and my three friends.

Somebody bad enough to surprise and overcome three combat vets, one of whom was as paranoid as hell.

Lucky had said he was covered, which meant the bad guy had a gun pointed at him, not a knife or blunt instrument and not an automatic or shotgun, because in that case Lucky would have said *totally covered*. If it had been a grenade, Lucky would have said *completely covered*.

So, a revolver . . .

Handcuffed, meaning the bad guy had come prepared. It wasn't a meth-head robbery. It had been planned.

Tinkertoy was down and out, meaning she was alive but incapacitated or unconscious.

Ripple was hung up, which didn't mean a damn thing so was to be taken literally—a double amputee tacked up where he couldn't hurt anybody.

That made me angry.

"Front door?" I asked.

"Apologies," Lucky said.

Apologies meant I was going to have to simply walk in. If Lucky thought it was worth me coming in hot, guns a-blazing, he'd have said *afraid so*.

Apologies meant that Lucky could see no alternatives, and Lucky was very, very good at seeing alternatives.

I punched my enlistment date into the security pad near the center bay and, for the second time in a day, waited to see what surprises lurked on the other side of a roll-up garage door. (I was pretty sure this time it wouldn't be stone angels.) The door rolled up in near silence. Oasis Limo is an excellent neighbor, even in the middle of the night, facing mayhem and violence.

As advertised, Lucky was sitting on the floor, handcuffed to a vise on the workbench, otherwise unharmed.

I couldn't see the bad guy, but Lucky's right foot was pointed to his left so that's where the bad guy was, out of my sight line. I also couldn't see Tinkertoy, but the haunted Caddie blocked my view to the left. I stepped into the garage and hit the button to shut the door again. Now I could see Ripple hanging from the engine hoist, his wrists bound by an extension cord, his I LOVE JESUS BUT I STILL CUSS fanny pack twisted around onto his left hip, his mouth stuffed with oily rags, vomit visible beneath his nose and all over the gag. The boy had to be in agony, stomach acids in his airways, lungs, and sinuses, but Ripple's eyes did nothing but glitter hate. I felt a disorienting surge of affection for the tough little stoner son of a bitch.

Another step, another, and there was Tinkertoy, beyond her haunted Caddie, lying on her back, shirt ripped open, breasts exposed, eyes half shut. She looked dead but Lucky would have let me know. I waited for the door to close behind me, after which Sheriff's Detective Willeniec, A., stepped from the dispatch office, aiming a stainless steel .357 Magnum at my chest. Four-inch barrel. Seven shots. Lethal at this range if Willeniec was any kind of shot—which is something I just knew he prided himself on.

Shit.

"Remember me?" Willeniec asked, glittery eyed. (Coke? Panic? Meth? Red Bull? Ten cups of coffee? Insanity?)

When I didn't answer, Willeniec kicked Tinkertoy in the ribs, hard, without looking at her. When I still didn't say anything, he took three quick steps and struck Ripple with the butt of his weapon, in the solar plexus. The sound was sickening, both the impact itself and Ripple's gulping retch of agony.

Lucky let loose what must have sounded, to Willeniec, like an uncontrolled string of Farsi curses but was actually a terse and cogent warning: "Be careful. This one is evil."

"Ali Baba keeps insulting me in his gargly fucking language," Willeniec said. "I guess because he feels bad that these two get all the attention and I leave him alone. But that's just until I kill him."

I knew that if I said nothing he'd exact a blood tax, so I said, "What do you want?"

Willeniec kicked Tinkertoy again anyway, meaning this whole clusterfuck was going down the hard way.

"Stop, I beg you," said Lucky. "This Situation is Containable. Please tell Mr. Skellig what you require."

Smart. The "Mister" suggested to Willeniec that we weren't close, that these people were nothing more than employees to me. Why try to use them as leverage?

Lucky isn't only an interpreter. He's a trained hostage negotiator. Another reason he is so successful in his sexual life.

"Mr. Skellig knows what I want," Willeniec said.

"Barrels?" I asked.

"I told you he knew," Willeniec said.

"Today was my first day driving for Avila," I said. "I don't know anything about barrels. I thought being an asshole to you would earn me a bonus."

Willeniec struck Ripple again, this time using the butt of his gun to chop down onto Ripple's bladder. Ripple screamed behind the gag and pissed himself, his whole body shaking.

Willeniec laughed.

Lucky was right. Willeniec was the kind of sadist who dug secret torture chambers beneath his basement. The next time I told him I didn't know anything he'd up the ante by putting a bullet in someone's head. Probably Lucky's. Willeniec meant to kill us all— Lucky, then Ripple, then Tinkertoy, saving me for last so that he could show my corpse to Avila in order to get those barrels.

What I had to do first was open up the possibilities in this situation, expand the elements, take some small measure of control until the opportunity I needed presented itself. What did I have to barter with Willeniec?

(Pain.)

The man got off on inflicting pain. I'd show him a painful dilemma he could inflict on me and he'd take it like a cat after a baby bird.

"I get the situation. But let the boy down. And sit her up before she chokes to death."

"Which one do you like more?" Willeniec asked. "You can't have both."

He poked Ripple with the barrel of his Magnum and kicked Tinkertoy.

"Who do you pick? Gimp boy or nigger girl?"

I prevaricated, plastered a look of anguish on my face. "Sorry, Ripple." Then pointed at Tinkertoy.

I allowed my feelings to be heard in my voice, mostly for Willeniec's enjoyment, but for Ripple too, wondering if he could possibly understand.

Willeniec stepped back as I moved toward Tinkertoy to sit her up, ensuring that he was far enough away (eight feet) that I wouldn't have a chance to tackle him before he could pull the trigger—two, maybe three times—yet close enough that he wouldn't miss. As I sat Tinkertoy up against the wheel of the haunted limo, I saw that she clutched a twelve-inch dog-bone wrench in her hand.

And there was my opportunity.

I straightened up, purposely banging my head on the wheel well as hard as I could, opening my stitches. I cursed and bled. Willeniec laughed, enjoying himself immensely, which distracted him enough that I could palm Tinkertoy's wrench without his noticing. I slumped against the limo, blood streaming down my neck, and tilted my head back to regard Willeniec, needing the blood to flow but stay out of my eyes.

"Ouch," Willeniec said. "That has to hurt."

I reached out to pull Tinkertoy's shirt back across her breasts, keeping Willeniec's eyes moving where I wanted them moving.

"I'm going to ask once more," Willeniec said, stepping over toward Ripple. "I'm going to ask where the barrels are, and if you don't tell me, I'll shoot Cheeto boy's balls off."

He yanked Ripple's urine-soaked cargo shorts down and off his stumps in one swift movement, pushed Ripple's penis aside with the barrel of his gun, grabbed a pair of pliers from Tinkertoy's workbench, seized one of Ripple's testicles in the jaws, and squeezed.

Ripple cries out in agony.

I leap to my feet, blood streaming, holding out my left hand in supplication, drawing Willeniec's eye again.

"Stop. Please. Jesus Christ!"

Willeniec releases Ripple. Through what must be sheets of pain, Ripple lashes out with the stump of his right leg and catches Willeniec on the side of the head; it's like being hit with a roast beef. Willeniec stumbles back, wrenching his revolver up to shoot Ripple in the center of his body mass.

I throw the socket wrench like a tomahawk. The wrench strikes Willeniec in the face, busting his nose. Willeniec swings his gun around and fires at where I was but I'm not there anymore; I'm chasing the wrench, following its trajectory as fast as I can. I seize Willeniec's pistol, twisting, dislocating his thumb, breaking his wrist.

I strike him in the throat with the barrel. I feel his larynx crumple.

Willeniec stumbles and gasps, his mouth moving like a goldfish's. He collapses against the hood of the Caddie, amazed and angry, not yet understanding that he is Alpha Mike Foxtrot.

Willeniec kicked and retched while I yanked the gag from Ripple's mouth and lowered the hoist, then used the same pliers Willeniec had used to torture Ripple to cut through the extension cords that bound his wrists. Ripple sobbed in agony, but he reached for his pants, so I helped him pull them on. I opened the back door of One and set Ripple down on his back on the seat. I reached for a bottle of water in the door and opened it for him, but he wasn't interested.

I headed over to Willeniec and rifled through his pockets, searching for the handcuff key that would free Lucky. Tinkertoy still slumped against the front wheel of Three, her large, liquid eyes fixed on Willeniec's face as he died.

Willeniec gargled in panic, making almost the exact same sound he'd made mocking Lucky's Farsi, heels kicking at the floor like he was trying to escape. He clutched at my clothing, weakening fast, perhaps realizing at last that he was about to die. I didn't see the precise moment when Willeniec knew for certain he was dead because I was getting the handcuffs off Lucky and helping him to his feet. By the time I turned around, Willeniec was all but gone.

"Wait! Hold me over him," Ripple sobbed from the backseat of One. "I want to shit on his face while he still knows what's happening."

"Too late," Lucky said, "he's dead," flicking his eyes at me in accusation.

"He had a gun pointed at Ripple and his finger on the trigger," I said. "I had to kill him."

Lucky nodded but did not meet my eyes.

"Go outside, see if anybody heard the shot."

"If they did, then what? Shall I kill them?"

Lucky was unhappy with me.

"Then come back in, find where the bullet Willeniec fired at me, *to kill me*, ended up."

Lucky looked once more at Willeniec, looked at me, nodded his apology, and went outside.

"I was waiting. For him. To come close. Enough to hit. With the wrench," Tinkertoy said. "I never thought. Of throwing it."

"That wrench saved us," I said.

Lucky reentered and shook his head. No sign that anyone in the neighborhood had heard the shot. The criminal who had run this place as a chop shop had done a lot of soundproofing so that cars could be taken apart at night.

"The bullet. Is in. The wooden beam." Tinkertoy pointed at the rough-hewn beam between doors one and two.

"Gouge it out," I told Lucky, "and hang something over the hole."

"For the Sake of Clarification, you intend to cover up what's happened here tonight?" Lucky asked.

"That's exactly what I intend."

Ripple leaned out of One and gagged. Tinkertoy placed a wastebasket in front of him and he vomited.

Rubbing his chafed wrists, Lucky asked, "Why don't we call the authorities and tell them we were attacked by this sadistic intruder whom you killed in self-defense?"

"This sadistic intruder *is* the authorities."

"What kind of authority?"

"He's an LA County sheriff's detective."

"Still, Skellig, you have a trusting relationship with Detective Delilah Groopman—"

"Who is the lead investigator in the murder of a bodyguard in which my role is unclear. It shouldn't be, but it is."

"Still—?"

"We have to make it so that this . . ."

". . . murder . . . ?"

". . . *killing* never happened. We don't know how many other cops are involved. I'm already a suspect. No matter what, you'll be deported back to Afghanistan. Tinkertoy's psychiatric history won't help. They could pop her back into the loony bin. That leaves Ripple, on his own, to convince a court of law that we were in the right to kill a cop."

Even Lucky knew that Ripple lacked a certain credibility.

Lucky groaned and clasped his hands beneath his chin, moving them like he was a nervous monk at prayer. Ripple vomited again. Tinkertoy dragged herself to where the wrench I'd thrown at Willeniec lay on the floor. She picked it up, hauled herself to her workbench, and scrubbed it with a wire brush, using solvent, working her strong brown hands, being useful.

"A cop," Lucky said. "Very bad. Very bad indeed."

"Suck it up, Buttercup," Ripple said.

"Additional consideration: we call the police, it becomes a

matter of record that Willeniec came here looking for those barrels. Who knows who else is after them?"

"Yes," Lucky said, "I see. But I wish we could take some time before Initiating a Cover-Up—"

"I'm glad Skellig killed the fucker," Ripple said, "even if I get executed for it."

I regarded the lifeless corpse of the man I'd killed and confronted the age-old question of murderers.

How long until daylight?

PERTURBATIONS AND OBFUSCATIONS

Following Phase 2 of my plan to get away with murdering a police-man, I treat my ragtag band of murderous adventurers to breakfast at Callahan's Diner, just up the street from the scene of the crime. I figure the sooner the staff of Oasis Limo are out in the neighbor-hood, normalizing our situation, the better.

But I've jumped too far ahead because breakfast occurred more than six hours after Willeniec choked to death on the ragged gristle of his own crushed Adam's apple.

Phase 1 consisted of cleaning up the crime scene.

There wasn't much blood and most of it was mine from pur-posely smacking my head on Three's wheel well and opening up my stitches. I decided to leave all that mess where it was. No one ever got put on death row for their own blood.

Of course, Willeniec had bled from his broken nose, but most of that blood was on his suit jacket. Some had pooled in one half-closed eyeball, but his heart wasn't beating long enough to produce much more than half a pint.

Minute traces of blood and skin on the wrench would make for DNA evidence, but Tinkertoy cleaned that up before Willeniec even achieved official brain death. The rest of Willeniec's blood coagulated down the sides of his head into his ears and hair, with a very small amount ending up on a bit of matting near Tinkertoy's tool bench.

Tinkertoy burned the mat to ashes with a blowtorch while I hoisted Ripple onto my back and—preceded by Lucky, opening doors and pulling down ladders—carried the kid up to the hot tub on the roof beside my penthouse. Ripple waved off my offer of Vicodin in favor of rummaging through his I LOVE JESUS fanny pack for medical marijuana, choosing between candies, chocolate, tongue sprays, tinctures, tea, vaporizers, eatables, and smokables.

While Ripple let himself float away from the pain, Lucky entered with the first aid kit to clean and restitch my scalp wound.

In order to ensure that Ripple didn't slide happily to the bottom of my hot tub and drown, I secured him to the handrail with a belt and headed back downstairs, where Lucky and I hoisted Willeniec's body onto a blue polyethylene tarp that we used for tying down loose loads. We spread out an inventory of Willeniec's belongings on the same tarp.

Weapon. One bullet discharged.

Cell phone. Battery removed.

"When he's reported missing," I said, "at least his GPS won't lead here."

"Perhaps he didn't want anyone zeroing in on his location," Lucky said, "indicating that he Strayed from Protocol."

"Good for us," I said.

Watch. High-quality quartz Seiko.

"Just for telling time and date," Lucky said, "not one of the smart watches tethered to satellites."

Despite the fact that he looked like a runner, Willeniec was not wearing a fitness bracelet of the kind that connects to your computer or mobile phone to record heart rate, distance covered, altitude changes, or how many calories you've burned walking.

"No wedding ring."

"Thank God," Lucky said.

"That doesn't mean he doesn't have somebody," I said.

Car keys.

Gun, wallet, the bullet we gouged out of the beam, the watch, cell phone, battery, his weapon; all of these we shoved inside Willeniec's sports coat pockets. The car keys I kept.

We swaddled Willeniec, A., like a baby in the blue tarp and duct-taped the whole enchilada.

Lucky and I hoisted said corpse-size blue enchilada into one of the two 2011 Ford Transits I'd bought from a bankrupt florist and which we now rented out on a jobber basis to local businesses.

We climbed back upstairs to extract Ripple from my hot tub before he parboiled. I wanted to put him in my bed, but stoned Ripple got stubborn on the issue and insisted upon coming downstairs to help, despite his ashen color.

I loaned him basketball shorts and a sweatshirt. We carried Ripple back down to Dispatch and put him on the couch, hoping he'd get some sleep.

I left with Willeniec's car keys and trotted in a slow, clockwise spiral, keeping the world headquarters of Oasis Limo Services at the epicenter, regularly pushing the lock/unlock button on the fob until blinking running lights told me I'd found Willeniec's vehicle— a nondescript black Chevy Tahoe—three blocks away from Oasis, tucked behind a guitar store called Truetone Music.

What to do next merited careful consideration.

Willeniec, on his own time, not on the job, wouldn't be reported missing until he failed to show up for his next scheduled shift at the Whittier sheriff's station, whenever that was. Since he'd been driving an official vehicle when he executed the warrant at Avila's place, it was best to assume that Willeniec hadn't taken vacation time or a leave of absence to threaten and torture civilians.

For a moment I wondered if he might have been impersonating a cop but decided, in the end, that it didn't matter. The most prudent course was to assume he was the sheriff's son-in-law and the mayor's best friend since childhood.

In the same spirit, it was smart to be conservative and assume that Willeniec, A., was due to start his shift at, say, seven tomorrow morning, maybe eight, given that some detectives think that eating breakfast is part of their workday. By about nine or ten A.M., someone might start asking questions. How much vigor was put into the subsequent search would depend upon Willeniec's work habits, whether he had a partner, and how much his coworkers gave a shit.

Safest bet: behave as though Willeniec was popular and high-profile, with a partner who owed him his life; assume that every cop and sheriff's deputy in the county would go on high alert when Willeniec didn't show up for the following shift. They'd know that he hadn't come home, and everybody he knew (girlfriends, boyfriends, buddies, landlords, personal trainers, busybodies, moms, and assorted other concerned human beings) was personally calling his boss to demand Willeniec's whereabouts.

Ain'tnobodynobodyain'tnobody, Willeniec rasped in my ear.

Nary a diphthong of regret or apology or anger in his ruined voice, no sense of irony that he was now helping the man who'd killed him less than an hour ago.

All my ghost voices are like that.

Maybe the people I've killed are appreciative. (Does that make me sound like some kind of psychopath?) Maybe the Great Beyond is so fantastically wonderful that the people I send there are compelled to come back to help me out of sheer, unfettered gratitude for releasing them from this torturous world.

Like Ripple says, we are all inmates of God's concentration camp.

The guitar sellers at Truetone might wait until noon to have the Tahoe towed from their minuscule parking lot, which would (presuming it was registered to Willeniec) shortly thereafter set off alarm bells.

If the Tahoe was discovered here, would anyone make the cognitive leap to Oasis Limo three blocks away?

Was Willeniec working this barrel deal alone?

Had he confided in anyone where he was going?

The battery removed from the phone suggested that Willeniec was a rogue cop, but that didn't mean he didn't have partners in crime or wasn't working for someone. I was tempted to walk away clean, because the second I even touched that Tahoe, much less got inside, I'd be shedding forensic clues: hair, skin, DNA (you know what I'm talking about; you watch TV).

All law enforcement needed was a partial fingerprint, and mine are stored in the FBI's Integrated Automated Fingerprint Identification System because I was in the military.

Ergo, the smart thing to do might be to stay a minimum of ten feet from Willeniec's Tahoe, go home, nap for a few hours, and then saunter down to watch the sun come up from the end of the Santa Monica Pier, wait until all the fishermen and surfers looked the other way, and toss Willeniec's car keys into the bay.

Except—Willeniec was after Avila and it didn't take Sherlock Holmes to deduce that Willeniec's Tahoe had been found only a few blocks from Avila's driver's place of business.

Notebookmynotebooknotebook, Willeniec whispered.

At Avila's place, Willeniec had written my info in a brand-new notebook.

At the storage unit, I'd (idiot!) handed him my business card with an obnoxious attitude that practically dared him to come after me.

Neither the notebook nor my business card was on Willeniec's cold, dead person.

Which left me hoping they were in his Tahoe.

First, I satisfied myself that the Tahoe wasn't in range of any security cameras, though I figured Willeniec was wily or paranoid enough to have chosen this spot with that in mind, given his homicidal intentions. Which meant I could probably count on his not having LoJack.

(I hoped Willeniec was as smart as I was giving him credit for.)

Smarterthanyou, Willeniec rasped.

"Deader than me too," I muttered.

I pulled on my standard-issue limo-driver leather driving gloves and climbed into Willeniec's Tahoe.

Nothing on the seats. In fact, nothing in the car at all. Willeniec must have been a clean freak. I wondered if that was a common personality trait for sadists. I checked the glove compartment, and there it was. His notebook. I opened it. There was my name with the curt annotation *asshole.*

Avila's address in Calabasas.

The address of the storage unit.

A list of other addresses that looked familiar. One, at least, I remembered from Willeniec's warrant. An Avila property.

My business card stuck between the pages.

(Take this now and walk away?)

Nope. I was committed (see above observations re: forensics).

I started the Tahoe and drove it home. Up goes the garage door, in drives Skellig, down goes the door, the alley left empty and quiet and cool, the light in the east emanating not from the rising sun but from the car dealerships along Santa Monica Boulevard.

It was still night (and miles to go before I sleep).

Now, here's the thing about getting rid of five and a half thousand pounds of SUV: it's not easy. Lucky suggested we drive it out into the desert and set it on fire with Willeniec's body behind the wheel. Stoned Ripple made fun of Lucky for wanting to place a flaming beacon over a dead body in the middle of nowhere. Ripple advised driving the truck to Tijuana and leaving it on the street with the keys in the ignition, which wasn't an awful notion. It was Tinkertoy who came up with the golden idea: *enforced entropy.* Meaning take it apart.

Make it cease to be a Tahoe.

I liked that plan because there are only a few parts of an automobile that can be uniquely identified as a definite part of a specific vehicle using serial numbers, including the VIN. I liked Tinkertoy's plan even more when she pointed out we weren't even facing that problem.

When Ripple asked why, Tinkertoy tapped on the front windshield on the driver's side as though that was explanation enough. When it wasn't, she read off the VIN number as though that was explanation enough. When it wasn't, she explained that what she'd just read was the VIN for a 2006 Suburban. When none of us reacted properly to that information, Tinkertoy explained that Willeniec's vehicle must have been cobbled together in a chop shop, a Frankenstein made up of stolen and chopped vehicles, and, accordingly, just like Frankenstein's monster, once it was taken apart it wouldn't be identifiable as a particular, specific vehicle.

"Are you certain?" Lucky asked, meaning, *Can it be that easy?*

Tinkertoy shut down for a minute, searching for secret messages in Lucky's simple question before responding, "I'll check. The drivetrain. And. Transmission but. Yeah."

All we had to do was spend about six hours reducing the Tahoe to the parts that made up a whole, then a day or two selling off pieces to salvage yards and local mechanics.

Of course it was Ripple who asked (way too eagerly) if we were going to do the same thing to Willeniec's corpse.

"Take him apart? Piece by piece?"

I looked at my watch.

Three A.M.

I told Lucky, Ripple, and Tinkertoy to get going on dismantling Willeniec's Tahoe. I told them that I'd take care of Phase 2 myself: getting rid of Willeniec's body. We'd meet for breakfast at Callahan's in six hours. If anything went wrong, and the place was swarmed by cops while I was away, all they knew was that I'd brought in a Chevy Tahoe and told them to take it apart. That's it. They didn't know where it came from and they didn't know where I'd gone.

"What Skellig is telling us," Lucky said, "is that getting rid of this policeman's murdered corpse is an Irrevocable Step. There is no coming back from that."

It's good to have a personal translator.

"Through a glass darkly and down the rabbit hole," I said.

"Wait. I'd've thought crushing the guy's larynx the actual irrevocable step," Ripple said, "because that's what murdered him."

"Skellig killed him, not us."

"Don't rub it in," Ripple said.

Tinkertoy asked what I was going to do with the remains. Lucky explained that it was better she didn't know.

Ripple, his voice dulled by pain and cannabis, asked yet again what I was going to do with Willeniec's body. Patient Lucky reiterated that the less they knew, the better.

"We'll see you at breakfast."

I nodded and went to Tinkertoy's workbench and looked around.

"What do? You need?" Tinkertoy asked, very possessive of her work space.

I didn't answer.

"Everything from Here On In is Need to Know," Lucky said.

"Need. To know," Tinkertoy repeated.

"That's all Skellig's stuff anyway," Ripple said. "Tools. Parts. Everything. None of your business if he wants to take something. It's his, not yours."

Bickering. Good. Things were getting back to normal.

By the time I pulled out of the garage in the Transit, Willeniec's mortal remains hermetically sealed in the back, Lucky, Tinkertoy, and Ripple were busy wreaking entropy upon Willeniec's Frankenstein chop shop vehicle, Ripple and Tinkertoy moving real slow (like people in pain), but moving.

When one is obliged to dispose of a murdered body, one faces a Gordian knot wrapped around Pandora's box, which contains Occam's razor. One can hide the body somewhere and hope it is never discovered, the downside being that most places filling that requirement, like the foundation of a building, a backyard, a crawl space, are also places that preserve the body for long periods of time. The continuing downside being that if the body is found, it's still identifiable and brimming with clues.

The other option is for one to get rid of the body completely, say, through incineration or dissolving or feeding to wild animals, but that tends to involve a lot of noticeable, dramatic, attention-getting behaviors and/or the need for facilities like giant furnaces or acid baths or shark tanks or dens of hyenas, all of which are mostly the purview of supervillains. Therefore, the best way for an everyman limo driver without criminal connections is to dispose of a body in a place where it will never be found.

Duh, you may say. But we live in a very crowded world. Even if I were to take Willeniec's body out in a boat, wrap it in chains, and dump it into the Catalina Trench, someone would be watching me on radar, maybe photographing me from a drone or satellites.

All in all, it's best for society that body disposal is a fraught enterprise because if it weren't, people might get away with murder (exactly as I intended to do).

I pulled the Transit out onto Santa Monica Boulevard, pointed it east to the interstate, and headed north. Even at four o'clock in the morning, there's traffic on the 405, though I can't say how many other vehicles were transporting dead LA County sheriff's detectives. I turned on KNX 1070 AM—"Southern California's Only All-News Radio Station"—and cruised over the Sepulveda Pass and across the Ventura Freeway and kept going. Less and less traffic traveling my way but more and more coming toward me, hardworking, honest people who lived out in the Valley and beyond, heading to their jobs, drinking coffee from insulated sports team mugs, and cursing their daily commutes.

Past Mission Hills to North Hills to where 405 joins the Golden State, climbing out of the Southland basin (holding my breath superstitiously as I passed the LAPD training center), up and up and up through the darkness, I drove five miles per hour over the speed limit, which is the least suspicious speed a man can drive when there's a corpse in the vehicle.

An hour later I grabbed a Styrofoam cup of acidic, hyperstrong coffee at the McDonald's in Castaic because it occurred to me that everything I'd done in the last couple of days was extremely fatiguing. I considered popping a Vicodin but figured I should keep all my wits about me and told myself the throbbing pain in my head would keep me sharp. By the time I reached Pyramid Lake, the sky was lightening, which I tried to deny as a figment of my imagination, but no, the mountains were definitely outlined against the eastern horizon. I crested the Tejon Pass, the San Joaquin Valley stretching out in front of me, the lights of Bakersfield in the distance. Daylight was coming too fast, so I risked increasing my speed.

It was five thirty when I exited the 5 at Maricopa Highway and headed west.

My destination was a patch of land near Capitola Park not far past the town of Maricopa.

I'd been there once before with a charity client after an Oilers game at the Staples Center. I was supposed to take him directly back to his room at a seniors' facility in Bakersfield, but he asked me if I'd mind taking a small detour to what he called his home place, adding that he had liver cancer and was not expected to live long. Would you have said no? (I didn't think so.)

The old codger's name was Danny Marler, a small man wearing cardboard-stiff overalls, hunched from a life of hard labor, with giant ears and a weird mop of white hair, crazy eyebrows.

"You don't mind me saying, Mr. Marler," I said, "I never met anybody who looks less like a hockey fan."

Mr. Marler wheezed (which I took for a laugh) and admitted that as long as he'd been living in the senior center, he'd entered every contest that might get him the hell out of his room.

"You're right, I don't know nothing about hockey, but I loved that game tonight," Mr. Marler said. "Loved it!"

Mr. Marler told me his intention was to leave these sixty desiccated acres outside Maricopa to his children, who he hoped would redevelop an interest in what used to be a pretty sweet orchard.

"After the damn drought ends," he said.

Four years before we met, Mr. Marler had tried to save his tangerine trees by drilling a six-hundred-foot well. It worked for exactly two months before his neighbor, a giant industrial almond company, drilled a thousand feet down.

And that was that for Danny Marler and his beloved tangerine trees and his sixty acres.

His ten-thousand-dollar well drained dry in a matter of minutes.

"Fickle finger of fate," Mr. Marler said, pointing his own gnarled index finger up at the sky.

Danny Marler capped the well, got cancer, and moved into the senior center in Bakersfield, where he was the hundredth caller to a radio contest to get limo-driven to an Oilers game.

I said something lame to Mr. Marler, nothing more than the usual sympathetic human noise. Mr. Marler wheezed and said he wouldn't expect me to understand how much he loved this piece of land because I'd never seen it before the drought, supporting him and his wife and a bunch of kids. For forty years, Mr. Marler said he'd felt like Adam doing God's work in his own private Garden of Eden. If he got to Heaven and it didn't look exactly like this, he'd be disappointed. We stayed there for an hour, Mr. Marler giving me a tour of a place that looked to be about ready to dry up and blow away.

"Like me," he joked, making his wheezing sound.

A couple of weeks later, I called Danny Marler up to offer another hockey game on me, and an impatient woman at the hospice told me Mr. Marler had died three days after showing me his desiccated slice of paradise.

My intention was to drop Willeniec's corpse down Danny Marler's useless dry well.

To my great relief, Mr. Marler's faded wooden farmhouse remained boarded up and abandoned and his tangerine trees remained so much vertical firewood.

I trotted around the area Mr. Marler had flapped his hand at in disgust when he told me about his well. By which time I no longer needed my flashlight. I hustled back to the Transit and backed as close as I could get to the wellhead, which was capped by a hatch twenty-four inches across, topped by a bolted-down manhole cover with rocks placed on top. I put on my leather driving gloves, removed the rocks, then used the ratchet wrench and penetrating oil I'd taken from Tinkertoy's bench to unbolt the hatch. It weighed about two hundred pounds, but at least it wasn't rusted in place.

When I shifted the hatch, a dank, cool miasma rose from the hole and I stumbled backward with vertigo. I assumed it was my aching head and lack of sleep, but it felt like that six-hundred-foot hole wanted to suck me into it.

I opened the ambulance doors on the Transit and tilted Willeniec's tarp-shrouded corpse directly into the hole without it ever touching the ground. I heard a *shoosh* as the body slid down the tube. Lucky for me, Willeniec was not a fat man or particularly wide shouldered, because I heard that sound for long seconds before it finally faded.

I stood over the hole feeling both severe fear of heights and intense claustrophobia, feeling bad that I'd sent the sadistic bastard down headfirst (as though that mattered), and wondered just for a moment if I might be losing my shit. But, like when you're shooting coyotes, doubt and fear should come before the decision is made, not when the action is taken.

Did I say a prayer for Sheriff's Detective Willeniec, A.?

No, I did not but, just in case God existed and wasn't a sadistic superalien, I said one for myself and my people. I prayed that if anyone ever opened this wellhead again, they would simply fill it with rocks or sand and not try to drill deeper for water. I prayed that nobody would even stand here again until after I was long dead. I prayed that if they did find Willeniec's body they wouldn't be able to find any evidence tracing it back to me and mine. Then I rebolted the hatch, replaced the rocks, shut the ambulance doors, and drove back out to the road. I shuffled back and forth to the wellhead dragging a branch in case there were tire tracks I couldn't see, then resolved to replace the tires on the Transit when I got back to Santa Monica just to be sure. I drove through Maricopa without a single person seeing me, smelling the Midway-Sunset Oil Field to the north, and I didn't stop again until I pulled into Oasis Limo Services and put the Transit onto the lift to remind me to change out the tires.

No sign of Tinkertoy, Lucky, and Ripple, but the Tahoe's quarter panels leaned against the far wall, like they'd always been there, and the engine was on the same hoist Willeniec had used to suspend Ripple only a few hours before.

Out back I found four tires, a drivetrain, and the frame. What they'd done with the seats I did not know.

I changed my clothes, then dropped the lightweight black suit

I'd been wearing for nearly twenty-four hours into the donation bin at the Santa Monica Goodwill along with the leather driving gloves.

It had been five and a half hours nearly to the minute since I'd left, and for most non-murderers the day was just beginning, so I went to join my friends and coworkers at Callahan's Diner for breakfast.

When I got there, nobody had ordered food. But once I tucked in, starving, one by one the others discovered they could eat as well. We ate without speaking, which was exactly as it should be, in silence, then ordered more coffee, except for Lucky, who likes tea.

I cleared my throat. They all looked at me like I was their leader, like we were a military unit.

Are you aware that a five-star general feels less responsibility than the lowliest second-grade lieutenant facing a platoon of grunts? An admiral doesn't look sailors in the eye. Go ahead, ask any of the big muck-a-mucks who command thousands (or hundreds of thousands) of troops about his or her toughest command, and you will hear about the first day a newly minted junior officer faces thirty individuals.

You know who feels an even greater burden? A noncommissioned officer. We bear an even greater responsibility for the personal well-being of our subordinates because there are maybe eight or fifteen people in a squad and we know them well. Real people. In fact, you could say that officers from generals down to lieutenants have prime objectives designed to get soldiers killed. Sergeants work to keep their people alive. To send them all home.

That's why being a sergeant is the highest calling available in the military.

(I may be biased.)

"Interesting phenomenon," I announced.

Lucky reacted to the tone of my voice, relaxing a little because he's the one who tends to read my mind and so knew whatever I'd been up to had gone as well as could be expected. "Interesting phenomenon a cop once told me," I continued.

Tinkertoy blew on her coffee and winced, her sore breast giving her pain, maybe even a broken rib grating.

"Crimes, especially murders, are always solved by three things." I held up three fingers. "One: people talking. Two: evidence at the crime scene. Three: evidence on the body."

"What about eyewitnesses?" Ripple asked.

"Falls Under the Aegis of finger one," Lucky said, grabbing my index finger to illustrate. (Again, Afghans display different personal boundaries from your average American male.)

"If nobody talks," I said, reclaiming my finger, "the crime cannot be solved. If there is no crime scene, the crime cannot be solved. If there is no body, the crime cannot be solved. So, if those three things either don't exist or can't be found, you know what you have?"

"Perfect crime?" Ripple was looking green under his stoned smirk. His balls must be aching like Jesus's right hand.

"No crime at all," I corrected him. "Like the tree in the forest falling down, it never happened."

"The Allegory of the Tree Falling does not concern the Fact of the Occurrence," Lucky corrected me. "It concerns the Fact of the Sound the tree does or does not make when it falls as a Perception of the Occurrence."

(Which blather reassured me that Lucky had made his peace with the night's events.)

"In this case the tree made no sound because it never fell," I said, showing my three fingers with my right hand, then knocking them down with a flick of the thumb and forefinger on my left. "And anyone will tell you it's stupid to worry about something that never happened."

Lucky nodded. So did Ripple.

"Tinkertoy?"

Without taking her face out of her coffee mug, Tinkertoy said, "None of this. Bothers me. None. I got some seats. From the Tahoe. Need exchanging. With the Suburban. That's all. I got on my mind."

At least that told me what her plan was with the Tahoe's upholstery.

"Nobody's gonna talk," Ripple said.

"As for evidence of the crime scene, the only blood at the garage is yours," Lucky said.

"And I took care of finger number three."

I gulped my coffee and rubbed my eyes.

"When you think you've Thought of Everything," Lucky said, "that is exactly when the Heavens Collapse Upon You."

"There is one thing outside our control," I admitted, "which I gotta deal with."

"What?" Ripple asked.

"I told Delilah Groopman about Willeniec showing up with a warrant at Avila's place yesterday."

"Is that bad?"

"Delilah's a really good cop," I said. "That's what's bad. But what happened didn't happen, and this, right now, is the last we speak of it."

They nodded. They trusted me. They had faith in me.

Goddammit.

EVERYTHING IS FINE

Can you believe I have to leave the comfort of that diner and my friends, haul myself behind the wheel of One, gas her up, and drive my fatigued self all the way up to Bismarck Avila's lunatic mansion in Calabasas? It's a good thing that sleep is something I've always been able to go without (although the fact that I hear the voices of people I've killed might indicate otherwise). I consider borrowing some of Ripple's Ritalin (adult attention deficit due to post-traumatic stress), but I'm reasonably confident that this pounding headache will keep me awake through at least one more watch.

You want me to write here that it's guilt that keeps me awake, not a headache.

You realize that would make guilt a force about as powerful as a can of Rip It?

You do remember what an awful person Willeniec, A., was, right? (Kicking Tinkertoy? Torturing a teenage war-veteran amputee?)

What? You still want me to feel guilty for killing him?

Are you sure it isn't shame you require?

Or remorse?

Disgrace?

Do you want me to bemoan a lapse of rectitude or a lack of probity?

I ask because these are all different sentiments that people lump together into one ball of wax and call it conscience. Perhaps it's your opinion that a good man in my position should be hearing rattling chains in the night, beating hearts beneath the floorboards, out-out-damn-spotting, hair shirts and fig leaves. What you are demanding is that I bear a penitential burden. Ideally a cross. You want me to suffer for killing Willeniec. Which means you resent my decision to kill him more than my subsequent action of actually taking his life.

No? You say you don't resent me for what I did? Then you must resent me for not feeling the way you think I should feel after doing something of which you tacitly approve?

(I'll leave you to cogitate upon the nature of guilt while I continue to live my day-to-day life.)

At the fake concrete / wood / Greco-Roman columns of Avila's gate, I rang the buzzer and waved at the camera angled down at me from Olympus. Nobody spoke, but the gate swung open, and just like that, I was back on King Kong's Skull Island, crunching along the driveway toward the crazy mansion with the gigantic vertical ramp built behind.

Nina waited for me at the door wearing nothing but an American flag bikini (which made me feel violently patriotic) and a skimpy, gauzy throw-over that all but disappeared when viewed from almost every angle.

"Biz is still asleep," she informed me.

"Late night?"

"He was up skating 'til all hours. Biz does that when he's worried."

"What's he worried about?"

"Oh, I dunno, maybe people taking shots at him and cops sniffing around looking for mysterious barrels. What you think he's worried about?"

"I had a pretty late night myself," I said, hoping she'd suggest I go home and wait for Avila's call. No such luck.

"Doing what?" she asked, as though I had no life aside from driving her famous boyfriend around.

If Nina knew what I'd been doing she probably wouldn't be traipsing through her house wearing nothing but Betsy Ross's bathing suit and spiderwebs, me following behind like a poodle, gaping in surprise because the outwardly schizophrenic, theme-confused mansion was decorated in a low-key, beautiful, and tasteful manner.

"Nice place," I said.

"What did you expect? Video games and leather and big screens and shark tanks?"

I couldn't tell if she was accusing me of being racist or angling for my support if she tried to get Avila to spice up the place. Sure as hell, there was no way to ask without coming off as racist, so I shut up and followed her through a foyer, then a library, then a dining room suitable for seating forty of Avila's closest friends and family, into an industrial-size kitchen featuring granite and chrome and copper.

Nina indicated a box full of liquor in what was either an aircraft hangar or a pantry.

"I need that to go out to the island," she said.

"I'm Avila's driver."

"*Mr.* Avila's driver."

"I'm not a day laborer."

"Fine. Put it in your scabby limo and drive that shit out to my island."

"Not gonna happen," I said. "I'll go wait out in the car for Avila to wake up; then I'll drive him wherever he wants to go."

"Because you're a *driver*."

"That's correct."

"Too proud to carry stuff."

"Not my rationale but identical outcome."

"I'm gonna have Biz rip you a new asshole when he wakes up."

"Do me one better," I suggested. "Get him to fire me."

I retraced my steps to the front of the house (without the need for bread crumbs), returned to One, reclined in the front seat, clicked the satellite over to piano trio sleep music, and shut my eyes . . .

. . . and awoke to the sound of cursing as Nina appeared, box of booze in her arms, leaning back, trying not to topple off her spiky heels as she tottered across the driveway. Extremely entertaining. Nina wobbled across the paving stones, then stopped to rest, propping the box on a decorative rock wall, refusing to glance my way, before hoisting the box to resume her stagger toward the dwarf pirate ship at its stubby dock, where she put the box down and headed back inside for more.

I followed her back to the kitchen, where I picked up two dozen beers and a string bag full of limes. Then I went back for two seven-fifties of tequila and a hundred pounds of ice. It wasn't until all that was loaded onto Nina's pirate ship that I noticed the first box she'd carried out was completely empty.

"Ha!" she crowed, noticing me notice.

"I underestimated you."

"Everyone does," Nina said, "especially men. I suppose now you're not gonna help me unload."

"You got me," I said.

(There you go. Menial labor: my penance for killing the bad man. Feel better?)

Nina pushed a tiny lever at the base of the mainmast, which was the width of a pie plate and eight feet tall, Jolly Roger fluttering on wires at the top, and Nina's miniature *Queen Anne's Revenge* lurched across the man-made pond to her desert-island getaway maybe thirty yards from the mainland. At the stern of the ship, a fake cannon pointed at any Royal Navy pursuers who might appear. I sat on the barrel of gunpowder, nudged immovable cannonballs with my feet. When we bumped against the dock, Nina grabbed my arm (totally unnecessary) to support herself before leaping to the sand and tottering on six-inch heels toward the hammock between the two palm trees while I hefted boxes of party goods onto the dock.

"This is where I come when I get stressed," Nina said, lighting a huge, slightly moist (and, I assume, salty) doobie she extracted from between her breasts.

"You suffer a lot of stress?"

Nina was focused on holding the smoke in her lungs and she sure as hell wasn't allowing a conversation with me to interfere with her process.

"Fuck you!" she said finally, expelling lungfuls of smoke. (Nina smoking weed was a beauteous thing to behold.) "Living in a pretty place don't convey lack of stress." She offered me the doobie, but I shook my head.

"You don't smoke?"

"I'm on duty."

"What if you wasn't?"

"Never developed the taste."

"I thought you was some nature of soldier."

"Some nature, yeah."

"Soldiers *love* weed."

"I'm independent in thought and deed."

"Biz don't smoke neither. Biz don't do nothing, recreationally speaking, on account his mother was a crackhead. But he don't care what I do. Biz is not a judgmental type of man. He understands people got different coping mechanisms for life. What you got for a coping mechanism?"

"Good works, prayer, and Bible study."

"Don't be ironic on religion. It's one thing you should not be ironic on."

"You said don't be judgmental."

"I said *Biz* ain't judgmental. Never said I weren't. What Biz copes with is coffee or energy drinks mixed with half booze."

"Poor man's speedball."

"Biz ain't not a poor man's nothing," Nina said, losing focus.

If the booze was any indication, her weed was top grade: only the best stuff out here on stress-free Treasure Island.

"Biz's last driver used to smoke with me," Nina said.

"Where's he now?"

"Dead."

"That's too bad."

"Not for you. If it weren't for Rocky getting killed, you wouldn't have a job. Rocky got killed in a carjacking. Rocky was short for Rakim or some such shit. Sweet kid. Rocky and Biz were close, like this." (You know what she did with her thumb and index finger.) "Cousins. Biz's mother had a real dark half sister and that sister had Rocky. Who, even though he was a driver, did not mind bringing all my shit out here to the island because he liked me. Six foot six and arms like this." (You know what she did with her hands.)

If weed made Nina talk this fast, what the hell would cocaine do to her?

"Eighteen years old," she said. "You know what else Rocky did? He built most of the stuff on the boat there for me. Used his carpentry skills to turn it from a boring barge into a full-on pirate ship. Fanciful. Put in a hundred hours just to delight me. Sometimes I think maybe Rocky liked me more than Biz."

I wondered if Nina and Rocky had done more than smoke weed together.

"I don't see you being satisfied with a mere driver," I said.

"Damn right you don't see me being happy with the driver! Who I belong with is someone like Biz. Owns a whole company by himself. Someone at the top of the heap. See all this we got now? That's nothing. Biz is gonna take this shit public. You know what happens then?" Nina made an explosion noise, accompanied by a cloud of smoke. "Billionaire time, baby. Chairman-of-the-board money. That happens, we're gonna look back on this place like some kind of shack."

Obviously, Nina was not concerned about being seen as a gold digger. She wore her ambitions like a crown. Nina flapped her hand at the treasure chest to illustrate for my benefit that it featured both refrigerator and freezer sections that needed filling. I loaded beer into the refrigerator and vodka and ice into the freezer.

"I hope it doesn't become a pattern," I said.

"You hope what doesn't become a pattern?"

"Avila's drivers getting shot."

"You should call him *Mr.* Avila."

"Especially if he's gonna get me killed," I said. "Let's hope Avila decides to lay low here at home, give the cops a chance to figure out who wants him dead."

"You should call him Mr. Avila. Cops ain't worth shit to Biz. They don't care if he gets killed. They like to kill Biz themself. I tell him don't never wear a hoodie."

"The name Keet mean anything to you?" I asked.

"Poet?" she answered, shocking the hell out of me. Which must have showed on my face.

"Fuck you, racist," she said.

Acting insulted was Nina's way of hiding the fact that the name scared her; otherwise, she'd never have flicked that fat unfinished roach into the pond like it was an ordinary cigarette butt.

"That's gotta be bad for the ducks."

"Thank you for helping me carry shit," Nina said, laying herself down in the hammock, shutting her eyes like daring me to stare. "Biz'll tip you something. You can take the boat back yourself. Don't forget to release the brake or the little electric motor burns out."

"Aye, aye," I said. But she was done with me, not in the least amused.

Nina was still buried in that hammock, immersed in her phone, two hours later when I drove off with Avila to keep an appointment at his lawyer's office in Beverly Hills.

101, 405, Santa Monica Boulevard.

When I asked Avila if he was concerned about any more attempts on his life, he informed me that as long as we kept moving, nobody would take a shot at him.

"You tell the last guy that?" I asked.

"You heard about my cousin?"

"Rakim or some shit."

"When he got shot, Rocky was driving a tricked-out hundred-thousand-dollar Escalade, in the middle of the night in Leimert Park," Avila said. "Stupid."

"Interesting fact: more daylight jackings are successful than nighttime jackings."

"You got an odd idea what makes a fact interesting."

"It's a counterintuitive statistic."

"Why would you ask Nina about Rocky and Keet?"

"I only asked about Keet. She offered up Rocky all on her own."

"Why'd you ask her about Keet?"

"I'm interested in poetry."

"You about half as funny as you think."

"I get forced against my will to work for a guy who two skater kids try to kill in a bar, but who do they kill instead? His bodyguard. Before that, his driver gets gunned down. Your employees die at an alarming, *Game of Thrones* rate. That gives me the right to ask a few questions."

"Who told you about Keet?"

I didn't feel like I should answer that question by saying it was a woman cop upon whom I was crushing. I decided to lie like a lying-dog liar.

"That cop from the other day? He came to where I work and asked me if I knew a guy named Asher Keet."

Avila made a sucking noise through his teeth that didn't provide any information except that I was annoying him.

I honked my horn at a texting Beemer drifting into my lane.

"I got a question," Avila said. "Why'd you shoot the ceiling in that bar? Why didn't you aim at those boys who killed Chris?"

"I try not to shoot kids."

"I bet you shot kids over there when you was Army. Women too."

I saw no upside in explaining why that fact made me less likely to do it again.

"And dogs. We're here," I said.

"Drop me in front. I'll text when I need you."

"I'll drop you at the elevator in the underground garage," I said. "Not in front on the street."

"I appreciate your concern," Avila said, "but even though you got ninja bodyguard skills, I didn't hire you for protection."

"Why did you hire me?"

"On account that same white cop asking about Keet and looking for barrels has been harassing me. Every time I turn around, there he is. I figure he's less likely to shoot me in cold blood I got a white guy with me."

I couldn't argue with that, the world currently being the way it is. Too bad I couldn't tell Avila that he could stop worrying about that particular white cop.

I removed my sunglasses and pulled in beneath the building on Roxbury just south of Wilshire Boulevard in the heart of Beverly Hills. The garage was full of Jags and Lambos and Ferraris and Bentleys. It smelled like rubber and polish and money. Avila fit right in, even wearing his crazy oversize skater costume and un-laced Jordans. I looped around and opened the door for him like an honest-to-God chauffeur. He took to it like a birthright.

"Thank you, Mickey."

"I prefer you call me Skellig."

"And I prefer you call me Mr. Avila. Which you think is gonna occur first?"

Avila was at the elevator doors punching the up button. It was quiet and cool in that dim Beverly Hills basement, surrounded by millions of dollars' worth of automobiles (I didn't even have to raise my voice).

"You ever consider the possibility that the cop and Keet are working together?"

Avila stared at me for a moment, then said, "Shit," in a tone meant to convey that he was miles ahead of me, but that wasn't true. The thought had never crossed his mind.

Avila stepped into the elevator and kept jabbing at the button until the doors closed.

I spent the next forty-five minutes on my phone, checking break-ing news to see if any sheriff's department detectives had been re-ported missing, until the elevator disgorged Avila, escorted by a uniformed security heavy.

Avila plumped himself down in the backseat and said, "Home."

He reclined there in silence, not answering his phone, not star-ing out the window, not listening to music.

As we approached the gate to the mansion, a guy I'd never seen before, dressed in khaki pants and a green polo shirt, waved us through.

"Security?" I asked.

"My managers and lawyers set it up. Said I wouldn't even notice."

"Yeah? My podiatrist told me the same thing about my orthot-ics. You know what? I notice them every time I take a step."

"But they fix your feet, though, right?"

"It's a metaphor," I said. "There's nothing wrong with my feet."

"It's a lie, you mean. Just say you lied, brah."

The pirate ship was docked on the driveway side and Nina was nowhere to be seen. Even though it was only midafternoon, Avila said he didn't need me anymore and sent me home.

Avila's new security umbrella was aiming to impress. Guard at the front door, another couple visible patrolling the perimeter, gym fit and moving like military or paramilitary, all of them wearing the same hunter-green polo shirt, dark khakis, and soft, black, tactical-team-type boots.

I stopped on the way out to roll down my window and talk to the guy at the gate.

"Hey, crew cut. What service were you in?" I asked.

"Have a good afternoon," he said.

"Not blue-water Navy; that's for sure."

"Good afternoon."

"I'm guessing Marines."

"Drive carefully."

"You're slouching. Marines tend to slouch. Probably from try-ing to present a smaller target."

He sighed, realizing that I wasn't going to drive away and leave him in peace.

"You look like you're gonna duck and cover any second," he said. "So, what . . . Army?"

"That's right. You allowed to say what security company you work for?"

"Mr. Skellig," he said (in a tone meant to convey that even though he possessed bottomless reserves of patience, he preferred not to draw upon them), "our instructions are to meld. You aren't supposed to notice us."

"Tell your boss that if he doesn't want you to be noticed, he shouldn't deck you out in such an eye-catching wardrobe."

"I'll tell him. Have a good afternoon, Mr. Skellig."

"I get it. You know my name. But what am I supposed to call you?"

"You don't call me anything."

"Because you don't exist?"

"Because we're invisible."

"That comes across as aloof."

"It's an unfriendly world, sir. Thank Christ; otherwise, I wouldn't have a job."

He said this without attitude or condescension, and the *sir* indicated that he'd subconsciously registered that I outranked him.

"If you don't tell me what to call you, I'll have to make something up."

"Have a good afternoon, Mr. Skellig."

"You have a good evening too, Nestor."

"Nestor?"

"Google it."

Nestor laughed, but not much and not very loudly.

"Semper fi," I said and drove home.

When I pulled into bay three at Oasis, Tinkertoy was standing directly in front of me, wiping her hands with a rag. She wanted me to ask what was wrong.

"What's wrong?"

"Ripple ain't. Doing so. Good."

I entered Dispatch. Ripple's wheelchair was at the desk but Ripple wasn't in it. He was lying supine on the floor, pinching his temples with his left hand, his right hand balling up the fabric of his shorts. That's what pain looks like.

"Let's go," I said.

"Fuck," he said, which was Ripple-speak for *okay*.

He let me help him into the backseat of the Caddie; then I stowed his wheelchair in the trunk.

"I hope you brought your medical marijuana card," I said, "because the lab is most definitely going to find traces of THC in your blood."

"More like they're gonna find blood in my THC."

At the emergency room I asked if Dr. Quan was on duty. The nurse said he'd try but reminded me that the Emergency Department wasn't a hairdressing salon where you requested your favorite stylist.

"Wait, who's Dr. Quan?" Ripple asked.

I explained that she'd taken care of me when I got smacked on the head and I got attached.

"A *girl* is going to check out my nards?"

I couldn't tell if Ripple relished the idea or hated it, because his voice was strained through waves of pain, his skin clammy and pale, his freckles and moles standing out like crimson stars on a bone-white sky.

The nurse showed us into a curtained cubicle right at the very end. I helped Ripple out of his wheelchair and up onto the bed. He kept shutting his eyes and going to some other place (this from a kid who'd been through wounds as bad as they come).

Dr. Quan came in, still chewing on her energy bar.

"Nice to see you again, Mr. Skellig, but you don't really get to request whatever doctor you want in Emergency."

"Dr. Quan, this is Darren Monning—"

"Ripple."

"He hurt himself the other day."

"Hello, Darren."

"Ripple."

"How did you hurt yourself, Ripple?"

"You want me to tell her?" I asked, because I'd come up with a credible lie featuring Ripple, a pair of crutches, and a cat.

Ripple said, "I was hoisting from my wheelchair to the toilet and I slipped and squared myself on the rim of the toilet."

That must've been something that actually happened to Ripple, it came out so easy.

"When did the accident occur?" Dr. Quan asked.

"Couple days," Ripple said.

Dr. Quan suggested that I go out to the waiting room and she'd speak to me after she examined Ripple. I said I'd like to stay. She asked if I was a relative or Ripple's significant other.

"Just my boss," Ripple said. "I don't need a babysitter."

Which is how I ended up watching TV in the Emergency waiting room.

Twenty minutes later, Dr. Quan came out to find me, distress written all over her fine, intelligent face.

"Darren authorized me to keep you in the loop regarding his condition," she said, "so I'm here to tell you this did not happen because he slipped on a toilet."

"How can you tell?"

"There's not enough bruising or abrasion on the scrotum to explain the damage to the testicle."

"No damage? It looks like a grapefruit."

"All the damage is inside. Darren's left testicle appears to have been crushed, Mr. Skellig. In addition, there's a nasty bruise above his pubic bone that leads me to believe he was struck."

"Struck? By what?"

(The butt of Willeniec's pistol.)

"I don't know. Perhaps a hammer? But the point is his wounds show at least two separate incidents and that doesn't include the fact that his wrists are chafed."

"Ripple was tied up?"

"I don't know, but what I can say is that this damage doesn't correspond with his explanation."

"What's your theory?" I asked.

"Assault. Or a psychological problem in which he did damage to himself. Maybe a sex game that went wrong."

"What?"

"S and M can go wrong. I've seen the results before."

(Excellent!)

"You get a pretty warped point of view on the world working in this place."

"It's an emergency room," she said. "In Los Angeles."

The kinky one-night-stand story sounded perfect to me if I could plant it in Ripple's ear, especially including the chafing to his wrists. Ripple could say he never got the girl's name, that he'd found her on Craigslist or on some dominatrix website.

"Mr. Skellig. I can see you are thinking about this and that you're concerned. Do you have any idea what really happened to Darren?"

"The kid's been through hell," I said. "He has PTSD, anger and impulse issues. But I've never known him to lie."

"People lie all the time in here, especially about sexual injuries."

"What happens now?"

"The hospital social worker and a psychiatrist will take a look at the file and decide whether to interview Darren, try to ascertain if he's being victimized or doing damage to himself. If they decide that someone else did this to him, then a police report will be filed."

A man with a blood-soaked tea towel wrapped around his hand groaned. A mother with a glassy-eyed sick child looked hopefully at Dr. Quan, wondering if we were finished yet.

"Can I take him home?"

"What's his living situation?"

"I own a duplex on Euclid. I rent it out to him and another employee."

"There's no chance this other employee abused him?"

"No chance."

"Does he have a girlfriend?"

"Not since he was wounded. I dunno, maybe . . . some kind of Internet hookup? Maybe if I took him home, I could have a serious talk? Get to the truth?"

"Darren's too badly hurt for that. We've admitted him. We're trying to bring the swelling down with steroids and compresses. We'll sedate him and do a couple more ultrasounds, after which it's possible we'll be obliged to go in and remove damaged tissue or blood clots. Without immediate improvement, we'll be forced to perform an orchiectomy."

"Tell me that has something to do with orchids."

"We'll have to remove the damaged testicle."

"He's nineteen!"

"He's got two of them."

"I wouldn't use that argument on him."

"Because . . . ?"

"Because that's what they told him about his legs."

Dr. Quan blinked at me like I'd slapped her.

She took me back to see Ripple, but he was out cold. He looked about twelve and I didn't have the heart to wake him up to plant a kinky S and M cover story.

I treated Lucky and Tinkertoy to dinner at Callahan's. Lucky was worried that Ripple might reveal Certain Truths under the effects of anesthesia.

"Good point," I said. "I'll call the hospital and tell them to forget anesthesia. Just make him bite down on a twig like they do in your hometown."

"Ripple might. Calm down if they. Take one away," Tinkertoy said.

"Like fixing a dog?"

"An Apt Metaphor."

I counted to ten so that I wouldn't stand up and toss the table like a Real Housewife. What was wrong with me?

Lucky, seeing I was biting back on my temper, grabbed my hand and kissed it.

"You really gotta try harder to join the melting pot of America," I told him.

Tinkertoy pointed at the television.

There, on the local news, was the official departmental photo of Los Angeles County Sheriff's Detective Willeniec, A., looking noble in his dress uniform. The caption beneath him read *Local Sheriff's Deputy Reported Missing* next to an animated logo in which Homer Simpson strangled Bart, which I suspect had nothing to do with the story.

The sheriff's department had no comment and the graphic beside the newsreader changed to a puppy who'd been rescued from an overpass along the LA River.

"It's going to be okay," I said.

"For that puppy?"

"For Ripple. For us."

Tinkertoy pushed her ice cream away.

"Why don't you kiss Tinkertoy's hand?" I asked Lucky. "Looks like she could use an emotional boost."

"No. Thanks," Tinkertoy said. "Things are. Bad. Enough."

AYN RAND IS BULLSHIT

While we are all spending a fitful night sleeping badly and wondering if Ripple will have to undergo yet another humiliating mutilation in order to save his life, I'd like to tell you about my mother.

Hippocrates would define Mom as an invigorating combination of blood, yellow bile, and black bile, meaning that she resists categorization but is ruled by a fractious tribunal made up of her spleen, liver, and heart. At the risk of describing my mother as something you might order as a Szechuan lunch special, she is dry and fiery, ambitious, restless and courageous, and so dedicated to being useful in the world that she can come off as distressingly utilitarian.

My brother, Brendan, and I were still students at Carmel High when Mom sprang from school board to the Republican state senator representing the Seventeenth District. You might have heard of Mom because she once tripped Governor Arnold Schwarzenegger when he made the mistake of turning his back on her and walking away before she'd finished what she was saying to him.

Yes, California state senator Dolores "Dolly" Shipton is my mother.

Most people assume prickly Dolly Shipton is divorced. Mom encourages that misapprehension because Dad values his privacy and she enjoys Dad as much as any wife enjoys her husband, except that enjoyment occurs exclusively on the weekends. Mom drives the same sea-salt-rusted '89 Jeep Comanche she used to commute from Rancho Pico Blanco into Monterey when she worked as principal of a high school catering to at-risk youth.

Picture Mom's swearing in.

Mom in her conservative skirt and pearls, Dad in his best jeans, cowboy boots, and corduroy suit jacket, shaking his head in amiable disagreement with Mom's conservative views, fifteen-year-old Brendan, combative, out and proud and here and queer in eyeliner and a TAKE YOUR MAMA OUT TONIGHT! Scissor Sisters T-shirt, and me, sixteen, a high school wrestler sporting a black eye, gung ho in my JROTC uniform, all of us squabbling as they took our family photo, backed by the American flag.

You're thinking that the Skelligs must be a hellish dysfunctional family (but you're wrong). Brendan saw Mom's election leaflet for the first time when the whole family was out door-to-dooring the ootsy backstreets of Carmel-by-the-Sea. Brendan got huffy and pointed out that, according to her brochure, I was Mom's only political asset.

"You boys aren't assets or debits. You're my sons and I love you."

"That's true," Dad said. "She even says so behind your backs."

"Apparently, not enough to include me and Dad in your brochure," Brendan insisted.

"I *begged* not to be in the brochure," Dad said.

"I only see Michael there, wearing his soldier costume."

"It's called a uniform, Froot Loop."

"News flash, you're not an actual, real soldier, Mikey. Ergo, that's a costume."

"They did a great job Photoshopping out your black eye," Dad said.

"Mom left me out of her brochure because they can't Photoshop out queer."

"Bullshit," Mom said.

"I don't think you should be shouting *bullshit* in the street while campaigning," I said. "You're a Republican."

"Your mother's calling bullshit because it is bullshit," Dad said.

Mom took Brendan's hands in hers, like they were about to play slap hands. "Look at you. Pretty little charismatic homosexual."

(The fact is, Brendan was never pretty—he looks more like a boxer than a dancer—but apparently, Mom and Brendan think otherwise.)

"If I put you on that brochure, what happens? You get me votes from people who would not otherwise support the Republican Party, and excuse me for thinking a dope-smoking, environmentally inclined queer like you wants to throw any influence to the Republican Party."

Brendan looked at me.

"At least she said *queer*," I told him.

"Is Mom telling me the truth?" he asked me.

"I'd pretty much count on that," I answered.

"While we're on the subject of dope smoking, Brendan," Dad said, "I wish you would cut it out until you're at least twenty-five. Your brain is still developing."

"We have to accept that ship has sailed, Abel," Mom said, releasing Brendan's hands. "Brendan's a total stoner, a tendency he inherited from your father the hippie."

That was true too. Mom has an unerring nose for bullshit.

One time, when I picked Mom up at the Salinas train station to drive her back out to the ranch for the weekend, I complained that Dad was dismissive of my interest in the writings and philosophies of the author Ayn Rand.

"If you want to have a conversation with your father about Ayn Rand, then you have it with him, not with me."

"Mom, her name is not Ann. It's *Ayn*. Rhymes with *cane*."

"Bullshit on that, Mikey. People can't just decide how they want their names pronounced. It undermines civilization."

"Dad is wrong to write Ayn Rand off, is all I'm saying."

"We don't drive wedges in this family, Mikey. We slug it out and hug it out at the kitchen table."

"Only problem is Dad won't listen."

"What did I just tell you about wedges?"

I turned the car radio on. Mom turned it off.

"Your dad does too listen. In fact, he listens too much, if you ask me. What it is, he *disagrees* with you and you assume he isn't listening because your adolescent logic is unassailable."

I turned the car radio on. Mom turned it off.

"You're seventeen so it's understandable you like Ayn Rand. Adolescent boys respond to her simplistic ranting because Ayn Rand herself was basically an angry adolescent boy who had all the answers but felt like nobody listened to her."

"You're a Republican. How can you not like Ayn Rand?"

"She's bullshit you grow out of, like costume parties or thinking farts are hilarious. I mean, go ahead and like her *now*, Mikey, but have the grace to look back in a few years and be embarrassed."

"Embarrassed! Have you really read *Atlas Shrugged*? I mean, really read it?"

"Is that the one where all the greatest minds in the world run away and hide? Or the one about the rapey architect?"

"The greatest minds in the world disappear because they're tired of being impeded by lesser minds."

"Bullshit."

"*Bullshit?*"

"It's Atlas's job to hold up the world. All of a sudden he's tired and doesn't feel appreciated? *Wah-wah-wah!* She should have called that bullshit book *Big Baby Shrugs.*"

"Mom, in order to restart the motor of the world, you have to stop it first."

"Bullshit."

"Stop saying *bullshit!*"

"There's a lot of things we don't get to choose, Mikey. How smart we are, how talented—but we do get to choose how we use the gifts God gives us. You and me, we've got something in common. We're leaders."

"You're just saying that because you think I'll like it."

"Bullshit."

"Again!"

"God put you and me on planet Earth to lead. We don't whine and bitch and complain and hide on a secret invisible island; we change the world through taking action. Not by stopping the motor of the world! We *are* the motor of the world. It's a mortal sin to stop yourself from doing good. It's a sin to withhold the best part of yourself."

Back then I thought Mom had missed the point because Ayn Rand's leaders didn't hide on a secret invisible island; they hid in a secret valley in Colorado. That particular detail, in my adolescent boy opinion, indicated why Mom was incapable of venerating Ayn Rand's beautiful vision of geniuses sweeping floors while civilization crumbled.

A few years later, when I became the leader my mother expected me to become, I realized she'd been right. I think my thoughts like my father, and I make my decisions like my father, but to this day when I give orders I give them in my mother's voice, only without shouting, "Bullshit!" quite as often or as loudly.

Why do I bring up this story now?

It was me who killed Willeniec, A., which means that those who followed me (Lucky, Tinkertoy, and poor Ripple, lying in the hospital) are my responsibility.

I am their leader and Ayn Rand is bullshit. No shrugging.

"We're a family," Mom told me as we turned off the Old Coast Road to start the series of switchbacks leading up to our house on the ranch. "We hardly agree on anything between the four of us, and maybe not all of us make the bullshit political brochure, but we are stuck in this life together."

In my head I thought *Bullshit!* and considered driving off the road and into the Pacific Ocean just to make Mom scream, but now I'm amazed and thankful I had the sense to keep my mouth shut and hold the course.

SORRY, LINDA

Midmorning the next day, I'm driving Avila from his ludicrous Calabasas mansion to his business manager's office in Century City, when I get a call from a loopy Ripple telling me he's scheduled for surgery later that afternoon.

"They're taking one ball," he said, "but they're gonna replace it."

"With what? A pig's ball?"

"With a prosthetic. Why would I want a pig's ball?"

"Why would you want a fake ball?"

"I don't want a fake ball."

"Then why bother?"

"Wait. Why bother which? Removing? Or replacing?"

"I know why they're removing your ball, Ripple. It's *dead*. It goes toxic, it'll kill you. Heads up, they aren't buying the squared-on-the-toilet-bowl scenario."

"I know. They keep asking me for the truth, but I'm sticking to my story."

"Taking a ball? You mean like a testicle?" Avila asked from the backseat.

"Personal conversation," I said, "if you don't mind."

"You have a conversation on my time, it's my conversation."

"Who's that?" asked Ripple.

"Bismarck Avila."

"Don't say where we are at," Avila said. "Nobody's supposed to know my whereabouts."

"Says who?"

"My new security people, who cost a fortune."

"If you really don't want anyone to know where you are, you'd turn off your phone, take out the battery."

"I did that already," Avila said. "Why do you think I'm listening to you discuss some random person's maracas problems?"

"Wait, is that really Bismarck Avila?" Ripple asked.

"Listen, Ripple, what they think is maybe you had casual rough sex with somebody who grabbed your ball."

"Like, for fun? Who does that?"

"It's a fetish," I said. "People do it. People do anything you can think of. The doctors think maybe you hooked up with somebody you found online and now you're ashamed and made up the toilet story. So if that's what happened, I think it's time for you to come clean and tell them the truth."

I cracked the window for some air and heard Willeniec's raspy voice in the wind *Looklooklooklooklooklook* . . .

So I look-look-looked.

"I'm down with that! Rough sex with a stranger is way more epic than slipping off a toilet. Ask Bismarck Avila if he ever did such a thing."

I had a more important question for Avila. "Your security people aren't following us?"

"No," Avila said. "Why?"

The answer was a late-model burgundy Ford Taurus, three cars back. I saw no reason to share that information with Avila until I confirmed my suspicion. So I scraped his attention off on Ripple.

"The kid I'm talking to is my dispatcher," I said. "He's gotta have a testicle removed."

"What happened?"

"Better he explains."

I handed my phone to Avila, jiggered lickety-split onto the 405 off-ramp to Olympic, and took advantage of a left turn on a yellow light at Sawtelle to spurt through.

"Bismarck Avila speaking," Avila said into the phone. Very formal.

Behind us the Taurus burned through the red. So not a sophisticated tail, or they'd have played it subtle and handed me off to somebody up ahead.

Behind me Avila said, "My condolences, but yeah, that shit can get out of hand, but no, I never got permanently hurt playing none of those games. I came pretty close to losing a maraca myself, once. European championships, twenty years old, vertical ramp, I square myself on my own board . . . you remember that injury? You a fan? . . . Yeah, the groin muscle was a cover story, brah, a complete lie. What really happened was I crushed one of my maracas but my PR people said that if the world knew the truth, it would be all the world ever talked about when they talked about me. It would detract from my brand, brah! So that was the big lie, a groin injury. But the point is the German doctors operated, fixed my scrotal hematoma and my parenchyma, stitched the sack back up, good as new. Told me if I'd waited another six hours they'd have had to remove the ball."

Which was a helluva way to discover that I should have taken Ripple to the hospital immediately after Willeniec hurt him instead of waiting. Meaning that losing this testicle was due to my faulty judgment.

Heading east on Olympic, crossing Veteran, approaching West-wood, I ran through a number of possible alternatives. Overland was coming up and that would be my fastest route to the 10 freeway. From there I could head toward downtown. At least on the freeway nobody could jump out at a red light, use a carjacking as cover to pump bullets into me.

"The reason they put in the fake ball is for cosmetics," Avila told Ripple.

Avila listened for a moment, then made a sucking sound with his teeth (sympathetic) and said, "All due respect, just because you got no legs don't mean give up on making sure your junk presents. Bright side, at least you damaged a redundancy. Could've been worse. Could've been the main diggity."

Up ahead I could see the towers of Century City and, to the right, the Plaza Hotel that overlooks the Fox Studios Lot. The burgundy Taurus was still there, three cars back, playing it cool.

"Okay, Ripple, you rest up for your operation. Good luck."

Avila hung up and gave me back my phone.

"Nice kid," said Avila.

"Not how I'd describe him."

"He's alive, at least," Avila said. "You meet some of these kinky sex people online, you end up buried in the backyard. Gotta take the positive view sometimes. Least he's got a story to tell."

Avila stared out the window a minute, then said, "I'll stay in tonight. That way you can be there when the kid comes out of his operation."

I was pretty sure it was only the Taurus following us. No flanking vehicles and no air support meant that if they were cops, then we were either a low-priority tail or the police wanted us to make them.

Or they weren't law enforcement at all. They were bad guys waiting for the right time to kill Avila and (worse) his driver.

"Avila. Keep facing forward."

"*Mr.* Avila."

"Do not turn around."

"I wasn't going to turn around, but now I want to."

"Don't."

"Why the hell not?"

"We're being followed and I need a couple minutes to figure out how to lose them, and if you look back, they'll know we made them and they'll be ready when I make my move."

"Are you good at this?" Avila asked.

"I'm extremely good at this."

Century City provides the usual dodges (alleys, underground parking, pedestrian walkways, nooks and crannies) but while One is comfortable, she is not agile. In a freeway chase, One would be my first choice. Great top speed. Excellent suspension. And enough gas in her for about two hundred miles at high speeds. But if our followers had access to a helicopter, then we would cease being a quiet matter and burst into the news/entertainment matrix.

I debated if that was good or bad and decided on bad.

"You gonna do something?" Avila asked.

We sailed past Beverly Glen, high concrete walls rising above us to the south as Olympic passed beneath the Avenue of the Stars. Up ahead rose the Fox Plaza, which in real life houses Rupert Murdoch's army of lawyers but is on the tourist maps as the *Die Hard* building.

Which gave me a notion that I hoped was the beginning of an idea.

"Turn around and stare at the burgundy Ford Taurus that's following us."

"You want me to do what you just told me don't do?"

"Make sure they see you seeing them."

"You got a very gymnastic mind," Avila said, but he did as I asked, and then, with an extra flourish, he extended his middle finger.

"They see you?"

"Uh-huh."

I floored One. Avila bounced around a little in the backseat before he managed to get his seat belt fastened. We gathered speed beneath the overpass and looped to the right, tires squealing, onto a tight ramp leading around and up onto Avenue of the Stars, g-forces driving my left shoulder into the car door and thunking Avila's head into the window.

"They hit the curb!" Avila shouted.

"They still coming?"

"Yeah," he said. "Too bad they missed the trees."

Easy for him to say. Last thing I needed was to kill another couple of cops. If they were cops.

I straightened out, but just for a second or two before jamming into a hard left turn onto Avenue of the Stars, the globular shapes of pedestrians, shocked faces turning toward us, lawyers or agents or Fox executives.

We lost a hubcap.

The car leveled out like a boat just in time for me to crank her into a tight fast right onto Galaxy.

"Dead end!" Avila shouted.

He was only partially right. It was a dead end but it was bracketed by two parking structures. The one on the right serviced the *Die Hard* lawyer building, which we'd now circumnavigated, and the one on the left serviced the Fox Lot studios themselves, parking for visitors and lower-level assistants and crew members.

That's the structure I chose.

A Lexus checking in at the entrance left me with no choice but to crash through the drop-down barrier. In through the out door. Avila shouted at me, but I suspected that his protests were not germane to our situation. There were two parking floors above us, culminating in the roof, but I drilled downward, keeping an eye out for which level which would bring us even with the Fox Lot surface streets. If I overshot, we'd be in a real dead end three floors farther down in the basement with no way out.

One floor, two floors, tires squealing, security guards following, hilariously, in golf carts, which, if the frantic honking I heard was any indication, were slowing down the Taurus. More guards barked into walkie-talkies, setting off alarm protocols across the lot, warning people to stay in their offices or trailers or on dozens of soundstages. One particularly motivated and physically fit guard was pretty much keeping level with us, charging down the stairs on the western side of the parking garage, moving fast, like a pro ball player. Down we went, tires screeching, leaning on the horn, two more levels. I prayed out loud that nobody would back out of a stall and end the chase here.

There was the exit!

I saw daylight through a gate that led to the main thoroughfare on the lot, between Stages 22 and 20, lined by tall Mexican fan palms, the gleaming-glass modern network building to the left and the Spanishy old-timey movie studio offices to the right.

"Can you see the Taurus?" I asked.

"No," Avila said, craning his neck. "But there's six golf carts and about a hundred people running after us."

"Good."

"*Good?*"

I killed the engine, slowed down to a stately crawl, and coasted into the no-parking area at the grand front of the Fox television network building, where a large black ball sat in a fountain to the left of the main entrance, water shimmering down the surface, symbolizing, I don't know, maybe existential despair due to rampant materialism?

"Good girl," I said, patting the dash.

It was peaceful there, near the black-ball water feature with a dozen security people moving toward us, some with hands on their sidearms, others with their sidearms fully drawn.

"What the hell?" Avila asked. "Let's get out of here, man! There's the main gate, right there! Let 'er rip. Let's go."

"Stay in the car."

"Stay in the car? Maybe you're mistaking me for your personal bitch? *You* stay in the car."

I exited the car with my hands up.

"Sorry," I said. "Sorry, everybody."

I emulated a major in Army Intelligence I'd known who had fucked up hugely and tried to get me to forgive him for nearly getting me and my people killed. I made a big act out of leaning on the hood of the car as though I'd just survived the most terrifying experience.

Twenty-five yards behind us, the Taurus stopped beneath a looming mural of Mary Poppins twirling in the Alps. I could discern two figures in the Taurus, no faces.

"My accelerator jammed," I told the nearest security guard, who had his gun trained on me. "It jammed. I didn't know what else to do. Anybody hurt? I'm really sorry. Tell me everybody's okay."

"Your accelerator jammed?" he said.

"I heard of that happening," someone said.

"Took off on its own," I said. "My life flashed before my eyes. Anybody hurt? Please tell me nobody got hurt."

"Nobody got hurt," the guard said. It was the superhero who'd run down the stairs. He was buying it.

The Taurus drove by us, on its way to the main gate. Whoever they were, they were leaving, averting their heads. The driver was a white male, but that's the most I could tell.

I leaned inside the car and told Avila to step out.

"We had business on the lot," I said. "Mr. Bismarck Avila. Here for a meeting."

Avila stepped out of the car. Everybody there recognized him.

"Howzit goin'?" Avila asked.

The security guard holstered his sidearm, which prompted everyone else to do the same. Everybody relaxed. What could be wrong? There was a celebrity present! One of their own. In another five minutes Avila would be signing autographs. Nobody was going to get shot today.

"You want us to call a tow truck?" asked the guard.

"That's okay. I got a guy," I said, dialing my phone. "You need to inform the police?"

"Nah," said the guard. "We're law enforcement on the lot here. Nobody's hurt. No damage done."

My usual tow-truck driver is a buddy who sells secondhand Land Rovers, Broncos, FJ40s, and some Czech military four-by-fours from his lot on Lincoln Avenue. Most of his stock originated in Louisiana about the time of Hurricane Katrina, which means that they spent time under the waters of Lake Pontchartrain or the Gulf of Mexico. As a result, their electrical systems tend to fail, which is why he requires his own in-house tow truck.

He appeared half an hour later, Lucky in the passenger seat. Of course by then I'd fixed the nonexistent accelerator problem myself and had my fixes confirmed by Lucky, who everybody bought as an accomplished mechanic because he was brown and wearing grimy overalls.

It was a long half hour, though, because there's always at least one person on the job who is smart and competent. In this case it was a dumpy Hispanic woman who worked as a liaison between Security and Facilities on the Fox Lot. She wore a pantsuit in a color my mother's political advisers would have called Screaming Babyshit with matching shoes. Her name was Linda. Linda was troubled because there was no record of Bismarck Avila having an appointment on the books at the Fox network. I bought an extra five minutes by suggesting to Linda that perhaps the meeting was at the

Fox News Channel due to Mr. Avila's recent experience as a victim of violence. I got another reprieve when I said the meeting could be at the Fox Business Network because Mr. Avila was also a respected businessman who was about to take his company public.

Linda found no record there either. Nor at Fox Sports when I informed her that Mr. Avila was a respected athlete. Nor at any of the cable networks or any other satellites, including film companies.

Avila, catching on, took Linda's veiled accusations and turned them into apologies—*No problem!*—and struck a perfect note of good-guy conciliatory and superstar noblesse oblige. He made everyone feel that the less said on the subject, the better.

Except for competent Linda. Doing the job she was paid to do.

Avila suggested helpfully that perhaps he'd gotten the date or time wrong, at which time Linda said there was no meeting on the books for any date or time ever, anywhere on the lot. Avila winced and suggested his assistant might have gotten the whole thing wrong and the meeting might have been down the street at Sony. How awkward!

Poor competent, smart, observant, embarrassing Linda was packed away, by order of the head of Security, when she suggested that the police should be notified because nobody could account for Avila's presence on the lot. A presence that had endangered hundreds of Fox employees. Nor could anyone account for the burgundy Taurus, which had followed us onto the lot, sideswiped a Bentley, and then disappeared during the ensuing hubbub.

Typical that the person most committed to and competent at her work was hustled out of sight because she was indiscreet.

Sorry, Linda.

Kudos to you.

Respect.

DELTA SIERRA CHARLIE

After waving good-bye to approximately thousands of well-wishers and fans, Avila and I exit the Fox Lot through the main gate and head back to Calabasas, keeping our eyes peeled for the Taurus, which is nowhere to be seen.

"I don't suppose you're going to tell me about what's really going on?" I asked.

"What do you mean?"

"Skaters trying to kill you in nightclubs. Getting chased on city streets in broad daylight?"

"That today? Paparazzi, brah. TMZ."

"I'm more useful if I know what's going on."

"Don't worry about it. You're useful the exact amount I want you to be useful."

"How did you know Willeniec was coming with the warrant?"

I was watching Avila in the rearview mirror when I asked that question, and Avila's eyes shot straight to mine. His pupils dilated like he'd taken a bong hit.

"Remember who's the boss here, Mickey."

"Remember who's up shit creek here, Biz."

Insubordination made Avila cranky. What made me cranky was not being able to see who'd been following us. For all I knew, I'd been the target and not Avila.

"You're the driver."

"I know I'm the driver."

"So be the driver. Drive."

But after a moment, Avila's curiosity got the best of him.

"What makes you think I knew he was coming?"

"You moved barrels out of that storage unit just ahead of the warrant."

Avila leaned his head back and shut his eyes. It wasn't chilly nonchalance; he was hiding.

"There were crescent-shaped scuff marks on the floor," I continued. "You scraped your knuckles on the door."

Avila glanced at the gauze on his knuckles.

"That there's a skating injury."

"What's the use of being a high-life business titan if you gotta hide evidence from the police all by yourself in the middle of the night? Don't you have low-life people to handle that kind of thing for you?"

Avila tilted his head back and pretended to sleep until we approached his gate in Calabasas.

Which was blocked by flashing lights.

"What now?" he asked.

"Ambulance."

Nestor, my pal the invisible security guard, was being tended by an EMT. Nestor was conscious and scowling while the EMT poked at his head. A man I took to be Nestor's boss (same khaki pants and tac boots but his polo shirt was authoritatively black) watched from a couple of yards away. Big man. Arms crossed. Calm as a glacier if glaciers were Samoan.

A minion in a green polo shirt talked into his walkie-talkie and the gate yawned open to beckon us forward.

"Hold up," Avila said, exiting the car.

While Avila approached the Samoan glacier, I ambled over to speak with Nestor, peon to peon.

"You okay there, Nestor?"

"You asking me questions all the time makes it tough to stay invisible and do my job."

"Can I ask you if he's okay?" I said to the EMT, a good-looking Hispanic kid in his midtwenties.

"He's fine," the EMT said, "for somebody who got cracked on the head with a blunt object."

"What happened to doctor-client privilege?" Nestor asked.

"I'm not a doctor," the EMT said.

As the EMT applied butterfly bandages to Nestor's scalp, I asked him if he knew Dr. Quan at the UCLA Medical Center in Santa Monica. It turned out he did. Dr. Quan's first name was Grace and she was always too busy to go out with him, even though he usually went out with (his exact words) better-looking women.

"Gracie's not wicked hot," he said, "but there's something about her."

"Y'ever consider that she turned you down because she picked up on your attitude?" I asked.

"What attitude?"

"That you think she's not good-looking enough for you."

"You mean like she's psychic?"

"Dr. Quan seems like the kind of a woman who knows if a guy figures he's wrestling a weight class down."

"It's a curse being this handsome," the EMT said. "I'm just being honest."

"You get a piece of whoever attacked you, Nestor?" I asked.

"Why you keep calling me *Nestor*?"

"It's got a meaning. I told you, look it up."

"Nestor was one of the Argonauts," the EMT said.

"Argonauts? What's that?"

"The Argonauts were ancient Greek heroes who backed up Jason on his quest for the Golden Fleece," the EMT said.

"Why are you wasting a classical education cleaning up after car accidents?"

"I'm really an actor. I played a bad-guy extra in a low-budget sci-fi version set in space. Got my head chopped off by Nestor. In slow motion," the EMT said, patting Nestor on the shoulder to show he was done with the butterfly bandages. "My pay was they let me take my head home in a box."

"I guess that explains why you need to moonlight as an EMT."

Nestor laughed but swallowed it when the Samoan and Avila approached.

"All good?" the Samoan asked.

He waved a new green-shirt guy into position, this one packing a Taser and a look of firm resolve not to end up like Nestor.

"Any idea who did this?" I asked.

"Nothing for you to worry about," the Samoan said.

He turned to Avila. "We have some security footage for you to look at, Mr. Avila."

"See?" Avila said to me. "*Mister.* Why can't you do that?"

"You want me to drive Nestor home?"

"Who's Nestor?"

I pointed at Nestor, who was patting his aching head like a church lady checking her blue hair.

"You told him your name is Nestor?"

Nestor looked at the Samoan and made a face like, *How can you even ask such a question?*

"His name is not Nestor."

"He wouldn't tell me his name. I had to give him one. How's Nestor getting home?"

"We'll take care of getting him home, thank you. Nothing for you to worry about."

"Looks like I got nothing in this world to worry about."

The Samoan was working at not being irritated. I found this heartening.

"So, how's the no-name thing work? You assign your people numbers?"

"Mr. Avila?" the Samoan asked. "Could we head up to the house? No use standing out here on the street in public."

"In public? Nobody's even driven by here in twenty minutes."

The Samoan looked at Avila, who shrugged and said, "He's annoying, right? It's not just me?"

The Samoan glanced at me again. Obviously a pro. Ex–federal agent of some kind. He possessed the unnatural patience of a federal marshal. Which made it all the more challenging and fun.

"Want me to drive you up to the house?" I asked. "Or are you taking a golf cart?"

"We'll take the car," Avila said, to the Samoan's disappointment.

I opened the car door for Avila. The Samoan got into the front seat with me, identifying himself as one of Avila's employees, not as an equal—meaning he was somebody whose ego existed outside the apparent hierarchy.

"I'm Michael Skellig," I said to the Samoan and extended my hand to shake.

"I know who you are, sir."

"You look into my background?"

"I told him not to bother about you," Avila said from the backseat. "If he's any good at his job, he ignored you."

"I know all about you, Mr. Skellig," the Samoan said, and then over his shoulder to Avila, "Special Forces Weapons Sergeant Michael Skellig, three Silver Stars and a Delta Sierra Charlie."

Not a military man, because we don't call the Distinguished Service Cross *Delta Sierra Charlie*, but hey, nice effort, Samoan guy.

"I never won any Silver Delta Charlies but I got six world championships," said Avila.

The Samoan finally accepted my hand, looking me in the eye. "I asked some contacts in a couple federal agencies about you, Mr. Skellig. Turns out the best stuff you did isn't in the public record."

"Nothing for you to worry about," I said.

He nodded at me and crinkled his eyes, admitting he deserved that, keeping a grip on my hand long enough to give me my props. And hard enough to show me he was not a man to be fucked with.

Definitely a fed.

"You being who you are is the only reason I allowed Mr. Avila to leave the house today."

"Excuse me? *Allowed?* You know you work for me, right?"

The Samoan winced in the manner of somebody who has spent time being a human shield for puffed-up egomaniacs who don't know any better. You see that quality in a lot of publicists and second wives in LA.

And the Secret Service.

"I misspoke, Mr. Avila. I should have used the verb *advised* instead of *allowed.*"

"Damn right use your verbs," Avila said. "Nobody *allows* me."

"Hey, John Frederick Parker, we were followed today," I said.

The Samoan laughed.

"That's not his name," said Avila.

"If a man refuses to tell me his name, I gotta call him something."

"That's what you come up with? John Parker?"

"John Frederick Parker."

"Why not Jay Z, or Kendrick, or some such normal name?"

"Mr. Skellig is making a joke. John Frederick Parker was the Secret Service agent assigned to guard President Abraham Lincoln the night he was assassinated."

"Shit. That's not funny, Mickey."

I said I thought it was kind of funny.

"It's not funny because if he's Lincoln's bodyguard, then I'm Lincoln and that night ended up bad for Lincoln!"

"I'm not John Frederick Parker, Mr. Avila."

"His name's Cody, okay, Mickey? Jesus Christ, why'n't you just put a curse on me?"

"Cody is not a scary name. Tell me you at least got an intimidating nickname."

"What the fuck is it with you and names?" Avila asked. "You got a fixation!"

"What do you mean you were followed?" Cody asked.

He listened carefully as Avila described our short car chase, glancing at me in the mirror.

"Fox Lot," Cody said. "Clever."

"I'd be more impressed if we actually got away," Avila said.

"Mr. Skellig knew you couldn't get away from them due to your vehicle, so he took you to a place with lots of cameras and an armed security force where there were too many people for them to do whatever it is they intended to do."

"We're here!" I said, jabbing the brake so that Cody had to brace himself on the dash and Avila thumped against the back of the front seat.

I stayed in the car as Cody and Avila bailed. Nina appeared at the front door wearing a shiny, clinging, cream-colored deal with a plunging neckline, and bare feet. Avila kissed Nina, and Cody nodded at her like she was just another ugly dude. (That's what I call a pro!) The three of them conferred for a couple of minutes and then all three turned to look at me in unison. What could I do?

I waved.

Nina thrust her hip out and crossed her arms, Cody adjusted his sunglasses, and Avila beckoned me.

Cody led us to where his technical guy sat at a folding card table set up in the foyer. I knew he was the technical guy because he was soft and had a beard and wore glasses and his polo shirt was baby blue, not green or black.

"Let me save us all a lot of pain. This is Seth," Cody said.

Seth showed us surveillance footage from two angles. One was from a camera mounted on the left column of the entrance gate, the other from a camera mounted on the dashboard of a golf cart parked in the street.

The golf-cart cam showed a late-model white F-350 pickup pulling up and disgorging two figures, both carrying aluminum baseball bats. They entered from screen right on the column camera, much closer, much more identifiable. I realized that Nestor had set up the camera that way on purpose, showing a wide shot and a close shot. Everybody in LA wants to be in movies.

One of Nestor's attackers was a biker-looking guy, very hairy, with a filthy beard, truly obese (over three hundred pounds), slow but intimidating. The other one was much younger and weighed at least a hundred and a half less and bounced around on his toes a lot like he'd hoovered up a nostril or two of meth before the attack. When fatso biker rolled up to Nestor and took a swing, Nestor ducked, then came up and cracked him in the forehead with his elbow, Krav Maga style, which gave the speeding younger dude the opening he needed to pop Nestor on the noggin with his base-ball bat.

Which did not deter Nestor. He spun-kicked fatso in the chest and punched the younger kid in the kidneys.

"That boy might be better at attacking people if he pulled up his pants," Nina said.

Nestor made sure that the big one never got a chance to land a blow, while the kid walked off a bit to get his breath, grimacing and holding his kidneys with his back arched. After a moment, they fled back to the truck. Nestor stepped back out of the way when they tried to run him over. It was only when the truck was out of sight that Nestor took a knee and held his head.

Cody told Seth that was enough and Seth stopped the playback.

"Recognize anybody?" Cody asked.

"No," said Avila.

Nobody asked, but Nina shook her head anyway. Cody looked at me, so I shrugged (which is not the same as lying).

"Fans who wanted to see Biz," Nina said.

"Sure," I said, "just like the TMZ guys in the Taurus today."

"Fans show up all the time at that gate. Some people are really rude when they get told no."

"You get a lot of fat, white-supremacist-type biker fans?" I asked.

"Biz got all kinds of fans," Nina said.

I nodded, trying to decide if Avila genuinely didn't recognize Nestor's smaller assailant or if he was trying to send me some kind of message to shut up, because it was unmistakably the stocky, buzz-cut, zitty Slavic skater boy who'd shot Avila's bodyguard in the gut and killed him.

"Mr. Skellig?" Cody asked.

I decided to back Avila. "Those no-goodniks mean zilch to me.

But major props to Nestor, taking a conk like that and coming back hard."

"Go on home, Mickey," Avila said. "Tell the kid good luck with his operation."

Seth was replaying the footage again when I left.

THE AFGHAN SCOWL

Waiting at the hospital for Ripple to come out of surgery, Lucky and I drink coffee and fidget in a room put aside for the friends and loved ones of patients undergoing surgery on their man parts. Lucky reads me excerpts from a pamphlet on the prostate that warns against sitting all day—not particularly constructive advice for a limo driver. Lucky encourages me to emulate him by executing a series of squat thrusts several times a day and demonstrates a series of stretches despite my complete lack of interest.

To my surprise, it was Dr. Quan who came looking for us.

"Are you doing a testicle rotation in your residency?" I asked.

"No," she said, turning red.

Of course, with a minimum of coaching, Ripple had changed his story from innocent toilet accident to victim of sexual perversion and, knowing him, relished the description of his supposed depravities more than, say, a normal young man would.

"Dr. Quan," I said, "this is Luqmaan Qadir Yosufzai, but it's easier to call him Lucky. He shares the duplex with Ripple. Lucky, this is my personal physician, Dr. Grace Quan."

"Do you bring news concerning our Ripple?" Lucky continued (which, when you think about it, was the more appropriate conversation opener than a testicle joke).

"The surgery was a success," Dr. Quan said, sitting down on the coffee table to face us.

"*Success* and *ball removal* don't fit comfortably into the same sentence."

"Please, Skellig," Lucky said. "I know you deal with Upset by Making Light, but I hope you won't make such Insensitive Remarks when Ripple awakens."

Lucky glanced at Dr. Quan in a way that might appear to an outsider that he was begging her pardon for my vulgarities but which I recognized as his initial foray into a potential love connection. I gave Lucky *Are you serious?* eyeballs, but he came back at me hard with the Afghan Scowl.

(It's a historical fact that the Afghan Scowl is what defeated Alexander the Great in 330 BC, Genghis Khan in AD 1219, the Persians, the Arabs, Tamerlane, Queen Victoria twice, and the Soviets. But don't worry, I'm sure we will fare differently—USA! USA! USA!)

"I don't recall telling you my first name," she said.

"I heard it from an EMT who asked you out."

"Skellig," Lucky said, "I think you have to be much more specific than that. I can't imagine there is any EMT who hasn't asked Dr. Grace Quan out."

"Is he for real?" Dr. Quan asked me, jerking a thumb at Lucky.

"Totally sincere," I said. "I know it sounds like a cheesy line, but he's in dead earnest. Can we see Ripple?"

"He's still unconscious," Dr. Quan said.

"It would do us good just to see him breathing," Lucky said, laying on the sensitive-soul crap pretty thick, not that Dr. Quan minded.

In fact, she must have found Lucky reassuring, because she led us through to the recovery area, where we looked at Ripple through glass.

At least I assumed it was Ripple. There was a smudge of orange in a sea of complicated white and blue medical linens and tubing, bandages, and machines. We stared at Ripple for a long moment; then Lucky nodded and I realized that this display of love and compassion was only fifty percent to seduce Dr. Quan. The other fifty percent was one hundred percent sincere concern.

Dr. Quan walked us out saying that we should come back the next morning. She'd make sure that Ripple knew we'd both been here and concerned for his well-being.

"He won't care," I said.

"He will pretend not to care," Lucky clarified. "Our Ripple pretends not to give a shit but in fact he gives a Large Shit," said Lucky, illustrating that even trained communicators who speak many languages can have trouble conveying exactly what they mean.

Dr. Quan smiled and (lo!) Lucky had achieved his goal. Mentally, I jumped ahead in time to where Dr. Quan introduced Mom and Dad Quan (both doctors, I presumed) to her diminutive, illegal-alien, limo-driving, Afghan boyfriend and hoped, for Lucky's sake, they weren't Dragon Parents.

At the main doors to the hospital, Lucky took Dr. Quan's hand and thanked her for her concern.

"Please don't thank me," she said. "I've just about called Detective Groopman a hundred times to tell her I'm suspicious."

"Suspicious? Of what?" I asked.

"If I could answer that," she said, "I'd know what to say to Detective Groopman. Maybe I just want to ask her if she thinks you're a good man or not."

I wondered how to answer her implied question, given the fact that I'd recently slid the corpse of a man I'd murdered headfirst down a bottomless dry hole.

"Lucky thinks I'm okay," I said. "I've always trusted his judgment."

"You two," she said. "I can't tell if you're legit or, like, epic wingmen for each other."

"A doctor is much like a detective," Lucky said. "You must listen to your instincts."

"Darren said a few things after he was sedated," Dr. Quan said.

Thank God Delilah wasn't there to see panic flicker across my face.

"About his time in Afghanistan," she continued.

My gut unclenched an iota.

"What about it?"

"He never got a chance to prove himself," she said. "He said he never even got a chance to fire his gun at the enemy, much less be a hero."

"Being a hero is overrated," I said.

"You'd know," she said, "according to Darren."

"It's true," Lucky said. "Our Skellig is Brave and True and Much Decorated."

"A man brings in a woman and she's hurt. Broken nose, say. Eyes swollen shut. Some doctors can tell instantly if the man is helping her or if he's the one who did it to her. Not just men and women either. Adults and children. I'm not good at that. I recognize that my instincts don't always serve me well. Who's good? Who's bad? I honestly can't tell."

"That's an overrated skill," I said. "My advice is to worry about whether *you* are good or bad. If you're mostly good, you'll be drawn to mostly good people. If you're mostly bad . . ."

"I am a Very Mostly Good Person," Lucky said. "And I love Skellig like a brother."

Dr. Quan shook her head and grimaced at Lucky's unbearable sincerity.

"I know," I said, half apology, half boast.

"It would be good for Darren if you could find a way to convince him that he has nothing to prove."

I've led enough human beings into harm's way to know that even though Gracie Quan was right about Ripple, her insights probably came about because of her own issues having to do with proving her own self-worth.

"You are concerned that a young man like Darren, who feels that he has not proven himself courageous In His Own Eyes, may search out Inappropriate and Dangerous Opportunities to prove himself."

"Like the situation that put him here," she said, shaking our hands. She chose to shake my hand first and Lucky's second. Every man in the world knows that the last hand shaken is the preferred hand, and nobody knows that better than Lucky.

"So pleased to meet you, Grace," he said, firing me the Afghan Gloat.

Lucky and I watched Dr. Quan head back in through the automatic doors. Lucky asked what I wanted to do for dinner. I told him that I wanted to grab some take-out Mexican to eat in the car while we checked out a few properties.

"What kind of properties?"

"That's what I need to check out."

I showed Lucky the warrant Willeniec had produced to search for barrels at Avila's home. My finger skipped by the storage unit and indicated the other addresses that matched the addresses written down in Willeniec's notebook.

But first we had to decide between Gilbert's and Benny's for the tacos (we chose Gilbert's), after which we started our real estate tour downtown.

Three crap hotels, all within spitting distance of Skid Row. Two of them four stories high, the third six.

"None of these would survive an earthquake," Lucky said.

"Looks like they already have. Barely."

None of the buildings showed lights in the windows above the second floor.

That's a lot of empty hotel rooms—unless you count squatters, hypes, crackheads, meth heads, and hustlers.

Since Lucky had driven us downtown, I got behind the wheel and drove us out to the next series of addresses out in the Valley.

The Armenian section of Van Nuys.

North Hollywood.

Panorama City.

Arleta.

The addresses were not diverse. The properties were much of a muchness: shitboxes, mostly abandoned, overrun by rats and fleas, squatters, and the homeless. All multiunit: apartments, hotels, or motels. All at least partly deserted. Some were boarded up completely.

"Mr. Avila appears to be a slumlord," Lucky said.

"Maybe he's involved in one of those things where he knows where the state's gonna put through a bullet train or redevelop so he's just holding on to the land until it triples in value."

"Is that legal?"

"Sure—as long as Avila doesn't have any kind of inside knowledge. And even if he did, what do deserted buildings have to do with barrels?"

"These would all be Grand Places to Hide Contraband," Lucky said. "Would you like to search one of them?"

"No. Willeniec did that already. Let's call it a night."

Lucky drove us back over the Sepulveda Pass to Oasis in Santa Monica, both of us glad that we were heading south on the 405 instead of north with the last vestiges of rush-hour traffic heading from the LA Basin into the Valley.

A burgundy Ford Taurus was parked diagonally in front of the mechanic's bay doors. It sported a dent in the side of the sort that might result from, say, sideswiping a Bentley during a car chase on the Fox Lot.

"What Crapola is this Encroaching Upon Us now?" Lucky asked.

"Where's Tinkertoy?" I asked.

"She was sealed up tight inside her room when I left," Lucky said. "Why?"

The driver's door of the Taurus opened and Detective Delilah Groopman of the LAPD, Pacific Division, Major Crimes, stepped out, leaned one hip against the car, and crossed her arms.

DELILAH AND I ENJOY
A COLD ONE

Delilah and I decide to conduct our conversation on the porch of my penthouse on the roof. Having never been up here before, Delilah is surprised to find that my porch is a delightful terrace, three sides of which are enclosed by handmade Thai teak screens commissioned (then rejected) by Quentin Tarantino for his movie about girls with swords. The fourth side opens to the west, where we can see the top half of the Santa Monica Pier Ferris wheel rolling above the beach in a multicolored nimbus of flashing lights.

I present herewith a heavily paraphrased transcript of our conversation, made suitable for Disneyland and 1950s prime-time network television programming.

Delilah proceeded. "Skellig, whatever could you have been thinking when you decided to elude the officers of the law who were endeavoring to fulfill nothing less than their sworn duty when they followed you earlier today?"

"Why, Delilah, I find I am amazed! Were you in that vehicle?"

Delilah conceded that she was not personally in the burgundy Taurus but that as a member of the siblinghood of law enforcement, she found herself piqued on behalf of all peace officers because I had eluded them.

I inquired if Delilah had contrived to arrive tonight in the burgundy Ford Taurus in a transparent effort to startle me and she allowed that she had hoped such a dramatic and illustrative move might drive home to me the fucking importance of fucking candor in our current fucking conversation.

When I responded that I'd had no fucking idea who the fuck was in the fucking burgundy Ford Taurus when I'd made asses of them, the quality of our colloquy flung itself into a temporary briar patch of nonproductive vitriol, invective, and personal insults from both sides (she felt I was lying; I was insulted by the charge), until we counted to ten and agreed to return to the pertinent essence of the conversation.

When I queried as to why the police were following me, Delilah responded with "Oh, you fool, you were not the object of this surveillance; Bismarck Avila was the object, but pray tell why you would think otherwise? Are you plagued by some manner of guilty conscience?"

(I told you Delilah is an excellent cop with a top-notch bullshit detector and motive sniffer, because I was, of course, stewing in anxiety as, let's call it what it is, a cop killer.)

Fresh from my success deflecting Dr. Quan with semantics, I suggested that when I said *follow me*, I was extending the umbrella of a collective entity over both my client and myself, at which point Delilah told me, again, to fuck myself.

I guess I'm no longer paraphrasing.

Delilah and I both stared at the whirling wheel of lights on the pier, struggling to remember that we were friends who would be much more than friends if it weren't for the fact that the woman whom I unrequitedly loved with all my heart was her actual best friend.

"I didn't know it was cops."

"Liar."

"I couldn't take a chance with Avila's safety. Somebody wants him dead. And you have to know if I'd seen you in the car, I'd never even have told him we were being tailed."

Delilah recognizes the truth when she hears it. She nodded, slightly mollified. I pressed my tiny advantage.

"Do I get to know why the police were following Avila?"

What I really meant was: *It's definitely Bismarck Avila who was being followed, right? Not me? For murdering a cop?*

Delilah thought about answering honestly, but the cop part of her was still majorly irked with me, so she changed the subject. But she switched from asking questions to making observations, so I figured I was halfway out of the woods.

"I never took you for a reader," she said, indicating the piles of books shoved under my glass coffee table.

"My dad's effort to make me a better man. I have to read them in case he springs a pop quiz. Could you at least tell me if what has you all hot and bothered is the killing of Avila's bodyguard or the disappearance of Willeniec, A.?"

Delilah pressed her lips together like an annoyed child and wrinkled her nose. (Very fetching.)

"There's been no official response from the sheriff on Willeniec yet."

"Is that what they ordered you to say?"

"No, Skellig, what they ordered us to say is absolutely nothing. I'm stretching the rules for you."

"That instruction is coming down on you from a great height?"

"Like piss from Mount Olympus."

"LAPD or sheriff?"

Delilah didn't answer but made a big show of looking at me quizzically and smacking her lips like her tongue was parched. I got the point.

"Want a beer?"

"A little sensitivity if you please, fuckwit. I'm currently not drinking."

"Fizzy water with lemon?"

"Thank you."

Which definitely meant that Detective Groopman was about to punch out for the evening, leaving me to chat with my pal and unhealthy crush, Delilah. When I returned with a tall glass of iced mineral water with lemon for her and a bottle of beer for me, Delilah was standing at the lip of the roof, gazing down Santa Monica Boulevard toward the ocean, letting the sea breeze ruffle her hair. We tapped beverages and drank.

"Tell me about Ripple."

I had to remind myself that it wasn't a question so this was Delilah being solicitous, not Detective Groopman probing for connections to Willeniec's disappearance.

I told her. She winced but obviously bought the rough-sex-with-an-Internet-stranger cover story. Then she peered at me through lowered lids and said, "Detective Antony Willeniec is attached to the sheriff's Commercial Crimes Unit."

"That's shocking."

"Why?"

"The *A* stands for Antony? I did not see that coming. I thought for sure it was Asshole."

"You want to hear this or you want to be a fuckwit?"

"Both?"

"There's no record of Willeniec applying for a warrant to search Avila's place."

"I saw the warrant, Delilah."

"You're the kind of person who might remember the name of the judge who signed."

"Last name, Kellog."

"Judge Kellog died last year."

"Kudos to Willeniec, persuading a dead judge to sign a warrant."

Delilah laughed because, unlike many, she thinks I'm funny. She drank her lemon water again, the ice cubes bumping up against her lips. (Lucky ice cubes.) I like to watch Delilah drink deeply because there's no bobbing Adam's apple, just a sensual throb in the throat, like a sob but sexy instead of sad.

"Pervert," she said, catching me at it, pleased.

"Willeniec falsified the warrant?"

"What warrant?"

"The one he showed Avila and me."

"We have only your say-so on the existence of said alleged warrant."

I reached into my breast pocket and presented her with said alleged warrant.

"Fuck," Delilah said.

She looked at it for a moment, then held it up to the light.

"He took an old warrant, used Wite-Out on the names and objectives, photocopied it, then typed his own shit in."

"Very old-school crooked cop."

"Fuck," she said again, unhappy that she had in her hand actual tangible proof that one of her own was walking the wrong side of the tracks.

"The other night, when I brought you coffee at work, this is why you got all excited when I told you about Willeniec?"

"I'd like to keep this," she said, flapping the warrant.

"Technically, it's Avila's, so maybe give me a receipt?"

"No wonder Avila wanted you to be his driver; he gets a paralegal with the package."

"You pick a few things up when you sleep with a lawyer."

I immediately wished I hadn't said it because a shadow crossed Delilah's face.

(Change the subject.)

"What's Willeniec up to?"

"Maybe searching for something he knew he wouldn't be able to use as evidence in court."

"You like that scenario?"

"Beats the alternative."

"Which is . . . Willeniec trying to steal evidence for himself?"

"Depends what's in the barrels."

"Liquid cocaine? Human organs? Blood diamonds. Like that?"

Delilah plucked the lemon from her glass and scraped the pulp out with her lovely teeth. (Lucky pulp.)

"We learned from Sir Thomas More that silence indicates consent," I said.

"Your face is stupid and it fools me into forgetting that you read books and went to college," she said.

I figured this was as far as I was getting and I was about to suggest dinner, when Delilah said, "Willeniec was being watched," which startled me enough that it must have shown on my face for at least a microsecond, which is all Delilah needed. (Good cop.) And she switched back to asking questions.

"What?"

"What what?"

"Why did you flinch?"

"I stifled a beer burp," I said, "hurt my sinuses."

"Cone of silence?"

I zipped my lips, sealing them forever.

"Willeniec was a couple days from suspension and indictment."

"Indictment? For what?"

"An internal sheriff's investigation found an illicit income stream. Three months ago, an ex-girlfriend disappeared."

I was starting to feel better about ending the guy. On the other hand, if I'd known all this, I could have called Delilah immediately after I killed Willeniec, told her what happened, and be free and clear of the whole mess.

"The ex-girlfriend who disappeared . . . Nice woman?"

"Not at all. White-collar embezzler in Orange County who avoided jail by ratting out her boss."

"Faking warrants, Willeniec was sure to get caught, right?"

Delilah nodded.

"So Willeniec was desperate? Out of options?"

"Fuck you, Skellig. Say what you think."

"I think Willeniec figured out you were following him, panicked, and took off."

"Hey, I wasn't following Willeniec," she said. "I only found out about any of this after somebody tried to kill Avila on my watch."

"Where'd Willeniec get his illicit income stream?"

"Kickbacks from crooks. Payoffs. Maybe even a couple of hits."

"You mean killing people, right? Not moonlighting as a singer-songwriter?"

To my great relief, Delilah laughed. We listened to the breeze rattle the palm trees, watched a siren flash past over on Lincoln, heading south, toward the airport.

"How about this?" I said. "The girlfriend vanishes herself, goes someplace warm with no fear of extradition, sets up a new life on a beach. Willeniec stays behind to make one more big score before joining her."

"The last big score being Avila's barrels?"

"Right. Willeniec finds the barrels and whatever's in them and then joins her in paradise. That's why he's missing."

"Makes sense," she said evenly. "It scans."

When cops say two things encouraging about a case quickly in succession, like *makes sense* followed by *it scans*, it means that they are trying to convince themselves and failing. Personally (for selfish reasons), I was a big fan of the theory in which Willeniec makes one last score, changes his identity, and vanishes forever, because if enough cops and prosecutors bought into that, then the physical search for Willeniec's actual, corporeal self in the real world would grind to a halt. The only place they'd be looking for Willeniec was on the Internet.

Excellent outcome for me and mine.

I had no evidence to push Delilah in that direction, so I tried the next best thing: innuendo.

"Something happened today," I said.

"Aside from you ditching the cops following you?"

"Yes. Aside from that. Didn't I already apologize?"

"Sorry. Yes, you did. What else happened?"

I hesitated in an artful manner.

"I showed you mine," she said, taking the bait. "Show me yours."

I told her about Nestor getting bonked on the head by the Slavic-looking kid who shot Avila's bodyguard in the gut.

"You're positive it was the same kid?"

"It's getting to the point where I'd recognize his ass crack in a lineup."

"Skellig!"

"What? The kid should wear underpants."

"No, not that, fuckwit. How long were you gonna wait before telling me? I'm the lead investigator in that homicide, at least until Robbery-Homicide steps in to take it over."

I explained to Delilah that it had been my intention to come home, have a beer, and then call the lead investigator in the homicide of the bodyguard, which was her, but unfortunately I'd been waylaid and unfairly maligned for ditching some cops earlier in the day.

"Which," I said, "raises an interesting question."

"About what, now?"

"You're all over the place, Delilah. You're the investigator on the bodyguard's murder, but it feels like what you're really interested in is whatever's going on with Willeniec."

"So?"

"Willeniec's a sheriff's deputy from Whittier! You're Pacific Division LAPD. The Royal Canadian Mounted Police have as much jurisdiction as you."

"Did Avila recognize the Slavic kid?"

My mother always told me that when you argue with someone, if they head for the back door in an effort to escape, let them go. Winning is not the most desirable outcome of an argument; getting what you want is the most desirable outcome.

Delilah was headed for the back door. I not only let her go there; I ran ahead and opened it for her.

"If Avila recognized the kid, he didn't tell his security guy."

"Did Avila have any explanation for the assault?"

"Avila told his security guy that it was probably a crazy fan."

"Who's this security guy?"

"Avila called him Cody."

"Cody Fiso?"

"Is Fiso a Samoan name?"

"Did your Cody look Samoan?"

"What self-respecting Samoan would name their kid Cody?"

"Skellig! Did the security guy look Samoan?"

"Yes. Do you know him?"

"Cody Fiso. Heads up Fiso Security Outcomes. Very highly regarded. Did Cody get actual footage of the attack?"

"Yep, both attackers show up Charlie Foxtrot Bravo."

"What's that? Some Army acronym?"

"CFB . . . clear as a fucking bell."

"Did you recognize the other guy?"

"No. Obese biker type, early thirties, tatted up, beard, lice, swastikas, etcetera."

"So, definitely not the other kid from the hit?"

"Ten years older, two hundred pounds heavier. Smelled like sour milk."

"How the fuck you know that? You only saw him on video."

"You could see how he smelled on the video."

"Avila didn't recognize either one?"

"He told Samoan Cody he didn't."

Delilah sighed.

"To be fair," I said, "Avila might not have gotten a good look at the kid who shot at him. There was a lot of panic and he got pushed to the floor."

"Oh, please."

"I know I'm not a professional investigator and I'm sure you're ahead of me on this—"

"Fuck! Skellig! Just say it!"

I tossed Keet into the salad by reminding Delilah that Keet had biker ties, and the obese guy was a biker, and that she'd told me that Keet was linked to Avila, and that maybe that link was being investigated by Commercial Crimes.

"Willeniec's specialty in Commercial Crimes was money laundering."

"There you go. Barrels are an excellent place to store and transport cash that needs laundering," I said. "Willeniec is trying to find barrels. He thinks Avila has the barrels. Delilah, what we have here is a fiery nexus."

"Just say *pattern*. Fiery nexus my ass."

"Is anybody working that angle?"

"I can't discuss that with you!"

"Because you're only supposed to be solving the part where Avila's bodyguard got killed?"

Delilah grimaced.

Bingo.

Delilah had been shouldered aside. She wasn't part of the investigation into Willeniec's disappearance. Which sucked for me because if Delilah was a principal in that investigation, then I could use her to muddy it up (which sounds like a terrible way to use a friend, I know, but you have to admit, I was juggling a lot of friends in this circus, all with conflicting needs).

"That explains why you weren't in the car following me and Avila today, which means you should be thanking me for making them look like idiots, not hollering at me."

"Wow," Delilah said, giving me a sarcastic slow clap, "that was beautiful. I bet you never had to shoot anyone in the war. I bet you could talk the enemy into shooting himself."

"Who was following me?"

"My promotion to Robbery-Homicide; that's who was following you."

Delilah's deep professional desire is to be a member of the LAPD's elite Robbery-Homicide Division. It figures Robbery-Homicide would help the sheriff investigate the disappearance of a sheriff's detective—especially if the detective in question was corrupt, suspected of murder, and maybe murdered himself.

"Delilah, if I'd known it was Robbery-Homicide, I'd have done anything in my power to make you look good to them."

"Thank you, Skellig. The opportunity has passed."

"Don't give up. All you need is to provide them with a link between Avila and Keet."

Delilah looked at me in a way that showed that while I'd been showing her my back door, she'd been showing me to hers. She'd made me look at her throat drinking her fizzy lemon instead of her eyes, and now I was trapped.

"Oh," I said, "you horrible, evil, manipulative lady."

"I'm just standing here with a friend, enjoying the evening air and some bubbly water."

"That's why Robbery-Homicide is following Avila," I said. "To see if he'll lead them back to Keet."

"Not Robbery-Homicide. A task force."

"LAPD and sheriff's department?"

"And the Bureau of Investigative Services."

"So yesterday I embarrassed LAPD, the sheriff's department, and the California Bureau of Investigation?"

"And the FBI. It's a task force, Skellig."

I felt a little sick. Task forces are well-funded political entities that never give up without an indictment, a whirring multibladed machine where careers in law enforcement are made or ground up like cheap beef. That's why ambitious Delilah wanted on board. If this task force figured out what happened to Willeniec, then she'd be certain to get promoted to Robbery-Homicide. I had a sudden horrible thought: what if this whole multijurisdiction task force only existed because Willeniec was a hero, working undercover, pretending to be a crooked cop in order to catch Keet?

"Willeniec's a full-on bad guy, right, Delilah?"

I know I sounded like a ten-year-old putting it that way, but that's how cops label enemies: bad guys. Soldiers don't think that way, or at least we didn't before the Global War on Terror.

"What?"

"He wasn't undercover working Keet?"

"No."

"Because that would explain the task force."

"No, Skellig. Willeniec was a corrupt son of a bitch who probably murdered his girlfriend."

Thank you, Jesus, I thought. My lips might even have moved.

"This task force exists because, dirty or not, Willeniec was one of ours. You understand? Ours to catch and punish. Maybe we'll get some additional bad guys along the way, like Keet or Avila, but the main thrust is the identification and apprehension, pure and simple, of whoever murdered Antony Willeniec."

"You aren't buying that he's happy on a beach in Belize?"

"We have reason to believe Willeniec's been murdered."

I could see only one way to keep tabs on the task force and, if at all possible, influence their investigation. "Tell the task force that you have someone next to Avila."

"Who?"

"Me. That's what you've been angling for, isn't it? You win. Tell them I'll work for you but I won't even talk to anyone else."

Delilah blinked.

She was touched.

"Do you want another fizzy water?"

She seemed to consider that for a moment, but it was something else she had on her mind. "There's two kinds of people," Delilah said abruptly.

Words do not just slip out of Delilah Groopman. She uses them like silver bullets, always with a point.

"People who like jazz guitar and people who don't?"

"People who work on the surface of the earth and people who fly above us all and change history. Connie is a flying, change-history person."

"Where does that leave the people who like jazz guitar?"

What Delilah said was "Fuck you, Skellig," but she said it fondly.

Delilah was trying to talk about me and her (or was it me and

Connie?) or was it Connie and her? One thing I knew for sure was that we weren't talking about Willeniec and task forces.

"Somehow I feel like it would be a mistake to say anything more about jazz guitar," I said.

"The flying people spend their lives fixing big problems, and to do that they mostly ignore, or never see, smaller problems, like the people around them or their families. Then there's the people who walk on the ground, take care of their families and the people they love, and let history take care of itself."

"Surface-of-the-earth people," I said.

She said nothing for a moment. Then she said, "I'm being silent because apparently silence means consent."

"I know what you mean," I said finally. It was generals and sergeants all over again. Of course I understood. "Steve Jobs. Martin Luther King. They make the world better but they treat the people closest to them like crap."

"Maybe you have to be a fucktard to make the world a better place."

Had Delilah just called Connie a fucktard? Or was she suggesting that she and I were surface-of-the-earth types who'd be a better mix?

It felt like the room was thrumming, that if I told Delilah that I agreed with her, she and I would be having full-on, jolly, fun, man-on-woman, Olympic-caliber sex in about five mikes.

"Mother Teresa, Thomas Mann, Christopher Columbus," I said, "Thomas Edison, Martha Stewart, Kobe Bryant—"

"All right, Skellig."

"Gandhi, Thomas Jefferson, all the Kennedys—"

"You can stop. Relax," Delilah said. "I'm not looking to seduce you, asswipe."

"Einstein, Picasso—"

Delilah said, "You are such an asshole," but she was laughing.

"All I offered was fizzy water," I said, "with lemon."

"I like the way you take care of those around you. I like that you left the big world of politics to run a limo company and hire veterans down here on the surface of the earth where people actually live."

But Connie *didn't* find the surface of the earth extremely attractive? Was Delilah telling me that was the reason that I had no future with Connie? My life was too small?

Delilah put down her empty glass, crunching on the last piece of ice. "You'll either think about it or you won't. I'll find my own way out."

I said nothing because silence is consent.

ARKS, PROJECTILES, AND VECTORS

Seven o'clock the next morning, right in the middle of a six-mile run along the Santa Monica Bluffs, dodging street-corner preachers, the homeless, tai chi enthusiasts, yoga dorks, and Segway douches, I get a call from Connie. She wants me to go with her to see Ripple in the hospital. She has a get-well gift for him. I tell her that if her gift isn't a donor maraca, then Ripple is unlikely to be gracious.

"Maraca?"

"Single form of *maracas*," I said, following up with my best vocal impression of maracas, hoping to get a laugh.

"Thanks for the clarification, Skellig, me being Hispanic and all, the definition of *maracas* could've remained a mystery."

"*Maracas*, in this case, being slang for testicles."

"Where'd you get the idea that get-well gifts should be replacement parts?"

The answer is my pragmatic mother (who else?), though Mom is the first to say that such gifts can be symbolic on the subconscious level, which is why I was bringing Ripple a bag of almonds. (I know. Almonds aren't nuts; they are seeds. But Ripple didn't know that.)

"No offense to Dolly, but the best gifts are simply reminders that a person isn't all alone in this world," Connie said.

You've probably guessed that Connie and my mom do not like each other. It could be a communist/fascist thing (yes, that's how they refer to each other) but it's obvious to me that Hippocrates would say they were made of the same humors in proportions just different enough to make them hate each other.

"What did you get him?" I asked Connie. "Something engraved: *You are not alone in this world?*"

In fact, what Connie had found for Ripple was an antique walnut lap desk with a top that swung up on brass hinges to reveal a sketching pen and a ream of thick cream-colored sketch paper.

Even unmanned (literally) by the operation and nauseous from the general anesthesia hangover, it was obvious from the way Ripple ran his hands over the desk and the paper that he loved Connie's gift.

"I guess that's all my lap is good for now," he said, not wanting to admit he was thrilled, "holding up a sketch pad."

"I know quite a few men would do better with a sketch pad in their laps than what they got there," Connie replied.

I admired the way she managed to call Ripple a man without making a huge deal out of it. Perfect PsyOps.

"Thank you," Ripple whispered.

I tried (and failed) to remember the last time I'd ever heard him say those words.

"*De nada*, Darren," Connie said, and kissed his pale, downy, freckly cheek. "Maybe you could sketch my portrait."

"Ripple only draws portraits of severed heads," I said.

"I'm sure that's not true," Connie said, which made Ripple smile again because it was true.

Heading toward the parking lot, Connie told me I had to be more *conducive* when it came to Ripple and less *enabling*.

"Nothing you are saying to me makes any sense," I said.

"Buy a dictionary, why don't you?"

"No way you're using the dictionary definitions of those words."

"You have to *elevate* Darren," Connie said, "both by example and by how you speak to him."

"What self-help spiritualist crap have you been reading?"

"I like to elevate myself and those around me."

"You mean the way you elevate me?" Waggling my eyebrows so she'd know I was being ironically saucy.

"Sometimes when you think you're being funny," Connie said, "you're being corny. Like you only know jokes told by old men and high school boys."

"I don't think you mean *corny*," I said. "I think you mean *cheesy*. Small but important distinction."

"Thank you for proving my point. Like it or not, you're the best example of how to be a man to Darren. You have to show him there's more to life than being decisive and courageous and good-hearted."

I stopped and stared at her, suddenly very pleased that I hadn't succumbed to temptation and electric chemistry and slept with Delilah Groopman.

"What?" Connie asked.

"That's the nicest thing you've ever said about me."

"That's because you only heard the part you liked."

"How about I come over later?"

"*Mi amigo*, this is the problem. Every time we sleep together you think we're going to do it regularly."

"What's wrong with that?"

"You know what's wrong. This thing we have? *El romance entre nosotros?* We agreed that it would be casual."

"I can do casual. What about right now? In this handicap spot."

"See? *Cheesy*. Besides, you can't do casual. You *enciendes* every time we spend time together."

"Have you found anyone else to catch fire with who's as fun as me? Maybe someone who isn't wasting a couple of doctorates by being a limo driver?"

"*Idiota*," she said, patting me on the face, "that's got nothing to do with us," before getting into her Prius and driving away.

THIS AIN'T HOLLYWOOD

An hour later, I pull up to Avila's gate, where Nestor waves me through, giving Two (the vintage '54 New Yorker that Avila hates) a thumbs-up. There's another green-polo-shirted guardian in the driveway, but I do not see Samoan Cody, which makes sense because Avila can't be his only client. Tragically, there is no sign of Nina.

I exited Two and immediately received a text from Avila reading: **RND BK**. So I took a wild guess, went *rnd bk*, and found Avila reclining at a forty-five-degree angle near the bottom of his ramp, watching his skateboard roll back and forth in lower and lower arcs before coming to a rest at the vertex so that he could reach out desultorily and push it again. I had the sense he'd been playing this game for quite some time.

"You know what they call the shape of this ramp?" Avila asked. "A parabola."

His breath smelled of coffee and alcohol and he was sodden

with sweat. Not the healthy kind that comes from exertion; the unhealthy kind that comes from hard liquor and anxiety.

"It's not a parabola," I said.

"Why not?"

"Parabolas are defined by the curve formed by the intersection of the surface of a cone with a plane parallel to one of its sides."

"What the hell you saying?"

"It's a simple mathematical equation. Y equals AX to the power of N—"

"No one gives a shit what Y equals! Why do you know that shit?"

"I have a PhD in mathematics."

"Now you're Dr. Sergeant Skellig? How many more titles you got?"

"My thesis was entitled 'Arcs, Parabolas, and Vectors Particular to Projectiles.' Are you fresh wasted this morning or still working on last night?"

"Why you always working to get fired?" Avila asked, scrambling to his feet and trying to smell his own breath by exhaling into his hands. "What's so terrible about working for me?"

"Ask your last driver."

"That's cold, brah."

"Plus, you're the prime suspect in a murder investigation."

Avila stepped back like a photographer trying to get an entire cathedral into the viewfinder.

"The fuck?"

"Willeniec, the cop who came sniffing around for barrels? He's missing, presumed murdered, and you are everybody's favorite suspect."

"How do you know?"

"Cops. The same ones who were following us yesterday. They

want me to spy on you. Looks like everybody wants me working for them. You aren't nearly as special as you think."

"You're lying."

"I'd fire me if I were you."

"I didn't kill no cop. Look at all this! Why am I gonna kill a cop?"

"Maybe to keep all this?"

"Fuck you, Mickey. You tell the cops about me moving the barrels?"

"Nope."

"Why not?"

"I'm giving you the opportunity to buy my silence."

"How much?"

"Ten grand."

"You tell the cops anything?"

"I told them about your security guard getting attacked by a fat man and a kid. I told them it was the same kid who killed your body-guard. I told them that you pretended not to recognize the boy."

"Maybe I never got a look at him."

"Yeah, I floated that. They didn't buy it."

"How do I know you're telling me the truth?"

"You forced me to work for you because you're afraid of Willeniec. Willeniec is gone. Maybe the cops are right and you had him killed. Maybe you had your cousin killed too, for fucking your girlfriend on that island while you were back here playing on your skateboard."

Avila swung the skateboard back like a baseball bat, intending to whack me with it, so I shoved him, both hands to his chest, extending with a snap, sending him flying five feet or so, legs in the air, before he crashed down onto the nadir of his not-a-parabola vertical ramp.

Too late I remembered the first rule of PsyOps: know exactly which specific psychological lever you are pulling. I didn't know if

Avila took a swing at me because (a) I'd accused him of killing a cop or (b) I'd accused him of killing his cousin or (c) I'd suggested he'd been cuckolded by an eighteen-year-old kid or (d) I was blackmailing him for ten grand.

I was just spraying buckshot. Which revealed nothing useful.

I must have been more upset than I thought by (a) killing Willeniec or (b) being rejected by Connie or (c) not moving forward the way I should with Delilah or (d) Ripple's getting mutilated because of me.

Avila stood up, the anger gone.

"You want me to fire you, I'll fire you."

"Thank you," I said.

"I'll pay you that ten grand if you drive me one more place. I gotta take a shower first."

"Maybe have something to eat too. Pull yourself together. Sober up."

"Fuck you, driver."

Half an hour later, Avila came out and saw me standing beside Two.

"I hate that old shit."

I tried again to tell him that the New Yorker was a noble, vintage vehicle of the sort that nobody makes anymore. Avila got bored and got in behind the passenger seat and stared out at his lake and his house as we pulled away.

"Where to?"

"Temecula."

"What's in Temecula?" I asked.

"Keet."

Delilah was going to love this. She wanted a connection between Avila and Keet and she was about to get it.

Assuming she'd persuaded the task force to follow me.

"Wouldn't it make more sense to go where Keet *isn't?*"

"Maybe I want you to kill Keet for me," Avila said. "Maybe that's why I hired you in the first place. War hero who's killed plenty of people."

"I'm not killing anyone for you," I said. "Do you still want to go?"

"I got other reasons to see Keet besides killing him. Who knows? Maybe you'll change your mind on the way."

We waited for Nestor to open the gate. Nestor signaled at me to open the window.

"Good morning, Nestor," I said.

"Not my name. Boss said that if you left, ask if you could be accompanied discreetly by a second vehicle."

"No," Avila said from the backseat.

"Take three minutes to pull it together," Nestor said.

"No."

"Would you mind telling us your destination, Mr. Avila?"

"Just open the gate," Avila said.

"Yes, sir," Nestor said, pushing a button so that the gate opened. Not for the first time I felt like King Kong about to leave his half of Skull Island.

"Sir, do you mind if I ask you why you aren't giving us the information we need to keep you safe?"

"Tell Cody the cops are all over me," Avila said.

I was startled for a moment, wondering what he knew, before I realized he was making a wry joke about me.

"Go," Avila said as soon as the gate was open enough for us to slip through. I made a face at Nestor meaning, *Out of my hands, brah!* and drove Avila out into the wide and dangerous world.

I said, "10—5—60—"

"You're the driver. Go however you want as long as your Oasis Limo place is on the way."

"Why?"

"I want to swing by and switch to that Mercedes. I like that Mercedes. I hate this classic piece of vintage shit."

"You're the boss," I said, "at least for the rest of today."

At Oasis, Tinkertoy watched as we swapped Two for One. Avila did a double take, Tinkertoy towering over him in her baggy sweat top and dark-blue janitor pants.

"How you doing?" Avila asked.

Tinkertoy nodded at Avila and turned back to her work.

I tooted my horn and waved as we pulled out onto Santa Monica Boulevard. Tinkertoy stood and watched us leave without waving back.

"Sister be a lesbian woman; am I right?" Avila asked.

"As her employer I'm not legally allowed to ask."

"Usually I get a better reaction from bitches. I'm not boasting; it's just a fact of my life since before it even mattered to me."

"You truly are a beautiful specimen."

"Don't say it sarcastic. It's true. I am a beautiful specimen!"

After that, Avila sat silent, wrestling with himself. I kept an eye out for a tail, wondering if Delilah had had enough time to convince the task force to follow us today. It was also possible that if they said no, she'd follow us on her own. Not to mention Cody might disregard Avila's instruction to Nestor and follow us for Avila's own good. Hell, given the number of interested parties, somebody had to be following us.

We grabbed the 10 at Lincoln, headed east to the 60, by which time I'd identified two possible tails: a gray Ford Expedition with heavily tinted windows, and a battered Nissan Altima with one of those crazy expensive chameleon paint jobs, a hood scoop, and spinning hubcaps. Both looked like the kind of cars that might be impounded during a drug bust and so readily available to the task force.

The 71 took us south to the 91, where I headed east and then quickly, without signaling, rabbited onto the exit leading to Sixth Avenue into the town of Corona. Cranky in the midst of his hangover, Avila demanded to know what the hell I was doing, driving like a maniac when he was trying to sleep.

"I've always wanted to drive on Grand Boulevard in Corona," I told him. "It forms a perfect circle around the downtown commercial area, featuring views of mountains on two sides. Beautiful."

"Why can't you just say you're checking to see if we're being followed?"

We only did a quarter of the circle, right on Main, dumping out onto Ontario Avenue, crossing the 15, continuing east to Temescal Canyon Road, paralleling the freeway before rejoining the flow of traffic just north of Lake Elsinore.

"What do you think?"

"Nothing," I said.

It was the truth. If Delilah was following us, then she was doing a great job or using satellites or drones.

"Are you good at this shit?"

"You keep asking me that. The answer's always yes. Bonus, I'm a natural tour guide. For example, little-known fact: Lake Elsinore is an actual natural lake, very rare in Southern California."

"Something else they got in Elsinore is a couple skate parks," Avila said. "I caught a ride here with a few of my boys from surfers in a short bus. I was thirteen, fourteen. Surfers robbed us, dumped us outside Elsinore."

"How'd you get back home?"

"Caught a ride with a couple other surfers going the other way." Avila laughed. "They knew the guys who robbed us too!"

Talking about being a kid loosened something in Avila.

"Wanna know why we're going to see Keet?"

"Something to do with those barrels, I guess."

"My cousin Rocky? Rakim? He stole those barrels. From Keet.

Keet killed him for it. Not me, for the reasons you said, which I won't grace with a response."

"What's in the barrels?"

Avila ignored my question. "I had no idea Willeniec was coming to the house with a warrant when I moved those barrels. I moved 'em because those kids tried to shoot me."

"Keet sent the shooters?"

"That's right."

"You think Willeniec was working for Keet?"

"I don't know nothing about Willeniec," Avila said. "Keet figures I got those barrels and hid them somewhere easy to find if I get killed. Which was true until I moved them. That's what I'm going to inform Keet today. He kills me, he never finds those barrels."

"You're saying it's a coincidence that Willeniec showed up the day after you moved the barrels?"

"I didn't know he was coming, if that makes it a coincidence. What I know for sure is if I get killed, Keet never finds those barrels."

"You know what would be smart? You tell Keet where to find the barrels and in return he stops sending people to kill you. That would be the really, really smart thing to do."

"Tell you what: you be the driver, I'll be the mastermind. Those barrels of money are the only thing between me and a bullet in the head."

(Barrels of *money*.)

"Great," I said, "you tell me one more drive and there's a pretty good chance it's gonna get us killed."

"This ain't Hollywood, brah. You don't get ten grand for doing nothing. Keet won't risk losing those barrels. You got no idea how much money's in them."

"I can guess."

"Hell you can."

"It's just math."

"Fuck you, brah. Money's a whole other item from parabolas."

"If it's American money, there's about ten thousand bills per cubic foot—"

"How you know that?"

"I've loaded up money on pallets to buy off warlords."

"In Afghanistan?"

"Other places too. We have a very desirable currency. A fifty-five-gallon drum holds a little under seven and a half cubic feet. Say we lose half a cubic foot because drums are cylindrical and bills are rectangular, which is awkward. Seven cubic feet is seventy thousand American bills. If it's all one-dollar bills, which I doubt, that comes to seventy grand per barrel."

Avila stopped muttering to himself and paid attention. It occurred to me that he had no idea how much money was inside those barrels.

"Five-dollar bills brings that to three hundred and fifty grand. Ten-dollar bills, double it, seven hundred K. Twenty-dollar bills equals one and a half million. Hundred-dollar bills, around seven mil per barrel. Are you double-checking my math?"

"I'm gonna trust you on that, Dr. Sergeant Parabola."

"Or do it by weight. Five hundred American bills weigh about a pound if they aren't soaked in cocaine or blood. How much did those barrels weigh when you moved them?"

"I got no idea. You know why? Because I don't work at the carnival."

"Let's estimate a minimum of one million dollars per barrel," I said.

"Take the turnoff to Pechanga," Avila said.

Pechanga isn't a town; it's an Indian casino outside the city of Temecula off County Road 16. Lots of traffic, and I was relieved to see the gray Ford Expedition five cars back. As well as having an escort, I could think of nothing better (for me) than meeting Keet safe and sound inside a crowded Indian casino chock-full of fully manned security cameras on high alert for card counters and other cheaters.

But alas, 'twas not to be.

The casino slipped by on our right and we headed straight for the Pechanga Indian Reservation itself, the Black Hills rising beyond. County Road 16 clipped the chunk of the reservation that jutted toward the town of Temecula to the northwest. All right, that was okay too; don't panic, because we were coming up into some reputable neighborhoods raised in the foothills to look down on the town itself. Keet wouldn't want to murder us in a suburban idyll.

But alas, 'twas not to be; we kept heading south. The mountains rose to our right and we passed a few scringey vineyards to the east. Rising before us as the road twisted was another of the crazy, boulder-strewn hills that had to be crawling with rattlesnakes and crawling things that rattlesnakes eat.

"This is not good," I said. "We're getting into some pretty isolated territory."

"Lots of old, deserted mines out here," Avila said. "Spooky shit."

As someone who had recently slid a dead body into a bottomless pit, I could appreciate the allure of deserted mines for hiding corpses. I did not relish the thought of being one of those dead bodies.

"Turn left here."

"Into what?"

"There! See?"

He was pointing at a barely visible double track through the scrub.

"Are you sure this is a road? It doesn't show on my GPS. This is a Mercedes sedan, not a four-by-four."

"It paves up again in a while."

I made the turn and we squirreled our way down a canyon through gnarled oak trees and scrub and boulders and deer grass, but then, a hundred yards farther along, as Avila had promised, the gravel turned to macadam. There was even a fluorescent line along the soft shoulder, indicating that people drove this road in the pitch-black night.

"How far?"

"A ways yet."

"Did you bring a gun?"

"No, brah, that's what I pay you for."

"Brah, you pay me to drive you places. Not to kill people. And especially not to get killed."

"For a Dr. Sergeant, you sure get nervous."

I was nervous because I knew what it was like not only to get shot at but to actually be struck by a bullet (it's a life-changing experience). I understand that Avila had probably seen some ugly things growing up the way he did (crackhead hooker for a mom), but he'd never been shot.

Ten minutes later we were still driving, seldom reaching speeds above twenty-five miles per hour, the Mercedes bobbling and tossing like a ship on her soft suspension on the twisty road.

"How much farther?"

"Brah, I told you. A *ways*."

It's extremely frustrating for military or former military to take instructions from civilians. Soldiers tend to be precise in time and distance (mikes and klicks), and Avila's fondness for meaningless measurements like *a ways* and *a while* did not help. We skirted the mountain before descending into a dry mishmash of hummocky hills and dry washes. One thing I knew for sure was that our tail, if we had one, would have to stay well out of sight behind us. Even a helicopter would draw too much attention back here on the ass end of beyond. We were being provided with plenty of time and space to get ourselves into shitloads of trouble and desperation.

The road veered south along an arroyo, directly into the sun, which made everything even harder to see, a kaleidoscope of glare and silhouette that was unnerving.

I'd spent some time on various exercises and maneuvers in and around Camp Pendleton, which wasn't far to the southwest, and I tried to recall if the Marines had any kind of eyes that swung over this far. I realized that all the stuff I was currently finding disconcerting was disconcerting because Keet knew exactly what he was doing.

"Lots of white supremacists in this area," I told Avila, "in case you didn't know."

"Lots of white supremacists everywhere, brah," he said.

"You aren't apprehensive?"

"Shit," he said, meaning, *I ain't scared of shit.*

"I can't see why we didn't bring a few of your tough guys with green polo shirts and guns."

"When you got barrels of money," Avila said, "you don't need guns."

"Is that Gandhi you're quoting?"

Beneath Avila's hip-hop mogul veneer, he was exactly what Delilah said he was: a street kid who made his fortune leaping off fifty-foot plywood cliffs with nothing but faith in his own abilities and a plank nailed to acrylic wheels (all of which made him brave and stupid where I prefer to think of myself as courageous and smart).

"Slow down," Avila said, and I allowed myself to hope for one glorious moment that he had no idea where we were, that we were hopelessly lost and we'd simply turn around and get a steak and martinis at the Indian casino on the way back to Los Angeles. But Avila knew what he was looking for: a turnoff marked by one of those old-fashioned Western-style ranch gates. This one was topped with sheet-metal work that had mostly rusted but clearly read HARBOR RANCH, bracketed by a brace of what appeared to be civil war–era cannons.

"This is it."

"Harbor Ranch?"

"Turn in."

I stopped dead in the road, hoping that the task force tail would rear-end us or at least catch up a couple of miles.

"I gotta ask. What's cannons got to do with a harbor?"

"You don't gotta ask because who the fuck cares?"

"For that matter, why call a ranch a harbor? They're two completely different things. One is made of water and the other is made of dirt."

"Brah. Go!"

"Is this even really a ranch? Does Keet raise cattle?"

"Why you always talking about things I don't give a slick shit about?"

"He built a sign saying *Harbor Ranch*, festooned with cannons," I said. "I'm intrigued by the psychology."

Avila looked at me for a moment and must have decided that the only way we'd get moving again was if he explained the situation fully.

"The cannon is to protect the harbor. A harbor is a protected place, out of the storm, right? Keet's been to prison, so his psychology wants to feel safe and protected. Like in a harbor. Maybe you disagree with his symbolism. Probably you think he should have called it Castle Ranch or Fortress Ranch or Bunker Ranch, but what I think is that *you should ask him for yourself if we ever get there!*"

Avila was now yelling at me, which meant that he was scared, which made me feel better, so I put the Mercedes in drive and said, "There's a harbor for ships and there's a harbor that is a verb meaning *to take in* or *protect*—like *harbor a fugitive*."

But Avila had managed to calm himself. "You're lucky I didn't bring a gun, Mickey. Right at this moment, you are the luckiest son of a bitch in the history of the world I don't have a gun."

We bounced along the dusty road for almost a mile in silence, twice barely clearing boulders at the side of the road before we popped out of the arroyo to see Keet's place laid out on a shelf on the other side of a dry wash. A bridge rated for four tons carried us over the wash and through a fantastical double row of King palm trees, as straight as the horizon, as though we were driving up to the lobby of some fancy desert hotel in Palm Springs. I counted a dozen palms on each side. But at the end of the driveway, instead of a hotel, there was a comically king-size log cabin, probably made from a kit sent in a hundred one-ton trucks from Wyoming because no way a full-size tractor-trailer could get past those boulders. To the left and right of the log cabin were two surplus Korean War–era Air Force Quonset huts. Outside of the one on the left, close to the driveway, leaned a fully tricked-out Harley Electra Glide, gleaming with care and chrome and aftermarket extras. On the right was a free-weights setup that looked like it had been transported straight from the yard at San Quentin—except the weight bag was hanging from a towable sixty-foot crane rated to lift two tons.

All completely deserted.

I pulled up in front of the log cabin, ensuring that the nose of the Mercedes was pointed back toward freedom and safety, both of which were, by my best guesstimates, ten miles and a century and a half away.

"Nobody home," I said. "Oh well, maybe another day with some other clueless nitwit driving you."

"Keet's got cameras all the way out to the state road," Avila said. "He knew we were coming for the last half hour. The man likes to make an entrance."

Avila let himself out of the Mercedes. I sighed and got out as well in time to see Avila place his arms on the roof and wince from the burn. It was well over a hundred degrees out here. It felt like Kandahar in July except not as safe.

A couple of minutes later, a tall, heavyset man exited the cabin's front door and waved at Avila.

"Biz! Good to see you here in my front yard. Come on in out of the sun," he said in a disconcertingly pleasant voice.

"That's Keet," Avila said.

"We got air-conditioning," Keet continued. "We got cold beer. We got comfortable chairs. Bring your friend with you."

Keet had to be telling the truth about the air-conditioning because he was dressed for autumn in the Brazos Mountains: a light-blue plaid shirt with a turquoise bolo tie hanging loose, turquoise and silver bracelets and rings, a turquoise belt buckle on a belt circled with pounded-out silver coins. Also flip-flops.

"Stylish," I said to Avila.

"C'mon up and sit a minute," Keet said.

"What I got to say won't take long," Avila said, not moving an inch toward the log cabin.

"Will you at least come up onto the porch? It's a hundred degrees and the porch is where we keep the shade."

Avila stood, still as a pond, staring at the porch, not moving.

This was nothing more or less than an elemental tussle of wills between a street rat and an ex-con, even if the street rat was dressed up as a lifestyle mogul and the criminal was dressed like a Latvian schoolteacher's fantasy of a Navajo mountain surfer cowboy.

Keet pulled a sweat-stained tractor cap out of his back pocket, slapped it against his thigh to remove imaginary dust, pulled it over his pomaded hair, and ambled out into the sun toward Avila and me. Honest to God it was like aliens had heard a description of how John Wayne walked, took a stab at it, and almost got close enough to fool you from a distance.

Lookathiseyeslookathiseyeslookathiseyes, Willeniec whispered in my ear when a puff of air-conditioning somehow made it all the way from Paul Bunyan's log cabin to where I stood in the driveway without being obliterated by sun and dust. I couldn't take Willeniec's advice because Keet was too far away, but the smell of cologne and hair product preceded the man like an advertisement—*here be a vainglorious and a dangerous man*, a man who'd worked out plenty on that heavy bag and probably on more than one poor bastard hung up on that hook.

Had Willeniec been here? Was this where he got the idea to hang Ripple from the engine hoist?

When Keet finally did come close enough to reveal his eyes, I wished he hadn't. They were milky-blue zombie eyes. Occluded. Hippocrates would have had to invent another class of humors (based on gonorrhea ooze) to describe Keet. As he walked toward us, Keet whistled through his teeth like he was calling a pack of dogs. A tricky, ventriloquist's whistle. If I hadn't been looking directly at him, I'd have thought that whistle came from somewhere else entirely. But it wasn't dogs who responded to Keet's whistle.

A number of vexing questions were instantly answered, theories confirmed, suspicions verified. Two men emerged from the Quonset hut on the left, the hut that acted as an extended garage housing cars, trucks, ATVs, and motorcycles. The first man was my old friend from the alley, Chelsea Boots, still wearing his fancy footwear but otherwise dressed like a Mormon missionary in khakis and a white dress shirt. Behind Chelsea Boots was the fat biker who'd attacked Nestor at Avila's gate. From the other Quonset hut, the one decked out like a prison gym, strode the two skater delinquents who'd attacked Avila in the swanky bar. The kids were both in wifebeaters and had obviously been pushing weights around because they walked as though their muscles were about five times bigger than they were, aggressive and hostile and stupid with testosterone. The stocky Slavic-looking kid who eschewed underwear was carrying a sawed-off shotgun, which was dispiriting because that particular weapon took absolutely no skill to operate in a lethal manner. Behind him was the skinny Goth boy with dyed hair and lurid tattoos. In the absence of a shotgun, he was dragging behind him what appeared to be the same aluminum baseball bat his buddy had used to crack Nestor on the head.

I uttered the following to Avila in the comically fast manner of someone listing side effects at the end of a drug commercial, "These are the two kids who tried to kill you in Santa Monica and the black guy was their getaway driver."

"Santa Anas!" Chelsea Boots said, pointing at me in recognition, like he was delighted to see me again. "Wife with a knife!"

"Hey," I said, doing my best to sound companionable.

"These two little shits tried to kill me," Avila told Keet. "They shot my bodyguard in the gut."

"Kill you, Biz?" Keet widened his eyes in fake surprise. "I don't think so. That's a reckless charge to level indiscriminately."

Avila decided to play it completely humorless with Keet, not be sucked into sarcastic badinage, which I considered to be a good decision. Goth Boy must have missed the life-skills class on self-incrimination because he pointed at me with his bat and said, "That's the motherfucker who stopped us from finishing the job!"

"You little pussy," I said, dredging up my best drill-sergeant contempt, "how about you try another somersault? Maybe get your boyfriend to hold your dick, though, so you don't lose it halfway through."

(You understand that my own personal evolution has brought me to a place where the use of *pussy* as an implication of cowardice, and implied homosexuality as a base insult, are both meaningless and wrongheaded, but I've found that when insulting someone, it's best to use terms that *they* find upsetting, which means stooping to their level. Sorry.)

Proving my theory, Goth Boy took the insult hard, vibrated with fury, and demanded that Slavic Kid immediately swap the shotgun for the bat, spit spraying from his mouth, the gist being that he wanted to jam the shotgun up my ass and blow my head off.

"Go get your own gun," Slavic Kid told Goth Boy.

That made Chelsea Boots laugh, which infuriated Goth Boy. He grabbed Slavic Kid's shotgun by the barrel and started a tug-of-war. I'm not sure there are many more dangerous pastimes than playing push-me-pull-you with a loaded shotgun, and I fully expected (hoped?) to see one of these dipshits blow the other in half.

"Stop it, you boys," the fat biker said in a mellow tone.

The boys ignored him.

"The fact is my boys did what they were told," Keet informed Avila.

"You told them to kill my bodyguard?"

"In fact, I ordered them to kill both bodyguards but to use their judgment and don't risk getting caught. These boys did a bang-up job for me."

"Even the one who dropped his gun?" Avila asked.

The professional hitters who had done such a bang-up job were still tussling over the shotgun. Like an indulgent father, Keet nodded at the biker, who stepped over and cracked the two boys' heads together like coconuts. Goth Boy went out like a light, his stream of invective ending with the clunk as he crumpled to the ground in a heap, his knees bending together like a Victorian horsewoman riding sidesaddle, his tattooed arms comically limp at his sides, ending up left cheek in the dirt, facing the log cabin. Slavic Kid had a thicker skull. He staggered, made a halfhearted kick at the fat biker, then stumbled drunkenly back toward one of the weight benches, sat down, cradled his head in his hands, and cried softly like he didn't want us to hear.

Chelsea Boots could not have been more amused. On the downside, the fat biker picked up the shotgun, and he handled it a lot more authoritatively than the boy had.

"You sent him and him to my house." Avila pointed at the biker and Slavic Kid. "They assaulted one of my security guards. You consider that a bang-up job too?"

"My name is X-Ray," Slavic Kid said through his tears.

"What's the matter with you, X-Ray," I asked, "sagging your shorts so low with no underpants?"

"It gets him girls," Keet said.

"Why? Because your ass crack draws their eyes away from your ass face?"

Chelsea Boots chortled and repeated, "Ass face!"

"What do you want me to do?" the biker asked Keet, hefting the shotgun.

"Shoot his head off," X-Ray said.

"I wasn't asking you."

"What's your name?" I asked the biker, hoping to delay a horrible death if Keet agreed with X-Ray. "I'm guessing Tiny or Beanpole?"

Chelsea Boots guffawed. "It's Slim! I wish we did call him Beanpole. Maybe we will from now on!"

"He didn't ask you, Tums," the biker said.

"Tums?" I said. "What's with you people and whimsical names?"

"Maybe I got a nervous stomach," Tums said, chortling through a cloud of smoke.

"You know everybody's name. X-Ray. Slim. Tums," Keet said. "You might as well know the young man taking a nap is Nick, because now we got no choice but to kill you."

"I don't know anybody's *real* name," I pointed out.

"If you finished playing, I came to tell you that I got your barrels," Avila said.

"I know you have my barrels, Biz," Keet said, flapping his arms. Then to me: "You know we're the only ones here with brains, right? Too bad I'm gonna have to get Slim to blast yours all over my yard."

"I moved those barrels to a place where, if I die, you will never find them."

"People always think they can hide things, but things always get found if you look hard enough."

(I couldn't help but think of Willeniec's corpse, upside down at the bottom of a dried-up well far to the north of us, and wondered if I'd end up stuffed into one of the abandoned mines on this property. Karma's a bitch, baby.)

"Think about all those times cops came to bust us for drugs when I was a kid. Nobody never found my stash. Not once."

"That's true," Keet allowed, "even when they brought dogs." He spat into the dust near Goth Boy. Nick.

Who was not moving. I wondered if he might be dead even though there was no sign of blood.

"But how's about we kill your friend?"

(Pointing at me again.)

"Now?" Slim asked.

I was not happy. The death threats flying around were all landing on me like starlings on a wire.

"You have a very soothing voice," I told Slim.

What I fervently desired was the arrival of Delilah's task force. X-Ray and Slim could be taken into custody for assaulting Nestor (we had that on camera) and Goth Boy Nick (who was now endeavoring to sit up but seemed unable to coordinate his arms enough to provide the leverage) and Mr. Tums could be arrested as accessories for the attempted murder of Bismarck Avila, not to mention the actual murder of his bodyguard. Failing the appearance of the task force, I listened for the approach of a noisy helicopter full of law enforcement officers hovering overhead and filming everything. But the only sounds in that dry, hot air were the clicking of the cooling engine of my Mercedes and the soft groans of Nick as he gave up trying to stand and simply began crawling for the nearest shade, which was under my automobile.

It was looking more and more like I was going to get shot in the gut by a filthy fat biker, after which Keet would take the heavy bag off that crane, hang Avila in its place, and start clipping off his extremities with a pair of bolt cutters until Avila gave up the location of Keet's barrels of money. (These are the kinds of developments that result when you let civilians run an operation.)

"The reason I sent Slim and Nick to your place," Keet told Avila, "was to gauge your security levels. Slim's got an eye for that shit."

"Lemme shoot him," says Slim.

"I admire your focus," I tell him.

"Being nice to Slim ain't gonna help you none." Tums laughs, lighting another of his skunky, weed-packed cigarillo blunts.

"My head," Nick said, probing for the blood.

"How come poor little Nick doesn't get a nickname?" I asked.

"Tums is my real name. I bet you thought I have a nervous stomach, didn't you? But I don't," offered Mr. Tums. He carried a gun in a nylon holster in the small of his back. Not a big one, a .32. If I could just figure out how to cross twenty-five feet of dusty real estate, disarm Mr. Tums, flick off the safety, and shoot fat-boy Slim through the eye before he emptied two barrels of double-aught into my central body mass, I might have a chance of survival, assuming that Keet wasn't packing some surprise of his own.

"Why you wanna know who's guarding me if you don't want to kill me?" Avila asked.

Keet spit and said, "I been finding kids like you and raising 'em out of the gutter for years. Isn't that right, Tums?"

"It *is* right," Mr. Tums said, billowing smoke. "Dime a dozen." He pointed his blunt at Nick and X-Ray, not that either of them was paying attention, due to their respective headaches.

"I know how to deal with people like you," Keet said.

"Does it all the time," Mr. Tums said. "Every day."

"Street rats got an outsize opinion of theirselves," Keet told me. "The size of their brains. How tough they are." He turned to Avila. "You, Biz, you are the worst of all, given how far you've risen on those qualities. But what I'm going to do is kill him."

(Pointing at me again!)

"Then everyone who guards you. Other people around you."

(Bodyguard. Cousin Rocky . . .)

"Street kid wraps himself in layers of protection," Keet explained. "To make a point, you gotta cut through the layers, get to the heart. What's the girl's name, Tums?"

"Nina," Mr. Tums said, scratching his ankle, providing me with a side-view glimpse of his sidearm—a Seecamp LWS .32. Fine little gun, beautifully balanced, often loaded with hollow-point bullets to make up for its diminutive size, magazine of six rounds. Deadly in the right hands but not very accurate past about ten yards. Excellent for close-in work, bullet to the spine or back of the head and gone before the body hits the ground, bullet doesn't even exit, just rattles around your insides, wreaking havoc.

I revised my opinion of the amiable, stoned Mr. Tums.

"You've always been able to pull the fillies, Biz," Keet said. Then, to me, "Getting laid since before he first got hair on his cookie."

Was this a good time, I wondered, to point out to Keet the weird, molester vibe he gave off? I decided no.

"So I have no doubt you'll be able to replace . . . what's her name again?"

"Nina Sprey," Mr. Tums said.

"You'll be able to replace Nina Sprey in no time. But eventually, nobody will want to be anywhere near you and you'll get lonely and tell me where to find my barrels."

I knew it wasn't the best of times to let my mind wander, but it occurred to me that it was a good thing that Delilah wasn't here or listening in, because nothing Keet was saying in any way suggested that he'd been working with Willeniec, which was unfortunate, because if somehow I survived this afternoon, I'd like Willeniec's death to be attributable to Keet.

"Aside from the part where I get killed," I told Keet, "that's a solid plan."

"Can I shoot him?" Slim asked.

"What if Mr. Avila were to tell you where the barrels are right now?"

"Worth a shot," Keet allowed. "No pun intended."

"He'd kill both of us," Avila said. "I'm sorry, Dr. Sergeant, then he'll just kill us both."

I'm already moving toward Mr. Tums when Keet nods permission for Slim to kill me, even though I don't have a chance of evading Slim's double-barreled shotgun blast, but hey, sometimes you gotta spit in the eye of probability.

"No!" Keet barks.

I know what's happened without even glancing over my shoulder.

Avila has stepped between me and the fat man. Like a well-trained pit bull, Slim stops himself from pulling the trigger and I hit Mr. Tums low and hard, reaching around for the sweet little Seecamp, flipping off the safety, and jamming the barrel into Tums's right ear while I yank us both to our feet, maneuvering his body mass in front of me as a shield.

Mr. Tums doesn't struggle. He raises his hands to the heavens. It's astonishing how inspiring a hollow-point .32 can be when properly implied.

I peer past Tums. Avila steps up to Slim, still frozen by his boss's *No!*, and takes the shotgun. Keet has conjured up a Colt .45 from somewhere on his person, and aims it, expertly, at Avila, which is a prime example of irony in the Human Comedy because not five seconds before, he stopped Slim from blowing Avila in two.

"No matter what," Mr. Tums whispers, "you and me can come out of this alive, Santa Anas. You and me."

I tell him, "Stand up."

Avila points the shotgun at Keet's belly; Keet has his Colt pointed at Avila's head. Slim stands obesely. The two boys realize they might be expected to display an interest outside of their own aching heads.

"You want us to do something, Mr. Keet?" X-Ray asks.

"No," Keet says.

"I can take him," Slim says, meaning Avila.

"It's a *shotgun*, Slim. Four-aught buck," Keet says, "but I appreciate the thought. You see a way out of this?"

Asking me.

(Finally someone had the sense to ask an expert.)

"I do see a way out."

"Let's hear it."

"Nick, you drop your shorts around your ankles and lie down and look away," I say.

"Fuck you, faggot."

"Do what he says," Keet says.

Through the corner of my eye, I see Nick drop his pants and lie down. I motivate the pliable Tums toward Avila, tightening my grip and pulling him close. Tums's arms drop to his sides like they are simply too heavy to hold up.

"You boys don't do a damn thing," Keet says.

"What I'd like to see is what happens when one of these hollow-points hits you in your big, fat, greasy guts," I tell Slim. "I bet you wish you'd shot me now, you greasy blimp."

"Slim," Keet says, "this is a serious motherfucker. He knocked out Tums with that choke hold and is using him like a shield."

Which is true. Mr. Tums is no longer conscious. Luckily for me, despite his height, Tums weighs a maximum of one fifty. I'd have been struggling pretty hard if the situation was different and Slim was my human shield.

"This goes on too much longer he'll have brain damage," I say. "Then he'll only be as smart as fuckfat."

Slim's eyes flicker. I'm getting to him.

"Not your fault," Keet tells Slim. "It's on me we didn't put this boy down first chance we had."

"What you wanna do for a next step?" Avila asks, his eyes never leaving Keet, the two of them locked to each other like a suicide pact.

"X-Ray?"

"Fuck you."

"You pick up that baseball bat."

"You aren't the boss of me," X-Ray says.

"Do every damn thing the man tells you," says Keet. "Don't make me say it every time."

X-Ray picks up the bat.

"Now hit Slim real hard on the top of his head. Overhand. Like chopping wood."

"What?"

Keet laughs.

"If fat boy is still conscious after you hit him, I'll shoot him in his belly. No way I can miss a target that big. So give it your best effort first time."

"I wanna watch," Nick says from the ground.

"Shut up, Nick," Keet says. "Do what he says, X-Ray. Put Slim down with one hit."

"Come on, now," Slim says.

"Here's hoping the kid kills you," I say.

Keet says, "Now."

Slim hollers just before X-Ray swings hard, over the top, like driving the last spike in the railroad, and the sound of the *whomp!* as the bat hits Slim's pumpkin-size head is spectacular. I suspect that X-Ray bears a grudge against Slim.

X-Ray says, "Sorry, Slim."

"You did a good job. He can't hear you," Keet says.

"Throw the bat over to me."

"Fuck you," X-Ray says.

"What'd I tell you?" Keet asks the boy. "Tums is purple."

X-Ray tosses the bat to me.

"Tums's eyes are open," Keet says, "but he ain't seeing nothing. He dies and I got no reason not to shoot you."

I shuffle me and the unconscious Mr. Tums over to within four feet of Keet and aim Tums's wicked little gun at his right eye.

"Mr. Avila, come over here and take Keet's pistol. If he doesn't like it, I'll shoot him."

"*Now* I'm Mr. Avila?"

Keet doesn't wait for Avila. He lays his gun down on the ground, winks at me with his creepy, milky eye, and walks toward the house, whistling his ventriloquist's whistle.

"Stop," Avila says.

"Pick up Keet's weapon," I tell Avila. And then to X-Ray: "Follow your boss."

"Do it," Keet says without looking back.

X-Ray spits at me, hits Tums with a wad of chewing tobacco, and follows Keet toward the house.

"What's going on?" asks Nick. I drop Mr. Tums like a sack of groceries, which also makes an interesting noise.

"You're driving," I tell Avila. "We should get out of here before Keet comes back with a machine gun."

When we left, Avila driving, Keet was still inside the log cabin. Mr. Tums lay on his back, eyes open, like a kid looking for animal shapes in the clouds, and Slim made a small mountain of lard, bleeding from what I hoped was a fractured skull, while poor, stupid Nick, pants around his ankles, missed everything because he kept on doing as he was told.

I emptied the shotgun into the decked-out Harley. It did that immensely satisfying thing that things seldom do in real life: it exploded and set the nearest of Keet's King palms on fire.

"What did you do that for?" Avila asked.

"I'm vindictive," I said, "and I don't like a loaded shotgun in the car."

I wiped my fingerprints and dropped it out the window.

About half a mile from the highway, we passed a gray Ford Expedition with tinted windows heading toward the Harbor Ranch. I wondered if Delilah was in there and what the hell they'd make of the mess we'd left behind.

"Who's that?" Avila said, craning his neck to look at the Expedition.

"Either more bad guys," I said, "or good guys who showed up too late to do us any good."

"You mean police?"

"Or your security team."

"I told them not to come."

"Yeah, well, you get killed, they don't get paid. Am I fired now?"

"You're fired now," Avila said.

"Thank you," I said, hoping I wouldn't suffer some kind of

flashback from the hellish smell of gunpowder and adrenaline that emanated from my torso. A gust of hot air from the open window and Willeniec whispered, *Oneofthesedaysoneofthesedays*, and I knew he was warning me that counting on good luck was a dead man's folly.

THE WAY A SOLDIER
THINKS

I'm toying with the idea of simply dropping Avila off at his gate, so Nestor or another one of the green-polo-shirt brigade can drive him the rest of the way up to the house in a golf cart, but once again, there are flashing lights at the end of his driveway.

This time it isn't EMTs.

"Cops," Avila said. "You think Keet sent someone after Nina?"

But it was a combined LAPD/sheriff's department team executing a search warrant. The lovely Nina was loudly unhappy about it. Avila was barely out of the car before Nina informed him that he was (I am quoting) "a pussy bitch." Of course, Nina hadn't seen Avila facing down a sociopath with a sawed-off shotgun earlier in the day, shielded by nothing but a sheen of sweat. Nina was also agitated that the police had already found a sandwich bag full of weed in the refrigerator, and she insisted that Avila tell them that it had been left by an employee (looking directly at me) so she wouldn't have to go through a bunch of (direct quote again) "legal-ass shit."

During that conversation, Cody waited a few yards up the driveway, his ears closed and his eyes fixed on the middle distance, convincingly demonstrating that he was deaf and blind when necessary. We could hear cops going through all the cupboards and closets in the house.

"What are they after?" Avila asked Cody after Nina flounced off to take her pirate ship across the shining water to her refuge on the island.

"Search warrant says *barrels*," Cody said.

"Can I see the warrant?" I asked.

Cody looked to Avila for permission. Avila shrugged and headed into the house, leaving Cody and me to come to terms without wasting any more of his time. No wonder he was running his own company.

"He didn't say *yes*," Cody informed me, glancing at my extended hand.

"Silence indicates consent," I informed Cody. (How come everybody doesn't know that?)

"Mr. Avila *shrugged*," Cody told me, "which is the kind of silent that indicates he doesn't give two shits if you see the warrant or not, which means he's leaving it to my discretion."

"If you're embarrassed sharing information with the hired help, it might make you feel better to know that he fired me."

"That does make me feel better, because now maybe he won't leave the house without me or one of my guys."

But he slapped the warrant into my hand. The wording was lifted directly from the fake warrant Willeniec had shown me just a few days before and which Delilah had taken from me.

This search was Delilah's doing. She was on the task force.

But Delilah wasn't here, which told me she'd probably been in the Expedition at Keet's place.

"Any chance you'll tell me what I'm up against?" Cody asked. So *that* was why he'd shown me the warrant. Fair enough.

"Avila is into some kind of clusterfuck with a wrongdoer named Asher Keet," I told him. "He's a local crime boss of some nature."

"I've heard of Keet," Cody said.

"Keet sent the two guys who tangled with Nestor—"

"Lou. You win. His name is Lou."

"Keet sent the two guys who messed with Lou to gauge the strength of your security forces. He threatened to start taking out your guys one by one to get what he wants out of Avila."

Cody's eyes narrowed when he heard the threat. It could have been ego, but I like to think it was concern for his people.

"When was this?"

"Couple of hours ago."

"What does Keet want from Mr. Avila?"

"Barrels of money."

I waved the warrant in his face before handing it back to him.

Which is when the gray Ford Expedition I'd last seen down in Temecula rolled into the driveway and disgorged, among others, Delilah.

"Mr. Fiso," Delilah said in an extremely neutral manner.

"Delilah," Cody said, matching her neutrality.

"Can I speak with you, Mr. Skellig?" Delilah asked, and she took my arm and dragged me several yards toward the observatory wing of Avila's ludicrous house.

But whatever Delilah wanted to know was superseded by the sight of Bismarck Avila, exiting his mansion, shedding his clothes as he went, stripping down to his banana-hammock underwear, striding out onto his playtime dock and diving into the lakelet and swimming toward his island. We both watched silently for a moment as he swam with the strong, steady strokes of a surfer.

"Dude!" Delilah said. "Clock the abs."

She waved at a passing member of the warrants team to get his attention and said, "Tell Deloitte to get a couple of divers into that lake. There's nothing saying those barrels aren't on the bottom."

Then she turned back to me.

"Thank you for providing a link between Keet and Avila," she said. "Though not one that would hold up in court."

"Why won't it hold up in court? Also, where were you today when I was almost killed?"

"We can't just trespass onto private property without a reason."

I hadn't thought of that.

"It wasn't until we saw a plume of smoke that we came up with the weakest excuse in law enforcement history to drive onto Keet's property to offer assistance."

"The burning Harley?"

"Was that you?"

"I decline to answer on the grounds that it would most definitely incriminate me."

"I'm not asking officially. I'm asking because Keet thanked us for our interest, then informed us that it was a case of spontaneous combustion brought on by the heat of the sun."

"More like spontaneous combustion brought on by the discharge of a sawed-off double-barreled shotgun into the gas tank."

"We did not see a shotgun."

"I dropped it on the driveway. I've been worried about my fingerprints being all over it."

"You did not come up in the conversation. There was an obese man lying semiconscious on the ground with a head injury and a baseball bat on the ground beside him."

"Semiconscious?"

"He couldn't tell us the date or his name but he was able to recite the Pledge of Allegiance."

"That was Slim. He must have a head like an anvil."

"Did you strike him with the baseball bat?"

"No, but I admit to ardently suggesting that one of Keet's juvenile delinquent thugs smack him in the head."

"*Ardently?* Does that mean you were pointing a gun at him at the time?"

"Not at the kid, no. It's complicated. What did Keet say happened?"

"Keet said that two of his spirited young employees had an argument that became violent. The obese man stepped in when one of the young men in question produced a baseball bat. The boy accidentally struck him in the head. The boy admitted to doing that and the obese man declined to press charges and refused transport to the hospital."

"You see a skinny black guy?"

"Yes. He was on the porch drinking ice water from a mason jar. Apparently, he had coincidentally suffered heatstroke and passed out at the same time the two boys and the obese man were fighting."

"You remember what he was wearing on his feet?"

Delilah looked at me for a moment, then said, "Shit."

"The Slavic-looking kid, the one who hit the obese man? He goes by the name X-Ray. He's the one who shot and killed Avila's bodyguard in the bar. The other kid, Nick, was the one who dropped his gun. You probably have fingerprints to match. It was him along with the fat biker who attacked one of your pal Cody's men here yesterday."

"What's that supposed to mean?"

"What?"

"Don't call Cody my *pal* using that tone."

"I'm sorry. I thought I picked up a vibe."

"Fuck you. I didn't sleep with Cody."

We both knew this was weird. Why should I care who Delilah slept with? Why should she care what I thought?

"I apologize."

"I need you to make an official statement that you recognized those boys. We can go back and pick them up."

"I will make that statement but you won't get them. Keet has a pretty effective early-warning system set up. His ranch is nothing but twisty canyons, bolt-holes, and abandoned mines."

"We'll get them eventually, and when we do we'll have the fingerprints, plus you can identify them in a lineup."

"What about Keet?"

"Keet didn't do anything wrong."

"He's on parole, isn't he? I'll give you a statement saying that I witnessed him brandishing a weapon. And I'll bet you my left ass cheek that fat biker is a former felon he shouldn't be associating with."

I knew as I said it that Keet was too smart for that. Not to mention, no fault of her own, it was getting harder for Delilah to concentrate on my excellent legal suggestions because Nina and Avila had crawled into the deep hammock tied between the two palm trees on the island. Avila's skimpy underpants came flying out of the hammock, followed by Nina's bikini. The hammock itself was bulging and rocking and swinging. The two palms the hammock was tied to swayed like there was an earthquake.

"Wow."

"Nina called Avila a pussy bitch in front of your people, so he's proving her wrong."

"I'll say he is."

Almost every single member of the warrant execution team, standing in windows or on the porch or in the driveway, was watching the famous Bismarck Avila perform exuberant, porn-worthy hammock sex.

"The barrels aren't here."

"Do you know that for sure?"

Please forgive me for lying to Delilah, a woman I really didn't want to lie to (because I wanted to lie *with* her), but what I said was "Avila told me Willeniec found the barrels and Keet killed him for it."

"Why'd Avila go see Keet today?"

"To ask if they were even."

"Are they even?"

"Not according to Keet."

"Why?"

"Keet wants more."

"More? More what?"

"Some kind of payoff. They argued, Keet threatened to kill me to show Avila he's serious, and all the rest of what happened happened."

"Exploded Harley, burning palm trees, everybody groaning and all beaten up. I'd love to hear the details of how you fucked them up so bad and not a mark on you."

I savored the note of grudging admiration in her voice.

"Keet will kill people until Avila gives him what he wants. Keet killed Avila's cousin and he sent those boys to kill Avila's bodyguards."

"He admitted that?"

(Not per se . . .)

"Too bad it's all hearsay you can't use."

"Why would he incriminate himself that way in front of a fucking witness?"

"You mean me? Because Keet had me booked for dead."

"Do I understand that Avila was not the target of the bar hit?"

"That's what Keet said."

"Do you believe him?"

"When Avila stood between me and our sweet Lord Jesus, Keet ordered Slim not to blow him to pieces, so yeah, I believe him."

Delilah ran that through her big brain.

"I know I said *sweet Lord Jesus* just now," I said, "but that was a euphemism for *sawed-off shotgun*."

"If Keet intends to kill the people around Avila, then you better be careful, Skellig."

"I'm not going to be around him anymore. I'm fired. But Cody and his guys better pay special attention. And her."

I pointed over toward the island, where, in the hammock, Nina was making a sound that was something between a moan and a siren. Avila was either doing a great job or Nina was flattering him in front of the police.

"We'll arrest him. That should get everyone off the hook."

"You're going to arrest Avila?"

"Could you please keep your fucking voice down?"

"Arrest him for what? Pleasuring a woman until she banshees?"

"We found drugs."

"Avila doesn't do drugs."

"His fucking house. His fucking drugs. That's the fucking law."

"Delilah, you put Avila in jail, Keet will have him killed before morning."

"You just told me that Keet wants him alive."

I told you. Delilah is smart. And she remembers things. And I'm no more or less pervy than the next guy, but the performance happening over in that hammock had charged the air between me and Delilah. Our animal selves wanted to prove that, given the chance, we could match or surpass Avila and Nina in the hammock.

"Let me rephrase. If you put Avila in jail, Keet will make him wish he were dead."

"Maybe that's why Avila wanted you to kill Keet."

(*WHAT?*)

"I beg your pardon?"

She waited while I did the math.

"You bugged my Chrysler?"

"You shouldn't have switched cars, Skellig. That's why we couldn't protect you properly. We had no cause to believe you required assistance."

"If you bugged the Chrysler and not the Mercedes, that means you did it here, while I was talking to Avila on his skateboard ramp."

Delilah remained conspicuously silent. *Silence indicates consent* and she knew it.

Blossoms of anger bloomed in my chest as I realized what had occurred behind my back.

"It was your pal, Cody."

"Don't you dare insinuate—"

"Insinuate? You talked Cody into bugging the Chrysler. Seems pretty pally to me. Did you even bother with a warrant?"

I had the moral high ground here and Delilah knew it.

"I got a warrant. And I have a recording of Bismarck Avila asking you to kill Keet."

The hammock had gone quiet, so perhaps Delilah and I could back down from the weird energy that was suffusing this strange conversation.

"Avila shows a proclivity for suborning murder," she said. "There are rumors that he used gang connections to have his previous driver killed. Most likely scenario, Avila got Keet to kill Willeniec. Avila maybe lives in a mansion in Calabasas but at heart he's a street rat."

I laughed.

"What's funny?"

"Keet called him the same thing. A street rat."

"You think because Avila stepped between you and a shotgun, he's better than that?"

"Yes."

"That's how a soldier thinks. Avila is no soldier."

"It was brave, Delilah."

"If you had been killed by that shotgun blast, what would have happened to Avila?"

I was getting caught up in my own lies here.

The truth was that if the sight of me being blown to bits didn't change Avila's mind, then Keet would have tortured him until he gave up the location of those barrels. But in the scenario I'd just sold Delilah, Keet had already gotten the barrels from Willeniec, then killed him.

"How would I know?"

"If Bismarck Avila saved your life, he did it for his own reasons. To save his own ass."

Either way, my conscience was served. I'd done my best. I was free and clear of the whole mess I'd brought down on me and my people by killing Willeniec. More important, Lucky, Tinkertoy, and Ripple were out of it, three innocent little ladybugs released from a child's fist. The task force was working Keet for Willeniec's murder, exactly as I'd hoped in my wildest hopes and dreamed in my wildest dreams. We had everything we wanted.

Me and my band of brothers (and sister), Lucky and Ripple and Tinkertoy, were in the clear.

EXPECTATIONS OF PRIVACY

There is something disconcerting about sitting between two women, best friends in their personal lives, because they are able to transcend the traditional cop/lawyer dynamic, who are tussling over your soul. Not to mention one of them I'm in love with and the other is a woman I'd definitely be exploring romantically in a serious way if the other woman weren't her best friend and the woman I'm in love with.

In an interview room in the LAPD Pacific Division station, Delilah sat across from me and Connie and played a recording, for the second time, of drunken Avila asking me to kill Asher Keet, followed, moments later, by a surprisingly adamant, loud, and irritated refusal, which did not, outside of the words, match my memory of the exchange.

"Well?" Delilah said, hitting a key to pause the recording.

"That's not a question," said my lawyer, Connie, in her most adversarial lawyer-to-cop voice.

"Oh, for Chrissakes," Delilah responded. "Interview is suspended for a short break." She stood and shut the laptop. "Could we please step into the corridor?"

Once outside the range of microphones, Delilah said to Connie, "Skellig is not suspected of anything. He's not being charged with anything. What we'd like to do is charge Bismarck Avila with suborning murder, which he did, and slap him in jail for a few days. For leverage. What's the fucking problem?"

"You are manipulating my client," Connie said.

Delilah made a long farting sound. Connie demanded that we go back into the interview room and continue the conversation in a professional manner.

Back at the scratched-up aluminum table, sitting on wooden chairs, Delilah reintroduced us to her laptop, providing time, date, and participants. In front of me on the table was a yellow legal pad and a stub of a pencil, placed there by Connie (so that I could write her secret notes), a tepid cup of Styrofoam coffee and a home-made chocolate chip cookie, both provided by Delilah before she knew Connie was going to stonewall. Since Delilah doesn't bake, I couldn't think how it got there unless some grateful citizen dropped off cookies for cops, in which case I hoped Delilah wasn't using me as a poison early-warning system.

"Mr. Skellig, will you stipulate that it is your voice on the recording?"

"Yes, but let the record show it's more nasal and higher pitched than what I hear in my head."

Connie cleared her throat. She'd warned me to answer *yes* or *no* with no other frills, addendums, modifiers, clarifications, or, most important, "things you think are funny but aren't."

"Will you stipulate that you are conversing with Bismarck Avila?"

"Yes."

"And that Avila clearly asked you to kill Asher Keet?'"

"Leading question," Connie said, "and also not a question."

"You mind explaining to me how something can be both a lead-ing question and not a question?"

Connie crossed her arms. Delilah made squinty eyes at her, then turned to me again and asked, "Did Bismarck Avila ask you to kill Asher Keet?"

"No," I said.

Even Connie raised her eyebrows.

"My lawyer instructed me to answer *yes* or *no*," I said. "If those are my only choices, then it's *no*."

"Maybe I should play the recording again," Delilah offered; then when Connie started to say that wasn't a question either, Delilah simply pressed a key on her laptop.

Where to?

Temecula.

What's in Temecula?

Keet.

Wouldn't it make more sense to go where Keet isn't?

Maybe I want you to kill Keet for me. Maybe that's why I hired you in the first place. War hero who's killed plenty of people.

I'm not killing anyone for you—

Delilah turned off the recording.

"Having refreshed your memory by playing the recording, I'll ask you again, Mr. Skellig. Did Bismarck Avila ask you to kill Asher Keet?"

"Avila wasn't suborning murder."

"*Yes* or *no*," Connie said.

"Avila had been drinking all night. He was drunk and goofing around because I'm always asking him why he insisted upon hiring me to drive him."

"None of those words were *yes* or *no*."

Delilah was annoyed but not angry because she knew I was telling the truth. She essayed a bunch of scattergun questions in an effort to find out what had happened out at Keet's place in Temecula, but Connie kept stopping her dead with phrases like *outside the purview* and *fishing expedition* and the like.

I doodled an owl on my legal pad. (Tip I learned from Ripple: you start with a figure eight.)

Delilah ended the interview and said that they didn't really need me to corroborate what was already plainly on tape so we were free to go. She didn't look up at either me or Connie as we left.

In Connie's Prius, Connie told me that it was obvious to her that Delilah's task force was determined to put Avila in jail with or without my help. They would use the drugs they found in his refrigerator or find some other pretext, but in the end the task force would throw their elbows in every direction until they found out what had happened to Sheriff's Detective Willeniec, A.

"The reason task forces love to include the FBI," Connie said, "is that it's a federal offense to lie to a federal agent. They catch you in a lie and use that as leverage to get you to do what they want. So don't tell a single lie, Skellig. *¿Lo entiendes?*"

"Keet will get to Avila in jail," I told Connie. "Have him gang-raped. Maybe bust his back so he's paralyzed. Maybe blind him with drain cleaner. Avila won't last the weekend."

"I'm your lawyer, not Bismarck Avila's. He has his own army of Beverly Hills lawyers."

"Connie. It's not right."

"Did you even hear what I said about task forces?" Connie asked. "I don't want you or any client anywhere near them. You even get the edge of your sleeve caught in those gears, the next thing you know, you are so deep into the system that I can't promise I can help you before you get turned into *cenizas y polvo.*"

"What about Avila?"

"I don't understand why you care," Connie said, echoing Delilah.

"Is this a privileged conversation?"

"Skellig—"

"I'm serious."

"Yes. This is a privileged client-to-lawyer conversation."

"Avila put himself between me and a psychopath with a shotgun is why. He didn't have to do it."

"But you have a theory as to why."

"Because he realized it was his fault I was about to get killed."

"It's not your fault that his *cojones* are in the wringer now."

(Yes, it was. Largely. Almost totally.)

"That's true."

"Yet you feel you owe Avila for saving your life."

I was not getting very far with Connie. She was holding me at arm's distance by making statements. If I wanted to keep Avila alive, or at least in one piece, I had to get her to cave in and ask a few questions.

"A very bad man was going to shoot me with a sawed-off shotgun. It would have cut me in half. Avila stepped in the way. He definitely saved my life."

"I'm pretty sure you could come up with a reasonable scenario in which saving you saved his own ass."

Were Delilah and Connie both, in their own ways, extremely smart, or were they both, in their own ways, extremely cynical?

"There wasn't time for Avila to weigh pros and cons before he did what he did. He just did it."

Connie considered the situation. I was smart enough to let her do that. At the next red light, Connie said, "What can I do that his lawyers can't do?"

A question! Connie's door was ajar . . .

At the next red light, I said, "What if a judge were to find out that the police had a hard-on for Avila? What if my lawyer were to say it was obvious that there was a witch hunt and this task force was overstepping its legal bounds in order to railroad Bismarck Avila for Willeniec's probable murder?"

"That accusation being based on . . . ?"

"Delilah straight-up told us that they don't intend to pursue the suborning-to-murder charges all the way to trial. They only want leverage."

"You mean out in the corridor?"

"Yes."

"That entire conversation was off the record. Between friends."

A statement. I was losing her!

"Doesn't mean it wasn't the truth."

"Delilah would hate me if I took advantage that way. Not to mention it would impact her career."

"Okay."

"It's not okay, *pendejo*. Delilah's my best friend."

"Delilah wants to get promoted to Robbery-Homicide."

"Are you saying she's blinded by ambition?"

"Not blinded. Dazzled."

"You think I don't want Delilah to succeed? You don't think I'm ambitious too?"

"That task force is using Avila as a shortcut. He's an expendable innocent bystander as long as they get what they want."

"Innocent?"

"In this group, Avila's the most innocent."

"Wouldn't that be you?" Connie asked. "Aren't you the most innocent?"

I decided to let her percolate some more. Which she did. You could smell the coffee.

"Here's what bothers me," Connie said, finally.

"Bothers you more than a guy getting a sharpened toothbrush shoved between the vertebrae in the small of his back?"

"The portion of the surveillance audio in which Bismarck Avila asked you to kill Keet was recorded in your limo."

"The task force had a warrant."

"The limo is your private property. You were not the target of the surveillance. We know that because they weren't allowed to record anything said in your limo unless they had visual confirmation that Bismarck Avila was in the limo."

"Which he was."

"Avila had no expectation of privacy in a hired limo. But *you* did. There's a possible argument that they can't use the recording to charge Avila with suborning murder because it violates your civil rights."

"I certainly feel violated."

"Are you willing to state, under oath, in the presence of a judge, that you never gave anyone on that task force even the tiniest indication that it would be all right with you for them to bug your limo?"

(Like offering to work as an informant for Delilah? Or begging her to follow me? That kind of indication?)

"Yes."

"Skellig, I need you to tell me something and I need it to be the absolute truth, *¡que Dios me ayude!*"

"I love you. I want to marry you and have six children."

"I don't mean some random truth. Do you believe, in your *corazón*, in your heart of hearts, that Bismarck Avila wanted you to kill Asher Keet?"

"Avila was drunk and joking. He didn't mean it. He doesn't deserve to get blinded or crippled in jail so a bullshit task force can get medals and promotions for solving the disappearance of a crooked cop."

"I'll see what I can do."

What it turned out that Connie could do was perform miracles.

First, Connie had Bismarck Avila segregated in protective custody.

Then she had the surveillance recording made in Two disallowed and the charges of suborning murder dropped. Then she got Avila released. As a last-ditch effort, an angry assistant DA hauled me in front of a judge, hoping I'd support Delilah's contention that I'd agreed to have my limousine bugged when I offered to work as a confidential informant for her.

Delilah looked at me and shook her head in disappointment when I perjured myself and stated that although she had approached me, I had not in any way agreed to help her.

Footage of Bismarck Avila being released and escorted home by Cody Fiso and his green-polo-shirt brigade in a presidential-size motorcade was not only all over TV but went viral.

Commentators and pundits went berserk over the images of Avila's fans and followers gathering outside the (wrong) courthouse and rejoicing that he'd regained some of the thug-life street cred he'd lost over the years.

Internet sales of *B!$m@R©k!* gear spiked within hours.

At the Van Nuys county courthouse, Connie and Delilah engaged in a very quiet, very intense argument down the corridor from where I stood, and the two times I approached in order to play peacemaker I got blasted first by Delilah, then by Connie. Due to the fact that I had encouraged Connie to damage her friendship with Delilah by repeating Delilah's off-the-record admission that the task force was harassing Bismarck Avila for leverage, Connie refused to drive me home. Lucky had to come and fetch me in the haunted Caddie.

I zipped my lips at Lucky, then had him take us both to the Tacos Reyes food truck on Sherman Way (highly recommended even if you aren't paranoid about being bugged). For all I knew, Delilah had gotten a new warrant to cover all our limos. When I conveyed those concerns, while standing in line for tacos, Lucky swore in Arabic and promised that he and Tinkertoy would sweep not only the limos but Oasis Limo Services in total the next day.

Lucky also told me that he'd looked into the ownership of the seedy apartment buildings and dive hotels we'd checked out on our Depressing Real Estate Tour, but the trail, in every case, had quickly gone cold. There were holding companies and numbered companies, nested LLCs, offshore syndicates, partnerships, but no names. Hacking further into bank accounts, etcetera, was beyond Lucky's Internet capabilities.

He did discover two interesting facts: One was that all the properties had been purchased within the last three years. The second was that one of the addresses, the Skid Row hooker hotel we'd staked out with tacos, was described as "luxury lofts" in a printout of company assets.

"That description is inaccurate," Lucky said.

Lucky wondered if we should present Delilah with these facts.

"Perhaps law enforcement can find the truth."

"Since I totally betrayed her confidence and perjured myself," I said, "I'm pretty sure the next communication I can expect from Delilah is her reading me my Miranda rights."

I told Lucky about Keet and Avila and the confrontation at Harbor Ranch. I told him about Slim, Mr. Tums and his nasty little assassin's pistol, and the two damaged boys who did Keet's every bidding no matter what, including cracking one of their own over the head with a baseball bat.

Lucky figured it would be prudent for me to leave town for a few days.

"Keet is angry at you," Lucky said, "for what you Rendered Unto His Pride. Also the fact that you are Willing and Able to identify Mr. Tums, and the terrible boys, and the fat man, Slim, as Murderers, Thugs, and Assassins Wanted by the Law."

"What about you and Tinkertoy and Ripple?"

"Ripple is in the hospital. I am like the Wind and can disappear, a Phantom."

"You wanna please back down on the desert mysticism at least while you're scarfing down a taco in Encino? What about Tinkertoy?"

"You must take her with you."

I tried to imagine Tinkertoy on a ranch in Big Sur. Hell, there was plenty of stuff that needed tinkering.

I told Lucky I'd think about it, but I never really had the chance because at seven o'clock the next morning I awoke to the sound of Tinkertoy screaming. I leaped out of bed and threw myself down the ladder and into the garage wearing only my underwear and an antique seven-iron I keep under my bed just for such eventualities.

Oasis Limo Services was chockablock full of cops all shouting at me to drop my golf club and me shouting at them to let go of Tinkertoy and it was a good old-fashioned Mexican standoff until Delilah stepped forward and told them to put down their weapons and told me to put down my sports equipment, which is when Tinkertoy took the opportunity to make a bolt for her safe place beneath the worktables and through to her hidey-hole.

Delilah and I yelled at each other some more as she took the seven-iron away from me, slapped me with a warrant, and told her people to get back to work searching Oasis.

I glanced at the warrant: barrels.

"What is it with you people and barrels?"

"Thanks to you, we have to start from the beginning. Barrels are what Willeniec was looking for just before he disappeared."

It took all my willpower not to glance over at the stain on the floor where I'd killed Willeniec.

As Delilah's team spread out to look for barrels, I persuaded Delilah to let me crawl in after Tinkertoy, accompanied only by Delilah, to check for barrels and to tempt Tinkertoy back out into the world—which I did by convincing Tinkertoy to come out and work on Three (her haunted nemesis).

"What's. Wrong. This time?" Tinkertoy asked.

"The headlights flick from high beam to low and back again for no reason."

Tinkertoy nodded and threw herself into uncovering the mysterious source of the headlight beam problem. (Which I had not made up. It existed. That machete murder car is haunted.)

Hard at work on Three, Tinkertoy was oblivious to the warrant execution team swirling around her.

"Don't pretend you don't fucking deserve this," Delilah said.

"I'm sorry. I couldn't see another way to keep Avila from getting crippled in jail."

"Fear of getting crippled would've scared Avila into turning on Keet. That's a pretty good choice."

"Avila doesn't scare. Like you said, at heart he's a tough street rat."

"Just so you know, I never fucking fucked fucking Cody," Delilah said. "He's tried more than once and the bug was his way of trying again. But I'm pretty fussy about the guys I fuck. At least since I stopped drinking."

Two members of the warrant team headed into the dispatch office. I hoped that Ripple had been smart enough to restrict his dope supply to legal, medical marijuana.

"Are you positive Willeniec isn't drinking rum and cokes on some black-sand beach?" I asked Delilah.

"We found his fake passport. We found his stash of cash. We found his cache of weapons. We followed all his wire transfers. We found a chunk of land he bought in Uruguay under his ex's name. The FBI sent someone from the embassy in Montevideo to check it out. If Willeniec escaped to a better life, then he did it without money or a passport or laying any groundwork."

"You ever think Uruguay and the transfers and passport and cash were diversions?"

"Oh, please! He's not fucking Jason Bourne. Willeniec's dead.

Someone killed him before he could make a run for it. And you are helping that person. Judas."

Unfair as that accusation was, it was also totally true.

"Avila is our link between Keet and Willeniec. It's obvious that Willeniec and Keet were competitors when it came to getting those barrels from Avila. We just need to prove it."

"By searching my place?"

"Guess what. The task force believes me and not you," she said.

"You mean that I offered to work for you, then reneged?"

"That's right. It looks pretty guilty, Skellig."

I thought about what Connie had said about task forces and dark forces and ruined lives. Delilah poked me in the chest with her forefinger. "You're hiding something from me. Maybe you think it's for my own fucking good, but you know what? You don't get to decide that. It's my job to find the truth. I hate my job right now, but I'm still going to do it to the best of my fucking ability."

Which is when a member of the warrant execution team wearing yellow glasses and waving around an ultraviolet flashlight called over to Delilah that she'd found evidence of cleaned-up blood.

Exactly where I'd killed Willeniec.

"Are you allowed to find blood?" I asked. "The warrant says barrels."

"Call your lawyer," Delilah advised.

"That's *my* blood," I said. "After I got home from the hospital, I opened my stitches conking my head on the wheel well."

I showed her the stitches in my head. "You'll find more of my blood on the right front fender of the Caddie."

"These stitches are made with thread."

"So?"

"Cotton thread. Not surgical nylon. These stitches were not done in a hospital."

"Lucky did it."

"Lucky stitched your head wound, here, using normal, red cotton thread? What'd you do for anesthetic? Take a shot of whiskey and bite on a bullet?"

"Lucky has medic training."

"Did it hurt?"

(It had—and she was back to asking her dangerous questions.)

"You know I'm extremely manly and tough."

"This head injury occurred the same night Willeniec disappeared. Wasn't that the same night Ripple got hurt during an anonymous S and M sex encounter?"

Which is when a member of the forensics team tried to move Tinkertoy away from the Caddie to examine the wheel well.

I'd warned Delilah not to let anyone touch Tinkertoy, especially males, but it was too late because a cop took her arm when she didn't respond to verbal commands, so she started screaming. I stepped in and the cop pushed me back and I reacted instinctively and dislocated his shoulder. Which meant another cop stepped in so I broke his nose. It went on from there in an increasingly unproductive manner, ending with me taking on all comers and a bunch of angry cops aiming weapons at me, and Delilah shouting at me to surrender.

It was Lucky, coming in to work, lunch bucket in one hand and Starbucks in the other, who convinced me to lie down and let them cuff me, even though, as he said, the police were likely to be Retributive considering I'd done some damage to their Extremities and Pride.

Which they were. Retributive, I mean. Cops kneeling on your head is tough on the dignity, the skull, and the ears.

I ended up in police custody (impeding police officers in the pursuance of their duties) and Tinkertoy ended up being taken away on a 5150 for psychiatric evaluation.

A fair amount of time passed in a mostly tedious manner.

Affronted law enforcement professionals at every level did a clever job of losing paperwork, squirreling me away in the system so that Connie didn't find me for twenty-four hours, most of which time I spent paranoid that Keet would discover where I was before Connie did, so I was a little low on sleep by the time Lucky bailed me out.

Also chilly, because I was still dressed only in my underwear.

Lucky drove me straight to Connie's place on the canals, where, in very strict lawyer mode, she informed me that in executing the warrant on Oasis Limo Services, the police had found a number of questionable items in my domicile.

"Everything in the penthouse came with the penthouse," I said. "It's all itemized on the bill of sale."

"Quit calling it a penthouse," Connie advised. "It makes you sound *como un loco*. It's a mobile home craned up onto the roof of a garage."

"It is nicer than people think," Lucky offered.

"You're being charged with obstructing justice, assault on two peace officers, specifically Penal Code 243(b) and (c)."

"I bought the penthouse as is. I shouldn't be held accountable—"

"Pay attention. You have bigger problems. Under California law, battery on a peace officer is typically a misdemeanor in which, if found guilty, you can get up to a year in county jail and a fine of two thousand dollars. Unfortunately, if the assault results in injury re-quiring medical treatment"—here she read from a list—"dislocated shoulders, broken noses, cracked ribs, broken fingers, a crushed in-step, and a ruptured eardrum, then the district attorney may decide to lay a felony charge, which can result in three years in prison and a ten-thousand-dollar fine."

"Is this in total?" Lucky asked. "Or cumulative with each charge?"

"Like you said," I said. "That task force is coming after me."

"Well, you made it *muy fácil* for them, *¿no lo hizo?*"

"Skellig Acted Out of Concern for our Tinkertoy," Lucky said.

"Your Tinkertoy is being held on a 5150 for a minimum of seventy-two hours," Connie said, "for a thorough psychiatric evaluation."

"After which they'll let her out?" Lucky asked.

"Only if the attending psychiatrist finds that she's not a danger to herself or others. Then there's the matter of the blood they found in the garage."

"It's my blood. I bumped my head on the wheel well."

"Yeah, they found it's your blood," Connie said. "But there are minute traces of someone else's blood mixed with it. Explain that."

"Can't they test it?"

"DNA," Lucky suggested.

"There's not a big enough sample to run a DNA test."

(Thank God.)

"That sucks!" I said.

"I'm sure there's an explanation," Lucky said.

"Maybe Tinkertoy cut herself?" I said.

"I've seen her punch the Cadillac," Lucky said.

"She hates that Caddie," I said.

"Tinkertoy believes it is haunted and malignant and that it means her harm," Lucky said.

"That kind of statement won't make Tinkertoy appear any saner," Connie said. "And this back-and-forth routine you boys do? Does that work in the Army? Because to me it comes off as bobbing and weaving to obscure the truth."

Both Lucky and I played it smart and shut up. Lesson learned. *Gracias por* the input, Connie.

Connie bit her lip then and looked at me, then at Lucky, then back at me. "Lawyers aren't supposed to ask questions unless they already know the answer or don't care what the answer is."

"I've heard that before," Lucky said.

"What happened to Darren?"

Lucky and I looked at each other and communicated in the way we have for years. We both knew to say nothing. We both knew to let the question fade away until everyone forgot it had ever been asked.

"*Jesús lloró*," Connie said, shaking her head. Then to me, "*¿Quién eres tú?*"

"You know who I am."

"I hate being manipulated."

"Our Skellig is a good man," Lucky said. "He is Trustworthy Above All."

"Boys, I am not one of your Army buddies. I haven't been *tempered in war* or *forged in a Roman wilderness of pain* or any other poetic violence crap. I live *en el mundo real*, with all the good, solid, social contract rules that we agree to abide by because we're civilized. Unlike you, I'm normal."

"We'll go now," I said, standing.

"You should do that."

I felt my heart breaking, because even though Connie had always been clear about the eventual futility of our romance, I'd remained hopeful. What I heard in her voice now was the death of that hope.

"We should not leave," Lucky said to Connie hotly. "We should sit here in silence until the Anger and the Distrust dissipate, and then we can speak again."

"Like I said, I live in this world. And, Skellig, get yourself another lawyer."

"C'mon, now, Connie . . ."

"I'm done. You're lying to me or leaving something out, and I will not be manipulated. I'll e-mail you a list of referrals."

Connie left us sitting in her living room and headed for her bedroom. She shut the door on us.

"You should join her in there," Lucky advised, "not allow these Harsh Words to harden into a Reality."

"Let's go," I said. "You were right."

"About what?"

"It's time to get out of LA for a couple days."

VARROA DESTRUCTOR

I follow my father down a dusty game trail that meanders along the southern side of a scrubby dry hill festooned with cartoon-looking cacti. It's a microclimate on Rancho Pico Blanco in Big Sur, the warmest microclimate on the Central Coast, and if the hillside on our left wasn't covered with thorns, it'd be a great place for a blanket and a bottle of wine and bouncing bare bottoms. A thought that leads me to Connie's bare bottom, which leads me to despair, so I concentrate on the rhythms of Dad's cowboy boots and try to exclude all other thoughts, the same coping mechanism I learned as a young grunt, boots on the ground, trying not to think about me or my buddies getting shot or blown up.

Knowing I was sleep deprived and depressed, Dad asked if the pace he was setting was good for me and I told him I was fine and he grunted, which meant he had his doubts but didn't feel like challenging me on the subject. The old man sets a pretty fierce pace for a civilian. He'd have made one hell of a soldier if he wasn't so wrapped up in peace and love and harmony and all the good vibes he cloaks himself in on this ranch along one of the loneliest coasts in an otherwise crowded state.

I'd pulled into Dad's yard two hours before and sat on the hood of Three, knowing he'd seen me and my contrail of dust on the unpaved approach road from whatever ridge he was working on, and sure enough, forty-five minutes later he appeared behind the wheel of his hilariously (and continuously) modified vehicle that probably started as a Jeep CJ long before I was born. No windshield, no doors, no roof, and one seat. If you wanted to travel with Dad, you had to choose between a lawn chair placed where a passenger seat is usually found or bouncing around in the back like a sack of groceries.

When I informed Dad how (and why) Connie had dumped me both as a client and as a boyfriend, he whistled the three separate notes that make up the D minor chord. It's Dad's opinion that D minor is the saddest chord.

I told him that Keet might want to kill me as a way to motivate Bismarck Avila to give Keet something he wanted but also because I could connect Keet through his associates to the murder of Avila's bodyguard. That's when Dad whistled something a bit angrier than D minor and suggested that we hike out to his favorite, secret fishing hole.

It wasn't until we'd crossed the winding creek seven times (Dad wading through in the knee-high rubber boots he kept in his crazy vehicle for just this reason, me jumping like Gollum from rock to log to rock) and we set our lines in the water to catch and release steelhead that I dropped the really big bomb on him. Dad listened carefully, then reeled in his line because a man's emotional state travels along his line and into the water and he didn't want to scare the fish.

"Michael," he said, rubbing his eyes, "are you telling me you had absolutely no other option?"

"Not that I could see."

"You couldn't scare the man? Or bribe him? Or make a deal? Did you try to reason with him? Or knock sense into him?"

"I didn't have time for any of that, Dad. He was going to shoot one of my guys."

"You're absolutely certain he was going to kill one of you?"

"I absolutely am."

(I was.)

"Well, certainly it seems to me in that case you had to take him out."

"Yeah."

I thought Dad might cast his line back into the stream. But he didn't. "You broke his nose with a wrench, busted his fingers, took his gun—do I have that sequence correct in my mind?"

"Yes."

"And after all that ferocity, you still felt the need to crush his larynx? What danger was he to anyone at that point, Michael? It seems to me you should have considered more options before killing him."

"Like what?"

"Hell, tie him up, put him in the trunk of a car, and have a good think on the matter! You gonna tell me that you had to go all the way and commit to ending a man's life because you lack imagination?"

"Fine, Dad. Here we are. We have all the time in the world. I promise to feel really bad about killing him if between the two of us we can come up with another workable scenario."

"I should hope you already feel terrible, Mikey."

I did not feel terrible about killing Willeniec. (We've been through this, you and I.) I'd come to grips with my decision and my actions long before I slid Willeniec down that bottomless hole in a dead man's dried-up orchard on a barren farm on the arid edge of the Carrizo Plain. I told Dad that I felt terrible, but the only truth he heard in my voice sprang from the anger I still felt that Willeniec had come to my home and hurt my people and forced me to kill him.

"Dad, the man was a sociopath and a sadist."

"You had time to figure out his psychology but not enough time to figure out how to preserve his life?"

"Everything I've found out about him since has confirmed what he was."

"When you took his life you also took away any chance he had to live long enough to redeem himself, to become a better man."

"Or become even worse?"

"Mikey, it's not good for you. You have to stop adding voices who whisper to you from the wind."

Yes, I'd even told my father about the ghosts who haunt me. We all need somebody in the world who knows who we really are.

We began the five-mile hike back, Dad letting me set the pace— but only because he expected me to talk the whole way.

"I hope you don't intend to just abandon this Bismarck Avila fella," he said.

"Dad, there's nothing I can do with this task force looking at me now. Why do you think I'm here?"

"The police have fixated on him because they think he killed this corrupt cop—but that was *you*, Mikey."

"Christ, Dad. What do you want me to do? Confess?"

"Only if you can't find some other way to keep Bismarck Avila from paying the price for what you did," Dad said.

I often wonder how my father, a tough old cowboy with a moral code, would fare as a soldier in a war zone where right and wrong and black and white are subsumed in noise and chaos and terror.

Who would break first? Abel Skellig or War? (I can never imagine anything beyond a dead draw.)

"Why, after killing the man in self-defense, didn't you call the authorities and explain your actions?"

I told Dad that at the time I didn't know the police were aware that Willeniec was a corrupt cop. I didn't know how many other cops might be working with him. And if I called Delilah Groopman, whom I trust, and she tried to help me, how did I know she wouldn't get ground up by the same corrupt machine?

"Plus," I told Dad, "I didn't know who else was looking for those barrels and what they might do to get them. I still don't."

"Difficult," Dad admitted.

"All I want is to run my little limo company, do my bit, hire some vets who need jobs. Marry Connie . . ."

I don't know what Dad was thinking about while we walked past the wall of cactus, but I was trying to think of a way to do the right thing without getting lethally injected for killing a psychopathic corrupt cop who had every intention of shooting Ripple, Tinkertoy, Lucky, and me to get his hands on a couple of barrels of money.

Back at the house, I made dinner (hamburgers with fried eggs on top, Tabasco, raw onion on bread Mom brought Dad from Sacramento); then, before sunset, I accompanied Dad to check on one of his new enthusiasms, a collection of beehives. He had about twenty boxes up against a hillside, near one of his favorite cow pastures, tiny little humming honey factories. Dad checked each one of them, telling me about a mite called Varroa destructor that decimated beehives. Dad was trying out a bunch of different methods for fighting the mite, including synthetic chemicals like formic acid vapor (which he did not favor), powdered sugar (which he found amusing), thyme and lemon oils (which he found festive), physical methods like heat (which he found anxiety inducing due to the possibility of cooking the bees as well as the mites), and an involved method of moving the bees at crucial junctures in the honeybee and Varroa mite life cycle (which he found complicated).

It was more interesting than I'm making it sound.

On the way back to the house, we detoured up onto the ridge to watch the sun drop into the Pacific Ocean.

"There," Dad said when it did, as though he was the one who'd overseen the whole operation.

Back at the house, Dad decided to read and listen to music, but he suggested that I get to sleep early.

"You look terrible," Dad said. Which made sense, given that I hadn't had more than one good night's sleep since meeting Bismarck Avila.

When I stay with Dad, I sleep in the same room my brother and I shared growing up. Bunk beds. I fell asleep so hard it's possible I actually expired. Something to do with the top bunk in my childhood room (a glow-in-the-dark poster of the solar system plastered to the ceiling), maybe the fine, clean air in Big Sur, maybe the subconscious reassurance provided by knowing my father was awake in the other room; or maybe it was simply lack of sleep that caught up with me. Who knows how long I'd have slept if Dad hadn't pinched my nose shut the next morning (his tried-and-true method of waking sons for more than thirty years), thrust a tin cup of boiled, corrosive coffee into my hands, and said, "We have a problem."

I figured Dad was going to tell me that the parasitic Varroa destructor mites had somehow overnight won the battle and overpowered all his bees, but instead he led me out of the house and across the yard past the haunted Caddie and past his modified Jeep to the root cellar that had been dug into the hillside by the original ranchers, Spaniards, before the turn of, not this century, but the one before.

Dad grunted and heaved the oak doors open.

There, trussed up with duct tape, rags tied around their mouths, lying on their sides, facing away from each other, were Mr.

Tums (still in those Chelsea Boots) and X-Ray (ass hanging out). I stood there with my cup of coffee, gaping. I'd expected that Dad was going to show me evidence that pack rats or possums had found a way into the root cellar.

"Hi, guys," I said, because literally *nothing* else occurred to me.

"Damnedest thing," Dad said, in the same tone he used to talk about bees and coyotes and other minor threats to the ranch. "I turned in around midnight, but just after one in the morning I startled awake. I think what woke me was all the frogs singing and carrying on near the water hole stopped! *Hell*, I thought to myself, *there must be a mountain lion in the vicinity.*"

X-Ray did that thing that he must have learned from TV or movies where he started trying to talk through his gag.

"Trying to talk with a gag in your mouth is a TV trope," I told X-Ray. "People don't really do that."

He stopped.

"But it wasn't a mountain lion," Dad continued. "It was these two, and now, here we all are."

"You left out some important stuff in the middle, Dad."

Behind his gag, Mr. Tums chortled.

"I went to check it out. I waited near the road, figuring that's where I'd see whatever stopped the frogs from singing cross, and, sure enough, here comes the black fella there with a tiny little pistol in his hand and the young fella following along behind him with a sawed-off shotgun. I found that suspicious. You know them?"

"Yeah, I know them."

"They here just to frighten or do real harm?"

"They're here to kill me and probably you. I'm sorry, Dad. I didn't know Keet got this serious this fast."

I crossed the cellar to take a closer look. Dad had tied them up with duct tape, ankles and wrists separately, then ankles and wrists together and the strips of rag tied around their mouths. Mr. Tums had dried blood on his nose. X-Ray's left eye was swollen shut. The two of them looked to have passed a miserable night.

"Why didn't you wake me up?"

"You needed eight solid hours," Dad said.

"I guess I can see you didn't need help."

"You gotta remember being color-blind means I see pretty good in the dark."

"These two are usually with two other sons a' bitches," I said.

"There's no one else," Dad said. "They left their car parked a mile along the Old Coast Road, just this side of the bridge of the north fork of the Little Sur."

"Is it still there?"

"Nope, it's locked inside the trailer shed near the irrigation pumps."

"Gee, Dad," I said, "did you have to rough them up so much? X-Ray here is just a kid."

"Well, even though they had guns," Dad said, "you'll notice neither of them is dead."

Tums laughed again from behind his gag. I had to hand it to the guy—he enjoyed life in the moment.

"What do you want to do with them?"

"I don't suppose you'd be okay with killing them and burying them under a bunch of rocks on Pico Blanco?"

"Hell, Mikey, we don't have to bury them. We'll tell the sheriff they were here to steal cattle," Dad said. "It's still legal to hang rustlers. I'll go fetch a rope."

Dad left the cellar. It wasn't true about rustlers and hanging, but despite hanging out on Keet's death ranch, these two were city boys and Mr. Tums stopped laughing.

COLD COMFORT

Instead of hanging Mr. Tums and X-Ray from the nearest California oak, Dad calls his buddy California State Patrol Trooper Stan
Linmidis. Stan calls his girlfriend, Monterey County Deputy Sheriff Jana Isa. Both meet at the Crossroads in Carmel before driving
out to the ranch to hear the story.

Jana removed the gags while Stan stood back with his hand on
his weapon, wearing the serious face he wears when he's trying not
to grin. Jana Mirandized Tums and X-Ray both, put them in handcuffs, and placed X-Ray in the back of Stan's cruiser. Stan put Tums
in the back of Jana's Charger, and then they both called their bosses
with the result that a half dozen law enforcement officers showed up
on the Pico Blanco Ranch to dare each other to drink Dad's camp
coffee, get some fresh air, and debate jurisdiction.

There was a lot of joking about whether or not Dad should be
arrested for kidnapping and assault, which gave gullible X-Ray a
bucketload of false hope. He readjusted his expectations when he

complained that his rights had been violated and everybody laughed in his face. Dad gave Jana's boss, the sheriff, a statement against Mr. Tums and X-Ray as armed trespassers, and I gave Stan's boss, the highway patrol watch commander, a statement identifying X-Ray as the murderer of Bismarck Avila's bodyguard and Mr. Tums as a person of interest identified at the crime scene. I provided both jurisdictions with Detective Delilah Groopman's number as the LAPD Pacific Division investigating officer down in Los Angeles.

Mr. Tums and X-Ray were processed and on their way back to Los Angeles before I was.

Later that afternoon, as I was getting into my car to leave, Dad extended one of those old-fashioned plaid Thermos Kings full of coffee (like there weren't six hundred Starbucks on the way back to Los Angeles).

"Dad, I'm pretty sure it's just me Keet is after, but just in case, you gotta watch yourself. There's no way those two followed me up here without me making them. That means Keet has your GPS."

"How would he get that?"

Willeniec. I gave him my card. He ran my business through the system. He shared what he knew with Keet. Simple. Maybe even foreseeable.

When I told Dad my theory, he said, "Hell, Mikey, don't worry. Nobody can sneak up on me up here. I'm safer here than you are back in LA."

"We gotta warn Mom too. What if Keet knows she's my mother?"

"I'll take care of warning your mom. Stan already promised me the state troopers will keep an eye out. Drive carefully. Watch out, I'm pretty sure these old-fashioned thermoses actually make things hotter." (No use telling the man that physics made that impossible.)

Dad stood waving in my rearview mirror until I was out of sight, like always.

The next morning, Delilah came by Oasis to inform me and

Lucky that a deputy sheriff at the county jail had found X-Ray dead in his cell even though he'd been segregated due to his youth.

"Dead how?" I asked.

"He hung himself."

"Didn't the deputies take his shoelaces?"

"He used his underwear."

"The kid didn't wear underwear."

Delilah showed us a police photo of X-Ray's suicide. On the back was a typed label bearing his real name.

"Bogdan Milic," Lucky read. "What's that, Serbian?"

But it wasn't the kid's ethnic background that interested me.

"Delilah, he's wearing pants."

"You got the eye of a detective, Skellig."

"Does it scan for you that young Bogdan removed his cargo shorts, took off underpants he didn't own and never wore and wasn't wearing when he was arrested, put his cargo shorts back on, and then hung himself?"

"Maybe he didn't want anyone to think it was an autoerotic accident."

Delilah told us that Bogdan Milic had been in and out of the foster system and juvie since he was seven years old. He got his nickname, X-Ray, from the number of times he'd hurt himself doing backyard stunts and posting them on YouTube.

"Kid had a following," Delilah said.

"Why?" Lucky asked.

"People dig seeing other people hurt themselves on the Internet," she said. "He was half a quasicelebrity in that world."

I handed the photos back to Delilah.

"No way this kid killed himself."

"I know, Skellig," Delilah said. "I'm not an idiot. I want you to consider that maybe if you hadn't lied and taken away my leverage on Avila, this kid might still be alive."

"Are you trying to make *me* wear this?"

"You made your decision; you gotta live with it. Maybe trust me a bit more next time."

"Next time?"

But she was already moving out the door.

"The boy was Serbian," Lucky told Ripple an hour later, as though that explained everything. Ripple was dozing off and on as we waited for the hospital to finalize his release. He'd been given a generous dose of some strong pain meds in preparation for his trip home, so he was loopy.

"Who was Serbian?" Ripple asked, but we'd learned over the last twenty minutes that if we simply waited a few seconds, he'd drift off without requiring an answer.

Lucky showed me a video on his phone. In the video, X-Ray jumped between two buildings downtown. He had to take a run because he had to travel about fifteen feet across and another twelve feet down. He hit the edge of the building and scrambled to climb onto the roof, scraping his face and elbows, but he raised his arms to the sky and whooped in victory when he made it.

"Hell of a jump," I said, thinking how Delilah blamed me for his death and the way I'd find out if I was really responsible or not was if I heard his voice in the wind. I hoped I never would.

"Over a quarter of a million views," Lucky said.

"Poor little bastard," I said.

"I'm fine," Ripple said, waking up just long enough to think he was the poor little bastard being discussed.

"What about Mr. Tums?" Lucky wanted to know as soon as Ripple drifted off again.

"Tums could only be charged with trespassing," I told Lucky, repeating what Delilah had told me. "His gun is registered and he said he was carrying it because he was afraid of mountain lions. He's awaiting a bail hearing."

Mr. Tums had no YouTube presence, and according to Delilah, he was refusing to say a word about anything to anyone, which was probably the reason Keet let him live. Not to mention that my statement could only put him at the scene of the homicide, not definitively incriminate him as an accomplice.

I'd asked Delilah to please let the task force and district attorney's office know the truth: Tums had been sent up to Big Sur to kill me and probably my father. I hoped that would at least toss a couple of obstacles in Tums's path before he was allowed back out into the world with an evil little assassin's gun tucked into the small of his back.

I also told her my theory that the only way Keet could have found me up in Big Sur was through Willeniec. I told her this both because it was true and because it might help sway the task force over into thinking that maybe Willeniec had run afoul of Keet and gotten himself disappeared.

Lucky wondered if it was safe for us to resume normal lives. "Keet has lost two Valued Henchmen coming after us. One permanently."

"Tums is Keet's right-hand guy," I theorized. "We're safe until he's released."

"This is what I would call Cold Comfort," Lucky said.

"Cold Comfort!" Ripple hollered in his outdoors voice.

I agreed.

Tinkertoy was nearing the end of her involuntary seventy-two-hour psychiatric hold at Harbor-UCLA Medical Center down in Torrance, but Connie (who was not speaking to me) had told Delilah that Tinkertoy was resisting all treatment and medications and had no intention of admitting herself willingly for further psychiatric help, so a county psychiatrist was recommending a 5250 hold order.

"What's that mean?"

"Another two weeks," Lucky said, "but first the Law Requires

a probable-cause hearing, where Connie will argue for our Tinkertoy to be Set Free."

"Does Connie think she'll win that?"

"She said that while she is not pessimistic she is also not opti-
mistic."

"Fifty-fifty?"

Lucky nodded and looked worried. The Afghan Mope.

"Tinkertoy won't say anything," I told him.

"They are feeding our Tinkertoy psychotropic drugs. She is
Disoriented, Afraid, and Paranoid."

"You worried Tinkertoy will blab?" Ripple asked. And he was
looking at us apparently completely clear-eyed.

"Hi, Ripple," I said. "Good to see you."

"Tinkertoy won't blab," Ripple said—and fell back asleep.

Dr. Quan entered. She greeted us coolly and professionally,
which I eventually realized was not because she thought we were
evil murderers or mutilators of redheaded boys but because she was
smitten by Lucky.

"How's our Darren?" Lucky asked.

"Ask him," Dr. Quan said. "He's the one whose hand you're
holding."

"We did ask him," I said. "He sang us a song he performed at
his church when he was eight years old."

"He changed the lyrics to something less religious," Lucky said
in the understatement of the year.

I helped Dr. Quan move Ripple to a wheelchair. We placed him
gently upon a huge hemorrhoid doughnut, which Dr. Quan said we
could take home.

"He may be a little cranky as the pain medication wears off,"
she said.

"He's never not been cranky," Lucky said, smiling at her. She smiled back at him. (This was the exact point where I realized they had done some bonding when I wasn't looking.)

As we moved down the hallway and toward the elevators, Dr. Quan told us about the care and feeding of Ripple over the next few days. He should try to move, stay active, keep the stitches clean, there shouldn't be much pain, the remaining testicle wasn't bruised so we didn't have to keep wincing all the time.

"Lucky wants to bang you so hard!" Ripple hollered as we descended in the elevator.

Both Dr. Quan and Lucky looked shocked.

"I never said that, Gracie," Lucky said in a strangled voice after a very long ten seconds. "I especially never said it in that manner."

"I'm a witness," I told Dr. Quan. "Lucky only speaks of you with respect."

Lucky gave me a look of Afghan Appreciation, knowing that I had forgone the much more amusing route of making things worse.

As I left them to get the car, I heard Lucky ask Dr. Quan to have dinner with him after her shift. I couldn't make out the exact words of her response, but it didn't sound negative.

I dropped Lucky and Ripple off at their duplex around the corner from Oasis and then swapped the Transit for Three, the haunted Caddie, and headed out to Avila's place in Calabasas, figuring the least I could do was bring him up to date in person about Tums and X-Ray. Not to mention that we might be able to speak without the task force writing down every word.

My old friend Lou was at the gate and took no joy in notifying me that I wasn't on the list of approved visitors. I asked Lou to call Avila. Lou said that he was not authorized to do anything that would inform someone not on the list (like myself) whether or not Avila was on the grounds. I asked Lou to call Cody Fiso and tell him that if I wasn't through this gate in three minutes I would inform Avila that Cody had been the one who bugged my limo on behalf of the police which is why they had a recording of him suborning murder.

"Is that true?" Lou asked.

"You'll be able to tell by how Cody reacts."

Lou stewed for about six seconds, probably figuring out which course of action was more likely to get him fired, then made a call on his cell, turning away so I couldn't hear what he said.

Lou hung up. The gate swung open ahead of me.

"Thanks to you, I know something about Fiso I wish I didn't," Lou said. "And he knows I know it. So when I get fired, I'll be looking to you for a driving job."

"You're in the gravy, Lou. Fiso knows if he fires you, you'll tell everyone what he did and he'll be the one looking for a new job. My advice, ask for a raise."

I drove the Caddie up to the house and parked.

There was no one on Nina's island and no one on the vertical ramp, so I walked in the front door and headed for the kitchen, where I found a very drunk Avila struggling to make himself a toasted roast beef sandwich. I stepped in and made the sandwich for him.

"You mind if we go somewhere less likely to be bugged?" I asked.

"Like where?"

We ended up sitting on the edge of the vertical ramp in the backyard, our legs dangling like kids'. This was Avila's true domain. I brought him up to date, which seemed to sober him up pretty quickly.

"Keet sent them to kill you?"

"Me and my dad."

"You think Keet killed X-Ray in jail?"

"Yeah. You worried yet?"

"Keet's not gonna kill me."

"Not until he's killed everyone around you first."

"Keet's just talking, brah."

"They came up to my dad's place. That's a six-hour drive."

"And you got two of his guys. One's dead. Keet's done."

"If you think he's done, why are you so drunk?"

Avila chewed on his sandwich and shrugged.

In my brain, a few tumblers turned and clicked. (It's possible you got there before me.)

"I know you're laundering money for Keet."

Avila stared at me, forgetting to chew the sandwich I'd made him. Suddenly sober, he asked, "Are you wired?"

"Moron, I'm the one who suggested we come out here where no one could hear us."

"How do I know you aren't playing me?"

He made me strip to my boxers, toss my clothes down to the bottom of the ramp.

"Look at you," he said, "all stippled with scars and shit."

"You bought up all these shitty, deserted buildings. Empty lots. But on paper, they're occupied by premium renters paying premium rents."

Avila turned his attention back to his sandwich.

"Dirty barrels of cash in, clean rent out, probably to some off-shore setup? Simple. Cops are looking for the connection between you and Keet, and there it is—a bunch of companies in Belize or Luxembourg or somewhere else they don't ask questions."

"What buildings? You can't trace those buildings to me. No-body can."

"Willeniec did."

"Willeniec's gone, brah."

"Did you kill him?" (Just in case the task force was listening.)

"I got no idea what happened to that racist piece of shit."

"I wish you'd give Keet those barrels."

"Why?"

"So he'll stop killing people. By *people*, I mean *me.*"

"Them barrels are just one part of my beef with Keet."

And the tumblers in my brain turned again.

"You want to take your company public," I said. "And you can't do that as long as you own those bogus rental properties."

"Nobody can trace those properties to me."

"From the outside," I said. "But when you go public, you gotta open the books. Due diligence. Keet tells you no, he likes things the way they are. But you, you need to be world champion. You want what you want."

Avila's chin tilted up, an alpha-male tell he couldn't control.

"Why you wasting your life being a driver? You got mad skills."

"One thing I can't figure is why you'd take those barrels when you had real money at stake."

"Rocky took those barrels because he thought he could get away with it. Dumb-ass kid. There's only so many people had access. Took Tums about five minutes to figure out it was Rocky. You think you're smart? Multiply that by ten and you got Tums."

"How did Willeniec find out about the barrels?"

"He was a cop. Cops hear things."

"How'd he get a list of your properties? Who else knows Rocky took those barrels? Nina, Keet and his people, you, me. Anyone else?"

Avila shook his head. Nobody.

"Then one of them told Willeniec. It wasn't me."

"Shit," Avila said.

"No one on that list of people benefits from telling Willeniec about the barrels—except Keet."

"I get it."

"Give Keet his barrels of money," I suggested. "Then sign the real estate over to him or the dummy companies, whatever, let him have it all. Walk away."

"Let Keet win?"

"It's the only way you get to be chairman of the board."

Avila smiled.

"What's funny?"

"Get your clothes and follow me."

Avila led me into his media room and sat me down on the most comfortable couch in the world in front of an eighty-five-inch 4K TV. He plopped himself down at the other end of the couch and pulled a tablet out of a leather pouch on his onyx coffee table. He flipped through a database and tapped the screen. Images appeared on the TV, a rough, punk-style credit sequence that Avila fast-forwarded through before he froze on the image of a mahogany-colored kid sporting bright Day-Glo pink dreads at the Venice Skate Park, midteens, cocky as hell, jutting out his chin, stroking his bare chest with one hand, holding a battered skateboard in the other, shot from a real low angle, like a superhero.

"That's Biz," Nina said from behind us. She entered the room sucking on a doobie (glory!), buzzed out of her mind, wearing an untied Chinese silk robe and nothing else, the purple robe billowing to reveal gravity-defying breasts, pubic hair cut to a landing strip, weed smoke trailing her into the room like an entourage.

Avila said, "Your cha-cha's out."

Nina ignored him, threw herself down on the couch beside me, crossed her fine legs, and nodded at Avila to play the footage. Avila unpaused. Punky-rap-metal-surf music blares, adolescent, aggressive underscore for young Bismarck Avila striking testosterone poses for the camera.

Cut to: grainy footage in a club. The band on the stage is playing the aggressive music we've been hearing as sound track and, lo, there's young Bismarck Avila fronting the band, sixteen, pink hair, singing his little heart out, obscene graffiti behind him, and a banner spelling out his name, exclamation mark and all. (The branding started young.)

Cut to: the crowd of skaters, surfers, punks, girls, and burnouts, beer and dope, a mosh pit going crazy.

"I remember that place," Nina said. "House club just off the boardwalk back when Venice was proper Venice."

Cut to: grainy video footage of lead singer Avila seizing his groin in his right hand, his microphone in the left, screaming at the top of his lungs, veins cording in his neck and forehead. The boys in the crowd scream with Avila, like a pack of young coyotes; the girls scream at him.

What would it feel like to be young the way Avila was young? One day you're a street kid trying not to get your ass beat (or worse) by your mom's boyfriends; the next, you're a demigod. What happens to the soul of a kid like that?

Cut to: network-quality coverage of a huge athletic event. Young pink-haired Bismarck Avila skates on a gigantic ramp in front of thousands of people. A banner reads OI VERT JAM!

"Brazil," Nina said. "Two thousand six."

"I might be as impressed as you want me to be if I knew what Oi Vert is," I said.

"World championships!" Nina said, disgusted.

"My second run," Avila said, and he fast-forwarded to a slight mahogany elf on a skateboard with bright orange wheels, his burnt-orange shorts clashing with his pink hair, shooting a good twelve, fifteen feet above the lip of the vertical ramp, and something goes wrong (I don't know what), and to me it looks like he falls three stories before crashing into the nadir of the parabola. The music continues, but young Avila lies motionless as EMTs and officials converge.

"Christ," I said.

Cut to: a close-up of young Avila, his face twisted in pain.

Avila paused the footage again.

"I guess you know what happened next."

"You died and went to heaven?"

"No, brah! Don't you know *nothing* about me? I told you Google."

"He don't know the first bit of nothin' about you, Biz," Nina said.

Avila restarted the footage.

"Next day, now," Nina said.

Cut to: young Avila stands on the precipice of that humongous vertical ramp, apparently recovered from his fall the day before, all eyes on him, his face unreadable.

The song beneath the images changes. Faster, buzz-saw aggressive.

Cut to: a closer shot. Avila's face is like stone.

Cut to: the camera punches in even closer. Now we can see that Avila's sweating. The sweat could be from pain, but, hey, it's Brazil—it could be heat and humidity; the whole crowd is sweating too.

Cut to: the band in the Venice club; young Avila is rapping now but I can't understand the words because I'm white, for Chrissakes, a soldier straight outta the rural Central Coast of California.

Cut to: Brazil. A bead of sweat rolls down young Avila's nose. When it gets to the tip, the kid expands his cheeks and blows and the drop of sweat blasts out into the void and a microsecond later Avila follows it.

Cut to: Avila races down one side of the ramp and up the other side and he does a twirl (more than 360 degrees, possibly 405?) and a kick and waves his board over his head, then lands on it at exactly the same moment that the board crashes onto the surface of the ramp, and he does it again and again, and apparently whatever he's doing is miraculous because . . .

Cut to: the crowd goes apeshit. Ten years later, a continent away, it's like the kid can fly, like gravity is just some arbitrary rule to be broken because the usual rules do not apply to Bismarck Avila.

The image freezes.

I look at Avila the grown man. Drunk, proud, looking at me as though he's proved something.

"Biz won," Nina said. "World championships! He beat that red-haired tomato kid, all the Australian brothers, everybody."

"Congratulations."

"That's all you got to say? Congratulations?"

"I admire the pink hair. Very forward fashion choice."

Avila sucked air through his teeth in irritation.

"With a broken back," Nina said. "Get it?"

I tried to process that.

"What do you mean broken?"

"Broken, brah. My legs were tingling the whole time like I was getting shocked."

"Now you get it?" Nina said.

"He gets it," Avila said.

"Wanna commit a threesome?" Nina asked. It took a moment to realize what she was asking. "Biz told me how vicious you can be. I find that hot."

"Babe," Avila said. "You know I'm not into the two guys version. Not my thing."

Nina stood up and opened her robe, swaying a little, giving us a long look at what we were passing up—*Suit yourselves*—and left.

"You probably wonder why I put up with that shit."

"I just saw why you put up with her. What I wonder is what you're trying to tell me, showing me home movies."

"You say give Keet everything he wants and walk away."

"It's great advice, but . . ." I pointed at the room, then at my ears, telling Avila the task force could be listening. He didn't give a rat's ass. He pointed at the frozen image of his younger self on the TV, midair, face tight and calm in concentration as he broke gravity's rule.

"Fifteen years old, broken back. I skated when everyone told me no—and I won. The world championship." Avila indicated his whole house, the whole world. "That's why I got all this that I got. I never walk away from any challenge, brah. Not ever."

"Ah," I said.

When Nina had called him a pussy bitch, Avila responded by

making her scream in ecstasy in front of thirty cops. Feeding the legend. When I impugned his manhood by advising him to buy his safety, he showed me proof that he was more of a man at fifteen, with bright pink hair and a broken back, than I could ever hope to be.

I guess that answered my question about what happened to his soul back in the day as he transformed himself from Bismarck Avila to *B!$m@R©k!*

"What would you have done?" Avila asked, tapping his knuckle on his younger self. "Gone home, I guess."

"Without a doubt."

"That's right."

What I wanted to do then was say, *Suit yourself*, like Nina, leave Avila to kill himself one way or the other. But even though half of Avila's problems were of his own making, the ones that would actually destroy him existed because I'd killed Willeniec.

"My dad wouldn't have let me skate with a broken back."

"Nobody tells me what to do. Not then. Not ever."

"Somebody should have stopped you," I said.

"Brah, you think they didn't try? Trust me."

"I don't mean a manager or someone who *invested* in you. I mean someone who actually gave a shit about you as a human being."

"They loved me, brah."

"You were their meal ticket, brah."

Avila made a noise through his teeth like what I'd said wasn't worth the effort of forming words.

"Would you do that now?" I said, crossing to the TV and knocking on the frozen flying kid on the screen.

"Don't do that to my screen."

"Would you try that today with a broken back? No, because you're smarter. You grew up. This kid was brave, yeah, but mostly he was a moron. Kids are morons."

Avila showed me his middle finger. He didn't believe I could ever understand. But of course I understood. I'd been to war when I was not much older than Avila had been when he broke his back.

"You really want to beat Keet?"

"What you think?"

"Give him back what belongs to him."

Avila started huffing at me, but I took the remote and started the footage again. I turned up the volume until the air thrummed with surf-punk music and the applause of thousands. I leaned in close to Avila's ear.

"Give him the barrels. Put the shell companies in his name."

"Give him millions of dollars in real estate?"

"Cooperate with the task force, turn the tables on Keet, let him get charged with money laundering, say you found out what he was doing during prep for your due diligence."

Avila stared at me for a long moment.

"Return the barrels how?" he said.

"Call him up and tell him where they are."

"Look at us. Police are watching *everything*," he said. "Cody says my phones are tapped. I can't go nowhere or see anybody the police don't know about."

That was all true. Avila wouldn't be able to move without the task force knowing what he was doing.

"Tell me where the barrels are. I'll tell Keet."

Avila laughed at me, figuring this is where I'd been heading this whole time. He showed me his middle finger again and, forgetting where we were, spat on his own carpet.

"You gonna tell me I can trust you? Limo driver? I'm gonna trust millions of dollars, the only leverage I got, to a fuckin' driver? Go on, get the fuck out of my house."

He took the remote and turned off the TV. The silence rang louder than the music.

"Keet told you how it's gonna go. He'll murder everyone around you. Nina. Everybody. He already tried to kill me and my dad. He won't stop. You think I'd risk my people for money?"

"Yeah," he said. "You totally thinking about your people. It's all about your people. You like a saint."

Delilah was right: that thought was foreign to Avila; he wasn't a soldier. I'd never be able to convince him of the responsibility I bore for the well-being of my people. As far as Avila was concerned, Keet cared just as much about his people as I did about mine. And Keet had hung one of his own in jail.

If Hippocrates were here he'd tell you that people can only be persuaded by things and feelings they experience for themselves.

I knew how to use that, how to persuade Avila he could trust me with those barrels.

But I really didn't want to do it.

Make the decision slowly; act upon it quickly.

I wasted a full minute hoping that one of my ghost voices would advise me, but the funny thing is, they've never once answered when I've asked a question.

I turned up the TV again and leaned toward Avila, who cupped his ear to listen.

"Think about everything that's happened; think how I might be in this as far as you. Think about how we could possibly be partners in this with equal interests. Consider it a fact. Then work backward to explain to yourself how it could be possible."

Avila was smart, but more important, he was cunning. He thought hard. He took his time.

And he realized what I was trying to tell him.

"Fuck," he said.

"Don't say it out loud," I said.

"You did that?"

"That's out loud."

Avila thought again, then turned off the TV.

"You had chances to make that fall on me and walk away clean," Avila said. "Why didn't you?"

"You stepped between me and that shotgun," I said. "That's why."

"Shit. You naive, brah. If I hadn't, Keet would've staked me out in the desert, drive nails into my head until I told him everything. I've seen him do it."

"Keet is a homicidal maniac," I said. "The police know that he killed your cousin. He killed your bodyguard. He killed Willeniec. And he tried to kill me and my dad."

"Keet killed Willeniec," Avila said, but he wasn't agreeing; he was telling me he understood the deal we were making.

Keet killed Willeniec . . .

I nodded. Deal.

I hoped the task force was listening, that Delilah could hear this.

"Let me think on this," Avila said. "You mind making me another sandwich before you go? This time don't be so afraid of the mustard."

SANCTUARIES

A week passes without violent incident—which sounds great but feels like somebody in the shadows pointing a crossbow at your chest. For whatever reason—instinct, paranoia, or some other internal logic that escapes me—I don't feel like it's Keet aiming that crossbow at my chest; I feel like it's the task force.

The good guys, I remind myself.

What does that make me?

Connie protested twice to the appropriate authorities, with no discernible effect, that Tinkertoy was being denied her civil rights to freedom, once for each time Tinkertoy's competency hearings were postponed without warning. Lucky and I consoled each other by speculating that Tinkertoy was safer in the loony bin than out in the wide world with the crossbows.

Delilah, peace be upon her forever, swam against the prevailing currents to open an investigation into X-Ray's jailhouse death.

Oasis Limousine Services had its own problems. We were struggling. Our mechanic was incarcerated in a psych ward, our dispatcher was morose because he'd lost half his body in the preceding two years, and the president of the company was wallowing in self-pity due to guilt and heartbreak.

"Connie will Come Around," Lucky told me as the two of us struggled to replace the brakes on the haunted Caddie (brakes that absolutely should not need replacing).

"I have an ethical question for you."

"How soon is it permissible for you to Engage in Sexual Relations with another woman?"

"Not a generic woman. A specific woman."

"The answer is *immediately*."

"The specific woman is Delilah."

"The answer is *never*."

"What's wrong with Delilah?"

"Nothing," Lucky whispered in my ear in case we were bugged, "excepting the Fact that she is not only Delilah; she is also Detective Groopman, a police officer who is endeavoring to catch you for murder."

"She's not endeavoring to catch *me*," I said, wasting my breath. "She's endeavoring to catch *somebody*."

"She's endeavoring to catch the murderer!" Lucky stabbed his finger into my chest several times to drive home the fact that the murderer was me, his breath moist in my ear.

I dragged Lucky out into the alley just to keep myself from busting off his finger. I explained that Delilah and I had undeniable chemistry. I told him about her throat when she swallows a cold beverage and the way she presses her lips together when she's flummoxed, her foul, foul language, and how many times she and I had both felt real heat but let it dissipate because of Connie.

"Correct behavior." Lucky sniffed.

I told him Delilah's theory about history people and surface-of-the-earth people and how we were both on the surface of the earth while Connie was not.

"I reject all systems for the Categorization of People," Lucky said.

"You mean like citizenship, religion, sex, nationality—?"

"You did not let me address my *but*."

"Fine, go."

"In this case, Delilah is Absolutely Correct. It is true that if you want Connie back, you must live a Larger Life."

"What?"

"You must reenter Politics."

"Seriously?"

"Don't misunderstand me. Connie is not shallow. It is not *appearances* she cares about. It is how you appear in her eyes because of the way she sees herself."

"You realize that's all about appearance, right?"

"Connie sees herself Striding Across History," Lucky said. "Who will stride by her side? A driver?"

"I tried politics," I said. "I didn't get anything done. This is better."

"This?" Lucky asked, laughing, gesturing at our surroundings, the fact that we were whispering in an alley behind a garage. "This is better?"

"Yes."

"This I know about women," Lucky said in an unbearable, superior tone because he considers women to be his undisputed area of expertise. "Connie will never forgive you if you Engage in a Romantic Relationship with her best friend."

I explained that Delilah should sleep with me, and keep it secret from Connie, because I'd given her a sworn eyewitness statement identifying Bogdan Milic, aka X-Ray, as the murderer of Avila's bodyguard, and because I provided her with invaluable information linking Keet to the murder of Avila's cousin Rocky, and because I'd given her at least circumstantial evidence that Willeniec had been working for Keet when he died.

We repeated a version of that conversation every day for a week.

On the eighth day, Nina called to inform me that Avila had the money he'd promised me if I could spare the time to come by the mansion.

I'd never expected to actually collect the ten grand Avila had promised me for driving him out to Keet's ranch.

"Put it in the mail," I said, but she'd already hung up.

I drove out to Calabasas to find the front gate fully functional but blackened with char marks. Lou and another green polo shirt were there. Lou wore a Kevlar vest and his sidearm was visible on his hip.

"Hi," I said. "What happened to the gate?"

"Vandals," Lou said, checking his clipboard.

"Vandals packing Molotov cocktails?"

"Correct."

"That explains the body armor and ostentatious display of firepower."

"You're cleared to go straight on up to the house, sir. Mr. Avila says to walk right in."

I saw three other green shirts on the way up to the house. A fourth met me at the door and escorted me up to Avila's office on the second floor and left us alone.

"Whassup, Mickey?" Avila said.

"Whassup, Biz?"

Avila winced in a way that indicated that he was choosing to be a good sport. Avila pushed an envelope across his gigantic glass-and-pewter desk. It felt like he was performing, so I took the hint and assumed that everything we did and said was for the benefit of an unseen audience.

"What's this?" I said.

"Severance check and bonus," Avila said. "Thanks for everything."

"Too bad about your gate," I said.

Avila started clicking on his laptop to indicate that we were done.

"That's a TV trope," I said.

"What?"

"Dismissing someone you're done with by going back to work as though they don't exist. People don't actually do that except on TV."

"Thanks for the etiquette lesson," Avila said. "I'm gonna miss you, brah." He grinned at me without blinking until I left his office.

Back at Oasis, Ripple opened the check (the size of which made Lucky whistle because Avila had, indeed, made good on his ten-thousand-dollar bonus offer). But the check wasn't the main event.

"Wait," Ripple said, unfolding a second piece of paper. "What's this?"

It was a drawing, apparently done by a child, of what looked like the mangled skeleton of a fish. Above that, to the left, was a cartoon figure of an airborne skateboarder with pink hair, apparently jumping onto an X surrounded by a circle of a dozen cats. A red half sun bled off the left side of the page.

Lucky looked at the drawing and furrowed his brow. "An electric schematic, a little girl, a cross, the sun, and a circle of civets."

"Wait. What's a civet?" Ripple asked.

Lucky pointed to the cats.

"Those are cats," Ripple said. "This is America. We don't have civets. We have cats."

"What makes you So Certain these are not raccoons or rats?"

"Split lip, bushy tail, whiskers, definitely cats! And this is an X, not a cross."

"I hate to pile on, Lucky," I said, indicating the skateboarder, "but this isn't a little girl either."

"She has pink hair!" Lucky said. "Girls may also ride skateboards, you know. As Ripple said, this is America."

I decided we should decamp to one of the vans, out in the yard where we couldn't be bugged but could still get Wi-Fi.

"It's not a little girl because it's Bismarck Avila," I said, taking up where we left off.

I told them about the video footage Avila had shown me of him winning the vertical ramp world championships with a broken back and bright pink hair.

"Wait. What are we even supposed to do with this drawing?" Ripple asked. "Say it's original art from Bismarck Avila and sell it on eBay?"

"It's a map," I said.

"What kind of map?"

"A treasure map. Avila's telling us where to find the barrels."

"Ah, X marks the spot, yes, of course," Lucky said.

The map was mostly drawn in black ink, but there were a few red lines in the schematic.

The pink hair had been done with a highlighter.

"Wait. If it's a map, it doesn't make any sense," Ripple said, opening his Jesus fanny pack and popping a candy into his mouth.

"You eat too many of those marijuana bonbons," Lucky said. "It's a miracle anything makes sense to you."

"This map is intended to make sense to one person in the world," I said.

"Who?"

"Me."

"Does it make sense to you?"

For a map to be a map, it has to have a context. A landmark, for example, or labels. Like any code, a map requires a key; otherwise, it's just lines. The doodle was Avila, as a kid, on a skateboard, little squiggly lines putting him in motion.

I indicated the bottom right corner of the page. The only word written on Avila's map:

ROBBED!

All in caps, red ink, and with Avila's ubiquitous exclamation mark.

"There's the key," I said.

"Wait. What's that supposed to tell us?"

"Avila's reminding me that he got robbed when he was a kid by surfers in Lake Elsinore," I said.

"There's no place to surf in Lake Elsinore!"

A line extended from *ROBBED!* northward to a carefully drawn circle, obviously traced around a nickel.

"If that's Lake Elsinore, then this circle is Grand Boulevard in Corona," I said. "Which makes this line the 15."

"Wait, the lines are streets?"

Another line clipped the northern edge of the circle and extended almost all the way to the left side of the pages where Avila and the cats lived.

"The Western Reaches," Lucky said.

The main right-to-left line that started in Corona would be the 91. I followed that line westward with my finger: a short line angled up, then a short line angled down, then another short line angled down, and then another short line crossed the east-west line, and then, approximately halfway across the map, a jagged black line extended across the entire piece of paper from the bottom right to the top left.

Ripple pulled up a map of Corona on his computer. He placed Corona on the right side of his screen and pulled out until the Pacific Ocean was on the left side. We all tried to find roads, streets, or highways that corresponded with the overlay of lines on Avila's map.

"Anybody got anything?" I asked. Because to my eye, nothing lined up.

"Wait!" Ripple said. "Maybe Lucky's right and this is a civet and we should be looking at a map of Kabul."

But Lucky, trained in code breaking, among everything else, had a different take.

"This map is drawn without Care or Exactitude."

"Wait, what?"

"I am saying that it is symbolic in nature, not representational."

"Wait, what?"

"Lucky's saying that Avila's a civilian. Which is true. He doesn't measure distances and time the way soldiers do. Avila measures distance by how far it feels to him and time by how bored he is."

"That makes for one shitty-ass map," Ripple said.

"Hugely Shitty-Ass," Lucky said. "So let us assume that these lines are major thoroughfares but drawn to a totally subjective scale by a Drunken, Frightened man."

Brilliant.

The lines jutting up and down from the 91 could be labeled 71 and 57 to the north and 241, 55, and 57 to the south.

"Wait," Ripple said. "That makes this dark red line going from the bottom right to the top left Interstate 5."

The 605 was a short line transecting our main line, as was the 710. Our main line terminated at another inked line, which we decided was the 110 because that was where the 91 terminated. Intersecting the 110 was another line, which extended back to the east but did not reach the dominant red line we'd decided was the 5. Ripple grunted in appreciation when it turned out that the actual, real-life 105, which crossed the 110, did not extend all the way to the 5.

"I feel confident we have Broken the Code," Lucky said.

Lucky indicated another heavily inked red line extending on a slight angle right to left from the bottom of the page to the top.

"This is the 405."

Which meant that the X surrounded by cats was nestled just south of the 105 and just east of the 405.

"A Literal Crossroads," Lucky said.

As life is wont to do, it circles back to the beginning of things; origins and endings happen in the same place, like echoes or jumping. Bismarck Avila had aimed himself like a teenage missile away from where he'd grown up, but if we'd cracked the Avila code, then the barrels were just across the 105 from his old stomping grounds in Lennox.

"Wait. What do we do now?"

"Treasure hunt," I said.

Lucky and I chose to take the same Transit I'd used to transport Willeniec's body in case we found the barrels on our first try. Meanwhile, Ripple was complaining because he was not invited.

"My nuts don't hurt at all," Ripple protested.

I explained that Oasis was still a business, albeit a failing one, and needed someone manning the phone, but still the only thing that kept Ripple from coming along was jamming a broomstick through his wheelchair spokes and making a run for it.

It turned out that all he missed by staying in the office was traffic and frustration. Lucky and I drove for more than an hour and covered a measly ten miles.

We drove on the 405.

We drove on the 105.

We drove on all the various exit and entrance ramps in the area to and from every direction possible. There weren't even any of those barrels that Caltrans fills with water and places in various escape lanes and dead ends as a buffer for runaway vehicles.

We approached on surface streets from Avila's hometown, Lennox, thinking maybe we'd see something more clearly from his point of view.

"No cats," Lucky said. "No barrels."

We circled around all the surrounding streets in Hawthorne. We stood on 116th Street and stared up at the 405 above us; then we pretended to have engine trouble on the 405 and stared down at where the X marked the spot. We pulled into the parking lot of the New Life Community Church and stared at the treasure map and Ripple's printouts, and we stood eating Jack in the Box, watching a bunch of middle-aged Hispanic men play kickball on a vacant lot just off where the Imperial Highway (note: it is neither imperial nor a highway) intersects with Inglewood Avenue, telling each other that this was the precise location of the X.

No barrels.

No cats.

"I got it wrong," I said.

We piled into the Transit to head back to Oasis Limo, where Ripple informed us that our failure was pure karma. If we'd taken him, he'd have spotted the barrels or the cats because he was young and we were not and, by the way, the phone had not rung once.

I recommended that we grab a late lunch at Callahan's. But before we could even order, Lucky got a call from Connie (knife in my heart). Lucky nodded, asked a few questions, and then hung up.

"That was Connie," Lucky said.

"We suspected around the time you said, 'Hello, Connie,' that it might be Connie," Ripple said.

"She has obtained permission for us to visit Tinkertoy," Lucky said. He went on to say that Tinkertoy was no longer being held at Harbor-UCLA hospital in Torrance because Connie had worked magic to have Tinkertoy transferred to the West LA Veterans Administration hospital.

Ripple groaned. He'd done time there at Prosthetic Services being fitted and enduring painful rehab.

The VA encompasses more than 380 acres of prime real estate

adjacent to the upscale neighborhood of Brentwood. Aside from the main hospital, the VA was an almighty jumble of old buildings, bungalows, sheds, temporary structures more than fifty years old, and new office buildings—many of which are leased out to hotel laundries, movie studios, a rich private school's athletic complex, car rental companies, storage for a charter bus company, an oil-drilling company, and other properties that the VA shares with like-minded community organizations.

I figured we'd be forced to meet with Tinkertoy in a depressing puke-green interview room at the main psych unit, but Lucky said that her doctors were allowing us to meet outside in the fresh air, in a place Tinkertoy had chosen herself: the Parrot Sanctuary.

The Parrot Sanctuary is adjacent to Jackie Robinson Stadium, the best ballpark in Los Angeles. Old-school. Surrounded by eucalyptus. Free parking.

I was worried that Ripple might find the dirt track leading from the parking lot to the Parrot Sanctuary hard sledding in his wheelchair, but he said he felt fine and told me to please stop pushing him when I thought he wouldn't notice.

We heard the Parrot Sanctuary long before we saw it. By the time we approached the five-foot wrought-iron fence around the sanctuary, we'd given up trying to talk. We stopped at a sign proclaiming SERENITY PARK—VETERANS STILL CARING FOR LIFE in patriotic red, white, and blue lettering, flanked by plywood cutouts of two colorful parrots, and wondered what to do next.

I peeked through the gate.

Tinkertoy sat bolt upright near some potted plants at a French café–style table with a faded tile top, the screened-in parrot cages rising behind her. She wore an Army sweat suit with black civilian flip-flops, a huge blue-and-gold bird perched on her forearm, biting her hair, then tucking its head into the hollow of her neck beneath her ear.

Just like that, all the birds stopped squawking at the same time.

"Allah be praised," Lucky said.

"Tinkertoy," I called, giving her plenty of warning from thirty feet away.

Tinkertoy looked up.

I'd been apprehensive that when we came face-to-face, Tinkertoy might be so heavily drugged and traumatized that I wouldn't be able to see the spark of herself in her dark eyes. But even though Tinkertoy didn't smile or wave when she saw us, everything was fine—because there she was.

I could not have been more surprised when both Lucky and Ripple got wet eyes as they approached and the three of them huddled together, heads bumping, hugging, saying nothing, while the parrot screeched in jealousy, setting off the whole flock again.

A dozen feet away stood an orderly. Not a big, scary guy, like you might expect to keep Tinkertoy in line if she went berserk; a small Filipino, all in white, with a big smile, who nodded at me, obviously enjoying the reunion.

The parrot nipped Lucky's ear and they separated. I walked over to Tinkertoy. She hugged me and whispered in my ear, "I didn't. Say anything. Nothing."

The Filipino orderly, who identified himself as Walter, dug up another two chairs, and the four of us sat together at the wobbly café table like we were waiting to be served coffee and pastries.

"One of those parrots is missing a wing," Ripple said, pointing at some birds sitting on what looked to be obstacle-course netting from boot camp, "and that one is missing a foot."

Tinkertoy mostly wanted to hear what she'd missed but succumbed to Lucky's incessant questions. Yes, she'd been sedated, but, thanks to Connie, she hadn't been pumped full of any of the buffalo-stomping, drool-making psychotropics.

"Connie. Says. I'll get out. If. I. Move," Tinkertoy said.

"Wait, like, to another city?" Ripple asked.

"I'm guessing they want you out of your crazy-lady hidey-hole at the back of the garage," I said.

Tinkertoy nodded.

"We'll find you a better place," I said.

Tinkertoy argued that she loved her cubby. That it suited her. That she felt safe back there. Lucky suggested that Tinkertoy take his half of the duplex and he would move in with Ripple. Ripple's protests and fury and invective were accepted by everyone as de rigueur and nonbinding.

"That bird sure does love you," I said.

"His name. Is. Bacardi," Tinkertoy said. She pointed to others. Joey. Molly. Dandelion.

"Wait. Five of these birds got yellow heads," Ripple said, "but it's the mangy gray bird who gets named Dandelion?"

Ripple and Tinkertoy argued about Dandelion for five minutes. It felt wonderful to close my eyes and listen to my people bicker, forget about elusive barrels, murderous cops, broken hearts, betrayed friendships, cop corpses, psycho teens, and broke-back skateboard moguls.

"When. I get out," Tinkertoy said. "I want. To come back."

"Wait, you mean this parrot place, or your rubber room in the hospital?"

Walter tutted gently from where he stood, pretending not to listen, twenty feet away.

"Every single. Day," Tinkertoy insisted.

Ripple pointed out that, wait, everyone wanted to go somewhere every single day but they can't, can they, because they have jobs and who would drive her? Tinkertoy said she used to be in transport. She could drive any vehicle put in front of her.

"What about an Ohio-class nuclear attack submarine?" Ripple asked. "You pretty confident you could drive that off the lot?"

Walter caught my eye and tapped his wrist even though he wasn't wearing a watch. I nodded.

Trying to delay our departure, Tinkertoy wanted to know what we were going to do next. Lucky told her about the map and she asked to look at it. Ripple and Lucky tag-teamed Tinkertoy with their theories and where we'd gone and how it wasn't working and how fucked it was that we couldn't call Avila to tell him his useless map sucked.

Tinkertoy blinked at the map.

I said, "Time to go." Walter nodded his thanks.

Tinkertoy said, "X isn't. What. You look for."

Ripple started in on how of course X marks the spot—that's what a treasure map is—all X's mark the spot.

"I mean. X isn't. What you. Look for *first*."

"What do we look for first? Cats?"

"Skateboarder," she said. "Who. Takes you to. Cats."

Well, that was crazy.

"I was. In transport," Tinkertoy reminded us. "I. Know. Bad maps."

A breeze blew up through the eucalyptus and I heard Willeniec rasp, *She'srightshe'sright.*

"Thanks," I said.

"Sorry. About you. And Connie," Tinkertoy said.

Jesus, how dire was my romantic situation that Connie and Tinkertoy were discussing it during downtime between psychiatric hearings?

"If she knew. The truth. She'd forgive. You," Tinkertoy said.

"No, Tinkertoy," I said, lowering my voice in case Walter had bat ears. "There's only one way we get through this and it doesn't involve telling an idealistic officer of the court what actually happened."

"Tree falls in the forest," Lucky said.

"I told Connie. You're. A good. Man. But she said. I don't take. Advice. About men. From lesbians. In. The loony bin."

I laughed. Tinkertoy patted my arm. I kissed her hand. She (in the nicest possible way) wiped her hand on her shirt.

There was a honk from outside the gate. It was an unmarked gray van. The backseats were separated from the driver by a heavy mesh screen.

"Our ride is here, Rose," Walter said.

"Leave. All your money. In the donation can," Tinkertoy ordered as she followed Walter to the van and drove away, Walter waving, Tinkertoy staring ahead through the screen like it wasn't there, probably wishing she could take the wheel and drive herself, the way she was trained.

I left what I had in my wallet in the donation can. Fifty bucks toward the welfare of a bunch of squawking birds.

Lucky put in eight dollars.

Ripple left thirty-five cents, three stale Twizzlers, and a pot cookie. I snuck the cookie out and tossed it in the garbage, worried somebody would feed it to the caged birds and they'd freak out.

WE ARE ALL MADE
OF DIRT

Back in the Transit, heading west along Wilshire, leaving the Veterans Administration behind, Lucky and Ripple are doubtful when I tell them that I think Tinkertoy is right.

"About parrots?"

"About the map," I said.

"Wait, we already checked there," Ripple said.

"We already checked there for barrels. Let's say Tinkertoy is right. Instead of looking for barrels, let's look for skateboarders."

"Skateboarders who will lead us to a place full of civets?" Lucky asked.

"Cats."

"I have a vague memory of a skate park," Lucky said. "Perhaps you could . . . ?" Lucky tapped on Ripple's phone. Ripple extended his middle finger at Lucky, then hunched over, using all his bony fingers on his phone, like a touch typist, instead of one meaty index-finger jab at a time, the way I do it.

"Eucalyptus Skate Plaza," Ripple said. "Inglewood and 120th."

Because we were crawling along in traffic, Ripple took the time to inform us that the park had originally been named after Mayor Larry Guidi.

"Until Larry stole city property and got charged with felony theft," Ripple said.

"What did Larry steal?"

"A rusted-out, broken-down, twenty-quart cement mixer. But that was enough to rename the park Eucalyptus Skate Plaza."

I dumped out of the 405 southbound traffic at Manchester onto La Cienega to hit the surface streets.

"Perhaps we'd do better with a Fresh Start tomorrow?" Lucky suggested.

"If you're hungry, just say so," Ripple said.

"I am Extremely Hungry," Lucky said. "I suggested A New Day only because it will be dark in less than an hour."

"Mayor Larry's skate park has lights and stays open until nine P.M."

"What if that setting sun on the map isn't there to tell us it's the west?" I asked. "What if it's there to tell us to be there at sunset?"

LAX slid by on the right; the 105 slid by overhead; we crossed Imperial Highway, passed a county courthouse, some apartment buildings, and a low-slung office building and crossed into a residential area.

"Left on 120th," Ripple said, glued to his phone.

We were in an area of house-proud one- and two-bedroom bungalows, reasonably late-model cars sheltered under carports, and older cars parked on the street.

"End of the street, straight ahead," Ripple said.

I pulled over two car lengths from the intersection of 121st and Inglewood beside a house with a tall, red, wooden fence. I turned off the Transit and we regarded the skate park through the windshield, the light angling down behind us while palm trees swayed in the breeze that rises as the sun goes down.

There were half a dozen young skateboarders in Larry's park: three boys, two unknowns, one girl. They were goofing around on the rails and ledges, intimidated, while older kids skated around the concrete bowls, trying not to collide with BMX bicycles.

"What's the plan?" Lucky asked.

"When one of these kids leaves, we'll follow him."

"To a cat refuge?"

"Wait, which kid will we follow?"

"Avila was fifteen, sixteen when he had pink hair. So forget all the little kids."

I had my eye on a boy and a girl, early high school age, the boy a skater, the girl a BMXer, both of whom left the fenced-in and supervised skate park to smoke cigarettes in the church parking lot next door.

"I'm starving," Ripple said.

"It's all the THC in your system," Lucky said disapprovingly.

"Fine," I said, "I'll stay here and watch while you two find a drive-through and—"

The lights in the skate park went on. The groms clapped but the boy and the girl I'd marked earlier obviously considered the lights a kind of signal and headed off together, directly away from us, across the grass, southeast across the park.

"Bogeys on the move," I said. "I'll follow them on foot, keep you apprised by cell phone; you guys station yourselves up ahead, out of sight."

I jumped out of the car and set off after them because I didn't want a debate.

Once off the grass on the other side of the park, the skater slammed down his board and hung on to his cyclist friend's saddle as she pedaled down a street, duplexes on one side and an apartment building on the other. They took a left at the next intersection, keeping to the sidewalk.

"East on Broadway," I said into my phone.

"We are ahead of you," Lucky said, "because the circle of civets is drawn to the east of the skateboarding little girl on the Map of Shit."

I saw the Transit was already parked ahead of the boy and the girl up on Hawthorne Boulevard.

They turned south again, both walking now, talking intently about something, though I couldn't make out distinct words.

They left the road and headed along a railway easement.

"Train tracks," I muttered into my phone.

They balanced along the rails, then shrunk into the deepening shadows against a graffiti-covered board fence, lighting cigarettes out of range of the streetlights thirty yards to the west.

Negatory. The smell was not tobacco.

Then they started making out.

I worried that my bogeys might hunker down for sex and drugs, but they disengaged and kept moving along a footpath beside the tracks, passing the joint back and forth, then jaywalked across Hawthorne. Lucky had guessed right again; the Transit was parked in a near-deserted parking area a block to the south.

"Your phone tell you what that dark building is?" I asked Ripple.

"It's a mall," Ripple said.

"Pretty damned depressed mall."

"It's abandoned."

"The whole mall is deserted?"

"Condemned and restricted. No public access."

Ahead of me, now on the north side of the tracks along the south end of the deserted mall, the bogeys finished the remainder of the joint, the skater ate the last soggy bit, and the biker clambered up a frost fence with barbed wire at the top and executed an impressive flip to land on her feet on the other side. The boy tossed his skateboard over, which the girl caught, then threw her bike—the girl ran from the bike instead of catching it, and the two of them doubled over in laughter, mellow and high, until the boy used the same technique as the girl to flip over the fence. Arms around each other's waists, they melted into the darkness between the deserted mall and a looming parking garage, destitute and deserted.

"Guard," Lucky warned me.

I pressed up against a concrete abutment across the track from the fence surrounding the mall. The guard was approaching from Hawthorne, but he was inside the fence, walking the perimeter. When he aimed his flashlight into the shadowed area between the parking structure and the mall, the bogeys were nowhere to be seen: nothing but weeds and detritus and crap and litter.

And a dozen pairs of red eyes staring at him before slipping away, first to shadow, then to nothing.

"Cats," I said into my phone. "Lots of cats."

"What now?" Lucky asked.

"I'll come to you."

I trotted along the railway back to well-lit Hawthorne, turned left, and got into the Transit with Lucky and Ripple.

"There's a ten-foot fence," I said, "barbed wire at the top."

"No razor wire?"

"Just rusty, dull stuff, easy to get over if you're wearing a jacket or a hoodie."

"I'm wearing a hoodie," Ripple said.

I explained that it wasn't exactly set up for the physically challenged.

"Wait, I know it's a pain, but don't make me stay in the car."

"Fine," I said.

Lucky had a tiny flashlight, but we figured if he used it the security guard would see us.

"The skaters come here when the lights go on at the skate park because they had to sneak in Under Cover of Darkness," Lucky said. "We must do the same."

I'll spare you the *Jackass* images of us getting Ripple down the train tracks and over the barbed wire while avoiding (in the following order) a train, three curious homeless people, a thousand feral cats, two security guards, and finally (I shit you not) a group of Satanists conducting a cat-sacrifice ritual on a spray-painted pentagram in the basement of the abandoned parking garage.

When Lucky ran at them, this solemn, occult gathering yelped and cursed and ran, stumbling over their stupid black robes, made from sheets or Halloween costumes, piling into somebody's mom's minivan, and screeched away, leaving behind a dead cat and a dozen burning black candles.

"Creep me out or what?" Ripple said.

"Terrible," Lucky said.

"We'll check back on the way out. If they're here, we'll sacrifice them to Satan and see how they like it."

"Avila must have driven in here the way they did," Lucky said.

We wound our way up the stairs to the second-highest level of the parking structure, where the chasm between us and the mall was spanned by three concrete pedestrian ramps. The ramps were obstructed by twenty-foot chain-link fences bolted to the concrete. In order to get around the barricade, it would be necessary to swing out over the thirty-foot abyss.

Of course a slightly stoned daredevil skater kid wouldn't think twice about the danger. Ripple offered to go first, maintaining that he wasn't afraid either.

"Because you have no legs," Lucky said, "you are high, and you have remarkable upper body strength."

"Avila came here alone with barrels," I said. "Assuming he either rolled them or brought a dolly, how'd he cross?"

We checked the barricades again, risking Lucky's flashlight.

One of them had been cut along the sides, and the bottom could be lifted like a large flap, far enough even for Ripple to get through in his wheelchair. After that, we simply crossed the concrete ramp to the mall the way thousands of shoppers had back in the early nineties when the place was a going commercial concern and the parking lot was used for parking, not sacrificing cats to the Dark Lord.

A trot around the eastern and southern sides of the mall (the northern and western sides were on busy, well-lit streets) confirmed that all of the entrances were welded shut. There was graffiti everywhere, graffiti on graffiti, some political (OBAMARAMA), some sexual (ANAL ROOLZ!), some existential (LIFE IS DA SHITZ), and some religious (JESUS SAVES AT BANK OF AMERICA).

"Now what?" Ripple asked. "Pound on a door until someone lets us in?"

I suggested that we station ourselves up against a dark wall at the southern end of the mall, where we could keep an eye on the entire eastern expanse of the mall and wait for a regular to show us the way.

Less than fifteen minutes later, a figure approached along the nearest pedestrian walkway, swung out over the chasm and back onto the ramp like a gibbon, and headed away from us along the outside of the mall.

"I'll go," said Lucky.

He disappeared into the shadows like an Afghan cat and returned five minutes later to lead us along the outside of the mall, passing two sets of welded doors before shining his flashlight on a mural-size rendering of a demon with his mouth wide open. Over the demon was a slogan in bloodred paint.

"'We Are All Made of Dirt,'" Ripple read.

Lucky, grinning, thrust his arm in and out of the demon's mouth to show that it was not, in fact, painted black, but was an actual hole leading into the mall.

We folded Ripple's wheelchair and Lucky muscled it through the demon's mouth while I played St. Christopher and carried baby Jesus Ripple through on my back. Lucky felt the need to tell me that he disagreed with the demon: "We are not all made of dirt. We are Divine in Origin."

"Just because you go through a doorway doesn't mean you agree with what's written above it," I said. "Work doesn't set you free. Disneyland isn't actually the happiest place on earth, and half the time I go through a door it's labeled NO ENTRY."

Once inside and past a glut of refuse and clutter, we stood a moment to let our eyes adjust.

Light pollution dribbled in from holes in the roof, enough to reveal a dim, rambling expanse of space marked by concrete columns and steel beams and treacherous holes in the floor meant for escalators and stairways or viewing galleries where shoppers could lean over and see what people were buying on the next level down.

And everywhere, the feathery shadows of cats, the smell of cat piss, dull red eyes watching us from the shadows.

"Hear that?" Lucky asked.

Yes. Music and hoots of derision or admiration from somewhere to the left, to the south.

Firelight flickered up from the main concourse beneath us.

Away from the walls and pillars, the concrete floor was surprisingly clear and Ripple demanded to be put back in his chair so he could roll himself. When we reached the fire hole, he gave me the heebie-jeebies by rolling right up to the edge so that he could look down to where thirty or more kids stood around a two-story plywood vertical ramp extending from the second floor down to the basement and back up again—utilizing what must once have been the food court.

The whole postapocalyptic, adolescent festival was lit by an array of hissing camp lanterns, heavy-duty flashlights, candles, a smoky barrel fire, traffic flares, and multiple strings of Christmas and Halloween lights rigged to a couple of car batteries.

"I hope when we get back to the Transit," Lucky said, reading my mind, "that there is still a battery in it."

"This is awesome," Ripple said.

Lucky made a near-silent whistle sound to get my attention and pointed.

The ends of the ramp were held in place by barrels. A dozen to sixteen per side. Ballast, to keep the ramp from shifting no matter how vigorous, fat, or numerous the skaters.

"They must pay the guard to look the other way," Lucky whispered.

"I'm guessing they pay him off in cheeba," Ripple said, indicating the haze of smoke heading toward holes chopped in the roof.

"Let's say howdy," I said.

As we descended the long-frozen escalator, me bumping Ripple down in his wheelchair, it seemed like the kids all saw us at the exact same time, concerned but not fearful, like a flock of birds seeing a cat who can't get at them. Lots of jerking chins.

I counted six under age fifteen—including the young couple who'd unwittingly led us here—maybe a dozen over eighteen, the rest in between, two boys for every girl, black kids, a few white kids, brown kids, fewer Asians, but the vast majority was a mix, undefinable, the future.

"The fuck?"

"You cops?"

"Stupid! Cops don't have no handicaps."

"They sure as fuck didn't come to skate."

Lucky explained that before he lost his legs in Afghanistan,

Ripple had been a serious skater. He'd read about this place online and wanted to come and see it, and we, his friends from work, had brought him to check it out.

Ripple nodded, playing his part.

"You get blown up?" one girl said, swaddled in Balkan military surplus, tilting back her head so she could regard Ripple from beneath her mirror aviators.

"Shot by a sniper," Ripple said, indicating his right leg. "Run over by a tank," indicating his left.

"Can I touch?" she asked, indicating Ripple's right stump, visible in the leg of his cargo shorts. She said it in a frankly sexual manner, which Ripple did not miss.

"Come and get it," he said.

And she did. But at the last moment she deked and reached way up for the much shorter left stump.

I looked at Lucky. He shrugged. The girl was obviously legal, over eighteen, pretty if a little dirty, tattoos on all the skin we could see, all up her arms and chest, her neck, and up into her hairline.

Freaky girl. None of which mattered to Ripple if the grin on his face was any indication as she groped him.

"All righty, then," said one heavily pierced young man, his earlobes stretched out and elongated by wooden disks. "It's good to be kind to our returning veterans."

The rest of the kids shrugged us off and drifted away to do what they'd been doing when we arrived. Skating. Screwing in the shadows. Smoking dope. Eating mushrooms. Taking pills. Telling each other stories.

"Did it hurt?" the girl asked Ripple, finally pulling her hand out of his pants.

"What's your name?" Ripple asked.

"Kink." (Very apt.)

"What's your real name?"

"Fuck-you is my real name. What's your name?"

"Ripple."

"What's your real name?"

"Darren."

She started laughing at that, but Ripple reached down to scratch the stump of his leg, which shut her up immediately, the way a spark of fire stops an arsonist dead.

Lucky muttered, "What is happening?"

"You okay here?" I asked Ripple.

He looked at me like I was nuts.

"Because if you are," I continued, "then me and Lucky will take a look around, check back with you later," at which point Ripple understood that I was being a good wingman.

"Later," he said.

"If I sit on your lap, will you take me for a ride?" Kink asked.

Ripple agreed that might be fun for both of them.

It took a lot less time to find Avila's barrels than you'd think: all but two of the many barrels stabilizing the ends of the vertical ramp were open, full of rubble, rebar, broken chunks of masonry, bricks, and garbage. Only two were welded shut.

Lucky removed the filler plug from one of the barrels and leaned over, flashlight pressed up to one eye, to look inside the barrel.

"Yes," he said, replacing the plug. "How do we get them out of here?"

"We don't," I said. "We tell Keet where they are and let him worry about it."

We headed back to where we'd left Ripple with the amputee fetishist, only to find half a dozen mall-rat skater kids rolling Ripple and Kink, both in his wheelchair, Kink straddling Ripple, up and down the vert ramp.

"He looks pretty happy," Lucky said.

At which point Kink grabbed Ripple's face and stuck her pierced tongue down his throat.

"Let's give him a minute," I said.

We sat against a column in the shadows.

"Grace Quan's mother is Korean," Lucky said, "but her father is Chinese. They moved here because of the stigma."

"Stigma? Against Koreans?"

"Yes, something to do with China and baseball. Grace's mother is a doctor and her father is a businessman. Grace defied her father to follow in her mother's footsteps."

"Her father is disappointed his daughter is a *doctor*?"

"Grace's father also blames her mother for the decision. Grace's mother is angry at Grace for causing a rift between her and her husband."

"Thanksgiving at the Quan house must be a blast."

"And they won't help her with her student loans."

"What did you do? Interrogate the woman?"

"I'm just pointing out that she is a lonely person and so deserving of kindness."

"Hippocrates would define Dr. Quan as a combination of *Melancholic* and *Phlegmatic*."

"That sounds very nice," Lucky said.

"It means she's thoughtful, patient, peaceful, analytical, and serious," I said, "but there's always a danger that she could fall into a sense of despondency."

"I believe I am a good Bulwark Against Despondency," Lucky said.

"That's for sure," I said. Which Lucky took to mean he and Gracie Quan had my blessing.

Five minutes later, Ripple pushed Kink off his lap and rolled over to see us, red-faced, sweating, and thrilled.

"I'm staying here tonight."

"We found the barrels."

"Good news. I'm staying here tonight."

"Ripple," I said, "just to be clear, you do realize that what you're dealing with here is a fetishist, right?"

He wanted to know what that was. Lucky told him it was someone with a very particular sexual taste, or even compulsion, Bordering on Perversion. I explained to Ripple that Kink obviously had a thing for amputees.

"More good news," he said. "Because I happen to be a double amputee. Triple, if you count my ball."

Ripple asked if we thought Kink might want to have sex with him tonight.

"I thought you did already," Lucky said.

"Ripple," I started—

Lucky was sorry to interrupt but wanted to remind me that Ripple was older than he looked, a war veteran, a divorced man, that he'd recently undergone surgery, and that I wasn't even his commanding officer, much less his parent, so I should allow him to make his own decisions.

"Call me when you need to be picked up," I said.

"Thanks, Dad," Ripple said.

"Do you have condoms in that Jesus fanny pack?"

"Glow in the dark."

"Because you don't want any other body parts falling off."

"Got it."

"Don't you start smoking cigarettes or chewing tobacco again to look cool," Lucky said. "Remember how hard it was for you to quit?"

"Thanks for the awesome advice, Mom," Ripple said.

Fifteen minutes later, after escaping the secret adolescent postapocalyptic world that had sprouted up in what Lucky called a Forgotten Palace of Materialism, we were in the Transit and headed home.

After a thoughtful silence, Lucky and I traded our kinkiest sexual experiences (we were soldiers once, and young). Lucky's trumped mine (kind of a traditionalist here), but we both knew that when we next saw Ripple he'd have us both beat in the kinky-sex department and we swore that we would never ask him for generalities, much less details.

DOG-PADDLING

I do not sleep well. Even though there's a cool breeze from the ocean, fresh sea air wafting through the penthouse, I toss and turn. I know I've always been insane in the middle of the night, even more so after returning from The Wars, something to do with the brain chemicals (or lack thereof) that diminish perspective and priorities and balance. I feel that the task force is watching me and that Keet is lying in wait for me and somehow they have put aside their differences and are working together against me.

After skipping rope for half an hour and breakfast and coffee, I descended from my sanctuary on the roof to find Lucky waiting in the bays.

"Aha," he said. I recognized the accusation in his voice, and he was right—I'd had every intention of sneaking off to Keet's ranch in the hopes of persuading Keet not to kill us all if we returned the barrels of money that Rakim had stolen from him.

When I told Lucky that there was no use in risking both our

lives, he cursed in Kashmiri, which I recognized but until then did not know Lucky spoke. He switched to English to reason with me. "If one person goes, Keet will believe the Situation is Contained. If two go, subconsciously Keet will feel that the Cat is Out of the Bag and, in fact, be less likely to kill two than one."

"I honestly can't tell if you're deeply insightful," I said, "or head gaming me. Also, when did you learn to speak Kashmiri?"

Lucky said, "I'll drive."

We agreed to take the Caddie.

We grabbed coffee and doughnuts to go from Callahan's before the two-and-a-half-hour drive. Lucky didn't start in on me until we passed downtown.

"I don't suppose you've Considered The Alternative of anonymously informing law enforcement of the barrel location?"

"Keet gets the barrels in return for not killing us. What do we get if the cops get to that money first?"

"Killed?"

"That's my math."

Lucky took this as a sign that we should indulge in a call-and-response discussion of all our options (as if I hadn't been doing that all night).

Call Keet anonymously and tell him where to find the barrels? No way the task force hasn't got Keet bugged; he'll know that and treat us as though we handed the barrels to the police and then kill us.

Take possession of the barrels ourselves and bring them to Keet? Keet thanks us for the moola and then kills us.

Take possession of the barrels and hide them from Keet and Avila and take our time to consider alternatives. Thus making ourselves a much more attractive target than Avila.

Steal the money for ourselves; or, as Lucky put it, "Beginning Life Anew in Alien Environs is the Only Plan which guarantees our survival."

"All four of us?" I asked. "One normal guy, a handsome but diminutive Afghan, an orange-haired, stoner teenage double amputee, and a lunatic black Amazon goddess? You figure we'd meld in pretty well no matter where we went, do you?"

"We could," Lucky said.

"Leaving Avila to face Keet alone?"

"I realize you are a Man of Honor," Lucky said, "but you are not admitting to your Real Reason for not taking the money and absconding. Which is the fact that you have not given up on Connie. Or is it Detective Groopman you haven't given up on?"

"All of the above," I admitted.

We turned south on the 15 and pulled over for more coffee at a Western-style cafe in Norco. (Lucky loves any diner that looks like it was built for the gold rush.)

In the parking lot, Lucky informed me that he felt we should confront Keet armed and wearing body armor.

"You don't think that'll provoke him?" I asked.

"Keet should know that it will cost him to fight us. I wish I could strap a nuclear weapon to my back."

"Really dedicated to playing into Muslim stereotypes, huh?"

Lucky informed me that he'd placed a duffel bag with suitable weaponry in the Caddie's trunk (which meant not only that he'd known where we were going and that I'd agree to bring him along but which vehicle we would take).

As we approached Temecula, I made a call to Delilah.

"Delilah, am I under surveillance?"

"Why the fuck would I tell you?"

"What about Keet?"

"Why would I discuss that with you?"

"Are you set up to tail Keet if he leaves Harbor Ranch?"

"Why do you keep asking me questions?"

"Trust me."

"Like the last fucking time I trusted you?"

"Delilah," I said, "you know I'm dog-paddling the best I can in deep, muddy, snake-infested waters. That's why you aren't really mad at me. You get it. Surface of the earth, right? So trust me, put a watcher at the end of Keet's road, make yourself a hero, get promoted to Robbery-Homicide."

Delilah hung up.

Because she hadn't come at me with another question, I didn't feel delusional in assuming that the abrupt cutoff meant she'd rushed off to make things happen, not that she had decided to ignore me.

"You intend for Keet to attain the barrels and immediately be arrested?" Lucky said.

"That'd be the second-best outcome."

"And first would be . . . ?"

"Keet dies in a shootout with police."

A couple of miles before Keet's unmarked private turnoff from Highway 16, where his security cameras began covering the long approach to Harbor Ranch, I pulled the Caddie over into a Caltrans gravel pit so we could pull on our bulletproof vests and check our weapons. Lucky had packed his trusty Smith & Wesson nine millimeter and, for me, my two favorites: a fairly new old-fashioned Ruger Redhawk revolver with speed loader (slow but accurate and dependable) and my show-offy high-tech Taurus 24/7. We argued the various merits of our weapons as we had every single time we put them on, a highly recommended way of not thinking both about what the weapons might have to be used for and about how the best-laid plans could go very wrong.

Lucky didn't like the isolated nature of Keet's ranch any more than I did.

"Tell you what makes it even better," I said. "The son of a bitch has at least half an hour warning we're coming."

"Good."

"Good?"

"Nothing beneficial ever resulted from Startling a Psychopath. Would you like to discuss our plan?" Lucky asked.

"Stay alive long enough to tell Keet where to find the barrels, get the hell out, let the task force do the rest, live happily ever after."

"The Merits of a Simple Plan," Lucky said.

We passed beneath the Harbor Ranch sign with its crossed cannons. Approaching Keet's home, we saw that a couple of his expensive King palms were now blackened stumps. There was a slight depression and discoloration of the ground where I'd blown up his Harley.

I stopped the Caddie equidistant between the Quonset huts and the crazy log cabin, angled for quick escape, left the engine running, and exited at the exact same time as Lucky. We'd learned long ago the benefits of simultaneously appearing both formidable and nonthreatening. Yes, we were wearing vests and carrying guns dangling at our sides, but our expressions said, *We are willing and able to wreak violence but would rather not.*

We stepped away from the car, spreading out but ready to leap behind the Caddie for cover if the situation deteriorated into a bag of dicks.

All of this impressive, psychologically effective choreography turned to liquid birds' turds when Keet kicked the screen door of his cabin open, swung a SMAW up to his shoulder, and fired a rocket into the Caddie, causing a primary explosion that knocked me to the ground, followed by a secondary explosion when the gas tank *whuffed* and ignited.

ADIOS, HAUNTED AMIGO

The secondary gas-tank explosion I do not hear because I am left deafened and insensible from the first, though I do feel a wash of warmth across my back, which I hope is not blood. My brain is confused but my soldier's cells know exactly what's happening and my first question—when I'm capable of forming a thought in my tumbled brain—is if Lucky is alive or dead, and my second question is how alive or dead Lucky might be.

(I put my own proportions at approximately fifty-fifty.)

Somebody turned me over on my back, and there was the sky (so blue!) and a pillar of smoke rising from what used to be my Caddie. (Adios, haunted amigo!)

Rough hands removed my PPE. I had no clue where my two weapons had gone, but they were most certainly not in my hands, which were reflexively clenching and unclenching the dust of the driveway beneath me as though reassuring themselves that they were still connected to a living human being and that the human being was still attached to the earth. Summoning all my strength and focus, I turned my head to see Nick standing over a prostrate Lucky, tugging at his Kevlar. Somebody seized my chin and turned my head back toward the sky.

Crazy milky blue eyes on me like creepy bloated baby corpse fingers.

I heard Keet's voice from a great distance even though his mouth was moving less than a foot away, saying, "That's what you get for blowing up my Harley."

It came to me (CFB) that Lucky and I were screwed.

I had underestimated Keet. He was one of those guys who, if you have a gun with bullets in it, you should shoot until all of those bullets are in him and none are left in your gun.

Keet straightened, waiting for me to regain the power of speech, glancing over his shoulder every once in a while to see what Nick and Lucky were up to.

I tried to speak two or three times.

"Try again. Not getting any of that," Keet said.

I swallowed and tried again.

"Barrels."

I saw Keet's zombie-corpse eyes widen.

He looked over toward the Caddie, thinking I'd had the money in the Caddie, which made me laugh (it sounded like somebody trying to pull apart a wicker chair with his bare hands) because Keet had to deal with the very real possibility that he'd blown up and incinerated God knows how many millions of dollars.

When he raised one of my own pistols (Oh! There it was . . .) to shoot me in the face, I said, "I came to tell you where to find the barrels."

THE DRIVER

Keet lowered the gun.
Things were looking up.
"Where?" Keet asked.
I told him.
Then he kicked me in the head.

I COULD NOT HAVE BEEN
MORE WRONG

Metal music plays at ear-splitting volume. I can't see anything and worry that Keet kicked the sight out of me until I realize that I am also unable to breathe and I'm seized with claustrophobia and panic, tumbling in the dark. The metal music stops and there is the sound of a car door opening. I can smell Tums's primo weed.

Blood.

Urine.

Feces.

The urine was mine. I hoped the shit was Lucky's because that meant he was at least alive.

A bag was ripped from my head so I could see after a few moments. Slim stood in front of me, holding the nylon backpack that had been pulled over my head. Slim wore a filthy Mexican poncho. He carried his shotgun. Nick bent over me with a pair of pliers. I felt a slash of pain in my wrists and then in my ankles before Nick straightened up, holding blood-soaked wire.

I'd been bound with wire.

"Some war hero," Nick said to Tums. "He totally pissed himself."

"Arab shit hisself too," Slim said.

"Lucky's not Arab," I said.

Keet, leaning on the back bumper of a dove-gray Land Cruiser, fondling a nasty little Heckler & Koch MP7 mini-machine pistol with a thirty-round magazine, watched Slim and Nick drag me and Lucky out the back of what appeared to be an airbrushed molester van, letting us fall hard to the ground.

We were on the bottom level of the abandoned parking garage— the level where, the night before (was it only the night before?), the wannabe Satanists had sacrificed the cat. The cat corpse was still there, under the Land Cruiser.

"Can you please stand up?" Slim asked in his kindly vicar's voice, though the effect was tempered by the way he prodded me with his shotgun. When I fell, Slim said, "Help him up, Nick."

"He reeks," Nick said.

"So do you," Keet said. "Get him up."

Which Nick did, mostly by kicking and punching me to my feet in lieu of a steadying hand under the arm, which is how I helped Lucky stand.

Lucky looked bad.

"Water?" I asked.

Nick slugged me in the gut.

"Come on, now, Nick," Keet said. "Chill out."

Keet reached into the Land Cruiser behind him and gave me a can of Coke.

I drained a third and extended the rest to Lucky.

If I had to be in a bad situation like this, then I preferred to be accompanied by Luqmaan Qadir Yosufzai, especially when he had shit running down his leg because what these morons didn't know is that shit and piss are an effective way to keep people at a distance. We'd taken back at least a little power from these bastards, even if it was just stench. The side of my head ached where Keet had kicked me. One of the vertebrae in the middle of my back felt out of line. Lucky looked bad, both his eyes swollen and seeping bloody tears. The entire front of his white shirt was covered in goop and gore, I hoped all from his nose.

"You should know that I created Bismarck Avila into what he is," Keet informed me. "I made that boy at the skate park and plucked him out of the mob."

"Biz had star quality even when he was a kid," Tums said.

"I told you, I see potential in these boys," Keet said. "No one else does."

"What potential did you see in X-Ray," I asked, "before you had him murdered?"

"What?" Nick asked. "What happened to X-Ray?"

Keet thumped me with the Heckler, an unmistakable warning.

"X-Ray is dead because I failed to get protection from the Mexicans in time," Keet told Nick. "That's on me. Don't you worry. It won't happen again."

"I never liked X-Ray much anyways," Nick said. "I'm ready to take over his duties."

"I know that," Keet said, "because I see your potential."

"I worked corners for Mr. Keet when I was ten," said Tums. "In high school, he sent me to do collections after class. Then he put me through law school."

Christ, Keet was running some kind of criminal School for Ambitious Wayward Juvenile Psychopaths.

"Not a good law school, I bet."

Tums laughed and said, "Good enough."

Lucky handed me back the can of Coke. I palmed the pull tab, apparently not as smoothly as I'd hoped.

"Whaddaya gonna do with that?" Keet asked. "Cut my throat?"

I shrugged and held it out to him.

"Keep it," Keet said. "Best of luck to you. Where are my barrels?"

I explained where the barrels were and how to get to them. My hands were no longer numb. They felt like I'd reached into a fire. I was good with that because it meant they weren't dead. Also, it distracted me from my aching head where Keet had kicked me.

Keet decided that I would lead the way, followed by Lucky, which was not good for Lucky because every time I stumbled or hesitated, Slim took the shotgun from where it was hidden under his poncho and struck Lucky in the back. Keet came next, followed by Nick hefting Lucky's Smith & Wesson, aiming it at birds and airplanes, aching to fire it. Tums brought up the rear, smoking his pot, whistling "Killing Me Softly."

Both Lucky and I bled steadily from our wrists and ankles, like walking suicides, as we climbed up one floor in the parking garage and then took the ramp with the cut flap of fencing over to the abandoned mall.

I led our little sociopath parade to the alcove with the demon's head and the slogan: WE ARE ALL MADE OF DIRT.

"No way you fit through that demon's mouth," Nick told Slim.

Keet sent Nick through first, then me and Lucky, with Keet pointing his machine pistol at me the whole time, and then we all watched as skinny-bones Tums tried to push Slim through the hole from the other side.

"You're too fat," Nick said.

Slim asked if there was a beam or piece of lumber inside that he could use to bash on the hole to widen it. Keet covered me and Lucky with his machine pistol as Nick and Tums hefted a piece of concrete about five feet long and eight inches wide, lined with rebar, out to Slim. Slim ran at the demon like a battering ram four or five times, making the hole big enough for him to come through. It was an impressive display of strength, but the big man didn't have a lot of stamina, because he was gray-faced after and it was easy to see that Nick was itching to comment on that fact.

Keet ordered Slim to hold my right hand on the beam Slim had used to bash his way through the wall. Nick pointed my own gun at my face from a foot away. Keet picked up a broken cinder block in both hands.

"In case you're feeling rebellious," Keet said.

"No, no!" Lucky said, just before Keet hammered my hand three times, the bones busting like a basket.

"Suddenly the Paki can talk?" Keet said.

I reeled and vomited, my right hand pulped and useless when Slim let it go, flapping at the wrist, ruined. Then—"Lucky isn't an Arab and he's not Pakistani. He's Afghan." I vomited again.

Keet ordered everybody to move on, shoving Lucky in front to lead the way. I pushed my pulverized right hand into my shirt as a makeshift sling and placed my left hand on Lucky's shoulder for support. Lightning bolts of agony shot from my hand straight up my arm into my head. Slim prodded me with the shotgun, and behind my nausea and anger I realized there was absolutely no chance of my taking the shotgun off him now.

Keet continued to justify his actions against Avila.

"Bought those kids a couple of cheap cameras, stocked the house with food and beer, parceled out just enough dope to keep 'em happy, and told 'em to make little films, sell 'em on the Internet."

"What, like pornos with the local board betties?" Nick asked. "I'd get in on that action."

"Skate films," Tums corrected Nick. "The Internet was the thing, man. All that fragmentation of entertainment, shit going viral. I saw an opportunity."

I was starting to be able to breathe again, shuffling with my head down, clinging to Lucky, waiting for my chance, any chance, because I would not let another go by, no matter how desperate. I felt sudden empathy for Ripple, being whittled away piece by piece. I wondered where he was and hoped that his kinky little girlfriend was rocking his world to the good.

Lucky led us along the dim first floor of the mall, moving slow through the rubble, dodging holes in the floor left for conduits and escalators and elevators and air shafts. I hoped Lucky would find a chance to escape, leave me behind, but I knew he wouldn't.

I was convinced that the task force was out there watching us, but I was equally convinced that they wouldn't move on Keet until he left the building with the barrels—by which time Lucky and I would be dead, our bodies dumped in the basement of this abandoned building, a buffet for feral cats.

"What Biz did was forget that he's just another little mud boy with fast feet from Lennox."

"Not so fast he could steal a couple of barrels of money without us noticing," Tums said.

"Avila's cousin Rocky stole those barrels," I said, "not Avila."

"Rocky was okay with me," Nick said. "He set me up with some fine bitches."

"If Rocky stole those barrels, it's because Biz told him to," Tums said.

This didn't exactly match what Avila had told me.

"Why'd you kill Rocky if it wasn't really his fault?"

"We had nothing to do with Rocky getting killed," Keet said.

Was he lying? Or was Tums lying to Keet? Neither, I thought, but I had to wonder if I was losing it—loss of blood, pain, micro-fissures in my brain from getting blown up . . .

We arrived at the vertical ramp looming out of the perpetual twilight in the decrepit mall. No skateboard kids, but I could still smell a fire smoldering nearby. For a moment I hoped that security guard would show up but realized Keet would just kill the poor bastard.

"The barrels are anchoring the ramp," I said.

"Look for the ones that are welded shut," Lucky said.

Keet nodded at Tums and Nick to go down one floor to check out the barrels.

They used the double escalators, frozen, leading from this floor down to the first floor where the ramp bottomed out, Tums walking, Nick sliding down the handrails. Slim kept his eyes and shotgun trained on me and Lucky while Keet watched Nick and Tums, Nick taking the northern end of the vertical ramp and Tums the southern end.

A gust of wind blew through a hole in the roof and over the dying fire, and Willeniec whispered, *Youaredirtyouaredirtweeralldirt*, and I knew for certain that Keet was minutes away from giving Slim permission to kick us over the edge. If the fall didn't kill us, he'd come down and step on our throats until we were dead.

I caught Lucky's eye and knew he was thinking the same thing.

"Got one." Tums's voice echoed off the pitted concrete walls.

"Me too," Nick said.

"Check 'em for cash and find the other one," Keet said. I finished his sentence in my mind—*so I can kill these guys.*

The other one?

My brain ticked and tumbled and started to work again. There absolutely was not a third barrel. Maybe there was a God, because I'd been handed just enough leverage that it might save us to fight another day. One more barrel missing meant that Keet was out at least a million dollars, probably more.

Tums and Nick struggled to roll their respective barrels to where Keet could look down and see them. Tums repeated Lucky's trick with the flashlight, opening the plug to look inside.

"Full of cash," Tums said. "Right up to the top."

"But only two barrels," Keet said.

"All the other barrels down there are full of garbage," Nick said.

Keet beckoned Nick and Tums to rejoin us one floor up. Keet stared at me until they arrived, then gave Nick the Heckler and walked over to stand in front of me, hands on his hips.

"Where's my money?" he asked.

"I tell you, I'm dead," I said.

Keet looked at Tums. Tums shrugged and lit one of his blunts.

Keet said, "I'm sick of this whole clusterfuck."

"You think *you're* tired of it . . . ," I said. "I'm just a driver."

"Here's the deal—tell me where the barrel is or Nick shoots the Paki."

"Can't even one of you dumb fuckers understand that he's not Pakistani or Arab? He's *Afghan*. He's from Afghanistan. It's a proud, fierce culture that has kicked everyone's ass for thousands of years."

I had the very brief satisfaction of seeing Keet and his motley crew of lowlifes momentarily taken aback by my sergeant's tone while Lucky straightened his entire five-foot-five frame because he knew we were about to fight back.

In my ruined hand I still held the pop-top, which I'd straightened out into a tiny dull blade that would barely manage to leave a mark on even the most delicate and exposed skin.

But skin wasn't my target.

I slice across both of Slim's eyeballs before Keet can react, but I fail to follow up by taking the shotgun from him because my right hand is nothing more than seeping hamburger. Knowing Slim will pull the trigger, reflexively I yank the barrel under my armpit in an effort to aim it at Keet but I'm too slow. The buckshot grazes my ribs but blows away most of poor Nick's head. The dying boy pulls convulsively on the trigger of the Heckler but instead of cutting

Keet in half, which is my ardent desire, it fires straight up into the ceiling.

Lucky goes after Tums. They grapple, each trying to get their hands on Tums's murderous little assassin's gun.

Slim is still on the other end of the shotgun, screaming in fury and agony, his eyes leaking blood and tears and eyeball insides all over me as Keet moves to jam the Ruger into my stomach—so I tip me and Slim over the edge, hoping I'll be the one on top when we hit the floor below.

We fall . . .

. . . we hit the floor . . .

. . . *did I lose consciousness?*

I gain my feet.

How much time has passed? What's happened?

Slim lies on his side, nearby, groaning, his hip dislocated, but still reaching for me with both massive arms. He wants to pull me close enough to bury his thumbs in my throat.

I stomp on the base of Slim's skull. He keeps coming. I do it again, aiming more carefully. This time there is a pop and Slim stops moving.

I look up to see Lucky, still wrestling with Tums. Keet, framed by a hole in the roof, silhouetted against the blue, blue Los Angeles sky, is raising a gun (my gun!) to blow Lucky's life away.

I shout a useless warning and register a blur of orange plummeting from the blue sky toward Keet. It knocks Keet to the ground.

Lucky flips Tums over the edge. Tums screams as he plummets and strikes the nearer of the two money barrels, landing in a terrible way so that he is literally lying on his own legs, left ankle jutting out from behind left armpit. I see his little assassin's gun and I pick it up and hear authoritative voices yelling at everyone to stop and drop our weapons, but Keet is rising again, swinging his gun up to shoot Lucky, who is moving toward Keet, but Lucky doesn't have a hope of reaching Keet before Keet shoots him. I'm too late! I'm too late! I don't have the time I need to bring up the assassin's gun in my wrong hand and fire, but Keet screams and recoils and looks down at his feet again in surprise, like he's been bitten by a poisonous snake, and he fires the gun at the snake just as I snap off a first shot and, as trained, a second, as quickly as I'm capable, and one of those two hollow-point bullets strikes Keet in the head and down he goes, and I think—*We're okay! We're okay!*—and the police scream at me to drop my weapon and I can and I do because it's Delilah and the task force and I raise the one hand I can raise, and something tells me—maybe it's Lucky's face (heartbroken)—I could not be more wrong.

We are not okay.

We are not okay at all.

HOW TO FALL AND
HOW TO LAND

There is trauma in life. There are difficulties and obstacles. Our memories are not dependable even at the best of times, when our brains haven't been scrambled, when we haven't lost pints of blood, when we aren't grief-stricken and furious. That's why we check in with the people we trust (sometimes dozens of times a day) to confirm that our perceptions of reality match at least a predominance of their perceptions of reality, so that we can agree that we live together in the same world.

Here are some facts I discovered later that I wasn't able to absorb for a while:

The orange streak I saw falling from heaven that knocked Keet to the ground wasn't God tossing down a meteor. It was Ripple (you knew that right away). He'd spent the night up there on the roof, in a sleeping bag with his kinky girl, and saw his chance to save Lucky and threw himself down through a hole in the roof at Keet.

When Keet turned his attention from Lucky and fired down, it was Ripple's chest he was firing into because Ripple bit his Achilles tendon so hard it was severed.

The task force handcuffed me and would not let me go to Ripple and I couldn't fight them off because I was done. I was out.

Later, in the hospital, Lucky told me that the last thing Ripple heard was me shouting his name. Shouting thanks.

(Did these things happen? I don't remember. Is Lucky telling me the truth or just trying to make me feel better?)

Lucky said that Ripple gripped his hand hard and did his best to live—but our best is nothing more than the most we can offer in the moment at that time and place and isn't always good enough, especially with a severed aorta.

So Ripple bled out on the filthy floor of an abandoned mall next to the dead son of a bitch who'd killed him because I wasn't fast enough.

And then . . .

. . . life went on . . .

. . . in the chaotic, messy, contentious manner it does when several people have been killed and mysteries deepen and lies are told and careers are made and broken, and the vast machinery of law enforcement and justice must react and respond to a degree that allows it to maintain a semblance of validity.

I was in the hospital for a long time. Three separate operations on my mashed hand with more to come. Ruptured spleen, bruised liver, torn diaphragm, buckshot in my ribs and lung, near my heart. A piece of shrapnel lodged deep in my back from the explosion of the Caddie. Extensive blood loss from the wire cuts in my wrists and ankles.

Painkillers.

Anesthetic.

I admit I embraced every opportunity they gave me to retreat from the real. I pushed the button on my morphine pump as often as it would let me; I took every pill they put in front of me; I forced myself to sleep.

Mom and Dad showed up through the mist, the two of them giving me hell in tandem, though I'm unclear on the specifics, until Mom told Dad to leave so that she could be alone with me and God, so she could pray.

I apologized to Mom because when it got out into the general news cycle that the maniac limo driver who'd killed three was her oldest son, it would damage her standing.

Mom said, "Bullshit!" and laid her head on my chest.

One afternoon, the sun low in the sky, *magic hour* they call it, I opened my eyes to find Dr. Quan holding my hand.

"I'm so sorry," she said.

"I'm okay."

"I mean about Ripple," she said.

I nodded, not trusting myself to speak. She went on to tell me that, according to Lucky, Ripple died knowing he was brave, that his fellow soldiers could count on him. "That would have meant the world to him," she said.

Media types and commentators had a field day trying to piece together what had happened. I was described, variously, as a crook who double-crossed his criminal accomplices; an innocent by-stander who did what he had to, to save himself and his friends; an undercover agent; and a vigilante.

One story that was popular for a day or two surmised that drug-addicted Darren (Ripple) had run away to live on the streets and Lucky and I had set off to bring him home and blundered into a gang turf war.

After they found out that I was out on bail after assaulting members of a warrant execution team, I became the poster boy for post-traumatic stress. On cable news, I saw myself psychoanalyzed by a psychiatrist I'd never met. The outcome didn't exactly match the me that I knew and loved and sounded disconcertingly like my personal theory of Assholes Find Each Other and I was most definitely a prime asshole.

Delilah persuaded Connie that Lucky deserved the best legal representation he could get—which meant Connie—and it turned out that, tactically speaking, it would be best for Lucky if Lucky and I shared representation, which meant I got Connie as my lawyer too.

But that's all I got. Connie the Lawyer, not Connie of My Heart. That turned out to hurt more than any of my various wounds, even the actual shard of lead near my heart.

During the early days of the investigation, the police didn't allow me and Lucky to communicate. They didn't want us to come up with a common narrative to explain the sequence of events leading to all those deaths.

What they couldn't understand was that Lucky and I didn't *need* to speak because I knew that Lucky knew that I would follow a time-honored stratagem that had worked for us more than once in the past.

Lucky would blame me.

I would blame the dead guy.

Following those simple rules, here's how the basic Q and A played out:

Mr. Skellig, how did you know where to find those barrels of money?

When Dad and I caught X-Ray (blame the dead guy) and Mr. Tums up in Big Sur and I threatened to hang X-Ray from a tree, the frightened kid, out of earshot of Mr. Tums, offered to buy his life by saying he and Nick (blame another dead guy) stole two barrels of cash from their criminal boss, Asher Keet. X-Ray told me where to find those barrels and in return I promised not to hang him from a tree.

Why didn't I inform law enforcement?

Because I wanted to live!

Convinced that poor Bismarck Avila was a victim of Asher Keet (blame the dead guy), forced to launder money by threats on his life and those around him, including his cousin Rocky (blame another dead guy), my intent was to trade the barrels of money for freedom. If I'd informed the police, they'd have taken the barrels of money, and Asher Keet (dead guy) would have killed everyone around Avila, including me and the beautiful Nina Sprey.

I stuck with that basic narrative through line no matter what holes Connie, Delilah, assorted defense lawyers, prosecutors, and journalists found and probed.

Did everyone believe me?

Life lesson: not only does everybody not believe one hundred percent of any story; nobody believes one hundred percent of *any* story, so the best you can hope for is that each and every part of your story is believed by somebody.

Blame the bad dead guy. Everybody will believe at least a part of your story.

Connie is a very good lawyer and she worked especially hard to prove that Lucky was blameless so that he wouldn't be deported to Afghanistan and have his head cut off by the Taliban. In fact, over the first few months, the publicity surrounding Lucky's plight actually worked to his benefit, shining a light on the fact that our brave Afghan interpreters and their families have earned the support of the American people.

Lucky ended up getting a two-year working visa and a path to citizenship.

My legal journey was bumpier.

There were questions about whether I'd used too much force with Slim and Nick and Keet. (I did, after all, blind one of them before kicking his head so hard it separated from his spinal column. I blasted a teenager with a shotgun. I shot the last through the eyeball with a hollow-point bullet.) But Connie persuaded Tums and his lawyer to demonize Keet (the legal version of blame the dead guy) in order to ameliorate Tums's own dire legal situation.

Tums and his public defender ran with the concept far beyond Connie's wildest hopes. Not only did the cunning Mr. Tums imply that I had no choice but to kill the psychotic bad guys, but Tums confessed that the money-laundering scheme had been his idea and forced upon an oblivious (and somewhat stupid) Avila, who, once he discovered the money laundering, tried to stop it and, if it hadn't been for me, would have been killed.

Mr. Tums also stated that he had heard from Slim (blame the dead guy) that Keet had ordered Slim to kill Willeniec when the crooked cop demanded a percentage of the money-laundering scheme.

Tums said Keet had ordered X-Ray murdered in jail for his part in stealing the barrels.

Every ray of light the cooperative Mr. Tums shone on the task force investigation resulted in a corresponding generous plea deal.

A few months later, in July, Tums provided me with another insight. Our lawyers left us alone together in a courthouse corridor, Tums in his wheelchair (he would never walk again), me on a cane (a prop to garner sympathy).

Tums said, "Hey, Santa Anas, you and me, we're gonna come out of this okay. I go to jail for a while; you pull probation. When I'm up for parole, you come and say nice things about me, right?"

A gust of the hot, unforgiving Santa Ana wind wafted through a broken window and I heard Keet and Nick laughing and, in his gentle vicar's voice, Slim whispered, *Tumsknowshowtofallandhowtoland.*

Tums called it. Connie got the serious charges against me dropped and got me probation on the misdemeanors. Keet got blamed for Willeniec's disappearance and presumed murder. The homicide investigation was closed.

Avila was cleared of most criminal charges attached to the money-laundering scheme and paid a hefty fine for the rest. Last I heard he was proceeding to take *B!$m@R©k!* public.

I went back to Oasis Limo.

Life went back to normal.

Except, of course, it didn't. How could it?

Lucky, Tinkertoy, and I had lost Ripple and we were hurting. We closed ranks around that pain, figuring no one else could understand.

Ripple's parents and widow (the divorce had not been finalized at the time of his death) claimed his body when it was finally released by the coroner. They wanted him buried in Three Rivers, a small town across the San Joaquin Valley, up against the Sierra mountains in Tulare County. It was Tinkertoy, now living in half the duplex while Lucky lived in the other half, who not only asked us to take her to Ripple's funeral but asked that the three of us dress up in our dress uniforms.

"Not a chance," I said.

"With. All. Our medals," Tinkertoy insisted.

"No uniform," I said. "No medals."

"Please," Tinkertoy said.

"She said *please*," Lucky said.

"No. Not gonna happen. The subject is closed."

Two o'clock in the morning, the night before Ripple's funeral, scheduled to leave Santa Monica for Ripple's hometown of Three Rivers at seven A.M., I awoke to knocking, shocking because no one ever knocks on my door because it is, when you come right down to it, a mobile home craned up onto the roof. I answered the door to reveal Lucky and, behind him, Tinkertoy, who had never in her life come up to my home on the roof.

Tinkertoy cradled an antique artist's desk in her arms—the one Connie had bought for Ripple as a get-well gift after his operation.

"Tinkertoy has Something To Share with you," Lucky said.

"We were supposed to turn all of Ripple's belongings over to his family," I said.

"We'll do it tomorrow after Ripple's funeral," Lucky said, "if you still think we should."

"Make. Some. Tea," Tinkertoy said.

Which I did, during which time Lucky and Tinkertoy made themselves comfortable at the small, round, flecked Formica table in my kitchen. The one I hardly ever use because I prefer to sit outside at my wooden picnic table.

"What's going on?" I said, placing mugs in front of everybody and dumping a handful of sugar cubes onto the table.

Tinkertoy looked at Lucky, everybody's translator.

"Tinkertoy found some things in Ripple's desk," Lucky said.

"And it's important to look at them now? In the middle of the night before an early-morning three-hour drive?"

"Yes."

Tinkertoy opens Ripple's lap desk and removes one of his pen-and-ink drawings. Typical Ripple, it features a row of dead children hanging from their necks from a gibbet while mangy, skinny curs snap at their dangling feet. One or two of the dogs have caught a foot and swing above the other dogs. Nearby a group of laughing, clapping people of all ages and races sit on bleachers, eating popcorn, drinking sodas, having a lovely time.

"So? Ripple was fucked-up. We all knew that. He'd have worked his way through it."

Tinkertoy looks at Lucky. Lucky nods. Tinkertoy pulls another drawing from the desk. I gird myself for whatever unpleasantness is coming.

But this drawing is different. It features Tinkertoy at her workbench in the mechanic's bay, rendered in pencil, almost like a photograph. Tinkertoy's face is calm and beautiful and focused on her work; her hands are strong and fluid and in motion, the line of her back indicating her strength and her dignity.

My throat tightens. I find I cannot speak.

Tinkertoy places a second drawing on the first.

This one is pen and ink. Comic. It features Lucky looking at the haunted Caddie askance. The Caddie has been subtly anthropomorphized, looking back at him—but it's Lucky's face that draws your eye: full of warmth and humor and skepticism and philosophy and wisdom and kindness.

"That's Lucky, all right," I say, stupidly, because it's an understatement.

Tinkertoy dips into Ripple's desk again and places a third drawing on top of the other two.

It's me.

You'll excuse me if I don't describe it in detail, but I will say that it shows the best version of me. The man I'd like to be. The man my family thinks I am. I want this to be true. I want to be that guy.

My heart aches to think that Ripple considered me to be this man.

Tinkertoy is not done.

She places a fourth drawing on top of the one Ripple did of me.

This one is of Ripple himself. I mean, you might not see it that way. In fact, only the three of us, me, Tinkertoy, and Lucky, hunkered over a sketch in the middle of the night, would know beyond a shadow of a doubt that it is a self-portrait, because the face is too small to make out. It's drawn from the point of view of the sniper who shot Ripple, moments before the shot, a brave young soldier, standing on two legs, confident in his manhood and his fine self, thinking he's immortal and untouchable, checking his fives and twenty-fives, doing his soldier's job and doing it well. In a moment, that boy's life will change; he'll be bleeding on the ground. He'll lose both his legs. He'll lose what he considered to be his life, but in this moment he is still whole, and that's the version of his self that Ripple drew in order to preserve himself from time and violence and inevitable disaster.

"Wait," I say. "Wait."

Trying, like Ripple, to stop time with a word.

Wait!

My vision narrows to where I see only Tinkertoy's calloused hands on my kitchen table and I see a tear plop onto her knuckle and I see Lucky's hand wipe that tear but I'm unable to look up at their faces; I can only look at Ripple's self-portrait in my own hands, one of them puckered and misshapen, months away from healing from this misshapen claw back into a real hand.

"Okay," I say.

"You'll wear your uniform?"

"I'll wear my uniform. And medals."

"Thank. You."

Tinkertoy and Lucky take Ripple's drawings with them when they leave. Except for one.

They also leave Ripple's desk.

It's now my desk. My inheritance. Inside it I keep Ripple's drawing of me so that when I see it I am reminded to be a better man because if I don't then I'll be disappointing the courageous, pale-assed, orange-haired stoner kid with no legs who sacrificed his life to save his friends.

Mom and Dad came to Ripple's funeral. So did Connie and Delilah. And Gracie Quan, holding hands with Lucky. Ripple's parents blinked when they saw the strange group of us all standing in the cemetery near the river, brokenhearted, including the fierce state senator who never left my side.

We watched Ripple's wife play up the grieving-widow routine and we disliked her intensely for abandoning Ripple, but, following Lucky's example, we were kind to her and her family and Ripple's mother and father.

What a shocking flash of orange Ripple must have been among that wan, colorless group.

After the graveside ceremony, everyone streaming out of the cemetery, I circled back on my own and placed my Distinguished Service Cross on Ripple's casket just before the cemetery workers filled in the grave. Maybe it's because ghost voices speak in my ear, but if there was any chance that I could convey to Ripple what I thought of his final act of bravery, well, I'd take it.

Afterward, in the parking lot along the road, I found myself standing with Mom, Delilah, and Connie.

"You look good in uniform," Connie said.

"Don't talk bullshit, Constanta," Mom said.

(You will recall that Mom and Connie do not like each other.)

"You don't think he looks good, Dolly?"

"You know that's not what I'm saying," Mom said, and Connie gritted her teeth. Senator versus lawyer. The System versus the Rebel.

"All right, now," Delilah said.

"It's not all right," Connie said. "Michael is lying and you say I'm talking bullshit and you expect me to *pasar por alto* about it."

"I expect you to be a grown-up about it," Mom said, "and maybe stop throwing in little Spanish phrases for no reason so you can feel special. Maybe stop smacking us with your statements, ask a question every now and then like you don't already know every-thing in the world worth knowing."

"All right, now," Delilah said again (the way you'd expect Gandhi to say it).

"You ever think if Michael tells you the truth you'd have to do something about it?" Mom asked Connie. "And if you didn't do something about it, you'd feel obliged to change your profession or your view of yourself? If Mikey asked my opinion, which he did not, I'd say go ahead and put that self-righteous prig on a razor's edge, see what she's made of."

"You called me a prick!"

"Prig! Prig! Look it up and see a photo of yourself."

"All right, now," Delilah said, using her cop voice this time, nipping a riot in the bud.

"It's a funeral," I said.

"Not mine," Mom said. "And not yours."

Mom walked one way. Connie walked the other.

Delilah said, "Holy shit."

"Yeah," I said. "She's terrific, isn't she?"

"Sure," Delilah said. "Which one?"

We looked at each for a couple of moments. She patted my chest three times—then poked the empty space where my DSC had been pinned. She raised her eyebrows at me. I shrugged. Delilah looked over to where Gracie Quan stood holding hands with Lucky, Tinkertoy standing a few feet away, looking up at the mountains, then over toward Mom and Dad, arm in arm, and she sighed.

"How's about I drive you home?" But it was a different kind of question this time.

So I nodded.

Delilah and I spent the next twelve hours in the Best Motel in Mojave. (That's not descriptive; the place is actually named the *Best Motel* and it happens to be in the town of Mojave.)

What we did there was wonderful. It shook me up. It set me up. It raised me up. Another kind of sanctuary. It reminded me that life is good and sweet and too fragile and too short.

"This is a onetime thing," Delilah said.

"Why?"

"Because I'm an investigator in an ongoing case that won't be resolved for a couple of years and you are a very active person of interest in much of that case and an outright suspect in some of the rest."

"We could compartmentalize."

"As a newly minted member of Robbery-Homicide, I can't afford to have a boyfriend who's on probation."

"What about when I'm off probation?"

"We'll see," she said.

But Delilah was happy that I'd asked and rewarded me with a reverse cowgirl that deserved a National Rodeo Gold Medal.

Delilah dropped me off at Oasis. When I leaned over to give her a kiss, she placed her hand on my chest and stopped me cold.

"Just so you know, I'm pretty sure I know what really happened."

"Yeah?"

"Even to Willeniec."

I said nothing. She laughed and I knew why. *Silence means consent.*

"Then why'd you take me to bed?"

"Surface of the earth," she said, smiling at me like Delilah. But seconds later it was Robbery-Homicide Detective Groopman who drove away, so that whole situation is about as clear as mud.

Which I took as a sign that it was time for me to leave the surface of the earth and take a swing at history.

THE RULE OF THREES

I don't know for absolute sure whether the voices I hear in the wind are supernatural or if they're just in my head. Do they tell me things I don't know or things I just don't know *consciously?* Are those voices my own guilty subconscious trying to tell me something and the only way to get my attention is to speak to me in the voices of those whose lives I've taken?

Or do ghosts actually exist?

A few days after Ripple's funeral, Keet whispered, *Avila-doesn'tknowaboutthethirdbarrel.*

My intention was to pull in the marker Avila owed me and sell him Oasis Limo with the caveat that he had to keep on Tinkertoy and Lucky for as long as they wanted to work there.

I asked my mom to ask her contacts for a place where a slightly infamous poster boy for PTSD could work to benefit veterans. She warned me that with all the criminal charges and probation, it would have to be behind the scenes. Maybe at one of the big charities.

I was thinking about those options, standing on my porch, when a breeze caressed my cheek and Willeniec chimed in to remind me about the third barrel.

Perhaps you thought I'd forgotten that there was a third barrel of money unaccounted for? I didn't forget; I just didn't care.

Until now.

I hurried down to where Lucky was sitting in Dispatch and reminded him that when the police opened the two barrels from the deserted mall, one of them contained 1.3 million dollars in cash and the other contained 3.1 million dollars in cash.

"You are Making Reference to the third barrel," he said.

"That's right."

"If you thought that blood money was out there and nobody had it, then you'd leave it. What you don't like is that you think somebody has that money and that they shouldn't."

Which goes to show that Mystical Voices That Tell The Truth don't come exclusively from the ghosts of those who die violently by my hand.

"Who do you think has that money?" Lucky asked.

"Gimme a second," I said. "This is new to me. I was thinking right up until this moment that the money was still hidden out there somewhere—that *nobody* has it—until you told me otherwise."

Lucky flapped his hands at Allah, sorry he'd said anything.

Like many mathematical equations, it wasn't that hard to figure out once you realized there was an equation just waiting to be figured out. (Ask Einstein.)

Lucky and I ran through it in less than fifteen minutes, much faster than deciphering Avila's map to find the first two barrels.

Three barrels of cash minus two in police hands equals one missing barrel of cash.

A constant (Avila) is a function of the variable (the missing barrel).

Avila is currently an associative property unaffected by the variable because he doesn't know it exists.

Avila's muscle-bound young cousin, Rocky, had stolen the barrels.

Constant: Rocky had stolen three barrels.

Constant: Rocky gave Avila two of those barrels.

Constant: Rocky was murdered.

Constant: Not by Keet.

Variable: What if Rocky hadn't stolen the barrels for Avila?

Variable: What if Rocky's murder hadn't been connected to the barrels?

"Oh," Lucky said.

We took the Mercedes because it has a spacious, lockable trunk. We placed two large, empty canvas duffel bags in that trunk as well as two shovels. We decided not to take weapons, partly because I was on probation and forbidden. I drove because I was extremely familiar with the route.

"What if Avila calls the police?"

"It's not stealing."

"How is this not stealing?"

"The money's not his."

"That is a Matter of Perception. Theft exists when you take something that does not belong to you. Thus it remains theft even if the person you stole it from is not the rightful owner."

"There is no rightful owner! It's like international law. Like salvage. Why do you have to be so negative?"

"We are discussing stealing well over a million dollars."

"We have no idea how much of that money is left. And it's not stealing!"

Then I told Lucky that I was thinking of selling Oasis Limo to Avila and that this money would provide for both him and Tinkertoy if it didn't work out. Plus, my share would give me the time I needed to find my place in the world.

"And be the type of man Connie will wed?"

It was an easy matter to get access to Avila's Calabasas mansion, especially now that Cody Fiso and his guards were no longer on the job because Avila no longer needed protection because Keet was dead and Avila's woes were all legal and so unlikely to get him killed, just financially bled to death.

"Since this place was searched both by the villain Willeniec and by a legitimate warrant-execution team, we must search where they didn't search," Lucky said as we pulled up in front of the mansion.

"Remembering," I said, "that they were looking for barrels."

"Yes."

"Which they didn't find."

"Yes."

"Meaning the cash was removed from the barrels and hidden somewhere else," I said.

"This place is huge."

"Avila's place is huge," I said. "Nina's place is not huge at all."

I pointed at her desert island.

We were in the miniature pirate ship heading across to Treasure Island when Avila exited his mansion and shouted at us. We waved in a friendly manner, pretending we couldn't hear him, which was ridiculous since he was only twenty-five yards away. Getting the point, Avila stopped yelling and watched us from the water's edge. After a moment, he was joined by my old pal Chris, aka Gargantua, aka Tweedledum, the giant who conked me on the head and tried to make it look like the correct response when X-Ray and Nick appeared in that bar waving guns so many months ago.

"Set the brake; it'll buy us some time," I told Lucky.

Lucky applied the brake. We watched for a couple of moments while Avila and Chris tried to recall the boat and then gave up.

The money wasn't on the island. My first thought was that we'd find it buried beneath the refrigerator / treasure chest, but I was wrong. By the time we'd dug her fridge up, Nina was on the shore with Avila, first yelling at us to stop whatever it was we were doing and then insisting that Avila and Chris swim across and kick our asses.

"But not, you'll notice," I said, "threatening to call the police."

Chris announced that he couldn't swim. Avila stripped to his underwear, dove in, and swam toward us.

"Hey, Nina?" I shouted.

"What?"

"Where is it?"

"Where's what?"

"The money."

"What money?" Avila asked, emerging from the pond and walking toward us along the beach.

"Ask Nina."

I leaned on my shovel while Avila blew water out of his nose.

"You are a beautiful swimmer," Lucky told him.

"I didn't ask Nina," Avila said. "I asked you."

"Turns out Rocky stole *three* barrels from Keet."

"He told me two."

I put on my weapons-sergeant poker face. I wanted to know how much Avila knew, or how much he'd guessed, without me providing him any hints. Avila wiped water off his body, using the web between his thumb and forefingers like a squeegee.

"What's he saying?" Nina shouted. "It's a lie."

"You're not the first guy who picked the wrong woman," I said.

Avila's mahogany skin rose in goose bumps as he realized the same inevitable sequence of events that Lucky and I had worked out. A puff of wind blew east to west, a miniature squall raising ripples on Avila's miniature lake.

"You fucked up in a major manner," I said.

"What do you want?"

"What do you think?"

Avila nodded at me and jumped back into the lake. This time he didn't swim on the water's surface; he swam along the bottom, invisible, and he stayed there so long Nina started shouting at the surface of the water when it started bubbling.

"What is it I Do Not Comprehend?" Lucky asked. "Why is he drowning himself?"

"He's not drowning. He's screaming."

Avila was upset because the rumors Delilah had heard around the Gangs Unit were true. Avila had his young muscle-head cousin Rakim or some shit killed because the kid slept with Nina and (I'd be willing to bet) because when Avila found out, Nina told Avila that the kid had forced himself on her, knowing that would be a mind-fogging trigger for Avila after what happened to his mother.

Avila rose from the water and said something to Nina and headed toward the house, calling poor, confused, lumbering Chris to come with him.

Whatever it was Avila said to Nina was bad enough that she crumpled to the ground. Avila shut the door on Nina in that way you know is final.

"You know," I told Lucky, "Nina once told me that it was Rocky who built most of this boat for her. Kid was good with his hands."

Nina's boat.

It was Nina who more or less told us where she'd hidden the money, the same way that so many Afghan and Iraqi civilians told us where to find stashes of weapons or explosives.

The closer we got to the money, the more Nina tried to distract us, like a child's game of getting-warmer.

Lucky, who'd helped my team search hundreds of huts and houses and apartments, clued in immediately. It was Lucky who found the money shoved into the barrel of the fake cannon. And it was me who found the rest in the fake gunpowder barrel.

Bundles of cash stuffed in garbage bags.

"What do we do now?" Lucky asked.

"We take it," I said.

"What about her?"

"Leave her cab fare," I said.

"You don't want to offer her a ride?"

"No," I said. "She's had her ride."

A PIECE OF PARADISE

To answer your first question: yes, this story is over.

To answer your second question: just over a million dollars.

To answer your third question: I split Keet's blood money equally with Tinkertoy and Lucky and then spent a chunk of my portion to buy a particular piece of parched and barren property just outside the town of Maricopa.

I explained this inexplicable action by telling the heartwarming story of a dying old farmer named Danny Marler I'd once driven to an Oilers game, his requested detour from the retirement home to his family orchard, Danny Marler's love of his land and his vision of its future. I said that I had decided to have faith in Mr. Marler's conviction that one day this drought would break and his land would sprout tangerines and almonds again no matter how far down his uncaring corporate neighbors dug their aqua-sucking wells.

Lucky is the only person who suspects the truth. And that's only because he helped me tilt twenty cubic yards of clean mixed fill into an abandoned dry well on the property.

Better safe than sorry, I told Lucky. Wouldn't want anyone falling down that hole now that I owned it. Who knows? Maybe old Danny Marler was right and it will bloom again someday.

At first Tinkertoy was determined to donate her entire share of the barrel money to the Parrot Sanctuary, but Lucky and I were able to persuade her that a sudden bequest of over a quarter of a million dollars from a former Army transport sergeant turned limo mechanic (with psych issues) to a bunch of colorful birds tucked away in the shadow of a minor league baseball stadium could raise eyebrows we didn't want raised. Tinkertoy agreed to parcel out smaller gifts anonymously over time.

She paid less than a thousand bucks for an old beater Toyota Corolla and rebuilt it (modifying a bunch of old Tahoe parts she got somewhere). She and Lucky painted it to resemble a parrot, and every single day she drove her loony-tunes car to visit the Parrot Sanctuary. The psych wizards at the Veterans Administration perceived her sudden engagement with the wider world around her as a giant stride forward in her personal progress.

Avila agreed to buy Oasis Limo Services, and Mom got me an interview with a big veterans charity that was trying to recover from a scandal where they paid more to themselves than they gave to the veterans who needed it.

Tinkertoy started hawking at me (in her gentle, insistent way) to go with her to the Parrot Sanctuary. I told her that I had to study up for my second interview, the one in which I presented a plan to remake the veterans charity and then take it to the national stage, but Tinkertoy kept staring at me with her dark, disappointed eyes before either turning back to her work or driving off in the parrotmobile to keep her date with her loud and talkative birds.

"Go with her," Lucky suggested.

"I don't have time."

"Seat. Belt," Tinkertoy said when I plopped myself into the passenger seat of her car. She drove like a confident hundred-year-old nun along Santa Monica Boulevard to Twenty-Sixth, up Twenty-Sixth to Wilshire, east on Wilshire toward the Veterans Administration. She parked in the shade of a keen-smelling green eucalyptus grove and led me to a folding chair at the same small round café table she'd been sitting at before Connie got her released from her 5150 psychiatric commitment.

She disappeared around some packing cases, then returned with a battered thermos and a tin cup and poured me a cup of astringent, burned coffee.

She was wearing Ripple's I LOVE JESUS BUT I STILL CUSS fanny pack.

"Exactly how much of Ripple's stuff did we steal?" I asked.

"He would've. Wanted. Me. To—"

"I think he would too," I said, "and Jesus will appreciate you filling his fanny pack with sunflower seeds and parrot pellets instead of marijuana."

But Tinkertoy was already moving away from me again, and if she answered, her response was masked by the parrots shrieking and clacking their bills on their stands and the wire screens.

Gradually, through the bird commotion, I heard another sound.

Someone in distress. I circled around the parrot cages toward the source.

"Take me back! Fuckin' take me back!"

These words were spoken by a young man, maybe twenty years old, long dirty brown hair. He wore shiny gray basketball shorts clownishly high on his waist, a black T-shirt sporting the slogan OBEY GRAVITY! On his feet were those ugly, soft rubber orange cartoon shoes that look like they were made for little children or mental patients—which is what I took him for because of the next thing he announced: "I want to go back."

There was no one there but me.

"I want to go back," he said again to nobody, close to tears.

(Who *doesn't* want to go back?)

He held a hand out in front of him, feeling the air.

He was blind, I realized. Which meant that I could simply sneak away without engaging. Which is what I was doing until I caught a glimpse of a tattoo on his calf above the rubber sandals.

A nautical star (Navy) and each point of the star was marked north (Lost).

I looked around for a volunteer or Tinkertoy, but there was only me. I heard the crack of a bat from over toward the baseball stadium and his head snapped over that way and a look crossed his face of complete desolation, the despair of a lost child. The parrots started shrieking again and the kid slumped down to the ground, cross-legged, and rocked forward, holding his head in his hands.

Feeling I was intruding, I turned to leave, only to find Tinkertoy standing behind me, hands on her hips, a huge blue-and-gold parrot on her shoulder, woman and parrot both staring me down.

"He. Needs. A job," Tinkertoy said. "And we. Need. A dispatcher."

To my surprise, my chest bloomed with tight anger. I felt my face change. "Is that why you brought me? To replace Ripple? Because Ripple is not replaceable."

Of course I didn't mean as a dispatcher. I meant that Ripple had thrown himself off a roof to save my life, to prove himself a hero, probably expecting me to save his life in return. Only I didn't, did I? Ripple's confidence in me had been misplaced. And now this kid—blind and obviously drowning in either sadness or depression or self-pity.

"I'm selling the place to Avila. You can bring Avila here, ask him to hire the kid."

"He's. Learning braille," Tinkertoy said. "His name is Rollo."

"Well, Rollo is *Navy*."

We're Army. Me and Tinkertoy and Lucky. Navy's a whole other culture. It would never work.

"And look at his stupid shoes."

The parrot on her shoulder stared at me, then tucked its head beneath Tinkertoy's ear. Stupid bird.

"Lemme think about it," I told Tinkertoy.

Make a decision, my Dad taught me.

Don't shrug, my mother taught me.

I remembered the way Ripple had drawn me.

Avila would have to go find himself some other limo company.

I crossed thirty feet of the surface of the earth and helped Rollo to his feet.

ACKNOWLEDGMENTS

Thank you, F. W. Watt, poet and professor, University College, University of Toronto, for being the first person to read my writing and still let me into your writing seminar. It changed my life.

Thank you to George McWhirter, writer, poet, translator, mastermind, and mad oracle, for your support, advice, and sheer Irishness.

Thank you to big shot novelists Scott Turow, Harlan Coben, Chris Ewan, Leif G. W. Persson, Richard Greener, and Kathy Reichs. Adapting your work for TV taught me buckets. Buckets of buckets.

Thank you to TV agent Matt Solo of WME (Los Angeles) for changing my life by bringing me to Los Angeles and then encouraging me to write a book even though you get paid only when I write TV scripts.

Thank you, New York hotshot literary agents Claudia Ballard and Eve Attermann at WME for being my hotshot New York book agents because actually having hotshot New York book agents has been a dream of mine since I found out about New York and literary agents.

Thank you to my editors at Dutton, Ben Sevier and Jessica Renheim, not only for publishing my book but for patiently shepherding me through this bizarre and magical process.

Thank you to Jeanne Newman, slayer of dragons and anxiety, bringer of calm, confidante, lawyer, and friend.

Thank you to my pal and cohort, Stephen Nathan, who was the first person to read *The Driver* and assure me that—with a few improvements—it was good enough to show other human beings.

Thank you to fancy novelist Steven Galloway for a much-needed and valuable early read and response.

Thank you to my sons, Hartwick and Joe, for being constantly amused by most of my endeavors and telling me many things I need to know.

Thanks to my dad, Paul, for making books a forbidden fruit by yelling at me to put down the damn book and go outside and do something on sunny days.

Thanks to my late mom, Brenda, for challenging me to typing competitions and for improving my spelling by cheating at Scrabble.

Thanks to my late stepdad, Art Macgregor, who, knowing that he would not live long enough to see this book published, asked to see it in manuscript—a much-appreciated compliment from a man whose time was too finite and so precious.

Huge thanks to novelist Jack Hodgins, friend of decades, a literary artist of the first rank who spent decades mentoring me.

And finally, thank you to the limo drivers of Los Angeles. Especially those who are military veterans. And most especially those who talked clearly and loudly on their cell phones while I feigned listening to music.

ABOUT THE AUTHOR

Hart Hanson wrote for Canadian television before moving to Los Angeles, where he worked on various TV programs before creating the series *Bones*, the longest-running, scripted, hour-long series on the FOX network.

Married with two sons, Hart lives with his wife, Brigitte, in Venice, California.

The Driver is his first novel unless you count the one he wrote in his midtwenties, which is rightfully buried away in his father's storage locker.

4/20/18 - 9/9/19